Hard to Feel Whole

MANDY THOMAS

For Barry, Archie and Mackenzie.

CONTENTS

Chapter One

Tears streamed down my cheeks at the vile sensations running through my body. I scrambled to the edge of my bed desperate to end the nightmare.

"No! Please no, not again!" My distressed plea, barely a whisper as I pressed the heels of my palms to my eyes, struggling to banish the horrific images from my head. *I can't take much more of this.*

Sweat beaded on my forehead and I reached for the glass of water on my nightstand. With shaking hands I brought the glass to my lips, the cool liquid clearing the debilitating lump from my throat. As my heartbeat slowed I eased back between the covers and took a deep breath; trying with all my might to force happier times into my mind's eye. After what seemed like an eternity my eyelids grew heavy and I was greeted with more pleasant memories…

Someone or something crashed into my side and flew over the top of me. His back pack hurled into the air before he face planted unceremoniously to the ground, howling in pain as various other parts of his anatomy followed his face.

"Watch it!" I cried after my butt hit the gravel.

He'd appeared out of nowhere. The boy finally skidded to a standstill outside the classroom. Gasps and shrieks from the kids close by filled the air as a young teacher ran quickly to his side.

"Jakey? Oh my goodness. It's okay, come on let's get you to the nurse," she said, "The rest of you can go into class quietly and take out your holiday assignments ready to hand in when I get back, I'll be five minutes tops."

"Oh my," I whispered under my breath, shocked at his battered appearance.

When the teacher took hold of his hand to help him up, the boy glanced in my direction. Staring back at me was the cutest boy. His dark blonde hair hinted at curls. He had a friendly face and even though blood covered his cheek from hitting the gravel, the few heavy freckles across his nose and cheeks were still visible. The boy's chest heaved up and down; his face turning red as he fought like crazy to blink back the tears that threatened to spill from his penetrating blue eyes.

"Sorry," he managed to mouth in my direction as the teacher helped him up. I moved towards my back pack giving him a sympathetic smile as the teacher led him away. Starting a new school and leaving Gran was bad enough without causing a stir on my first day.

"That's Jake," a girl said as I dusted myself off and picked up my scattered belongings. I didn't pay her much attention; I was too busy replaying the collision in my head.

"He's new too, he doesn't say much, he's a bit shy," she said. This piece of information broke my trance.

After a busy morning of mind blowing information on the ins and outs of Raven Elementary School my head hurt and my stomach grumbled ready for lunch. The cafeteria hummed with the mass of giddy bodies all dashing about, hugging and squealing with the excitement of not having seen each other for a whole weekend. I squeezed my way to the lunch line in the hopes of grabbing a drink.

"Hey," a voice behind me said, making me gasp in surprise. I turned quickly to come face to face with Jake, the boy from earlier.

"Err... Hello."

"I'm Jake... I'm really sorry about this morning... for knocking you over and everything..." He grinned widely and blushed a bit.

"It's okay... I'm okay... I'm Abbie," I said as a warm blush spread up my own face, "Are you alright, it looked really bad. There was a lot of blood."

"Yeah, I'm good; it was my own stupid fault for running round the corner. I got up late... should have woken up when my mom shouted me instead of sleeping in."

The warmth I felt flooding my body as my mind took me to happier times pulled me into a deeper, more restful sleep. I snuggled into the cool covers of my bed, smiling at the now extremely clear picture of Jake in my head.

At eight-years-old when we'd met; Jake was older than me by three months. We quickly learned we had a lot in common. He had a four-year-old sister called Lucy whereas Martin, my brother was six. Jake lived on the army base in the next town. Though we spent little time hanging out together out of school hours, my mom would occasionally drive me over for a visit. I'd attended two different elementary schools by the time we met, but Jake, because of his dad's job in the army, had already attended four. We grew inseparable and both really looked forward to seeing each other at school…

"Ouch!" I screamed in fits of laughter. "Stop it already! Jaaaaake!" My eyes tearing up I was laughing that hard.

"Softie," he said, grinning as he stopped tickling me and moved to my side, panting for breath.

"You're mean."

"Nah I'm not, you're just soft. I told you I'd get you back for the other day."

4

"Hmm, I didn't deserve that though. You really freaked me out, Jake. I didn't know it was you."

"Who else is as strong as me?" he asked, raising an eyebrow and smirking at me.

"Well... I still think you're mean," I said, taking a deep breath before looking at him again and breaking into giggles when he stuck out his bottom lip. Then he winked and made me blush.

"Come on," he said, holding out his hand.

"Hey, guess what?" I remembered the phone call to my gran the night before.

"What?"

"I'm going to visit my gran at Christmas," I said, my smile spreading from ear to ear.

"That's great, Abs. How long are you going for?"

"I'm not sure. My mom said something about going the week before term break because the air fares will be a bit cheaper. It will probably be a week, it depends on Dad's work I suppose," I said, realizing that as soon as the holidays came it would be three weeks until I saw Jake again. The thought left me down in the dumps and he noticed the change in my mood at once.

"What's wrong?"

"I'm gonna miss you, Jakey. Three weeks is ages..." I didn't understand why I was so upset. It wasn't like I'd never see him again. He gave me his cute Jake smile.

"It's not that long, Abs." He gave my shoulder a gentle squeeze.

5

The switch of mood disturbed my sleep and I became restless, sensing where this story was heading. My heart began to race and I turned over in bed, searching for a cool spot, hoping to change the direction of my dream...

The door to the large truck opened and an old man climbed out of the cab. He didn't have a beard like my dad but he looked tall and he had messy gray hair. His eyes scanned the front of the building before settling on me as I peeped at him through the railings. He lifted his hand to his brow in order to shield his eyes from the midday sun and smiled in my direction, holding my gaze a while. I jerked back against the wall, embarrassed at being caught snooping. He smirked and then carried on towards the stairs which headed to the upper floors of our apartments.

With my heart still pounding in my chest another vehicle screeched to a halt. I turned to see a big white Ford parked in front of the removal truck. The doors to the back swung open and out clambered two boisterous teenage boys. The lone girl had short dark hair styled like a pixie in one of my old story books. She looked a bit older than me, maybe nine or ten. Either way she was a potential play mate. A middle aged woman with unruly red hair got out of the driver's side and locked the car as she followed the three of them into the building.

I struggled against the images swirling round my head but relaxed a touch as they began to morph back to Jake and our last week together before the Christmas break. But along with his image; a gut wrenching sorrow crept through my body as I slept...

The bell rang signaling the end of my semester and the start of the holidays. It seemed weird to be finishing up a week earlier than everyone else. Under normal circumstances the excitement of an early finish and seeing Gran would have been overwhelming. Instead, I had a strange emptiness deep in the pit of my stomach that confused me.

"Hey, Jake, have a great holiday," I shouted as my best friend walked towards me. The biggest lump stuck in my throat and I turned away from him as my eyes prickled with tears. He wrapped me in a bone crushing hug before kissing me lightly on the cheek.

"I'll miss you, Abs, don't worry we'll see each other soon and you can tell me all about your holiday. I'll ask my mom to bring me over to your house again when you get back."

"Okay." The word stuck in my throat as I tried hard to smile back at him before walking away, my tears now flowing freely down my cheeks.

My dream hit the fast-forward button and skipped to the car ride back from the airport...

"I've been talking to your father, Abigail."

"Uh oh."

"It's been really hard for us lately, especially with the trip back to Casey to see Gran. So we've decided that I will carry on at work through the holidays. I've spoken to Peter and Jillian and they will be around most days if you need anything."

7

"*Aww, Mom! I can't look after Martin, he's a pain.*" No way. I just wanted to relax. Now I had a crappy job and no free time at all.

"*You can and you will, my girl.*"

"*Abbie's no fun, Mom, she always bosses me around!*"

I squirmed across the bed again at the disturbing memories hijacking my dream before the pull became too great and the images had me in their grasp...

Mom woke us up early before she left for work the next morning, reminding me of her expectations. We weren't allowed further than the shops across the road from our apartment building and had to be home before dinner.

"*I'm bored,*" *Martin said. We'd exhausted every vaguely entertaining activity since we'd arrived back from Gran's.*

"*We could go to Claire's house,*" *I suggested.*

"*You go, I'm not.*"

I thought long and hard about leaving him on his own. I'd be in big trouble if anything happened to him while I was supposed to be looking after him.

Not too long later; I found myself standing outside Claire's apartment. I knocked eagerly on the blue door, hoping that my friend would be back from her holiday. The door swung open widely and filling the opening was Peter, Claire's dad.

"*Well, hello there, Abbie,*" *he said cheerfully. "How are you?*"

"*Good thanks. Is Claire home?*" *I asked eagerly.*

"She's in her room, go through, she'll be happy to see you."

"Thanks," I said, skipping through the lounge room to my friend's bedroom.

"Hey!" I called as I entered the last room down the hallway on the left.

"Hey, yourself. How was your gran?"

"Yeah, great thanks," I beamed.

Again the images from my dream faded and reality drifted into my consciousness, but only briefly as sleep tugged me back to a time I would have preferred to avoid; a time where without realizing it then, I was about to experience the most horrific period in my young life. One which would catapult me into a brand new existence…

I knocked on Claire's door after lunch on Wednesday as planned. No answer.

"Oh well," I muttered under my breath and turned to head back to Martin when I bowled into Peter's solid mass. He'd just appeared from out of nowhere and I hit him square on in the chest. I jumped and gasped, but then smiled as I recovered, seeing who it was.

"Sorry I didn't see you, is Claire here?" I blushed madly.

"Not yet, but she won't be long, come in and wait for her, Abbie. She told me you'd be calling."

I followed him inside his apartment for the second time that week without a second thought; I'd been there so many times it felt like my second home. I sat on the couch next to Peter. He was reading the

9

newspaper and chatting to me at the same time. It turned out that Claire and her brothers were at the dentist with Jillian, their mom and wouldn't be much longer.

As the conversation continued, I began to feel a bit weird. Peter started acting strange, he began patting my leg as he spoke and then told me how pretty I was. I squirmed in my seat. It didn't feel right that he was telling me this. He said he'd been watching me since moving in to the apartment block. My tummy started to churn a little, like there were little butterflies flying about inside me. Then he lifted his hand from my leg and stroked my cheek. My breath caught in my throat and tears began to prickle in my eyes at the sensations running through my body.

"No!"

Chapter Two

"Abbie!" *It can't be time to get up yet. Please, God!* I slid further under the covers, clinging onto the remnants of sleep with all my might. "Abbie! Are you up?"

"Jeez, Mom! Five more minutes!" My stomach churned at the thought of going back to school. But at least with senior year finally here a welcome relief seeped into my chest. The whole ordeal would be over in less than ten months. Though I did okay on the work side of things, I hated the idea of having to interact with other students. I rolled over in bed with the intention of grabbing another few minute's sleep before hitting the shower. With the decision made to run tomorrow morning, I closed my eyes and pondered the torture of a new day at Casey High.

My reputation for being standoffish and rude preceded me. For the most part, people who didn't know me considered me moody, aggressive even. The simple truth of the matter was I preferred my own company. I settled back under the covers contemplating all things Casey High *and* my reputation. I hated meeting new people and making small talk with giggling teenage girls. It all seemed a pointless exercise. I recognized that my aversion to company and socializing was a lot to do with my childhood and how things had panned out. But I made no excuse for preferring to be alone.

Once a bubbly young girl, popular and sensible, not dissimilar to any other eight-year-old; I'd changed when my parents left me and my brother to fend for ourselves while they went to work. With strangers as our support network, the horrific fallout from that one misguided decision changed everything. The stress of hiding my foul secret for the two years that followed, as well as the constant nightmares, altered my personality to the extreme. Coupled with the persistent arguing between Mom and Dad, the remnants of anything like a normal life came crashing down the day Dad announced he was leaving us.

He gave up on us. He gave up on *me*. It was too hard for him to cope with a moody pre-teen. I hated him more than ever in that moment. For taking us to Raven in the first place, for not keeping me safe; his leaving was the ultimate betrayal after everything I'd suffered. But ironically, his leaving also supplied a ticket out of my living hell. I shuddered at the horrific memory replaying yet again in my head and buried my face in my pillow.

I made the life altering decision at ten-years-old after we got back home to Casey to never let another man into my life. Peter, Jake, my dad; they'd all hurt me. Men wrecked everything and tore out your heart along the way. No one was worth that kind of pain and I for one would not take that crap ever again. Nothing was more certain in my mind… No boyfriends. Trust was for fools.

"Abbie, I thought you wanted to go for a run before school?"

"I'll go tomorrow!" I groaned.

As the five minutes I'd begged Mom for turned into ten the appeal of staying in bed today of all mornings became far too tempting. I eased back under the covers, snuggled into my pillow and after only moments slipped into a light sleep. Images of Jake floated into my mind from distant memories tucked away for safekeeping. His smile, his eyes and the way my tummy tingled when he touched me. I found my body sinking into my soft mattress, savoring the memory replaying in my mind when the mood shifted brutally… There it was again…like a blow to my stomach…

"No one will ever love you like I do, Abigail. You're my angel from heaven, mine! Only mine!" I gasped for breath as the stale stench of tobacco and beer drifted into my senses and he crushed his body against mine.

My eyes flew open in a blind panic. My body shuddered as I realized where I was and that the realism of the loathsome memory was a reflection of the past, replayed through yet another vicious dream. A dream sent nightly to punish me repeatedly for my wrong doing. I squeezed my eyes shut as I tried to force the dream away and concentrate on the voice I could hear trying to pull me from my sleep.

"Abigail! Are you awake? You're going to be late!" I shook the evil image from my mind, rubbed my eyes then dragged my butt out of bed and into the shower.

The hot water crashed down on me as I stood with my forehead against the cold wall. After a moment I reached for the sponge and shower gel, allowing the calming effect of the exotic scent seep into my limbs. I inhaled deeply, recovering for now from my troubled sleep.

With my thoughts back on school I dressed in my usual jeans and T-shirt with a pair of sneakers and hoodie allowing for the unpredictable weather. Not wasting time on my hair, I tied it into a casual bun. After searching the bottom of the closet for my school bag I checked its contents and headed towards the stairs.

"Martin, are you ready?"

"I'm walking with Howie," he shouted from his room. I'd figured he wouldn't want to walk with me; he was far too cool to be seen with his big sister these days.

"Bye, Mom, see you tonight!" I called, grabbing a piece of toast on my way through the kitchen.

After the ten minute walk to school I crossed the parking lot and headed towards the main entrance of the senior building. The decision to leave my run until tomorrow meant a quieter start to the day. With more than forty minutes to go until the bell, I'd avoided the crowds. My gut started to churn with an all too familiar dread. By recess swarms of boisterous teenagers would be littering every hallway and courtyard. I took a tentative step onto the locker lined hallway where I saw Jo, the exception to my *No Friends* rule.

"How are you, stranger? I thought we were meeting up when I got back from the lake last week," she said, wrapping me in her arms.

"Yeah, sorry about that..." I stumbled through my brain trying to think of an excuse that wouldn't upset her. "I spent a fair amount of time at my gran's. She hasn't been well and Mom was working so I helped out." It wasn't a total lie as Gran had been unwell.

"Oh, that's too bad, hope she's ok now."

"She's on the mend, thanks. You're early."

"Well I have this friend who's a little shy in crowds and I figured she might like an iced chocolate before school starts." Jo and I had known each other forever. Our moms were best friends growing up and so we ended up friends by default.

"I reckon your friend will think that's an awesome idea." I smiled, my heart swelling at Jo's gesture.

Apart from an odd letter, I'd lost touch with Jo when my family moved away to Raven. But since coming back to Casey when Mom and Dad split, we'd hooked up again. Mom had needed a friend to support her through the whole divorce thing. Pam, Jo's mom, was a perfect fit for the role. I was glad about that because I hadn't felt up to *being there for her* after what happened to me.

Mom and Dad's priority of work over family wrecked my life. It still floored me how, aged eight and six respectively, me and Martin were left home alone for four hours every day. They were oblivious as to how their lack of common sense had impacted on their daughter. So no, I wasn't overly sympathetic to Mom's needs at that time. But despite all that, I loved my mom and deep down I was grateful of Pam's support.

"Come on then. You can tell me all about the lake."

"You're on," she said, draping her arm across my shoulder as we headed to the cafeteria.

***

"Jake, breakfast!" Mom's voice rebounded through the house as she prepared my breakfast, breaking my dream.

A crazy turn of events brought me to Casey High at this late stage in my education. I needed to graduate or I wouldn't get to university and I wanted to be a vet more than anything. I worried that the disruption to my studies, yet again, would set me back and keep me from that illusive place at the country's top veterinary academy.

Despite my frustrations with the constant moving between schools because of my dad's postings, I'd always managed to stay on top of my studies and catch up. I'd lost count of the friends I'd made and lost during my childhood. The loss of one friend in particular had left a gaping hole inside of me, one I'd never be able to fill. My mind drifted as thoughts of my best friend filled my head.

We'd thought we'd be friends forever and always joked about getting married and growing old together. I smiled at the memory and then frowned when, in turn, I remembered the day my parents had told me we were moving away again. Not being able to tell Abbie goodbye had killed me. She probably hated me because I'd left without a word. I remembered screaming and shouting at my dad at the time for ruining my life. But no amount of begging changed the fact that I was leaving her behind and would never see her again.

Last year had thrown another challenge my way. I'd spent a week in hospital followed by another four weeks off school after being diagnosed with a life threatening bacterial infection. Catching up on the assignments and lessons I'd missed proved challenging, but nothing would stop me from reaching my goal.

With my first day at Casey High looming, I was excited to get started. We'd been in the area for a couple of weeks, I'd met the neighbors, Pam and David. We'd chatted over the fence the day they got back from vacation. They seemed nice enough and done a great job filling in some gaps about the school with the help of their overly excited daughter, Joanna.

I hit the shower, threw on my jeans, loose shirt and sneakers before hauling myself down the stairs to where my mom had breakfast waiting.

"Thought you could do with a good start."

"Thanks, Mom, it looks great," I said as I sat down at the breakfast bar and helped myself to a pile of pancakes and bacon.

"Don't suppose you noticed whether Lucy was up before you came down?"

"Nah, sorry."

"Luuucyy! Get a move on, you're going to be late!" Mom shouted at the foot of the stairs.

"So... You got everything you need? Money?"

"I'm good. Thanks."

I stood up and moved towards where my mom was loading the dishwasher. As she turned to face me I grabbed her round the waist and spun her round, giving her a kiss before lowering her back to the ground.

"Thanks for breakfast." She laughed and smacked my chest before continuing to clear the kitchen.

"Are you taking Lucy?" I asked, picking up my bag.

"Yes, it looks like it," she said, shaking her head.

***

I arrived in time to complete all the necessary enrolment stuff before heading off to my first class armed with schedule, a handbook and map of the campus. Casey was much larger than my last school and I felt a bit disorientated to say the least. I glanced at my schedule making sure I was in the right place before entering my first class. Double English Literature followed by Calculus. Neither were particular favorites, I was more into the sciences, but hey, that was fine. Science came later in the week I noticed.

I struggled not to fall asleep in English Lit while the teacher enthused about analyzing some poem or other. Forced to sit at the front of the class because there were no seats available anywhere else, it soon became apparent why the occupants preferred to be as far from the teacher as possible. The lesson dragged.

I arrived in Calculus after everyone had already taken their seats. After apologizing to the teacher I glanced round the room for a vacant seat and spotted one towards the back where I could take in the whole gathering of personalities. I hoped to avoid being singled out to answer any questions. Aware that I had a lot of catching up to do, I intended focusing in lessons without attracting too much attention. My plan was to find my feet and work things out for a while.

The lesson had just started when the classroom door opened and in strolled a late arrival. At first glance she appeared quite tall for a girl, but I blew out a slow breath when my eyes drifted lower to her smoking body. Try as I might I couldn't see her face because of the hoodie she hid beneath. I couldn't work out why she'd captured my interest. After apologizing to the teacher, the girl took a seat by the door. The teacher told her to remove her hood as she sat down but yes, you guessed it, she had her back to me by then. Any hope of grabbing a good look at her was hopeless.

I couldn't help but stare at her throughout the lesson. Her long, dark blonde hair was knotted up on top of her head in one of those *up do thingies* girls went for these days. But apart from rocking my imagination to the limit, I had little idea of her appearance.

The lesson passed in a bit of a blur and ended before I had time to digest any new information on the subject at hand. I had spent an hour totally mesmerized by the long haired beauty in front of me. Grabbing my bag and shoving my books and stuff into it, I scanned the desks in front wondering where the girl would head next, but she'd disappeared.

"Shit!" I said under my breath and headed for the door with my map in hand.

One of the guys from English Lit called over from the opposite classroom as I navigated the hordes in the hallway.

"Hey, Jake! Over here buddy. Fancy grabbing a bite to eat? We all usually head to the cafeteria for lunch. You up for it?"

"Why not... thanks."

Chapter Three

The morning sessions passed without surprises. The same stale jokes and stupid pranks in lessons, the same teachers' mundane deliveries of an even more mundane syllabus; nothing much changed from year to year at Casey High.

I met Jo after Calculus outside the cafeteria as planned. The hum of excited students sharing tales from their holidays made me nervous. I took in a deep breath as my stress levels elevated. Crowds didn't do it for me at all. I'd spent the holidays alone, retreating back to my safe place. Faced with the need to emerge from my protective shell, my heart pounded against my ribs. I always struggled after holidays to dig myself out of *my rut* as Jo called it. But she never took *no* for an answer. Trips to the movies or shopping at the local mall on weekends satisfied her need to show me what I'd been missing. Jo's mission- to have me back to my sociable self within the week.

I took a sandwich from the selection on offer and grabbed a soda from the cooler. Jo rambled on about her holiday at the lake, family gossip, new puppy; a boy that had moved in next door and goodness knows what else. Being so off the wall crazy, I often wondered how we ever became friends. But she understood me better than anyone else. Jo knew there was more to me than even she understood, but she never asked she just accepted that all I wanted was a *no strings friend*.

"So..." she continued without a breath, "Any boys on the horizon?" The mouthful of soda I'd poured down my throat exploded in every direction as I inhaled instead of swallowing. My eyes watered and soda filled my nasal cavity. I coughed like a woman possessed as the bubbles hit, what I imagined to be the top of my lungs.

"Oh My God, Abs! Calm down, what's your problem, I was kidding!" she said, grabbing her bottle of water and throwing it towards me. She'd only asked about boys. It was a normal question in teenage circles. Not too welcome a topic in my view, but nevertheless a perfectly acceptable question.

"Sorry," I spluttered, "My soda went down the wrong way. Maybe I should switch to water." My brain stumbled, but Jo nodded in agreement and returned to her account of the lake, much to my relief.

Jo went on dates, but I never showed interest. So for her to blurt out a question about boys was way off. I wondered for a moment why she'd raised the subject now, but was distracted when a group of boisterous jocks drifted into the canteen. I frowned as I caught a glimpse of a new guy among them. He seemed familiar somehow.

They sat close by us, though the new guy had his back to our table. They had their own following though I didn't give a crap who they banged or what car they parked in the school parking lot. That said; I was now majorly captivated by the stranger with his back to us.

The cafeteria hummed with the noise of crazy students falling over themselves to find that perfect spot to socialize with friends. It made it difficult to listen in on a conversation on the next table. Especially when the girl sat next to you had a voice capable of breaking glass.

"Pretty cool place," the new guy said as Callum White launched himself at another bunch of guys already at the table. They were stuffing their faces with fries, burgers and anything else for that matter.

"Hey, this is Ja... He's new to football so give him a go guys." Callum grinned as he shoveled a burger into his mouth.

Shit! I missed his name. I played around with my lunch, breaking my sandwich into bite sized pieces for a while not really enjoying it.

The bell for the end of lunch sounded and we all finished up.

"Here we go again," I mumbled, my voice lacking enthusiasm. We gathered our trays and turned towards the exit facing the jocks' table. As usual they were surrounded by the regular cheer squad, skirts so short they left nothing to the imagination.

"Who do you reckon will be screwing the new guy by the end of the week?" I asked Joey under my breath. She just giggled at me and climbed over the bench seat. Not watching what she was doing, she caught her foot and ended up on her butt. Her clumsiness attracted the attention of everyone within striking distance. The jocks and their tramps included.

My eyes were drawn to the stranger amongst them with his back to us. The only hint to his appearance was his dark blonde, wavy hair, which skimmed his upturned collar. As he turned to see what all the fuss was about he laughed at Jo's predicament. I frowned in confusion as my heartbeat reacted to his laughter. My gaze was pulled towards him as adrenaline flooded my body, taking my heartbeat to another level. I gasped as I was hit square in the face with a sight that couldn't be real.

"Abbie?"

"Fuck!" My eyes locked on his, the same bright blue eyes of the little boy whose dreams I used to share. Then confusion hit me. What was he doing here?

Frozen to the spot, my breath caught in my throat. My eyes flooded with tears as my head spun with the barrage of emotions bombarding it; the hurt of losing him all those years ago, the anger he'd the nerve to be here, a crushing sadness at what we'd missed out on, and the resentment of a broken promise. But what terrified me the most was him finding out my deepest, darkest secret.

"Abbie!" Jo shouted, waving her hand in front of my face to get my attention.

In that moment I caught myself and snapped my eyes shut, "S-sorry Jo, I…I've got to go... Sorry." With a sudden overwhelming urge to escape; I fled.

"Where are you going? We've got Music... Abbie!" she yelled at my back as I flew towards the cafeteria doors desperate to get away.

"Shit!" he said before the bench he'd been sitting on scraped across the polished concrete and hit the floor.

"What's going on?" Jo shouted as my legs carried me across the courtyard at a ridiculous pace.

It can't be him. No way.

"I'll explain later," I heard him respond as he took chase.

We'd moved all the way across the country years ago and I hadn't seen him since I was eight-years-old. He'd left me with no way of staying in touch. How could he be

26

here? How had he found me? Panic began to rise like a tidal wave through my body.

I'd toughened up and gotten over the hurt that shattered my heart after he'd disappeared. I'd been to hell and back without him around and I didn't need him thinking I was interested in raking up the past or adding an *old friend* to my contact list on Facebook.

"Wait! Abbie, wait!"

"Argghh! This isn't happening." I ran harder across the campus towards the lake. Tears streamed down my cheeks. I didn't understand what he was doing there, but I did recognize the terror coursing through my veins at the prospect of him finding out about Peter.

"What the hell, Abs. Hold up! It's me, Jake, Jake Ashton... Don't you remember me?" That brought me to a sudden stop. I swung round, my ragged emotions clearly displayed on my tear stained face.

"Urrrgghhh!" I growled out in frustration and anger as I squeezed my fists tightly at my sides, "Of course I fucking remember you, Jake! How could I not?"

"Hey... Abbie... Whoa!" he said, gesturing with both hands for me to slow down, but I continued...

"You were my only friend. When you left my life fell apart," I cried, swiping at the burning tears streaming down my cheeks. My voice trailed off as another sob threatened to escape. He looked completely stunned at my outburst and I almost caved. My heart craved physical contact with my long lost friend; I'd missed him so much, but my head screamed the complete opposite and I remained rooted to the spot.

"Jesus, Abbie, I was eight-years-old for Christ's sake! I didn't want to move...*again*," he said, stepping towards me.

"Don't!" I growled under my breath as I backed up, not wanting him to touch me. I saw the confusion in his eyes at my reaction. He took a step away from me, rubbing his hands up and down his face trying to work out what he should do or say next.

"I was upset too, Abbie, I cried for days after we moved," he sighed, his hands on his head. "All I heard from my mom was how I would make new friends eventually and how it was normal to miss you at first. It didn't wear off...I've always missed you!"

Jake took a deep breath and ran his hand through his hair, searching my eyes for a glimmer of the old Abbie. "I wondered where you were and what you were doing. You were my best friend. I thought you would always be with me. Hell, I thought about you just this morning." He lowered his head briefly before looking at me again. I could see the sincerity in his eyes as he continued to speak. "I thought I'd never see you again. But for whatever reason, I'm here now. Call it a coincidence or fate or whatever you like, but we moved here for my dad's latest posting."

Desperation dripped from his every word. He waited, searching my face for a reaction to this latest information. "I know it's been a long time, Abs, but...can we..." His voice faded away as though unsure of what to suggest, or what he wanted from me, but I wanted nothing from him.

I took a deep breath before I replied, looking him straight in the eyes, determined to get my point across and to leave no room for doubt.

"Whatever, Jake, just leave me the fuck alone. I don't need you in my life, you're nothing special. People change. Life goes on." My eyes stung as I turned away from him.

He grabbed my arm to keep me from leaving.

"Don't do this, Abbie, please!" he begged.

I reaction to the physical restraint was instinctive. My fist made contact with the side of his face. All control of the situation lost in that split second and in its place, regret and a deep sadness in the pit of my stomach. He looked devastated; I needed to get away from him. I couldn't bear the expression of undeniable hurt on his face. It tore my heart out to see how, after all these years I'd managed to treat him so cruelly. He didn't deserve that.

"Argghh!" I cried and with that I fled. Where to? I didn't know. I just had to get away.

"What the hell? Abbie!" he shouted, sounding deflated. "Abbie!"

***

Stood by the bridge across the lake with a migraine threatening I leaned on the hand rail, trying to make sense of what had happened. *Why did you have to move here, Jake?* He couldn't have known what happened after he left, I knew that… and he'd probably missed me as much as I'd missed him. But one thing was certain…he couldn't have recognized any part of the old Abbie in the raving lunatic he'd just encountered.

"Aarrgghhh! Shit! Shit! Shit!"

I took off again, heading for home. The streaks of my tears had dried on my cheeks by the time I clattered up the porch steps. My mom was still at work and wouldn't be home for at least five more hours. *Thank God!* I needed to get a grip and decide what I was going to do.

With my head pounding, I headed for the kitchen and pulled open the cupboard where Mom kept the first aid box. I needed some painkillers badly. After swallowing two tablets and draining a large glass of water I climbed the stairs to my bedroom and threw myself on my bed.

"Shit, shit, shit, shit!" I screamed into my pillow. "Arrrggghhhh! Okay, deep breaths, deep breaths." Focused for a moment on slowing my pounding heart I closed my eyes and breathed in deeply. I had to think this through in a logical manner without raking up all the Peter Stevens shit.

I struggled to function at an acceptable level in school and at home as it was. The nightmares were bad enough without the humiliation of Jake finding out. With his whole life in front of him, Jake didn't need any of my shit dragging him down and I didn't want him hating me. Deep inside me, the memory of our friendship lived on, even after all these years. It wasn't hate I felt towards him, it was regret, regret of losing what we once had together *and* that he hadn't been there when I needed a hug and someone to make the pain stop. It wasn't his fault, I knew that, but it was too late. We weren't friends anymore, we'd changed, I'd changed and there was no going back. Not now, not ever.

Lying on my bed I stared at the ceiling for what seemed like hours, thinking and planning my next move. My body relaxed as I made a decision, one that I was convinced of and my eyes grew heavy as exhaustion took over my body.

Chapter Four

The moon shone through my window as I stared at the ceiling, mulling over Abbie's outburst. I hadn't felt like facing the inevitable questions from Callum *or* Jo, so I'd skipped the afternoon session. Not my usual style, but I needed to clear my head.

"Fuck!" I rolled onto my stomach and buried my head in the covers. *Jeez, girls are confusing.*

Images of Abbie at the lake flooded my mind. I'd followed her to the bridge and crouched at the side of the path so she wouldn't see me. *Shit she was gorgeous.* She'd always been pretty, but standing on that bridge, and earlier right in front of me... *Wow.*

Her blue green eyes still sparkled with the determination I remembered from years ago. The urge to touch her flawless skin had almost floored me. I imagined her hair would flow way down her back in thick waves if she untied the ridiculous bun thing. But *her body... Oh My God.* A new emotion stirred deep in my gut at that memory. Her stomping up and down on the bridge reminded me of her tantrums when we were kids, but my smile turned to a frown with the memory of her right hook. *Jeez, she's one crazy girl now.*

"What the hell happened to her?"

As sleep pulled me under, my mind flooded with a stream of familiar images of eight-year-old Abbie. Under the tree at school, a sleepover at her place, a trip to the pool, laughing at my jokes…

I thrashed around the bed trying to get comfortable as mid-dream she morphed into the raging beauty of today. My body ached for her embrace as I woke to my usual early morning alarm call.

"You up, Jake?"

"Mmm," I groaned, pulling the covers over my eyes. Memories of the confrontation I'd had with Abbie flooded back. Sleep deprived, the last thing I needed was to face everyone at school. "Argh!"

"Jake?"

"I'm up, Mom! Jeez!"

"Hey? I heard that, young man."

It took me less than thirty minutes to shower, dress and get to school; pretty impressive in anyone's book. I rounded the corner onto the court yard five minutes before the bell and took a deep breath as I spotted Callum, "Here we go…"

"Hey Jake! Wait up!" I carried on walking down the hallway. I didn't want to talk to anyone at that moment or explain yesterday's outburst to a relative stranger.

"Jake! Hey, come on, man!"

I made the decision to keep mine and Abbie's history private and turned to face Cal. "Hey, how's it going, Callum?" I said, doing my best to come off calm and cheerful.

"Jeez, you must be deaf!" Callum replied with a big grin on his face.

"Sorry, I was miles away. What you up to? You going to Gym?"

"Just heading there. Hey, what went down between you and Freaky Abbie yesterday, dude?" My jaw clenched at Callum's comment. I searched my mind for something to keep mine and Abbie's history under wraps for now.

"Oh that! Yeah, sorry about that. She reminded me of someone from another school."

"You called her Abbie though."

"Yeah well... the girl next to her called her Abbie."

"Oh, okay. Whatever, anyway, you don't wanna go messing with that chick, dude, she's got serious anger issues. She only speaks to Jo. She's bonkers. They're both crazy."

That's where I know her friend from… It's Joanna, the girl from next door. I thought I recognized her from somewhere.

"Don't be lulled into thinking they're like any other hot chicks. They so aren't. I'm serious, man. She's not right in her head!" Uncomfortable with our conversation, I focused on *my* knowledge of Abbie. The Abbie *I* remembered would never have such a poor reputation. *My* Abbie was awesome and gorgeous. The girl Callum described was a stranger and it made me nervous. My heart picked up a notch as I considered why she'd gone all psycho on me yesterday. Maybe she'd split with a boyfriend or something. I shuddered at the idea.

***

"Did you see Jake just now, Abs?" Jo asked as we got ready for Gym.

"Nope," I said, trying my best to halt any conversation about Jake Ashton before it started. I watched as Jo rummaged through her bag for her water bottle. Today was track and field and one of my favorite lessons.

I leaned back against the bleacher seats blocking out Jo's mutterings about yesterday's little episode. I didn't owe her an explanation. It was nothing to do with anyone else, but I wasn't about to offend her. I'd let her have her say. I just wouldn't listen.

"Shit!" I said, catching sight of Jake, "Why does my life have to be such a fucking drama?"

"What's wrong now?" she asked, taken aback by yet another *Abbie* outburst.

"It's nothing, just thinking out loud," I said, bending to fasten my shoes.

Jo glanced over to what had sparked my mood change. "Hmm."

"What?" I asked, pulling my hair back and fixing it in a tighter pony tail.

"Nothing, I didn't say a thing."

"Yeah right. Don't go getting any funny ideas, Jo. I'm not in the mood for any fucking wise cracks."

"Okay, okay, keep your hair on. Jeez! Come on, Jackson's here."

With a glare in Jake's direction, I headed over to the long jump pit as he and Callum walked towards the Javelin.

Did he just wink? My mouth dropped open in disgust, "The nerve of him. If he thinks he can waltz straight back in at *Number One Best Friend* he's another thing coming."

I was no walkover. I would not share my past or future with any guy. No way. Jo sat on the grass looking smug.

I launched myself down the long jump run and into the sand several times over the next hour. The lesson passed in a blur, but I welcomed the physical activity, it helped to clear my mind of the craziness of the last twenty four hours.

"Jeez, Abs, you were on fire today, girl. You'll have to tear a shred or two off a random guy every time we have Gym," she said as we stood reading the bulletin board after our shower. Before I was able to respond Jake exited the male locker room and walked straight into Jo.

"Oops, sorry... Hey, Joanna isn't it? From next door?" he asked as he threw a glance in my direction. I rolled my eyes, watching the cogs going round in her brain as Jo processed his words.

"Oh my God, yeah! It was you yesterday, when Abs had her melt down at lunch."

I couldn't believe this, he was her new neighbor?

Fuck!

"I'll see you when you're done here," I said, picking up my bag.

"I guessed you hadn't recognized me. Anyway, I'll see you around, Joanna. You too, Abbie... It is Abbie isn't it?" I glared at him, *frickin cheek*.

"Yeah, she's Abbie. Don't you two know each other already though?" My mouth fell open.

"No, she reminded me of a girl from elementary school, my best friend when I was about eight. *She* was very different though," he said as our eyes locked. *Hello.*

37

I'm standing right here. "My mistake," he said without apology. I didn't bother trying to hide my anger from either of them. I could see the regret in Jake's eyes as he watched me. "Erm... Anyway, Callum's waiting for me." With a final sideways glance at me, he left.

"See you at home sometime," Jo said.

"What the hell was that?" I was livid.

"He's a bit of a hunk isn't he?" Jo was oblivious to my mood. Unable to speak, I left.

"Urggh!"

"Wow, he's got it bad for you, missy," she said, her lips quirking up at the corners in a knowing smirk.

"Excuse me?" I closed my eyes at the absurdity of her statement, "Forget it. I'll see you tomorrow." My heart was now pounding harder than ever. I stormed down the hallway in serious need of air. I'd had enough for one day.

"Abbie, hold up!" an all too familiar voice shouted.

"Fuck!" Could this day get any worse? I ignored him and kept walking.

"I won't give up, Abbie."

"Really?" I said, just loud enough for him to hear the irritation in my voice, "That's too bad!"

"For fuck's sake, Abs, what the hell happened to you?" It was obvious he didn't realize what he was asking. It was more to do with the radical change in my personality, but I was pissed off and ready for round two.

"You have got to be kidding!" I said, swinging round to face him, "What gives you the right to comment on anything to do with me?" My voice faltered as I struggled to breathe, "You don't know me, Jake. You never did. So why don't you run along to your new buddies and get on with your sad little life and leave me the fuck alone!" He looked stunned but didn't move, his eyes reflected the hurt rushing through my veins.

"Abbie?" He tried to appeal to the old me, reaching out to touch my arm, but I flinched away at the sudden contact. I struggled to hide my overreaction to his touch by folding my arms, but it was too late, the torment was clear in his eyes.

Not about to let him or his emotions get to me, I took a deep breath, "I'm sorry, Jake, just leave me alone. Please."

***

I'm not sure how long it took me to get home, but I heaved a huge sigh of relief when I arrived at the front door. I took the stairs two at a time, dumped my bag, pulled off my hoodie and headed for the bathroom. Splashing cold water on my overheated face, I stared at my flustered expression in the mirror. It took a couple of deep breaths to slow my racing heartbeat.

"Abbie, is that you up there?" My mom called from downstairs.

"Yes! Who else is it going to be?"

She grumbled under her breath and headed into the kitchen. I couldn't help being a bitch, I opened my mouth and out it came, every time. I felt sorry for my mom, she tried to appeal to my better nature- the old Abbie, but the harder she tried, the more difficult I got. The crap with Peter could have happened at any time, whether she and Dad had been at work or not, but I had a need to transfer my deep seated guilt to someone else. There was no other way to get my head round my pain, not at this stage anyway. Mom was an easy target.

Martin rolled up with Howie just as I'd changed into a pair of loose track pants and clean T-shirt.

"Hey, Abs," he said, "Jo asked if you were going over, something about helping her out with an assignment." I grabbed my cell phone off my bed.

Missed Call

"Yep?" she said, sounding as though she had a mouth full of food.

"Hi! We didn't get an assignment."

"I know that," she said, finishing her mouth full of food. "I just thought you might like to hang out for an hour or two. You seemed a bit stressed today. I've got money for pizza, my mom's working late and Dad's out with his friends. We could listen to a few tunes and hang out."

"Give me a minute and I'll call you back." I hung up, grabbed my hoodie off the bed and ran down the stairs.

"Mom, I'm going round to Jo's for an hour or so. She needs my help with something for school!" I slammed the front door behind me, my cell already on redial.

"You coming?"

"Yeah, I'll be there in ten." I tucked the phone into my pocket and pulled my hood up as it began to drizzle.

I arrived at Jo's house as a car pulled into the drive next door. My heartbeat increased tenfold when I realized the implications of *that* drive and *that* car. I kept my head down and rushed to Jo's door, eager to get inside. I hadn't stopped to consider the possibility of bumping into Jake. The subject of him and Jo being next door neighbors had come up at least three times in the last two days. I guess with the shock of seeing him again my head was mush.

"Hi." I breathed out with relief as I pushed past her when she opened the front door.

41

"Hi, yourself. Hey, where's the fire?" she asked, almost falling over her own feet from the force of my entrance.

"It's raining… Stick the kettle on will you?" She shook her head at my over exaggeration and moved into the kitchen.

The evening passed with comfortable conversation, pizza, hot chocolate and a cheesy movie. The adrenaline eased from my body with every minute that passed. Jo was easy to be around. She would have loved to talk about boys and stuff, but she understood it was a *no go zone*. She also knew she'd said enough about Jake for one day.

"Fancy a couple of days away at the lake this weekend?" she asked out of the blue, "My mom is going on a software course for work a few miles from the lake house. She wondered whether we would like to go too."

I grinned at her. "That sounds great, I'll have to check with my mom first, but it should be fine. She'll be glad to get rid of me."

"Cool bananas, that's settled then."

"I guess I'd better head off, I'm tired out."

"Why don't you stay here tonight? Your mom won't mind, you've stayed before, give her a call."

"Ermm, I don't know, Joey, I'm tired. We'll end up chatting all night if I stay."

"No we won't, anyway, I'm tired too. Go on, it'll mean you don't have to get up as early for school tomorrow. We can go in together with my mom."

"Fine, I'll stay, but I'm going to bed soon."

"Yay!" she squealed.

Mom hadn't minded at all; she was probably relieved. It cut down the chances of another confrontation.

"They'll fit you," Jo said laying out clothes for the next day. I huffed at the sight of the skinny jeans and snug purple T-shirt she'd selected for me.

"Yeah right!" I said, climbing into the double bed that we were sharing that night.

.

Chapter Five

Come on, Abbie, lie still, that's right angel, you know you like it...

Silent sobs caught in my throat as the monster forced his bulk against me, terror holding me captive. Tears streamed down my cheeks as I thrashed and struggled to get free. A frantic voice urged me to open my eyes. Someone was trying to stop him...

"Abbie! Come on, Abbie, wake up, you're dreaming," Jo urged, shaking me by the shoulders. My eyes flew open, and I bolted upright. My heart pounded in my chest as I swiped at the tears streaming down my cheeks. A stunned Jo moved forward and placed a hand on my leg. I recoiled from the sudden touch, but the wall prevented my escape.

"Abbie? Jeez, girl! What's the matter?" Sobs caught in my throat and I gasped for air. My fingers clawed at the bed covers beneath me as my eyes searched in anguish for my invisible assailant. With my body pressed up against the wall and my knees pulled tight against my chest; my panic reached its climax leaving me dry mouthed, sweating and with no control over my trembling limbs.

"For fuck's sake, Abbie! Jeez, it was a dream!" Jo tried her best to shake me from my nightmare without waking the entire house. She took hold of my arms forcing me to make eye contact with her. "Hey! Shh, Abbie…shh."

I sucked in a deep breath and tried to calm down. An overwhelming sense of embarrassment flooded my entire being. Now off the bed, Jo paced around the room, every few seconds casting anxious glances my way. I raked my fingers through my hair in desperation. My heart was beating so hard I could feel it in my throat. How was I going to explain this to her? She'd never believe me.

"What the hell was that, Abbie?"

Uncontrollable tremors racked my body as I eased myself towards the edge of the bed. I gripped the sheets, fearful of the words that threatened to betray me.

The nightmares were nothing new to me. But they'd intensified since Jake showed up out of the blue. His arrival had stirred up my past with Peter in grand style. I'd managed to keep my secret hidden for years, preferring to keep a low profile. In a few short days my mundane existence had flipped on its head.

I had to think of an acceptable excuse for my outburst. It was obvious Joey wouldn't settle for, *It was just a nightmare*, but I heard those feeble words leave my mouth anyway. She knelt on the floor in front of me, her hands on my knees.

"*That*…was not…*just* a nightmare, Abs! That was fucking real! You do not react like that to *just a nightmare!* Now… What…the fuck…just went down?" she demanded.

Jo wasn't known for her serious side, but when the shit hit the fan she was solid. She'd do anything for anyone. I hoped this was one of those occasions.

I knew Jo suspected I had deep seated issues, but she respected my privacy. She never pushed the subject of boyfriends; I was grateful for that. This whole Jake thing of late threatened to be my undoing, and I didn't want to lose her trust and support. I needed to be honest with her. I needed Joey in my life. If her knowing everything was going to push her away and wreck our friendship then so be it. But one way or another, it was time to share my burden. I couldn't carry it any longer on my own.

The worry in her eyes reflected the torment coursing through my veins as I struggled for the words to save our friendship.

"I… Erm I…"

"Hey, it's okay." Jo took my hands squeezing them tight. I pulled in a deep breath and blew out slow through trembling lips as I summoned the courage to begin.

"You can tell me, sweetie." Concern etched across Jo's brow as she willed me to continue.

"You…you remember…when we…moved away?" Jo nodded but remained silent. "Fuccckkk!" *This is going to be tough.* "We had to stay home alone…while Mom and Dad worked. And…" My breath caught in my throat as tears threatened to spill over again.

Jo squeezed my hands, "Go on…"

"They were supposed to look after us, Joey," I sobbed, looking away from Jo as I tried to compose myself enough to continue, "But…he… Fuck!" I growled in disgust at the memory, "I…I went inside to…to wait…for Claire… He told me to come in… We talked a bit…" My voice shook with anger as I recalled that first horrific time.

"He…he raped me, Jo. Over and over and over for almost two years!" As I recalled my secret shame silent tears streamed down my face. "Claire's dad raped me." I covered my face with my hands, unable to look at my best friend. "He broke me, Joey." Violent sobs racked my body as I catapulted back to a time when an eight-year-old girl lost her innocence to a monster.

"Oh my God, Abbie. No!" she gasped, her eyes pooling with tears. She pulled me into her arms, to ease her pain as much as mine.

"I can't…do…this…anymore, Joey," I said between sobs, "I just want to…"

"Don't you dare go there, don't!"

Our bond strengthened as we cried together and comforted one another for what seemed like hours.

"You should have told me."

A sense of relief crept through my body. With a cautious gulp of air, I leaned away from my friend and I wiped away her tears. As my eyes locked on Jo's I saw the incredible hurt that my revelation had put there.

"Abbie, I'm so sorry," she said, shaking her head. "How could... Who the fuck?" Jo's voice trembled as she began to process the shit I'd just dumped on her.

Full of regret and concern for my friend I tried to ease her rising anger, "It was my fault anyway."

"What the fuck! Abbie? Jeez, you don't believe that? Do you?" Irrational as it was, my brain had convinced me over the years that being raped as an eight-year-old was my fault. I had caused it to happen and allowed it to continue; simple as that.

"I kept going back for more, Jo... I didn't want anyone to find out." My stomach dropped at Jo's stunned expression. I lowered my head and squeezed my eyes shut, mistaking her silence for disgust.

"Never, ever, say that! You were a baby... A grown man- A vicious, evil, Satan spawned piece of shit raped an eight-year-old! It. Was. Not. Your. Fault!"

I shifted uncomfortably on the bed, stifling my sobs as my fingers fidgeted in my lap. Her eyes narrowed as she sensed I was still hiding something, "What? There's more isn't there?"

I had to explain about Jake. All of this was because of him. The nightmares, my moods; everything had fallen apart since he arrived in town.

"Shit, Abbie, what else did he do?"

"It's Jake…" My lip trembled as I spoke his name.

"What do you mean it's Jake? What's Jake? Which Jake?" Jo shook her head in confusion. I took a deep breath, and proceeded to tell her about Jake leaving. She remembered that I'd mentioned him in a couple of letters, though she'd forgotten his name until now. The fact that I hadn't mentioned him once since the day he left probably had a lot to do with her vacant expression. I went on to explain about Mom and Dad leaving us on our own while they went to work.

"We needed the money," I protested. Jo's frown deepened at my reasoning. I could tell she was pissed at this latest piece of information. I guess she recognized the obvious in that one statement. Who leaves two young kids alone all day to go to work? It was a massive error of judgment on their part, one which continued to haunt me. I told her how we'd made friends with Claire's family, but how everything had turned sour when her dad engineered every opportunity possible to fuck a little girl. Jo looked mortified. She took a steadying breath and let it out slowly while I continued.

"I thought things would improve when I got back to school and saw Jake." Another lone tear left the corner of my eye as I recalled the first day back at school. How the teacher said Jake wouldn't be coming back to Raven Elementary.

"Then he shows up here after ten years like nothing happened?" I lifted a trembling hand to my forehead as I heaved in a lungful of air. Jo's expression shifted from one of confusion to instant understanding.

"Oh my God! No way! Jake Ashton? Fuck!"

"Yep."

"Does he know?"

Panic took over as soon as the question left her mouth, "Please don't tell him, Joey! He can't ever find out! Please!"

"Hey…" She grabbed my shoulders and forced me to look at her. In her eyes I saw nothing but warmth and understanding. "I won't tell a soul, ever. I love you, Abbie. You're my best friend. What that fucker did was sick. You'll tell Jake yourself when you're ready."

I shook my head frantically at this, "I won't...he can't...he'll hate me."

"Okay, okay, shh. It's okay, he won't find out from me," Jo said with a reassuring smile.

We spoke more about my time away and what Jake and I had together. As the conversation continued Jo grew more and more pissed. Her eyes became glassy with unshed tears of anger. I'd spilled all the trauma of my childhood with no thought of sparing my friend its gruesome details. I lifted my hand and squeezed her arm.

"You okay?" I asked, regretting my lack of a filter.

Jo slumped forward resting her head in her hands as she considered my question before turning towards me.

"Am I okay? You've got to kidding me right? You just told me you were raped when you were eight by a fucking dirty old pervert and you ask me if *I'm* ok?" she cried, getting to her feet, "No. I'm fucking livid!" Jo's tears fell as she leaned against the back of the bed. "Who does something like that to a kid?"

"It's over, it doesn't matter anymore," I replied with a defiant tilt of my chin.

"Fucking dead set it still matters!" she almost yelled as she swung round to face me, "You never date, you cringe every time guys are mentioned. You've just been reunited with the love of your life after not seeing him for ten years and what do you do? You treat him like a leper!" I flinched at the suggestion that I loved Jake, but she continued, "You're a bitch to your mom! Fuck, Abbie, of course it matters!"

With my nerves in tatters and desperate to end this conversation for good, I took another deep breath.

"I know I'm a bitch to her, I try not to be. It's just so hard." Jo's sympathetic smile showed a level of understanding. "As for Jake. You've seen him. He's popular, smart, talented…"

"And?" she challenged.

"He can do so much better," I answered, my voice reflecting the conviction I felt.

"You have got to be kidding me!" Jo scoffed. I knew she meant well, but I wasn't ready to have this conversation.

"I need you to drop it, Joey… I've lived with it for long enough and gotten over it. It's taken years to build a new life since we came back to Casey. I don't need that shit dragging me down again."

"But…"

"Please, Jo. Let it drop. I can't talk about it…not now. Not ever. Please." My determination won through, for the moment anyway.

"Okay, I'll leave it…for now," she said, rubbing my upper arms. "But it's not done, and you know it. It's been over for years and you're still dreaming like this. It's not done, not by a long shot." Jo gave me a comforting hug before heading into the bathroom.

I wiped my face with my sleeve as I glanced at the clock next to the bed, "Jeez, another hour and we've got to get up for school." I climbed back into bed and pulled the covers up to my chin. A sense of relief washed over me as I digested what I'd shared with Jo.

"I'm so sorry, Jo," I said as she returned to the bedroom.

"You don't *ever* have to say sorry. Not for that. Never! Okay?"

"Okay."

With that she climbed back into bed beside me.

"Go back to sleep," she said, giving my shoulder a gentle squeeze. "Night."

"Night, Joey," I said on a sigh and turned towards the window where the moon shone through a crack in the curtains. My thoughts returned again to Jake and how, even after all this time, he still had a place in my heart. I hated it, but it was true. No matter what happened in the coming days, weeks or months he would not find out. I had perfect memories of us in my head, untainted by anything that had happened to me at the hands of that monster. As far as I was concerned, Jake had to think I'd changed.

I couldn't allow him to remember me differently, to be disgusted in me; to hate me. I just couldn't risk seeing those emotions in his beautiful blue eyes.

Chapter Six

"Jake, don't forget your lunch?"

"It's in my bag. I'm going, I'll see you later." I pulled the door shut behind me throwing my bag over my shoulder.

"Wonder what excitement lies in wait today," I said under my breath with a wry smile as I headed for the garage doors. Two familiar voices drifted over the fence as I grabbed my bike. One in particular caught my attention. With that recognition, tingles flew across the flesh of my arms. Curious as to the nature of their conversation, I took a hesitant step towards Jo's driveway.

"Thanks again for last night, Joey, sorry about keeping you awake," Abbie said as I leaned in a little.

"Hey, that's what I'm here for."

I frowned at Abbie's apology and Jo's subsequent support. What the hell was that about? I decided to alert them to my presence and coughed under my breath as I pushed my bike within feet of their discussion. Not paying any attention they carried on talking.

"Huh hmm!" I coughed again. Abbie stopped laughing and threw me a glare I swear should have turned me to stone. She seemed about to give me a piece of her mind for eavesdropping when Jo saved me.

"Oh, hey! Morning, Jake! How are you?"

"Yeah, good thanks. You guys sound like you're having fun." My grin reflected my relief at Jo's timing.

"Oh, yeah, well, Abbie stayed over last night, girl's night in…you know?"

"Right," I said with a glance in Abbie's direction. She seemed less than impressed with mine and Jo's chat. The tension flowed from her straight into my chest.

Jo looked between the two of us sensing our non-verbal exchange, "Erm, well we're heading into school, you going in today?"

"Yep, just sorting out my bike, then I'm off."

"There's room with us if you want a lift." Abbie gasped at Jo's offer and again tension lingered in the air above us as I considered my options.

"I'm good thanks. Need the exercise," I said, patting my stomach.

Abbie's relieved expression didn't escape my notice as she walked to the other side of Pam's car.

"See you around then," I said, climbing onto my bike.

My imagination kicked into overdrive on the journey into school. I couldn't stop thinking about Abbie. I replayed each of our confrontations from the last couple of days over and over in my mind as I rode down the country lane.

What now? I had to find a way in. *I have to win her back!* My commitment to that one statement was greater than anything I'd felt for a long time. The big question was, how? I longed to hear her infectious laughter, to see the twinkle in her eyes. We'd shared happy and sad times together. I remembered us being able to talk about anything. We hadn't known one another for that long, a matter of months, but those few months were long enough to make a lasting impression. I'd carried my memories of Abbie throughout my teenage years with the hope that one day I'd see her again.

It blew me away when the hot babe from class two days ago turned out to be Abbie. A smile tugged at the corner of my mouth at the image that popped into my head. Her stunning curves captured my attention as soon as she walked into the classroom with her hoodie pulled over her face.

My smile turned to confusion as I pondered the emptiness in her eyes. She said she'd changed, well yeah, I had too. The only difference, I hadn't undergone a major personality transplant. Abbie was very different, and I planned on getting to the bottom of why.

"I have to find out what happened to her!" Determination flooded my chest. I had no intention of letting her slip through my fingers again.

And so it began... *Operation Abbie*. I decided from that point to give her space. I had to coax her into trusting me again; become her friend and rebuild our friendship.

Just ease off a bit... Give her a bit of space. I nodded in response to the silent mantra running through my overactive mind.

With my bike secured to the rack in the designated compound at the back of the gym I headed off to the first science lesson of the week. I'd arranged to meet Callum outside. Before I'd crossed the bike compound the rain began to fall. Distant thunder rumbled overhead and some serious lightning lit up the sky. Soaked through to the skin in an instant, I flew towards the main entrance; racing through the courtyard filled with screaming students, before crashing through the doors of the science block and out of the torrential storm.

"Hey, Jake! Bit wet there dude?" Callum roared laughing as he spotted me staggering towards him looking like a drowned rat.

"Hey!" I groaned then laughed as well.

We headed towards our first lesson more interested in football practice later than what we'd be doing in science.

All talk revolved around positions, tactics, strengths within the team, weaknesses and the up and coming season.

Still immersed in our conversation as we entered class, we slumped into our seats. I pulled my text book from my bag while listening to Cal ramble on about football, offering an intermittent nod and yep to the conversation as the need arose.

The arrival of Abbie and Jo went unnoticed by Callum, who continued on about football practice. My breath however, caught in my throat at the sight of her. Abbie's drenched waves fell about her shoulders; her clothes clung to her like a second skin and my heart clenched.

"Fuck!"

At this point Callum stopped speaking and turned towards me, then looked at Abbie.

"You've got it bad, man."

"What? What d'you mean?" I grinned, knowing I'd been busted.

"You know exactly what I mean, Jakey Wakey," he said with a smirk.

Abbie met my gaze as the teacher entered and with a flood of confidence I smiled at her, willing her to smile back.

"Go on, sweetheart...go on," I whispered under my breath. A blush of color crossed her cheeks as she adjusted her top. Then, a slight smile pulled on her lips, acknowledging the humor in my glance. I sucked in a small breath. At that moment an overwhelming sense of promise came over me.

The lesson continued with little excitement after the wet start. Dr. Thomas seemed happy with our attempts in the practical. After giving receiving our term assignment instructions with an explanation that we were expected to do them in groups, we packed up and headed towards the cafeteria for a well-deserved hot drink.

"Hot chocolate?" I heard Abbie suggest as both her and Jo packed their bags.

"You're on." Jo said, flashing her brightest smile.

"I'll see you in there. I'm just gonna dry off a little first. My undies are soaked right through to my skin," she said, handing over the money. My heart skipped a beat as the image of Abbie in her wet underwear flooded my mind.

Oh my God!

"Right you are, see you in a mo," Jo said over her shoulder as she skipped away in the opposite direction.

This was my opportunity to make contact again. I entered the male locker room, stripped down, dried and dressed in my sports gear before throwing a towel over my head. Now to wait...

The door to the girl's locker room banged open and I grabbed my chance.

"You look better," I said with a chuckle, noting the length of her hair and imagining what it would be like to run my fingers through it. She gasped at my sudden appearance, but it was the flinch away from me that took me by surprise.

"Yep, I feel it too," she said, her arms wrapped tight across her chest. She remained tense as we walked in the same direction towards the cafeteria. "Erm…you're a bit drier too," she said after a moment, in what appeared to be an attempt at making polite conversation.

"Yeah, lucky it's sport later and I had a change of clothes." I kept an eye on Abbie as we headed into the cafeteria. Her whole body language shifted, her eyes flitting all over the place, taking in everything and everybody. It reminded me of a crime show and a cop taking in clues at the crime scene.

I scanned the room until I spotted Cal deep in conversation with Jo. Based on his suggestion to stay away from both her and Abbie yesterday, I found this ironic and raised an eyebrow questioning his motives.

"Hey, here's your drink, Abs, I got you a toasted bagel as well," Jo said, holding out the cup. I watched with amusement as Abbie took the cup from her friend and sat on the bench seat as far away from Cal as possible.

"So that's set then…we'll meet round at my place tomorrow after school to make a start on the assignment."

"Cool," he agreed.

"What…what assignment? Meet where?" Abbie spluttered her mouth already full of hot chocolate.

"The science assignment that we have to complete in groups," Jo replied, rolling her eyes. I saw her glance over to Callum at that point and then to me.

"So what are you saying, Jo! You've asked Callum to join us to work on the assignment?" Abbie asked, taking another drink.

I raised an eyebrow at the genius of my new friend. *Jeez, Callum, that's perfect.*

"Yep, him and Jake," she added.

"What?"

In that split second an explosion of hot chocolate hit me full on in the chest. Abbie's eyes watered as she coughed and spluttered in the aftermath of her spraying me with the contents of her mouth. The few friends sat close by erupted into fits of laughter at the sight of my surprised expression. Surprise that faded as soon as I realized Abbie was struggling to breathe. She continued to cough and gasp for breath. Her eyes watering as she failed to get air into her lungs. I reacted instinctively by grabbing her wrists and squeezing hard across the pulse point on each, looking straight into her eyes.

"Hey!" I urged, working hard to get her undivided attention. "Breathe, Abs! Slow it down." She fought at first to escape my grasp, but I held firm. "Hey, stop struggling and breathe!" I insisted a second time, tugging at her arms. She stopped her wriggling at my insistence and I saw recognition in her eyes. I'd explained to her once that whenever I would have a coughing fit my mom would squeeze my wrists to get the coughing to stop; she never offered a medical explanation, it just worked.

When she'd regained her composure Abbie snatched her hands from my grasp. The subtle flush to her cheeks as she pulled away sent a warm glow to my groin.

"I'm so sorry," Abbie said, throwing me an apologetic frown as her lip became trapped in her teeth.

"Don't worry about it, I've had worse." I held back the urge to wink as I sat, deciding instead that a simple smile would do.

Chapter Seven

With no time to dwell on the hot chocolate saga, Thursday arrived. My stomach churned as Jo and I prepared snacks for our study group; my state of mind, that of a condemned woman.

"So…my mom told me the trip this weekend is off." Disappointment hit my chest like a battering ram. I suspected this would happen. Who would want to spend the night with a bipolar Freak like me anyway? I kept my focus on slicing the ham for the sandwiches.

"Oh, okay." I tried to appear unfazed by Jo's news. I had wondered whether I'd still be welcome at the lake after my major meltdown. I'd been too embarrassed to bring it up in case Jo was uncomfortable about the idea of having me sleep over again.

"Yeah, apparently the course has moved to next weekend, something about the venue being double booked. So if it's okay with your mom, can you come then instead?" I grinned and felt a surge of relief.

"Sure…that'll be fine, no problem," I said, unable to keep the excitement from my voice.

"We'll have to pack warm and cold weather gear. It can get quite cool in the evenings." Jo slipped into her practical mode as she continued to grate the cheese.

"What? Oh, okay. Cool."

"Yeah, we went one year and it started off real hot. We were all in summer gear when we arrived, then by the next evening...torrential rain!"

A beam of sunlight streamed in through the kitchen window of Jo's kitchen, warming my face as we prepared the sandwiches. Music from the radio filled the air and created a relaxed atmosphere. Despite the relative calm in the kitchen my nerves were reaching breaking point over the imminent arrival of Callum and Jake. I knew if I appeared at all Freaked out by their visit, Jo would end up pushing the whole, *this isn't done,* conversation again and that was the last thing I needed. So with that in mind I would suck it up, do the work and get out of there.

Good. Sorted. Oh, who am I kidding? I continued to fight an internal battle in the middle of Joey's kitchen; my stomach tied in knots at the prospect of having to spend more than a few minutes in the same room as Jake. Since his arrival on Monday, everything had flooded back. Peter's voice haunted my dreams; visions of him plagued the shadows of my mind. My recent teenage years had faded into an abyss as my tormented childhood became prominent again for all the wrong reasons. Sleep deprivation was not helping my rattled nerves.

"What time's your mom home?" I liked Pam. We got on well, her arrival would be a welcome diversion.

"Any minute."

"Cool."

I hoped the assignment would be easy to organize. How hard could it be to decide on the subject of our investigation and then to break it up into manageable components? I sighed at the prospect of a simple science project turning out to be an overly complicated nightmare. I just wanted the whole thing done with so I could get back to my usual self as soon as possible.

With a preference for my own company, this was the first time I'd had to interact with more than one person on something compulsory and crucial to achieving a decent grade. It also registered with me that my input would have a bearing on how well everyone else in the group performed. The pressure stirred an unwelcome anxiety in my chest.

"Hi, Mom!" Jo greeted as Pam struggled through the kitchen door, her arms full of groceries.

"Hi, girls, how was your day?"

"Yeah, good."

"Not bad, thanks," I said.

"So what's all this about?" she asked, her eyes taking in the chaos around us.

"It's not that bad, Mom," a giggling Jo mumbled. "We'll have it cleared up in no time!"

"You'd better, my girl!" Her mom raised an eyebrow as she took in the disaster zone that was her kitchen.

"We'll be done in a jiffy," I said, recognizing that Pam's patience teetered at its limit having worked all day and done a full grocery shop after school. She smiled at me before leaving us to finish.

"Any chance of a coffee?" she shouted from the living room.

"I'll get it," I called as Jo was just about to complain. "Don't!" I whispered at her making her giggle again.

We'd agreed to work in the den. The huge coffee table sat on top of a huge seventies style shag pile rug would be an ideal work area. I loved that room with its floor to ceiling bookcases crammed full of every imaginable book, journal and DVD. We'd spent hours chilling on the leather sofas, listening to music, watching TV, chatting about nothing. It had a relaxed atmosphere, therapeutic almost.

With the kitchen now spotless and the snacks ready, the boys arrived. We heard them before we saw them. My breath caught in my throat at the sound of Jake's old truck pulling up onto the driveway next door.

"It'll be fine," Jo said with empathy for my nervous state. I nodded and let out a long breath as the front door opened.

"Hi, guys!" Callum called out with his usual enthusiasm as they stepped inside.

"Hello again, Jo…Abbie," Jake said.

I swallowed as he walked past me into the den. He had to be six feet tall. His tight white T-shirt stretched across his toned chest muscles, the sleeves gripping his killer biceps while his dark jeans hugged his perfect ass. *WOW!*

"Er…I'll just grab the food, Jo," I whispered and left the room. "I can do this, I can do this!" I leaned against the counter in the kitchen a nervous lump lodged in my throat, the heels of my palm pressed into my eyes.

After a moment I picked up the plate of sandwiches and carried them into the den. Jo, Cal and Jake had already started to unpack a lap top and other reference materials. Jake looked up as I entered the room. The heart shattering smile which spread across his face almost caused me to drop the plate. I squeezed me eyes shut, frowning at the unwelcomed attention I was still getting from him. My heart pounded an unnatural rhythm as I placed the food down on the table before returning to the kitchen.

"We'll need power for this," I heard Callum suggest as I opened a packet of chips and tipped them into the large bowl on the side.

"Hang on a tick, I'll grab an extension cable from out the back," Jo replied, dashing through the kitchen to the garage.

"Have you got any drinks, Jo?" I asked.

"Yeah, there's soda in the refrigerator. The glasses are in the tall cupboard. Hold up, I'll come give you a hand."

"Here let me," a deep, sexy voice behind me offered as I struggled to reach the glasses. My heart beat out of control in my chest when his arm brushed mine.

My reaction was immediate and unwelcomed; a loud gasp escaped from my throat as I flinched away from him almost dropping the glasses. A sudden overwhelming sadness flooded my chest. Even looking away from him, I could sense his eyes boring into me, though I couldn't bring myself to make eye contact. Jake lifted a hand and reached towards me, I tried to move away from his touch, but he was too fast. The warmth of his fingers round mine, stole my breath yet again. I turned my face away so he couldn't see the fear etched into my eyes. Frozen to the spot, I couldn't move. Tears threatened to spill from my eyes, but I fought to hold them back. He carefully turned me towards him and waited for me to respond.

"I…"

"Hey," he soothed, squeezing my hand; the gentle pressure caused a tingling sensation to travel up my arm. He lifted his right hand to tilt my chin upwards so that I would have to look into his eyes. He ducked down so that he was level with me, "Abbie, its okay. Look I'm just going to carry the drinks for you…okay?" His eyes searched mine as I looked up from under my brow and nodded. "Okay. Good." He let go of my hand and gathered up the four glasses as well as enough sodas for everyone before returning to the others.

"Come on, we've got work to do," he suggested over his shoulder.

With a sudden gush, the breath I'd been holding left my lungs and I grabbed hold of the counter next to me. "What the hell?" My heart skipped a beat at the memory of Jake's hand on mine.

Jo appeared from outside looking flustered, "I can't find an extension cable!" She walked straight by me, through the kitchen and back to the boys. "You coming?" she asked, turning back towards me as she reached the door.

"Erm…yeah," I replied.

The moment with Jake had thrown me, but I couldn't stand in the kitchen all night; I had to deal with it. We had things to sort out, together, the four of us. Jo reappeared at the door as I pulled myself together, "You okay, Abs?"

"Yep. I'm fine," I smiled, pushing myself away from the counter, grabbing the chips and following her into the lion's den.

Jake's eyes searched my face for evidence that I was okay. Once satisfied, he continued to browse the internet. Callum reckoned they had enough battery life for the computer to last a couple of hours.

"Great sandwich, girls," Callum said with his mouth still full of the cheesy food. Jake grinned while shaking his head at his new friend.

"Come on then, guys, let's get organized," Jo suggested, much to my relief.

Over the next few hours we finished the sandwiches, drank sodas, and chatted about all things school. Surprised by our efforts at planning and drafting out what we wanted to achieve in the assignment we managed to insert a fair bit of joking around into the proceedings. It surprised me at how relaxed I'd been all evening with Jake and Callum. I glanced around the group just as Jake looked up at me. His bright blue eyes held mine long enough for me to catch a reflection of the old Jake. It felt good seeing him again.

"So, I guess I'm gonna head off, guys, I've got an early start in the morning!" Callum announced, breaking into my thoughts. "Thanks for the food!" I grinned at him as he stood up to leave.

"See ya!" we said in unison as he closed the front door behind him.

"How are you getting home, Abs?" Jake asked me, causing my heart to jump up into my throat.

"Erm…well, I hadn't given it much thought…I guess I'll walk."

"I don't think so!" His words surprised both Jo and I and a frown appeared on his brow, "I'll take you. No arguments!" he insisted as I opened my mouth.

A familiar anxiety began to radiate outwards from my chest. *Oh my God!* I willed Jo to jump in with a counter offer, but she smiled at me, her eyes full of encouragement. I took in a deep breath through my nose as I tried to convince myself it was fine. *I don't suppose it would do any harm.* It was preferable to walking home in the dark on my own.

"Okay, let's go," I said before I spent too long thinking about it and changed my mind, "Thanks for tonight, Jo. See you tomorrow. Thanks, Pam," I shouted up the stairs on my way out.

I was aware of an exchange between Jo and Jake as I walked out of the front door.

"Erm…the truck's on our driveway," Jake explained.

Every inch of my body trembled as I walked beside him to his house. My hands rammed deep into the pockets of my hoodie as my heart pounded against my chest. I waited with patient apprehension as he unlocked the passenger side door for me. Once inside I wondered whether I'd made the right choice. *Maybe I should have walked.*

Jake interrupted my thoughts as he slid onto the bench seat next to me. I watched as he fastened his seatbelt. His concern was visible in his eyes as he glanced over at me, but he said nothing.

The ride home was quick enough I guess. The noise of the engine would have impaired any conversation so it didn't matter much that we both remained silent. I was grateful Jake had concentrated on his driving. The light on our porch was on when we pulled up at the front of my house.

"Thanks for the lift."

"No problem, Abs, any time," he replied, turning towards me, "Listen…"

My heart picked up speed as soon as the word left his mouth. *I knew he had to say more, I just knew it.* A frown tugged at my brow as I held my breath, waiting.

"Erm…I want you to know…" He looked down at his hands which were now rubbing his thighs. "There wasn't a day went by that I didn't think about you."

He looked up then, his eyes probing mine, "If you ever need to talk…" He stopped when he noticed the tears welling in my eyes.

"Shit, Abbie, I'm sorry. I didn't mean to upset you." He placed a gentle hand on my left shoulder. I breathed out slowly and looked towards the house, but didn't make a move to get out of the truck.

"It's okay, it's not you." His intense stare bore into me as I tried to unscramble my head. "What a mess!"

"You don't have to say anything, Abbie. I just wanted you to know. That's all. It's been a long time?" I nodded, giving him a hint of a smile.

"I missed you," he whispered under his breath. I cast a glance in his direction and saw such sincerity in his eyes, there was no mistaking the truth in his words.

"I missed you too, Jake." With that, I opened the truck door and climbed out. "Thanks again for the lift, I appreciate it."

"It was my pleasure. Night, Abs."

"Night." The truck roared away as I locked the front door of our house behind me.

Chapter Eight

"Argh! No… not today! I can't be sick today. I gotta see Abbie." Racked with pain, I crouched in front of the toilet. My arms supported my head as violent cramps caused me to throw up into the bowl. "What the fuck? Urgh!"

Not again!

"Jake? Are you ready yet?" my mom shouted as she ran up the stairs.

"Urgh!" I threw up again.

"Jake, come on, you're going to be late!" she shouted through the bathroom door. "Jake, are you in there?" She pushed open the door and gasped at the sight of me slumped over the toilet. "Jake? Oh my God, sweetheart! How long have you been like this?"

"A couple of hours…I'm not sure…it was still dark when it started." My grip on reality was hanging precariously as I hunched over the toilet. The pain in my gut took my breath away. I pressed hard on my stomach in an attempt to ease the cramps.

"Why the hell didn't you call me?" she cried, pulling her cell phone from her pocket. The urge to vomit came over me again and I made aim for the toilet for what seemed like the hundredth time.

"Urrgghhh!" I leaned against the bath as I wiped my mouth. "It might be food poisoning, I bought a kebab on the way back from Abbie's last night. It didn't taste too good."

"Why the hell did you eat it then?" she asked, holding the phone to her ear. "Yes, is that Dr. Sayor's office? Yes, it's my son. He's been vomiting for a couple of hours… Yes, violent. Yes, Peritonitis a year ago…no…okay. Yes he says that he ate a kebab late last night," she emphasized the last part just as I threw up again. "Yes, that was him. I'll do that now, thank you." She tucked her cell into her pocket before turning back to me.

"Okay, sweetheart, we have to get you to the clinic for an exam. The nurse said that if you don't stop throwing up you'll get dehydrated and that could be harmful."

"Great!" I replied. I took a sip of water to rinse my mouth before the next spasm.

"Can you manage to get up and get dressed, or do you need some help?"

"Yeah, I'll give it a shot. Give me a minute and I'll be down." I pulled myself to my feet and staggered into my bedroom. The idea of a shower to ease the aches and pain in my lower back held great appeal but I dragged on the pair of loose sweat pants and a T-shirt instead. Just as I turned to the door I doubled over in excruciating pain.

Another wave of nausea swept over me and by some miracle I made it to the bathroom in time to empty my gut yet again. After wiping my mouth I headed downstairs.

"Okay?" Mom asked.

"Yep, for now." I groaned at the sight of the plastic tub in my mom's hand.

It took us ten minutes in the car to get to the clinic, during which time I managed to vomit once more. It was understandable that my mom was anxious. A little over twelve months ago I'd been diagnosed with Peritonitis. It took a week in hospital with two days in intensive care on an intravenous drip of antibiotics to clear the infection. The scar tissue increased the likelihood of a repeat attack and Mom's eyes reflected that fear.

"I'll be fine, Mom!"

"Better to be safe though, sweetheart?"

We didn't have too long a wait for the doctor.

"If it's food poisoning, and everything points to that being the case at this stage then it needs to run its course. So you should go home, take in plenty of fluids and if you don't improve in the next twenty-four hours call us. You may need an anti-sickness injection.

"Are you sure it's not related to the Peritonitis?" my mom asked.

"I can't rule it out completely," the doctor replied, "However; I don't believe so, going by the displayed symptoms at this stage." One look at Mom told me she wasn't convinced, but she accepted the script for anti-sickness meds and agreed to call again if needed.

***

A slight smile tugged at the corner of my mouth as I replayed the moment in Jake's truck last night when he told me how much he'd missed me. It wasn't so much the revelation that caused me to smile; it was the realization that I'd missed him as well. Still the same kind, funny, caring boy I remembered; I felt safe with Jake. Despite my feelings for him, I still faced a massive dilemma. My brow knitted together as I considered the consequences of allowing him back into my life. *Why does everything always get so screwed up?*

My mind shifted as I wondered why Jake hadn't been in lessons this morning. He'd missed Calculus and English. Was he giving me breathing space? Was he regretting everything he'd said? I had a tendency to over think everything and this was no exception.

"There you are, weren't we supposed to meet in the cafeteria?" Jo asked with a worried expression on her face.

"Sorry…just enjoying the sun," I said, smiling up at her, "What's got you so uptight?"

"Oh, I'll tell you in a minute. First I want to hear everything." Jo said as she flopped down beside me on the courtyard wall.

"Everything about what?" I said, knowing exactly what she wanted to talk about.

"In the truck! Jeez, Abbie, how to make a girl sweat?"

"Well… I guess there was one thing…"

"I knew it!" she said, squirming on the wall.

"Jake, told me he'd missed me and…I said that I'd missed him too." My cheeks flooded with color as Jo leaped up in excitement.

"So what happens now?" Jo asked.

"Nothing, I need time to take it in before I make any decisions on that score," I took a deep breath. "I'm scared he'll end up finding out what happened."

"So? If he finds out, and I don't know how he would unless you tell him, he'll be fine. Pissed at first I would imagine, but fine in the end… But that's not even on the agenda is it? You aren't going to tell him. So that's no excuse." A smug grin spread across Jo's face as she assumed she'd presented a winning argument.

"But…we're older now, Jo." I lowered my eyes, embarrassed with the direction of my thoughts.

"And?" Realization dawned on her; it was like someone had flicked a switch. She took hold of my hand

and squeezed, "Hey, there's no rush for anything like that Hun. I'm sure he'll respect you, not all guys are assholes. Jake seems like a nice guy, Abs."

"Weren't you going to tell me something?" I said, desperate to change the subject, for now at least.

Jo heaved in a deep breath and took a seat beside me, "I just got off the phone to mom. It's her day off today. She wants me to grab something from the office for her before I go home. Anyway…"

"What?"

"About Jake… turns out he's sick. He had a dodgy kebab last night on his way home. He's been vomiting since the early hours. That's why he's absent today." My heart dropped to the pit of my stomach.

"Is he okay now?" I asked as my pulse thundered in my ears.

"Not sure, Karen told my mom he might have to have an injection to make him stop vomiting." I swallowed, I didn't want Jake to be sick, I wanted him to be okay, I needed him to be okay. I wanted to see him. My head began to spin as confusing emotions flooded my mind. Panic pulsed through my veins at the realization I had developed, or rather, rekindled strong feelings for Jake Ashton. An overwhelming urge to be with him and make sure he was okay, ripped through me.

The afternoon passed in a blur as I replayed Jo's words over and over; with every run through the outcome became more unbearable. My stomach churned at the thought of Jake lying at home alone and unwell. I shook my head trying to rid my mind of the recurring negative images as I rushed up our driveway after school.

Jeez, he was only throwing up. How serious can it be? It's not like its life threatening or anything.

"Mom! I'm home." Friday nights at our house were busy affairs under normal circumstances with Mom home first unless she changed shifts. As I searched for her downstairs it became obvious that Mom had made other plans. I remembered Martin saying something about going round to Howie's after school to hang out before heading to the movies later.

"Mom?" I wandered into the kitchen to make a drink before dinner and spotted a note on the counter.

Abbie,
Don't forget I'm at work till late tonight, swapped my shift.
Dinner's in the refrigerator.
See you in the morning.
Mom xx

"Great! Just me then. Nah! Not happening!" I picked up my bag and rummaged around in it until I found my cell phone and found Jo in my contacts.

"Hey! You haven't any plans for tonight have you?"

"Nope. Why?"

"Martin's round at your place and my mom's working late. I wondered whether you wanted to hang out here tonight."

"Erm, hang on a minute, I'll check." Within seconds Jo's voice pierced my head, "Mom's suggested you come over here, she said one more won't make much difference."

"Serious?"

"Yep."

"Cool. Thanks, Jo, it'll take me about ten minutes."

After throwing an overnight bag together I scribbled a note for my mom. I couldn't wait to get out of the house; I hated being in there alone.

It wasn't dark yet, but the street lights flickered in the dusk. The wind picked up as the light faded, I couldn't help the nervousness rumbling in my stomach as I peddled the short distance. I felt a sense of relief on rounding the corner of Jo's street, but relief turned to horror at the scene in front of me.

Two paramedics were pushing Jake on a stretcher. His groans as he clutched his stomach brought a lump to my throat. Instinct kicked in; I dropped my bike and raced towards him.

"Jake!" He turned his head in response to my voice. "What's happened?" My tears threatened to spill over at any second.

Jake tried to smile as I grabbed his hand. "Hi, Abs...I'll be fine...they're just...making sure."

I shot a glance at Karen who gave me a reassuring smile. The smile didn't match the overwhelming worry visible in her eyes. I turned back to Jake my heart crashing against my chest. *Please be okay, Jakey.* I bit down on my lip for fear of breaking down. His mom didn't need me coming over all emotional. He squeezed my hand as he flinched in pain.

"How long will he be in hospital, Mrs. Ashton?" I asked, not taking my eyes off Jake.

"They aren't sure. We'll know more after they've run the tests."

"Okay," I nodded. Jake managed a wink and squeezed my hand before the paramedics resumed their task of getting him into the back of the ambulance. "Can I visit?" I asked his mom.

"Of course, as soon as we know something."

"Thank you."

A lone tear trickled down my cheek as I watched the ambulance pull away.

"Hey, he'll be fine, Abs, don't worry. He's in good hands," Jo's mum said.

I learned that Pam and Karen had discussed Jake's condition at length while waiting for the paramedics to arrive.

"Karen's concerned about Jake's violent vomiting because he had this infection where he ended up in hospital. She thinks it could be happening again," Jo explained as we walked up her driveway.

"I think we could all do with a warm drink," Pam said.

After a mug of hot sweet tea and lots of reassurance from Pam that Jake would be fine, I began to relax.

"So, what you gonna do?" Jo asked as we moved into the den.

"What do you mean?"

"Abbie, I can see that you're falling for him." I pulled in a deep breath at her assessment and exhaled slowly. I didn't say anything. "The question is… What are you going to do about it?" My head pounded; confused didn't even begin to describe my emotional state.

"I haven't got a fucking clue to be perfectly honest, Jo."

Chapter Nine

A sea of shoppers milled in and out of the dozens of brightly lit stores lining the main section of our favorite weekend hangout. Though I preferred the sports shops Jo was more of a fashion victim.

We almost always ended up having a milkshake in the food court around the midpoint of our visits; followed by a burger or hotdog maybe an hour or so later. This enabled us to stretch the day out for as long as possible. A typical mall trip resulted in very sore feet, lots of shopping bags and empty purses. Today was different, today I was preoccupied.

"I want to get a card for Jake while we're here," I said as we did one final loop of the mall before heading home.

"No problem." Jo grinned, her eyes twinkling like a crazy woman.

"What?" I asked, knowing I was opening a can of worms, but I asked anyway.

"Nothing," she giggled.

"Doesn't sound like nothing!" I said, sarcasm dripping from my reply.

"It's just... it's just cool to see you like this, Abbie."

"Like what?"

"Happy."

***

The heavy stench of disinfectant overpowered us as we passed through the large automated glass doors into the bustling reception area of the hospital.

"Hi," Pam said, approaching the receptionist, "Could you tell us where we can find Jake Ashton please? He was admitted last night."

"One minute, please." She searched the computer for Jake's details, "Here we are… Down the corridor on the left, then take the elevator to the second floor. Mr. Ashton is in B ward, the fourth room on the right."

"Thanks!" Our response almost automatic as we turned from the desk and hurried towards the elevator. My stomach churned with nervous tension at the sight of Karen coming out of Jake's room, pulling the door closed behind her as we entered the ward. She looked tired, I assumed she'd been up most of the night and could only imagine her worry during the last day or so.

"Hi, Karen, how is he?" Pam asked, hugging her friend.

"Yeah, he's much better today. It's such a relief," she added, looking over to where Jo and I were anxiously waiting to visit Jake.

"Go in, girls, he's awake. He'll be happy you're here." I swallowed past the nervous lump lodged in my throat and paused at the door before taking hold of the handle. I didn't know what response I would get from Jake, or how I would react to him either for that matter.

"Go on," Jo encouraged, nudging me forward.

My breath hitched as I peeped round the door and saw Jake, propped up in a bed to the right of the room. The cool mint green color of the walls provided a contrast to the stark white of the bed sheets. A bedside cabinet stood to the right of Jake and a window filled the wall to the left. A TV positioned in the top right corner of the wall opposite his bed held Jake's attention as we crept into the room. He looked so peaceful; I almost didn't want to disturb him.

"Hey?" I said as I tiptoed further into the room clutching his card. He turned in response to my voice.

"Hey!" A grin spread across his face when he saw us. "Hi, Jo," he said, looking at her for a moment before turning his attention back to me. "I didn't think you'd come," he said, his voice hoarse from the violent sickness of the day before, I supposed.

"Why?" I was a bit surprised that he thought that.

"Well, I didn't know whether you would want to," he said, dropping his gaze.

"I'm gonna grab a soda, Abs, you want one?" Jo asked on her way out of the room.

"No, I'm good thanks."

"Glad to see you're getting better, Jake," Jo said before closing the door behind her.

"I got you a card." I walked cautiously towards his bed and placed the card on the cabinet beside him, my eyes taking in all the medical equipment that he was hooked up to.

"That's… thank you, you didn't need to do that, but… thanks."

I teared up at the sight of the pads stuck to his chest and the drip still in the back of his hand.

"Fuck!" I turned towards the door in the unrealistic hope that he wouldn't notice my ridiculous response.

"Hey, it's okay, Abs, I'm fine, it's all a precaution," he croaked, gesturing towards the heart monitor and the drip before taking hold of my left hand. "Come sit down," he invited, pulling me towards the edge of the bed and when I looked round for a chair he patted the covers, "No, here." I hesitated for a second before perching on the edge of his bed, close enough now to see just how tired he looked. His eyes weren't their usual bright twinkling blue and he looked sick. His complexion was gray instead of his usual tan. Even his hair looked different, flattened and lifeless.

"Are you sure you're okay? You look dreadful," I whispered, hardly trusting my voice.

"Much better than last night. I thought I was a goner yesterday, I thought my stomach was going to explode. I've never had pain that bad before. It's not so bad now I've stopped throwing up, it's more like a dull ache."

I realized at that point that I was squeezing his hand a little too tightly. He looked down at my fingers which were almost turning white at the knuckles.

"Oops, sorry," I said before easing off a bit and trying to let go.

"Don't be," he replied, reaching for my hand and lacing his much larger fingers between mine. I placed my other hand over his while my thoughts drifted to the endless possibilities of what might have happened, before returning to the present and the pure relief of him being okay.

"I'm glad you're going to be okay, Jakey." He gasped slightly and out of instinct I reached towards him, placing my hand against his cheek, "What? What is it Jake? Are you in pain?" I asked, searching his face for what had caused the sudden intake of breath.

"I'm fine, Abs, I..."

"What? Fucking hell, Jake, what's wrong?" I urged, a familiar panic rising in me. He took hold of my wrist and leaned into my palm, closing his eyes for a moment.

He took a deep breath before continuing, "You called me Jakey."

"Oh," I said, blushing as I reluctantly lowered my hand from his face.

"I haven't had anyone call me that for a long, long time, not the way you say it anyway."

I placed my hand on the covers across his waist as I sat down next to him again. He was still holding my right hand in his and I was sure he wouldn't let go, even if I wanted to. Which I realized, I didn't.

"Jake…"

"Don't, it's okay, Abbie, you don't have to say anything." Jake lowered his gaze, his brow pulling together in a slight frown.

"Jake?"

"I understand, it's fine."

"You understand what exactly?" I asked, getting a bit agitated now. It was bad enough that I had to contend with these new feelings without being interrupted as I tried to explain it all to him. He opened his mouth to answer, but I cut him off.

"Just stop for a minute will you?" I insisted, taking in yet another deep breath, "I know I've been a bitch since you arrived, but…it wasn't directed at you, Jake…" I paused again as I processed my scrambled thoughts. "Well, yes it was but…it was wrong to treat you like that… I mean… Shit!" I struggled to find the right words. His eyes never left mine. He remained silent, sensing my need to speak my mind.

"I'm so sorry I punched you the other day. I just… I mean, I wanted to take it back as soon as it happened but…" *Shit! This isn't going very well.* I stared down at the bed sheets, embarrassed as I apologized for my behavior. "I've said some awful things to you, I'm so sorry," I took in a quick breath and let it out before looking up at him again, "I meant it the other night when I said I'd missed you too." I felt a gentle squeeze of encouragement as his grip tightened on my hand.

"I thought I'd lost my chance yesterday." My voice quivered as my breath hitched in my throat.

"Your chance for what, exactly?" he asked, his eyes searching mine for clarification.

"When they took you away in the ambulance I…I thought… I thought you were going to die," I whispered, "I thought I'd lost you for good this time."

The last few words almost stuck in my throat as the sobs got the better of me. The tears I'd been hanging onto since I arrived overflowed. I turned away from him while swiping at my cheeks, desperate to get my emotions back in check.

Jake placed a hand on my lower back, "Hey, it's okay. I'm not going anywhere," his voice soft and soothing as he rubbed my back, "Abbie, look at me." Jake was so gentle in his encouragement that after a while I turned to face him. He eased himself away from the pillows, raised his hand and cupped my cheek. His thumb wiped away the tail of my tears. "I'm not going anywhere, I've missed you too, so much it's hurt at times. Okay?"

"Okay," I gulped, taking a deep breath, trying to steady my voice.

"That's my girl," he smiled and after a moment's hesitation, pulled me into his arms. In that second, a flame of hope ignited deep inside me. It felt right being with Jake, letting him in, I was surer of him and our friendship than anything so far.

We sat talking through his treatment and what had happened in his tests for a while before Pam stuck her head around the door.

"Hey! How you doing, big guy?"

"Much better thanks, Pam."

"That's great, Jake, really great. I'm sorry, but it's time to go, Abs."

"Oh, okay, I'll be right out." I would have loved to stay longer; I didn't want to go home just yet, but Jake would be home soon. Just as soon as the intravenous antibiotics took effect and the doctors were happy with him.

"Jo's outside, I'll see you both in the car." I nodded.

"Abbie?" he said as I moved off the bed to reach for my bag.

"Yes?"

"Come here a minute please." A slight frown appeared across his forehead as he spoke. I moved towards him, concerned at the seriousness in his tone and in the thoughtful expression on his face.

"What is it? Do you need more meds, should I call someone?"

"No, I'm fine... I...I just wondered..." he said as his eyes dropped to my mouth.

"Erm...if I could..." Without any hesitation I closed the distance between us and with the lightest pressure, touched my lips to his. His fingers caressed my cheek as he returned my kiss. His lips were soft, gentle...perfect. I pulled away after a moment and rested my forehead on his. A warmth radiated through me as Jake's breath tickled my lips. We both eased back a touch more and in his eyes I saw a reflection of the same depth of emotion that I had for him.

"Fuck, I've dreamed about kissing you for years," he whispered, his voice full of emotion.

"I've got to go," I replied, a slight smile playing with the corner of my mouth as I moved towards the door. "See you soon?"

"You will," he said, his smile beaming.

The door closed behind me and I pulled in a long deep breath, closing my eyes as I leaned against the corridor wall. The pounding of my heart rang in my ears as I pondered what had just happened.

"What have I done?" I whispered.

The hospital seemed busier as nurses and other hospital staff changed shifts. A couple of them threw concerned glances my way as they passed by.

"You okay, Abs?" My breathing became heavier all of a sudden.

What have I done?

Am I ready to let him back into my life?

Do I even want a deeper relationship with him?

Why did I kiss him?

What if he starts asking questions?

I didn't have any answers, but I knew I cared about Jake. I'd almost lost him, again. That was enough of a reason at this point in time to run with what ever happened. I wanted him in my life, my heart had confirmed that. Screw what was going on in my head. Thinking was shit.

"I over think everything," I whispered, my breathing erratic. Jo stared at me wide eyed. I'd just kissed Jake; I'd actually kissed him... *and* I'd liked it, but now I was nervous again. "Shit!"

"Hey! Abs, calm down," Jo soothed, taking hold of my upper arms and rubbing them up and down. I tried to smile at Jo, coming back to the here and now. She breathed out a sigh of relief. "You okay?" I nodded. "How is he?" she asked, giving me a huge hug.

"Yeah, he's going to be just fine."

"How are you doing?" she asked as we walked back towards the elevator her arm across my shoulders.

"I'm okay..." An undercurrent of nervousness ran through my reply, "I think I may be ready to give us a chance."

She knew what I meant. "You can do this…he's worth it, Abbie."

A nervous smile played at my lips, "I know he is…but am I?" She nudged me hard as we stepped into the elevator and threw me a glare that I swear, could have turned me to stone. "No, what I mean is... Can *I* do this?" I clarified, more to keep her quiet than to justify the previous comment.

In reality, I didn't feel I was worthy of him at all, damaged goods as they say. Jake ticked every box in the perfection category in my eyes. The prospect of a friendship developing with him scared the crap out of me, but kissing him was a game changer. I had to take the consequences now. Good or bad, I'd crossed the line.

"I kissed him, Jo," I muttered under my breath as though trying to keep a secret.

"Nooo waaaay! I knew it!" Jo bounced up and down so much I thought the elevator floor would fall through at any second.

"Shhh! Damn it, Jo, the whole hospital will hear you!" I cringed at her enthusiasm. "I hope he doesn't think too much into it now though," I added, embarrassed by my actions, "What if he thinks it's an open invitation to...you know..?"

"Hey, slow down, girl. Jeez, Abbie, he's not even out of hospital yet. Give him a chance."

"It's not funny, Jo, I've led him on. I shouldn't have done that."

"You haven't led him on. You kissed him because you wanted to. That's all. Under the circumstances I'd say it was a pretty appropriate thing to do." I wasn't too sure, but it was too late now. I'd kissed Jake because it felt right, more than right, I'd liked it. In actual fact, it felt wonderful.

Chapter Ten

By Sunday lunch time I was filled with a desperate urge to see Jake again, however I knew that any movement in that direction could backfire on me. I didn't want my actions to be misconstrued. Jake obviously had feelings for me, whether deep or just physical, I wasn't too sure at this stage. Either way, I didn't want to hurt him anymore than I wanted to get hurt myself. So I decided to back off a bit and take things slow.

I decided to leave off visiting him until Monday after school. Chances were his family would be there anyway if I went sooner and I would only be in the way.

Grabbing a jacket and gloves, I pushed open the garage door. After unlocking my bike and navigating a pathway through several boxes of the same useless stuff everyone seems to have in their garage, I locked the door behind me and headed for the lake.

The lake provided a safe haven for me when I needed to unravel pent up anxiety and stress. The great cycle track running around the edge gave me the freedom to kick back and let it all come out.

A wooden bridge cut across a narrow section leading to a wooded area which stretched out for miles. At this time of year the carpet of wild blue flowers covering the ground gave it an almost mystical feel. On the other side, the view opened up to a lush meadow where I sometimes watched the horses grazing.

Whenever I felt like clearing my head, I'd often cut through the woods, along the narrow graveled path. The natural beauty of the place soothed me when I felt down and relaxed me in times of stress. I would lose track of time there, sitting under a tree letting my mind wander, reading a book on a sunny day or even skipping stones across the lake.

Today however, I just felt like a bike ride. I needed to pass the time and riding in the cool, lakeside air beat moping in my room. I'd only reached half way round the lake when a text came through to my cell. With a squeak of my brakes I pulled over to the side of the track. Still breathing heavily from peddling like a mad woman I pulled my phone free from my pocket.

Hi u in? It was Jo.

Nope, wot u up 2?

I was gonna come over.

Okie dokie, but give me 10 I'm on my bike.

"Here we go again!" I grinned. I actually didn't mind discussing Jake with Jo; she understood where I was coming from. Having her as a sounding board was a good thing.

Another text...

Just given your cell number to Karen, Jake asked her for it

"What the hell, Jo! You could have asked first, Fuck!" My stomach did a massive flip at the realization I might actually have to chat with Jake today. I kicked off the ground and headed over to Jo's house, less than impressed with her innate ability to interfere in everyone else's business without apology.

I guess talking to Jake had to come at some point.

Less than ten minutes later I was striding up my driveway towards Jo, who from the expression on her face, recognized I was less than happy with her meddling.

"What were you thinking?" I snapped, closing the front door rather firmly behind her and making her jump before I stormed off to the kitchen.

"What did I do now?" she asked, following behind me, knowing full well what I was talking about. I threw her a, *You know what I'm talking about look,* which made her giggle. "Sorry, but what was I supposed to say?" she shrugged her shoulders, "Sorry I can't give it to you, Karen because

100

Abbie is embarrassed about kissing Jake so she'd probably rather I didn't give it to you!"

"Well I don't know. You could have said you didn't have it on you or something," I suggested, snatching the milk from the refrigerator. She raised an eyebrow at the ludicrous idea that Karen would have believed that for a second.

"Anyway, he might not even call you," she offered, passing me the box of hot chocolate from the cupboard.

"Hmmm," I breathed, turning my back to her and finishing our hot drinks.

"So, guess who I bumped into this afternoon?" Jo's voice held an air of mystery.

"Oh, I don't know, surprise me!" I said, rolling my eyes to emphasize the sarcasm.

"Callum... he didn't know about Jake, he was gutted, said something about stopping by the hospital later to check on him."

"Oh, okay," I said, raising my eyebrows in surprise, "Where did you see him?"

"I had to call back to the mall for my mom, she needed some stuff for dinner tonight and I saw him when I came out of the store. Think he'd been to Sports Mart, not sure. Anyway, we ended up grabbing a soda," she added under her breath as an after-thought.

"Oh yeah?"

"Yeah, he's actually an okay guy you know?" I couldn't help laughing at her coyness, it was sweet.

"Well, just be careful, he's got quite a reputation for kissing and telling."

"Jeez, Abbie, it was only a soda. We were talking about the assignment mostly and a bit about Jake."

"That's all well and good, girlie, but a soda can lead to… Well you know what I mean. Just be careful."

"Yes, Mom. So where were you earlier when I text you?" she asked.

"Just riding, I had to get out, clear my head; I was going crazy cooped up here," I said, nodding towards where my mom was hanging out the laundry.

"Oh okay, my mom said she'd spoken to your mom. Did you get the third degree?" she asked, sympathizing with my plight.

"No, actually she was fine; just asked how Jake was and then how I felt, she didn't even push it when I said I had a head ache and wanted to have a lie down."

"Oh, right, oh well." Jo said. We headed up to my room and chatted a bit more about Jake and Callum, before moving on to discuss our assignment and the trip to the lake the following weekend. We were both looking forward to it, but agreed it had been fate that we hadn't gone this weekend, what with Jake getting sick and all.

"Well, I'm off," Jo said after a couple of hours, "School tomorrow and I've got history homework due in the morning." I groaned at her lack of organization. "See you outside before school then?" she asked, climbing into the driver's seat of her mom's car. She waved out of the window before driving off down the street.

I'd just got up stairs intending to hop in the shower when my cell rang.

"Fuck!"

I had a strong suspicion who it was. I didn't recognize the number on the screen and my heart skipped a beat at the prospect of talking to him.

"Hey, Abbie's phone."

"Hi, Abbie's phone," Jake said, making me smile. I don't know why I'd been so nervous, I was really happy to hear his voice.

"How you feeling?"

"I'm not too shabby. Bit sore, but better than yesterday." There was a slight pause as though he was thinking what to say next. "How are you?"

"Yeah, I'm good. I went for a bike ride earlier to pass the time, then Jo called round. She told me she'd seen Cal. They went for a soda." I chatted on, aware that he wasn't really asking me what I'd been up to; he wanted to know how I *was* after yesterday.

"Oh, okay, cool. Callum's okay. He's a good guy."

"Good, because she's my friend and I don't want him getting up to his usual tricks with her."

"I'm sure they'll be fine, Abs, don't worry about them. Jo seems a tough cookie, and like I said, Callum's sound. Anyway…" he said, changing the subject. *Here we go* I thought and my mouth went dry in anticipation. "Are you okay? After yesterday I mean?"

"Why wouldn't I be?" I replied sharply, unsure of how best to answer and as a result it came out a bit abrupt, "Sorry, that sounded a bit harsh. I'm good, Jake, honestly. I'm really glad you're feeling better, your voice sounds a bit better too."

"I am. It is. I'm glad you came to see me, Abs."

"Me too," I replied softly. I was glad, it was true.

"Can I see you when I get home?" he asked cautiously and I could sense his self-confidence wavering.

"I'd like that," I said and he heaved a sigh of relief that I could hear down the phone, making me giggle.

"What?"

"I heard you sigh," I informed him, giggling again and he laughed too.

"I have to go. The nurse is here with my meds. I'll see you soon, Abs, I could be out tomorrow."

"Really? That's so good." It was great to hear he was almost well enough to come home. "Promise you'll call me when you get out."

"I will, I promise," he assured me and I could tell he was grinning.

"Bye,"

"Bye, Abbie."

I lay back on my bed and closed my eyes. A smile came to my lips, as the early signs of happiness tingled in my stomach alongside a touch of apprehension. Jo had been right the other day... at least partially anyway. I had feelings for Jake Ashton.

"Fuck!" I groaned, rubbing my eyes and rolling onto my stomach reaching for my cell phone.

It had hardly rung out before she answered. "Did he call?" Jo half screamed down the phone.

"He did."

"Woo hoo!" she whooped, making me laugh out loud. "And?" She waited for a reply.

"Not much really…"

"Not much!" she shouted almost deafening me in the process. "Abbie James, if you think that after all these years of no boy talk, that you're getting away without sharing every detail of your *nearly* relationship with Jake Ashton with me, your *bestest* friend in the whole wide world then you are sadly mistaken!" she said, and I knew she meant every word.

"No, seriously, there isn't much to say yet. He asked if I was okay about yesterday and I said I was. Then he asked if he could see me when he gets out and I agreed to that as well. So yeah, that's all at the minute. He's feeling better by the way, thanks for asking."

"Oh okay, good," she said, giggling at the oversight.

"Anyway, I'm going, I'm hungry and Mom's cooked a roast," I spoke just as my stomach rumbled loudly.

"See you tomorrow, chicky," she said, as I ended the call.

Chapter Eleven

Within seconds of the lunch bell sounding an avalanche of students streamed into the cafeteria, all scrambling for that premium seat. I spotted Callum with a few of the footballers, laughing and joking among themselves; surrounded as usual by a solid wall of groupies. I rolled my eyes at the trampish display going on in full view of anyone paying the slightest bit of attention.

"Hey, Abbie!" Callum called over, snapping me out of my thoughts of slutty tramps.

"How's Jake doing, have you heard anything?" he asked, as he headed my way.

My cheeks reddened at being singled out by a major player in the middle of the cafeteria. Right on cue the *girls* hanging off the jocks threw sideways glances of disgust my way. I didn't care what they thought of me; I had no desire to be liked by them or accepted by anyone for that matter, but I did care what impact talking to me would have on Callum and Jake.

"Hi. Yeah, he seemed a bit better on the phone yesterday afternoon. I think he may be home sometime. Weren't you heading up to the hospital last night?" I was surprised he didn't already know how Jake was feeling.

"Yeah, but in the end I didn't make it, my dad needed some help so yeah, ran out of time," he explained, completely unaware of the attention our conversation was attracting.

"Hey, Jess! Looks like Callum's into the Freak!" One of the tramps shouted so loud that the entire cafeteria heard, including Jo who had just made an appearance.

"Who are you calling a freak, slut?" she commented as she strutted past their table, making me giggle. Callum reddened with embarrassment and threw a look of disgust across the room at his so called friends.

"What's the matter, Callum? Touch a nerve did she?" another random jock shouted over, gaining rapturous applause from the rest of his group.

"Get me out of here," I mumbled, gutted that I'd landed in the middle of more drama.

"Don't worry about them, they're idiots," Callum said, heading back to where he'd been sitting a moment earlier. "See you later, Abbie!" he called, raising a few more eyebrows among his groupies. "What?" he barked at them, "Cut it out you lot, Abbie's okay." They didn't seem satisfied or very happy from the looks they threw my way.

I let out the breath I'd been holding onto in one long stream as Jo took a seat in front of me.

"You okay?" she asked, concern etched across her face.

"Yeah, I'm good," I said, forcing a smile, "They don't bother me. Fuck them!" She laughed, but I could tell she wasn't convinced. We'd heard it all before. Just because I kept to myself and Jo was my friend, she was guilty by association.

"Come on, let's get out of here," I suggested, feeling uncomfortable with the hostile glares boring into me.

We strolled towards the main block and sat on a bench outside just as my cell beeped.

"You gonna get that?" Jo asked. Her mouth twitched at the corners as she tried her best not to grin. "Well? Are you?"

"Jeez, Jo, you're pushy." I laughed, pulling my cell from my pocket.

"Who's it from?" she asked with a smirk. I raised an eyebrow in response.

"What's he say?

"He's coming home today." Relief flooded my chest at the news Jake was well again, but an overwhelming nervousness coursed through my body by the start of the afternoon sessions. I drifted through the rest of the day with little recollection of how I got to the bell.

With tension running high, I opted to walk home via the lake. The wooden decking of the bridge creaked with each step I took. I pushed my legs through the bottom rung of the hand rail and sat on the edge of the bridge. The shimmering water of the lake took me to my safe place; I needed to sort out my scattered thoughts. The view across the dense woodland and the water helped to balance my conflicting emotions. With my chin resting on the middle rail and my legs dangling inches from the water, I realized I must have changed tack at least three times. I doubted my chances of anything resembling a regular friendship developing with Jake.

Jeez, I must be delusional! I pulled myself to my feet and strolled along the remainder of the track, still confused about Jake. I did like him, a lot, but I was scared. The initial shock of his illness and the chance of losing him had vanished now. All that remained was a deep concern that I'd started something I was incapable of finishing.

After ten minutes I found myself outside Jo's place, "Hey!" My greeting lacked enthusiasm.

"What's wrong with you?" she asked, screwing up her nose.

"Nothing."

"O…kay."

I tried to put together a coherent sentence in my head before opening my mouth, but a heap of crap tumbled out anyway. "I thought I had everything worked out, Joey. I really thought I could move forward with Jake and everything would be okay…"

"And?"

"I don't know whether I can. I can't rationalize it, Jo. It's freaking me out." My voice began to tremble.

"Abbie, listen to me, it's natural to feel anxious. Jake's a great guy. You two already know each other, you have history. Just take it slow."

"So what should I do? I can't go round there in this state. I'll end up doing something stupid, again!" I threw my hands up in the air to emphasize the point.

"Jeez, Abbie, give yourself a break, girl!"

I stopped pacing around her kitchen, "I'm scared, Jo."

"I know you are, but Jake's awesome, Abbie, he'll help you through whatever happens." I nodded, Jake was great, I agreed, but that didn't help my confidence.

"Errmmm…" she said, in a tone that gave me tingles.

"What?"

"Well… I might have seen Karen after I text you earlier and…"

"Joey! What have you done?" I groaned. A sense of dread swamped over me.

"I told her, you were on your way over and that you'd probably call round."

"Damn it, Jo! You just can't help yourself can you?"

"I'm sorry, but sometimes friends have to lend a helping hand."

"You're incorrigible, Jo Johnson, I hate you," I snarled with a slight grin.

"He'll be there now, don't leave it too late, he'll be tired." With my eyes squeezed closed and hands covering my face, my mind whirled at the dilemma now facing me.

"Do I have to?" I groaned, dropping my hands in defeat.

"Yes, you do. Now move your ass, missy! He's waiting and he's tired," Jo said, her hands planted on her hips.

"Okay! Jeez. I'm going already."

"Come back when you're done. Okay?"

"Yeah, right!" I said with no intention of going back to Jo's after this particular visit.

My heart rate escalated beyond all recognition as I headed next door. With my hands balled into fists at my side I gathered the courage to ring the bell. The door opened after a short wait revealing a pale looking Jake, his cheeks lined with tiredness.

"Hey!" Jake pushed the screen door open and moved to the side to let me pass.

"Hi... how are you?" I tried not to sound too nervous as I stepped inside.

"Better, thanks," he said, narrowing his eyes slightly as if detecting my attitude had shifted since we last spoke. I swallowed back the lump threatening to choke me. "So, do you want a drink or something?"

"No, I'm good thanks, I can't stay long."

"Oh, okay." His eyes reflected his disappointment; I knew he'd probably expected more.

"Jake... About the other day, in the hospital..."

"Please don't, Abbie." He turned to face the kitchen window and leaned on the counter. I waited a second. I wanted to make sure I phrased it so he understood.

"Jake, I want us to be friends." I reached over and touched his arm. "I've only just got you back... I don't want to lose you again." My heart raced as Jake remained silent. I so badly wanted him to be okay with this. "Things were a bit crazy after you moved away and I... well I guess I need you to just..." My mind felt cluttered.

"Listen, Abbie I'm more than happy to be your friend if that's what you need from me right now. We never stopped being friends." The warmth in his smile filled me with hope. He took a sudden step towards me lifting his hand. I gasped and flinched; a sense of immediate regret and embarrassment flooded my chest. I froze when I saw the confusion in his eyes.

"Sorry," I whispered, turning away. I wanted to hug him, but his sudden movement set off an uncontrollable chain reaction deep inside me.

"Abbie?"

"This is so screwed," I said, shaking my head.

"Look, I don't know what's going on, or what's upset you, but I want to be with you, just so you know. I'll be your friend for as long as you need a friend and if you want more, I'll be waiting." His voice held the promise of understanding and support that I remembered from when we were little. "Just don't push me away, okay? Please." He smiled at me then. His eyes twinkled and his grin widened as he saw a glimpse of a smile on my lips. "I care about you and I know you care about me too, or you wouldn't be here. We've both already admitted how much we missed each other. Let's just see what happens."

"I'd like that." My hands twitched as I stepped a little closer. My head spun with indecision as I tried to work out what to do next. I'd settle for a hug.

"Come here," he said, pulling me towards his chest. I closed my eyes as the warmth of his embrace melted my frozen heart. His hands came to my arms as he kissed the top of my head, "Do you want that drink now?" I nodded as he pulled away, "Okay." Jake moved to the bench and grabbed two cups.

"I'm glad you're home, Jake."

"I'm glad to be home. It was rough being sick." I frowned at the memory of him being stretchered away. However it had been a turning point. I'd been a bitch towards him up until that point.

"Hey, you okay?"

"Yeah, just remembering last Friday," I whispered, giving him a slight smile that didn't quite reach my eyes. The supportive hand on my arm sent sparks across my skin and shivers down my spine.

"So…" A change of subject would go a long way to moving forward with the old friendship thing at this point, "This assignment? Do you think we are going to be able to finish it in time or what?"

"Erm, well…I don't see any reason why not. We've got a great starting point. Cal seems happy enough to contribute and he's not the easiest to motivate usually, or so I've heard. So yeah, I think we'll be okay." Jake took a long slurp of his coffee as his eyes searched mine for a hint at what else I might have on my mind.

"We're going to have to pick it up a bit, what with losing time over the weekend and everything. I don't think any of us managed to add anything to what we already started while you were sick. I guess you're out of action this week as well?" I only stated the facts; not for a second intending he'd jump into school assignments when he'd just got out of the hospital. My comment was more about building an interest level into our new friendship, finding a comfort zone in our conversation.

"Yeah, I guess. I am feeling a lot better, but the meds have knocked me sideways. I don't remember ever being so washed out." He passed me a coffee and pulled out a second stool before sitting next to me.

A smile crept onto my face as I became drawn to his features and compared this older Jake to how I remembered him as an eight year old. His hair with its warm shade of mocha that hinted at blonde in the evening sun, he still towered over me. As he turned in his seat to face me I was reminded of the similarities, his eyes hadn't changed. They glistened with a renewed interest as he spoke about our assignment and our friends. *Our friends,* I smiled to myself. I liked how that sounded.

"I guess they would," I answered, working hard at remaining focused on what he was saying, rather than how he looked and the fluttering sensations in my tummy.

"You still into animals?" I asked.

"Yeah, I'm hoping to get into uni next year. I still want to be a vet. I never stopped."

"That's great, you'll be awesome. You definitely have the right qualities." The grin that spread across his face at my appraisal almost took my breath away.

"You think so?"

I nodded, "I do, definitely." I took another sip of coffee as Jake's mood shifted.

"Sorry about putting you all under pressure with the assignment... Erm, what do you reckon to coming round here to work on it a bit, maybe tomorrow. I could call Callum. See if he can make it after practice and you could ask Jo?"

"Erm, yeah, okay, that sounds good. You sure you're up to it though?" I worried he was taking on too much too soon.

"Nah, I'm good. I need something to keep me from going crazy."

"Well, I guess I'd better head off while it's still daylight, I've no lights on my bike at the moment."

"Okay, thanks for coming over," he said, taking my cup from me.

"I was glad to. See you tomorrow then?"

"Yep, will do. Night, Abbie."

Chapter Twelve

A sense of ease embraced my body the morning after visiting Jake. A pleasant shortcut through the woods gave me an excuse to avoid the crowded bus to school. I maneuvered my bike into the rack by the gym while going over my schedule in my mind. Thoughts of Jake and science assignments filled my head as I struggled to secure the lock on my bike.

"Hey! Freak!"

Dread coursed through my veins, recognition sending a sudden shiver up my spine.

"What do you want?" I growled, determined not to show any sign of weakness.

"A friendly warning, Freak!" Jess poked me hard in the chest and I flinched at the sudden contact, my blood simmering to a boil.

"Fuck you!" I snarled, standing my ground. Jess's eyes widened in surprise. I didn't want a confrontation, but I wouldn't let her intimidate me.

"Seriously? Did she just say, *Fuck me*?" Jess asked, turning to Becca.

"She did," Becca said with an evil grin across her face.

"Thought so." Jess grabbed me by the shoulders and pushed me up against the wire mesh fence. Her fingers dug into my skin as she leaned towards my ear. "Keep away from our guys. If you so much as look in our direction, Freak, your life won't be worth living... Got it?" she growled, pushing me with emphasis back into the fence. "Come on, Bec, she's not worth the effort." With that she and Becca flounced off in the direction of the cafeteria.

My heart thundered in my chest as I struggled to recover my self-control enough for class. All I wanted now was to get through the day. I hugged the edge of the walkway as I plodded towards the main building and past the usual hordes of giddy students. Becca and Jess were already hanging off the jocks when I rounded the corner of the courtyard and glared at me. The last thing I needed was anymore hassle, so I dipped my head and scuttled past.

The morning's lessons provided an equal measure of useful information and extreme boredom. My stomach growled with discomfort way before the lunch bell and as I contemplated the hordes of bodies in the cafeteria I came to a decision. Rather than becoming the center of attention again today, I planned on regaining my low profile. I'd flown under the radar for years and it had served me well.

Satisfied with a seat at the far end of the cafeteria, I pulled my sandwich and drink from my bag. I'd just bitten into my chicken salad roll when Callum showed up.

"Hey, Abs?"

Fuck! So much for a low profile.

"Hey," I whispered, keeping my head down and continuing to chew my food.

"You okay for tonight?" I frowned at his question casting a nervous glance sideways.

"Erm, yeah," I said, not wanting to prolong our interaction. *Jeez, Callum, just go away hey?* I was desperate for him to leave before Jess and her cronies noticed us.

"Cool, see you then. Jake sounds better, hey?" he said just as Becca spotted him and nudged Jess who was draped across one of the jocks beside her. The vicious glare from Jess raised the hairs on the back of my neck. I hated how my position in school had shifted over the last week.

"Yeah. Okay, bye." I pushed past Callum, desperate to get away from the prying eyes. Once out of the cafeteria, my breathing began to slow. The tension seeped slowly from my body as I leaned my forehead against my locker in the deserted hallway. Punching in the combination, my skin began to prickle with expectation.

"Thought I told you to keep away from, Callum?"

With a roll of my eyes and my jaw set with determination, I turned and came face to face with Jess. "Thought I told you to fuck off!"

"You really are a freak aren't you? Don't you realize who you're dealing with?" Narrowing her eyes, she leaned inches from my face. "Keep away from him *or else!*"

"Screw you!" She didn't scare me. Just because I didn't want any attention didn't mean I was a pushover.

"You're one fucked up chick! Be careful, Abbie, don't cross me." She turned and flounced down the hallway.

The breath stuck in my lungs gushed out and I blinked back the unwelcome tears. Adrenaline coursed through my veins and my heart rate soared. I slammed my locker door into the casing and laid into the cold metal with a clenched fist until an excruciating pain shot up my arm.

"Shit!" I held my hand to my chest. Tears of frustration spilled from my eyes as I rushed to the girls' bathroom and struggled to turn on the cold faucet. I held my throbbing fingers under the icy water until the pain running through them numbed.

This is what happens when you get involved with other people. I'm over this shit.

The bell rang signaling the end of lunch. I headed to Gym with my head down and kept my hand in the pocket of my hoodie. As the session progressed a painful pulse ran up my arm with every stride round the track. By the end of the lesson I felt sick with the pain.

Jo hated running and tried every excuse to get away with as little as possible. I spotted her filling up her water bottle on the warm up lap and again twice after that. She also fastened her shoes, tied up her hair twice and went to the bathroom. She'd managed half of the required laps by the end of the session.

"Jeez, you're slack." Jo was well aware of her achievement as she approached the bleachers.

"What do you mean?" she asked, knowing full well what I meant, grinning while she removed her running shoes, "Come on then, get a move on." I shook my head at the nerve of my friend before grabbing my water bottle and following her into the locker room.

"So, we still on for tonight at Jake's?" she blurted out, stepping out of the shower wrapped in a towel. An immediate stab of panic hit my chest as I realized Becca was still within ear shot. My eyes widened at Jo, willing her to *shut the fuck up*!

"What? What did I say?" she asked in an exaggerated whisper. I shook my head and continued to dry off and dress in silence. At least she was intelligent enough to realize she'd said enough. The aggressive glares through the steamy air burned into the back of my head and a sense of dread left me unnerved.

"You walking or riding?" Jo asked as we stepped outside five minutes later.

"Riding."

"Hey, are you mad at me, Abbie?"

I took in a deep breath, "No...course not. It's just; those two bitches don't need to know our business...that's all. I can do without the agro, Joey."

Jo's shocked expression as we approached the bike racks pulled my attention to where my bike laid on the ground. No longer upright in the rack where I'd left it. The tires were flat and *FREAK* was carved into the seat.

"No!" My eyes welled up and my heart dropped. "Fucking tramps!" I slammed the gate so hard it bounced back and missed me by inches. "How could they do this?"

By the time we arrived at Jo's house my tears had dried on my cheeks. We'd made arrangements to eat there before heading round to Jake's house when Callum got back from practice.

"So what you gonna do?" Jo asked, eyeing me with caution as we began preparing dinner. My stomach flipped with the realization she was talking about my bike.

I breathed in, contemplating my answer for a moment, "Nothing."

"Nothing?" Jo frowned in dismay.

"No… Nothing."

"Fine." She busied herself with the pizza topping while chewing on her lip. "You know what? It's not fine! They shouldn't get away with it! They've damaged your property and you have to report them, Abbie." Desperation dripped from every word as Jo tried to make me see sense. I didn't answer her; I couldn't, my heart seemed lodged in my throat, robbing me of the power of speech.

"Whatever," she said, turning her attention back to the packs in front of us. I picked up one of the containers and took out the cheese.

"Where's your grater?" I asked after a moment, willing her to get back to normal as fast as possible. I heard her sigh before turning to collect the utensil from one of the wall cupboards.

"Here."

"Thanks."

Even though I knew reporting Jess and Becca was the right thing to do, I wasn't about to wreck the morsel of normality I'd managed to carve out of my fucked up life. It was bad enough that we were already associating with two of the most popular boys in school and upsetting their friends. Reporting those same friends, for the damage done to my bike wasn't worth the shit I'd get. *Who would believe me anyway?*

I picked up the block of cheese and proceeded to rub it against the metal grater, being careful not to get my knuckles in the process.

"Hey?" Jo cried grabbing my arm, "What the hell did you do to your hand?"

"I know, looks bad, hey?" I said, trying to make light of my bruises, "Got it caught in my locker at lunchtime, I wasn't paying attention." She narrowed her eyes and was about to say something, but Pam arrived home.

"Hi, girls," she called, coming into the kitchen, "How was today?"

Jo looked at me, "We've had better, but that's school for you."

"What happened?" Jo's mom asked, her eyes twinkling with amusement.

"Oh you know, Coach Jackson got us running millions of laps in gym, he seems to think we're all potential Olympians or something."

Pam grinned at me. She knew Jo was no athlete. "What time are you going round to Jake's?" she asked just as I was about to put the two prepared pizzas in the oven. How I didn't drop them at the mention of his name, I don't know.

"Err, about an hour, Callum has football first, so we're going when he gets here."

"Don't be too late tonight please, Jo. Jake's still recovering and Karen doesn't want him getting over tired. He's back in school tomorrow."

"We won't. The work should take an hour max," Jo said, pouring two milkshakes.

"Jo! My God, girl, how old are you?" Pam complained, throwing a cloth at her. "Clean the mess up please."

We were finishing our pizza and drinks at the breakfast bar when Callum strolled up the driveway and in through the back door. He grinned at our stuffed mouths and cast a quick glance at the plates in front of us.

"Left any for me, girls?" he asked.

"Nope, finished," I said, popping the last bite into my mouth and downing the last slurp of fresh banana milkshake.

"Jeez, Joey, that was such good pizza," I emphasized while grinning at a shocked Callum. Jo laughed out loud at the expression on the footballer's face.

"Good job I grabbed a burger on the way here." Cal pouted as he looked at the empty plates. "Guess we better get to Jay's."

A sudden sensation of butterflies took over in my stomach at the thought of seeing Jake, which confused me considering the events of the day. I couldn't rationalize my excitement.

***

"Thought you weren't coming," Jake said with a wide grin as we strolled up his driveway a few minutes later.

"Jeez, dude, you had us scared there for a second," Callum said, grabbing Jake in a man hug, "How you feeling now, big guy? You still on track for coming back to school tomorrow?"

"Yeah, I'm all good, just got to take it easy for a few days. I should be back to normal by next week." Jake said, throwing a subtle glance in my direction as he spoke making me smile. I noticed a twinkle when his eyes met mine. The butterflies in my stomach launched themselves in a frenzy and I coughed in response to the unnerving sensation.

"You okay?" Jo whispered, trying not to attract the attention of the guys.

"Yeah, I'm fine, just got a tickle in my throat."

"So, we better crack on, guys, the patient needs his bed rest if he's gonna keep up tomorrow," Callum said with a smirk.

"Yeah, yeah," Jake replied with a chuckle, punching Cal in the arm.

The hour passed much quicker than expected. We'd surpassed our target of divvying up the work load as well as drafting an introduction to the project.

"What's the go at school then, guys?" Jake asked as we packed up our papers.

"Not a lot," I said, struggling to hide the slight frown that played on my forehead.

Not missing a trick Jake's eyes narrowed, "You don't sound too sure."

"Nothing if you don't count your so called friends acting like prize bitches!" Jo's sarcastic outburst had me heading straight to the bathroom. I had no interest in being a part of this conversation.

"What happened?" Jake asked, casting a concerned glance at me as I fled the room.

"Jess and Becca vandalized Abbie's bike. You can see for yourself, it's outside on my driveway." I heard the shuffling of bodies and surmised they'd gone to take a look.

Once in the bathroom I stared at my pathetic reflection in the mirror. I sucked in a deep breath and willed the tears of humiliation to be absorbed back into my eyes rather than letting them stream down my cheeks. The sound of muffled voices as Jo and the boys came back indoors set my heart pounding.

"Abbie?"

With a defiant tilt of my chin at myself in the mirror I turned to the door.

"Leave it, Jake, I'm over it, don't say anything. It's just a bike." I could see the internal battle of concern and anger in his eyes.

"You sure?" he asked, placing his hand gently on my upper arm.

I nodded in response, "Yeah, come on, let's go back." He still looked hesitant. "Jake, I'm fine honest!" I insisted. He sucked in a breath not convinced, but nodded as he slid his hand down my arm and took hold of my hand.

I winced at the pain shooting up my arm and pulled my hand from his as my eyes watered. Jake's reaction was priceless. I could see the, *Here we go again* look on his face. Disappointment flooded through my chest and I tried to push past him.

"Whatever. Don't worry about it." I felt like a fool for thinking he'd have any patience or be any different from everybody else.

"Abbie? What's going on?" he asked, grabbing my arms with gentle, yet firm hands.

His eyes searched mine for an explanation for my sudden outburst. I looked down, not wanting to share what had happened. This was the exact reason I'd avoided him last week. He had always known when I was hiding something.

"I punched my locker! Alright?" I shouted, pissed off that he had this effect on me. With a great deal of care he took my hand and pushed me back into the bathroom.

"Fuck! Have you been to a doctor with this?" he asked, his frown deepening at the state of the dark purple bruise covering the swelling on the back of my hand.

"I'm fine," I choked out, attempting to pull my hand away from his grasp.

"This is not fine…and if you haven't already seen a doctor, you're going now."

"Jake, I said I'm fine. Now please…leave it," I said, managing to remove myself from his grip.

"Jo, I'm going home. Tell your mom thanks for dinner will you please? See you, Cal. See you tomorrow, Jake," I said, before rushing past him towards the door.

"Abbie!" he called, running his hands through his hair in frustration.

Chapter Thirteen

"Jake, leave her," Jo implored, pulling on my arm.

"What the hell happened, Jo?" I shouted desperately, trying to hold my emotions in check.

Jo hung her head, trying to avoid my question. Her big mouth had already dropped Abbie in the shit once tonight. "Jo, I'm dead serious! What happened?" My voice began to tremble and I ran my hands through my hair. "That wasn't just about her bike!"

"Search me, I haven't got a clue what's going on, Jay," Callum said, looking a little uncomfortable, "Sorry."

I huffed out a sigh and rubbed my hands over my face.

Cal turned away from us hovering near the door, "I'll leave you to it, see you both tomorrow, thanks for tonight, the work I mean." He offered a sympathetic smile on his way out.

I faced Jo again in the hope she'd throw some light on what had happened with Abbie's hand.

"Before you ask, I don't know anything either."

"You know more than I do, Jo?" I said, desperate for her to fill in the gaps.

"Abbie said she'd punched a locker."

"I didn't know that, honest. She told me she'd trapped it in a door at lunchtime. I only noticed it earlier when we were at my place." Jo looked gutted, her shoulders dropped and her hands hung in submission by her sides. I could tell she was being truthful from her expression.

"But..."

"But what, Jo?" I urged, closing the gap between us.

"There's been a bit of hassle this week," she said, pausing for a second as though she was trying to organize her thoughts before continuing, "The damage to Abbie's bike isn't the first time she's had trouble. That Jess girl and her friend, Becca...well they called Abs a freak yesterday in the cafeteria, in front of half the school just because Callum was talking to her."

My heart motored at the new piece of information.

"She told me they'd warned her to stay away from you guys," Jo's eyes teared up as she recognized the seriousness of what they'd said.

"Fucking hell, Jo!" I couldn't believe what I was hearing. "Are you telling me those bitches are bullying Abbie just for talking to us?"

"That's exactly what I'm saying, Jake, and I think they've been at her again today. I saw them hanging around this morning. I suspected something had been said at the time, but Abbie didn't want to talk about it."

Jo looked really worried. My blood bubbled close to boiling point; I felt so helpless. Why hadn't she told anyone? Jeez she could be stubborn.

I grabbed my truck keys, "I have to go to her."

"Jake, I don't think that's a good idea," Jo spoke softly but with firmness, lowering her head in an attempt to avoid any eye contact. At that point a sense of dread numbed my brain.

"Jo?" Still no eye contact and my heart picked up speed. "What?"

She shook her head as if battling an inner demon, "I can't say…it's not my place. Just give her time…it needs to come from Abbie."

I couldn't stand still. My feet were itching to run to her.

"Trust me, Jake. Just believe me, she needs you, more than you even know…please, give her time…" Jo begged. My hands flew up to my face and I pressed my palms to my eyes. Fear coursed through my veins as my imagination kicked into overdrive. What could be so bad that Jo wouldn't tell me? A sense of doubt drained my remaining energy.

Confused and deflated I took in another deep breath before slumping down into the arm chair next to me, staring desperately at Jo. All I'd thought about since our chance reunion last week was Abbie, and how we used to be. All I had now was an empty shell of my girl. The difference in Abbie broke my heart. She wasn't particularly nice anymore. My throat tightened and an unfamiliar sting prickled my eyes as the emotion of the situation got to me. I heard my voice croak.

"What's she like, Jo?" I needed to know about Abbie; the new Abbie. Jo's tearful eyes met mine then wandered off into the distance as she considered her response.

"She's my best friend and I love her," Jo said, taking a deep breath, "I'd do anything for her and I know she feels the same about me." She nibbled on her thumb nail as she recalled a memory from when we were all kids. "I remember her telling me all about you when she came home to visit her gran, do you remember that holiday?"

I instantly recalled the conversation at Raven when Abbie told me about going to visit her gran for Christmas. A frown crossed my brow at the sense of loss attached to the memory; I hadn't seen her after that holiday.

"We had a really good time that Christmas, just like old times. We promised to keep in touch, but..." Jo looked down again and scowled.

"But what?" I prompted.

"But she didn't answer my letters." she said, her voice full of regret. "Anyway, when she came back to Casey after her dad left, she was different; angry and distant. She didn't trust anyone. It took her ages to accept me as her friend again, and believe me I tried everything. She wasn't the old Abbie anymore." A tear rolled down Jo's cheek while she grew distant.

"She's pretty much only had me as a friend all through school, she doesn't mix with anyone, Jake. That's why they all call her Freak. She doesn't speak to anyone unless she has to."

My eyes searched Jo's face hoping for an explanation. I took hold of her upper arms so that she had to keep eye contact. "Tell me?" I whispered, desperate to know what it was that had changed my girl.

"I can't!" Jo stood in front of me shaking her head as tears streamed down her cheeks. "I can't, Jake... I'm sorry, I just can't."

"I'm sorry. I didn't mean to make you cry. Fuck!" I said, pulling her in for a hug.

She pushed me away gently before adding, "I'm not crying for me, I'm crying for Abbie." Stepping away, she picked up her laptop and school bag, "I'll see you tomorrow. Bye, Jake."

I froze to the spot, my mind racing with unanswered questions; a sense of impending dread rumbled deep in my gut. After several minutes I climbed the stairs to my room and flopped onto my bed. I pulled my cell from my pocket and scrolled to Abbie's number, hit call and waited. My heart pounded in my chest as it rang out.

"Argh! Why won't you answer?" I switched to text and punched the keys in frustration.

Abbie, I hope u got home safely, plz pick up, I'm worried.

It took less than a minute for a reply to light up my phone and with it relief swept through my body.

I'm fine, plz don't worry, c u tomorrow

I fumbled a reply, *Ok I'm here if u need me. Night Xx*

I raked my hands through my hair, images of our latest encounter flooding my mind; my gut aching as I lay on my bed staring at the ceiling. Minutes turned into hours before I began to relax. I had to get up for school in a little over five hours and to be honest; I was desperate to get there. I needed to see Abbie. The intense anxiety running through me in regards to Jo's partial disclosure had me tossing and turning. I finally slipped into a restless sleep plagued with confusion and tortured images of Abbie in distress.

"Jake, Mom says you need to get your butt out of bed if you're going to school," Lucy shouted through the door.

"Arrghh!" I was screwed. I squeezed my eyes shut, fighting the glare streaming in through the crack in the curtains. My head pounded as I eased myself up from the mattress and headed into the shower. The warm water crashed down on my aching body as I leaned against the cold tiles.

What the hell happened to you, Abbie?

The shower revived me and my sense of purpose. I dressed hurriedly in Jeans and T-shirt after drying off and bounded downstairs for some breakfast grabbing my sneakers on the way.

"Morning, sweetheart. How you feeling?" Mom asked. She looked relieved to see me up and about.

"Yeah, I'm good, tired, but good," I said, feigning an exaggerated picture of health and vitality for my mom's sake. I sat down at the breakfast bar and helped myself to bacon and pancakes from the pile on a large plate next to a mountain of toast.

"This is great, thanks." My appetite wasn't quite back to normal, but she had made a special effort.

"Well, you need to keep up your strength. I don't want you getting sick again," she said, grabbing her bag. "Right guys, I'm off. You going to be okay, honey?" She turned to me, worry clearly visible on her face.

"Mom, I'm fine, honest."

"Right, good, okay." Not sounding too convinced, but she nodded before leaving for work.

I felt much better physically. It was the emotional shit I was having trouble with. Not so much recovering from an attack of peritonitis but more about Abs. I reached for my rucksack and cell phone before following Lucy out of the house. She headed off in the opposite direction to meet her friends.

I wondered about the decision that I'd made in the shower. Instinct told me it was a risk, a big risk in fact, but I'd decided to call for Abbie. I couldn't, in my right mind, go to school without her after everything I'd been told and *not told* last night.

After ten minutes of mulling over the pros and cons of my decision, I knocked on her front door. It was still early and possible that she wouldn't be ready yet.

Beth's voice drifted from one of the upstairs rooms, "Someone get that!"

Seconds later Martin pulled open the screen door with unexpected enthusiasm, "Hey, Jake. How you doing?" he asked, slapping me on the shoulder as he moved to allow me in.

"Yeah, great, thanks. Erm…is Abbie still here?" I asked, trying to keep it casual.

"I guess so, I haven't seen her yet. Come on through, I'll go see if she's ready." I followed him into the kitchen and watched as he bounded up the stairs two at a time.

"Abbie?" There came a muffled response from one of the bedrooms as I waited at the foot of the stairs. "Jake's here, Abs, get up!" he yelled again through the door before heading back towards me. "I was just leaving, but you can wait for her if you like, I'm sure she won't mind." Martin then grabbed a packed lunch from the kitchen counter and paused briefly, waiting for a response to his suggestion.

"Err, yeah, sure okay," I said, feeling a tad uncomfortable as he shouted up the stairs.

"Abbie, I'm going to Howie's, Jake's waiting down here for you, see you later. Bye, Mom." Martin left, closing the door behind him. I turned to look around the room, wondering what the hell I was doing here. Last night's tearful heart to heart with Abbie's best friend had left me no clearer as to what the fuck was going on than before the evening began. I questioned my sanity and headed into the den. I took a seat on the sofa, leaned into the cushions and waited for Abbie to come downstairs .

Chapter Fourteen

My tummy rumbled with nervous tension as I headed downstairs. Jake showing up was a little surprising, considering the disastrous end to our evening yesterday; unless he wanted another argument?

When I got downstairs I expected him to be in the kitchen, but walking past the den, two feet poking out in front of the sofa caught my eye. My breath hitched in my throat at what I saw. Asleep on the soft leather sofa with his head cocked to one side he looked so peaceful, unlike the stressed Jake from last night. I leaned against the door frame, taking in his sleeping form.

"Fuck, Jake! When did you get to be so good looking?" I swallowed past the lump in my throat as I considered the impact I'd had on his recovery. I'd expected another confrontation when Martin said Jake was here, but rather than offloading my anger and frustration, guilt seeped into my system. Getting mixed up with my shit was the last thing he needed. I didn't want him involved and I didn't want to be affected by his involvement.

The fact that he was here after what had gone down last night confused me. Jake had always been supportive, but last night I'd been a prize bitch towards him, *again*. So why was he here now? I narrowed my eyes, considering the possibilities.

No matter what I threw at this boy, he kept coming back for more. I knew I was testing him. Deep down I expected him to leave again. It was just a matter of when. I guess I had to decide whether I wanted him in my life until he snapped under the pressure of having me in his.

I covered him with a soft throw before following the aroma of fresh coffee back to the kitchen. After pouring myself a cup and finishing a slice of toast I wandered over to where Jake slept. He'd moved a touch and snuggled into the cushions; he looked so relaxed. My heart skipped with unexpected emotion. I took a deep breath and pulled my cell from my pocket.

"Hi, Jo, listen Jake's turned up at my place..." I needed to find out what Jake's mom thought about the fact that her recovering son had crashed out on my sofa.

"No shit?" Jo screamed down the phone, causing me to pull my cell away from my ear until she calmed down.

"Yes shit! Can you do me a favor?"

"Sure, shoot."

"Can you get Karen's number for me please? It's just that...well, Jake fell asleep while he was waiting for me to get ready for school and..."

"Oh, really? Okay, hang on a sec… Here you go, you got a pen?"

"Nope, text it when I hang up and I'll save it. Thanks. I'll call you later."

"Okie dokie. Will you be in school today?"

"Not sure at the minute, didn't sleep that great last night, I feel like shit."

"I'm not surprised, yesterday was a bit of a bummer to say the least. Get some rest. I'll call round after school."

"Okay, bye."

Jo was quick to send Karen's number so I hit call. Jake still had time to get to school, if that's what his mom wanted.

"Hello, Karen Ashton speaking."

"Hi, Mrs. Ashton, it's Abbie James."

"Hello, Abbie. What can I do for you?" I chewed my lip for a second as I contemplated the best way to tell her about Jake.

"Erm, well, Jake called round for me this morning and well, while I was getting ready…"

"Oh my God! He's okay isn't he? What's happened?"

"No, no, sorry, he's fine. It's just…he fell asleep in the den while he was waiting. I wondered whether you thought I should wake him or let him sleep, that's all. He's crashed out, Mrs. Ashton." I spoke quickly so Karen didn't have a seizure at the other end of the phone.

"I knew he was taking things too fast," she said, "Are you in school today, Abbie?"

"Erm...no I'm not, I'm off sick today. So if you want, he can stay here," I said, frowning at the idea of spending any amount of time with Jake.

"If you're sure, Abbie, that would be very kind, thank you," she said, sounding more at ease than she had at the start of the call.

"Sure, no problem."

"Oh and Abbie..."

"Yes."

"Please call me Karen," she said and I grinned, remembering her saying the same thing when I was a little girl.

"Okay, Karen. Thanks, bye." With that I headed into the kitchen and poured myself another cup of coffee. School wasn't high up on my list of priorities today. I'd slept like shit, tossing and turning all night and planned on skipping school anyway. So the fact that Jake had arrived unannounced and fallen asleep changed nothing.

Finishing my coffee, I returned to the den and sat at the other end of the sofa from Jake. I picked up a random magazine from the rack and skimmed through the pages.

"What the hell is going on here?" I heard a voice bellow in my ear, waking me with a start. After a frantic mental rewind of the morning's events, a flush of embarrassment colored my face when I realized the warmth under my cheek was Jake's lap.

"It's not what you think, Mom," I declared, easing myself up so I wouldn't wake him. "Jake called for me for school earlier and fell asleep before I came down stairs. I called his mom and she asked if I could let him sleep."

"That's all well and good, Abbie, but why aren't you in school and why were you all over him?" she snapped, not at all happy with the scene she thought was playing out in front of her.

"I was sick when he arrived. I'm not going in today. And I was not lying all over him! I fell asleep because I'm sick, I must have just... Urgghh! Why bother!"

My mom shook her head as I stormed past her. I needed to take some time to gather my thoughts and calm down before this turned into a full scale screaming match. I didn't want Jake to be witness to that. He'd already heard enough from me over the last week.

"Abbie?" she said, following me into the kitchen. "I didn't mean anything by it. It's...well...it was a surprise that's all. This is what happens when you take on too much during the week. Not helped by the fact your bedroom light was still on way past midnight. You can't expect to be up with the birds if you're awake half the night, sweetheart." Mom continued to pack her lunch as she lectured me. "Well, I've got to go to work, make sure that you rest, both of you!" she said as she rushed around the room gathering her bag and jacket. "See you tonight."

"Bye."

Wandering back into the den after Mom left, I picked up a book from one of the shelves and took up a safe position away from Jake.

As if he sensed me watching him, his eyes fluttered open and a grin spread slowly across his face as he worked out what had happened.

"Hey," he whispered, his voice sounding a bit croaky with sleep.

"Hey," I said, watching closely as he pushed himself upright and ran his hands through his sleep tousled hair.

"Sorry, I must have dozed off."

"Don't worry about it... I called your mom; she knows you didn't make it into school. She said she was fine with you crashing here." I swallowed and his eyes searched mine, causing a tingling sensation in my stomach.

"Oh, okay, cool. Thanks for that," he replied, "I didn't get much sleep last night."

"What are you doing here, Jake?" I asked, not happy with the sarcasm in his tone.

"Oh I don't know… maybe I thought you'd be pleased to see me?" He looked away, taking in another breath. "I thought walking with you this morning would save any further confrontation between you and those two skanks at school." His eyes didn't leave mine.

"It's no concern of yours, Jake," I said, moving to the other end of the sofa. I hugged a loose cushion and brought my knees to my chest, creating a barrier between him and me.

"You know that's not true, Abbie. If you're hurt it does concern me. That's just the way it is."

"But we haven't seen each other for ten years."

"No shit, Sherlock!" he cried, throwing his hands up in the air in frustration. His eyes swam with unanswered questions, but instead of asking anything he appeared to think better of it and lowered his head into his hands.

"What do you want from me, Jake? Why are you even bothered?" It made no sense to me that he was even the remotest bit interested in me.

"For fuck's sake, Abbie! Haven't you heard anything I've been saying? I don't want anything from you!" he barked in frustration, running his hands through his hair. He leaned forward on the sofa, pressing his palms to his brow. "You really don't have a clue do you?" he whispered, looking up at me. I frowned in response which prompted him to continue. "Abbie, I've spent the last ten years hoping that one day we'd be together again. I've missed you every day. The second I looked into your eyes last week it felt like I was home." He sat up and paused for a moment. "I want to help you."

With that I flew from the sofa, pacing the length of the den in front of him.

"You have no clue who I am anymore!" My head was all over the place. I couldn't handle this. I couldn't handle Jake and his promises; the promises he wouldn't be able to keep when he found out the truth.

"Then tell me, tell me who you are." His voice trembled with desperation, pleading with me to open up.

"I don't know!" I covered my face, slumping down on the arm chair facing him. I looked up and caught my breath when I saw the intensity in his eyes as they bored into me. My heart raced as my eyes pooled with the tears of overwhelming sadness that our lives had come to this; I truly loved this boy all those years ago.

"I can't do this, Jake!" I said as the tears spilled from my eyes and trickled down my cheeks, "I'm not that little girl you loved. I never will be, it's too late for us." Jake moved toward the armchair and crouched down on the floor in front of me. He placed his hands on my knees, forcing me to look at him.

"Trust me," he whispered as he lifted his hand and tilted my chin upward, "Please, Abbie, I won't hurt you." His sincerity was impossible to disbelieve, yet I continued to battle my inner demons.

"I'm sorry, I can't," I cried, pulling his hand from my face, "Please don't."

"Please don't what? Jeez, Abbie, I want to help you, it's killing me to see you so cut up like this. You can't keep pushing me away."

"What do you mean pushing *you* away? You're not that fucking important!" I shouted at him, only inches from his face. I gasped for breath, staring into his piercing blue eyes, waiting for a reaction; tense and ready for an argument. It was the only way I could cope when things got too hard. I felt more in control being a bitch. It didn't hurt as much as losing loved ones; being rejected, being betrayed.

"Well I'm sorry, but you *are* that important to me!" His voice was frantic, "I won't lose you a second time!"

"You can't lose what you don't have." As soon as the words left my mouth I wanted desperately to take them back.

"You don't mean that," he whispered, his eyes filling with tears. I stood frozen, unable to move at the sight of Jake's tears.

"I don't, I'm sorry, I really don't," I whispered, desperately sorry for being so cruel, I clamped a hand over my mouth to halt the sobs. Jake strode towards me and hauled me into his chest. "I'm s-sorry, I didn't mean it." I cried, burying my face in the front of his shirt as he stroked my hair with one hand and held me as close as possible with the other.

"Shh... Don't cry, Abbie. I'm not going anywhere," he said, holding me tight.

"I'm so sorry." The pounding of my heart resonated in my head for the longest moment before I leaned away from Jake, regarding the sincerity in his eyes.

"I promise you... I'm here to stay, if you'll have me."

I raised my hand and wiped a tear from his cheek with my thumb. My head swam in confusion as I contemplated his words and my response.

"I can't make you any promises," I whispered, hoping for acceptance, "But I do want to try. You *are* important to me...I'm so sorry I said you weren't, I didn't mean it."

He cupped my face in his hands, his fingers caressing my cheeks, "Hey...you don't have to apologize to me." A single tear slipped down my cheek. "Please don't cry, baby," Jake whispered. He wiped my tears before touching his lips to the same spot, then to my lips. The gesture was so gentle my heart skipped a beat and without caution I relaxed into his arms as he showed me how much he cared. I wrapped my arms around his neck, my fears melted away with the tenderness of his kiss. My hands reached for his face, as we eased apart. I traced his jaw with my fingers.

"You're a beautiful person, Jake Ashton. I can't believe you picked me," I whispered.

He took my hand in his and kissed my fingertips, "Abbie, I didn't pick you. We were supposed to be together from the moment I collided with you on your first day at Raven Elementary. I didn't stand a chance. There's been a gaping hole inside me for the last ten years, an ache I didn't understand. But I've been aching for you all this time." A fresh tear escaped from the corner of his eye as he spoke and I reached up and pulled him towards me, gripping onto him with all my might.

"I haven't got the words for how I'm feeling." An overwhelming sense of belonging filled my heart.

"Thank you," he said, cupping my face in his hands, kissing me again before taking my hand in his.

I winced at the shooting pain following his touch. He looked down at the angry bruise covering the back of my hand. Jake's jaw clenched as he inspected my injury.

"You need to get this looked at." His eyes pleaded with me to listen to him.

I nodded, "Okay, I'll go to the ER." I could see the relief on his face.

"I'm not in my truck," he said, taking my hand.

"That's okay; we can maybe walk to your place and pick up your truck?"

Chapter Fifteen

"Are you going into school tomorrow?" Jake asked tensely as we drove back from the ER.

"I guess so," I said, rolling my eyes and lifting the offending limb, "It's not like it's a life threatening illness or anything." It turned out my hand was just badly bruised. I'd been bandaged and sent away with instructions to keep it elevated and to be careful to avoid future mishaps involving lockers.

Jake seemed deep in thought on the way back and I wondered what was going through his mind. I continued to look through the passenger window, the sun warming my face as we drove through town. Casey wasn't a bad place for shops and services; a large elementary school sat on the hill on one side of the suburb while Casey High skirted the edge of town. Even now, after all these years, I couldn't understand why we ever moved away. Thoughts of the move and subsequent events suddenly flooded my mind and I shifted uncomfortably in my seat. A frown crossed my brow as I squeezed my eyes closed, trying to shake the images from my head.

"Hey?" Jake reached over and gave my arm a gentle squeeze. "You okay?"

"Huh? Yes…sorry. I'm fine, just a twinge," I lied, forcing a smile and covering his hand with mine to reassure him. He smiled back, seeming to accept my excuse before moving his attention back to the road. I inhaled deeply and exhaled real slow to give me more thinking time.

"I'm seeing Jo later," I said, smiling brightly, "We've got plans for this coming weekend so we need to catch up with last minute arrangements."

"Oh, cool. What you doing?"

"Her mom and dad have a house at Crawford Lake. We're heading up there for a long weekend on Friday. Pam has a computer course at Scott's convention center and her dad is going fishing with a friend, so Jo asked if we could tag along."

"Wow! That sounds fantastic!" His enthusiastic response made me grin. I had a sudden urge to invite him along and chewed my lip with indecision. I couldn't really ask him, it wasn't my place, so I left it, biting my lip to stop me blurting out an invitation. He noticed I'd not said anything and glanced over at me.

"What?" he asked, with a face splitting grin, "It does sound fantastic."

"It does, you're right," I agreed, returning his grin. "So, you in school tomorrow, or you gonna crash round at some random chick's house in the morning?"

"Hey! I resent that accusation. Anyway, I wouldn't call it random. It's all part of my game plan." He wrenched on the handbrake as he pulled up in front of my house, turning towards me with the twinkle of mischief in his eye.

"Oh, yeah, and what game plan are you referring to, Mr. Ashton?" In one swift movement he slid towards me and kissed me on the cheek. My stomach flipped in response, but before I could say anything he opened his door. "Maybe I'll see you later when I call for Jo?"

I hoped I could squeeze in a meet with Jake as well as my best friend. They were neighbors after all. It wouldn't be too weird if we bumped into one another later when I went round after dinner.

"Cool, I'll catch you later," he said casually before hopping out of the truck and running round to my door. He then helped me down to ground level. His hands lingered on my waist as our eyes met. A smile played on his lips as he lowered his head to kiss me.

"See you later." He raised a hand and gently tucked my hair behind my ear before brushing his knuckles softly against my cheek.

"Kay," I managed to croak out, struggling to stay upright as he turned and walked back around the front of his truck pausing briefly to throw me a cheeky wink. I stood and watched him climb back into the truck with a stupid grin plastered across my face.

"Fuck!" I whispered on a long breath as he waved to me through his open window and sped off up the road. "Jeez, I'm screwed!"

A warm glow spread across my skin as I strolled towards the front door.

"Martin?"

"Yep, in here, sis." He appeared from the den, stuffing his face with a sandwich. His eyes went wide when he caught sight of my bandaged hand. "What the fuck?" he spluttered, his brow creasing into a deep frown.

"Oh, yeah, it's nothing, had a bit of a run in with my locker at school," I replied vaguely. My reputation for violent outbursts when things got a bit too much was widely known. However, as I'd gotten older occurrences had lessened; much to the relief of my mother. In my mid-teens the ER became a frequent excursion. I'd accrued an extensive list of minor injuries. My temper had been ridiculously fiery and at times completely out of control, but for a long time now I had held it at bay. I'd learned to deal with my issues without hurting myself or anyone else and was quite proud of that fact.

Looking down at my hand I felt a pang of disappointment. I didn't want to revisit those feelings. I'd buried them deep inside me for such a long time, but since Jake showed up the absolute horror of my past had returned. Nightmares about Peter and what he did to me over the years were regular sleep time visitors, but they were nothing to compare with the horrific ones I was having lately.

For this to work there had to be a tradeoff. Well... as long as Jake never found out what happened, I was willing to take the risk. It was wonderful having him back in my life, even if only for a day at a time. He'd dump my ass as soon as he found out. What ambitious, talented and attractive guy would want a defiled shell of a girl as their partner in life? My eyes narrowed at the thought as I walked away from Martin.

"Mom's on late shift. Dinner's in the fridge," I shouted from halfway up the stairs. I needed a shower. Today had been unexpected, but I was also tired and feeling a bit guilty for lying to Jake. I was soiled goods and the thought that he was getting somebody different to what I was in reality weighed heavily on my conscience.

The hot steam from the shower swirled around the room and I could resist its call no longer. I carefully removed the bandage from my hand and stepped under the stream of warm, inviting water. Taking in a deep breath the pent up anxiety running through my body slowly melted away. I leaned against the tiled wall of the shower and recalled the memory of Jake lying asleep this morning and of his breath catching smile when he woke and how it pleased me. He wanted to be with me. My heart beat quickened at the thought. I'd always known he was *my* Jake. Coming back to the here and now, my mood shifted again. What would I do if he left? I closed my eyes, pushing that awful possibility to the depths of my mind. I didn't want to think about it, not today.

Showering quickly I rinsed my hair before turning off the faucet and stepping carefully onto the soft mat on the tiled floor. I didn't bother dressing, opting for my robe and a towel wrapped round my head before descending the stairs to grab a quick bite before I headed round to Joey's.

Opening the cooler, I glanced inside and spotted a bowl of pasta in sauce.

"Martin, are you having some of this spaghetti?" I asked, pulling out the bowl.

"Yeah, why not?" I smiled to myself; it would be a cold day in hell before Martin turned down food of any description, especially if it was being prepared for him. I divided the dish between two smaller bowls and placed one into the microwave for a couple of minutes while I grabbed some cheese.

"Mart?" I shouted, placing the second dish in the oven. "Grab a couple of glasses will you and the soda?"

"Mmm, that smells good," he said, walking into the kitchen. He reached up to get the items from the cupboard and pulled two cokes out of the cooler.

"Mom made it last night." Collecting my food from the oven I sat down by him at the breakfast bar.

"So...." he said, making me cringe in expectation of what line his conversation would take, "You and Jake Ashton, hey?"

"It's not like that," I said, chewing a mouthful of pasta, my eyes narrowing at the implied meaning. I thought to myself, of course, it was *exactly* like that. Or at least, we were at the beginning of *that*.

"Course it's not," he said, laughing before taking a long slurp of his drink. "Do you like him?" His voice shifted from joking to serious. I didn't answer straight away, causing him to turn towards me and lower his fork in anticipation.

"Yes...yes I do," I said, nodding my head as if realizing the fact right then and there.

"That's cool… He's okay, Abs. Jake's a sound guy."
He finished off his food and got up to place his bowl in
the dishwasher. I smiled at his attempt at giving mine and
Jake's friendship his brotherly seal of approval.

"I'm off round to Jo's in a while, I won't be late,
remind Mom when she gets home will you?"

"Yeah sure. You seeing Jake while you're there?" he
asked, ducking as I swiped at his head.

"Hey! Cheeky!" I heard my phone ringing upstairs as I
turned to go get dressed. Towel drying my hair before
picking up my cell from the bed I noticed a text message
notification.

Hey, just wanted to check ur okay.

Smiling, I replied, *I'm fine x*

Throwing my cell down onto my bed I went into the
bathroom to clean my teeth before plaiting my hair to one
side so that it hung over my shoulder, fastening it with a
black hair tie. I'd just finished dressing in my black jeans
and a sweatshirt when another text came through.

Good xxx

"See you later, Martin," I hollered on my way out of
the front door.

I turned the corner of our street and spotted a familiar
figure walking towards me. I recognized Jake's confident

swagger and I felt a warm glow begin to spread through my body.

"Hey!"

"Hey, yourself," I said, walking towards him, placing my hand in his as he held it out to me. "What you doing here?" I asked, loving the fact that he was.

"I didn't want you walking round to Jo's on your own." Jake's thoughtful reply made me blush.

"How did you know I was on my way?"

"I didn't, but I knew you were coming at some point," he said, grinning before his expression turned to one of concern when he noticed my hand, "How's your hand? Where's the bandage?"

"It's aching a bit, I could do with a little help getting it back on," I said, holding up the dressing.

"Here." He held out his other hand, "I'll do it for you if you like." I passed him the bandage and sat down on the wall by the side of the footpath. Pulling up my sleeve I raised my hand. "Jeez, Abbie, you did a good job," he commented, noting the deep purple bruise.

Carefully, Jake placed the end against my wrist, taking care not to catch my knuckles. He wound it precisely round my hand towards my fingers and then back up to my wrist, securing it with the elasticated fastener that came with it.

"Thanks," I said as he pulled me up to my feet.

"You're very welcome," he replied, bending slightly and kissing the top of my head. We continued on our way, his arm slung casually across my shoulders and mine around his waist. The closeness made me feel at ease, protected. I liked it.

"So…what's the go with this weekend away?" Jake asked when we'd gone another block down the road.

"Just a break away. Nothing too exciting. It is stunning up there though, I've seen photos. You should see the lake, it looks so beautiful." I smiled as I recalled the photographs Jo had shown me the week before. I was looking forward to getting away. Then narrowing my eyes I considered the events of the last couple of weeks. My mind was working overtime due to the mixed emotions of having Jake back in my life.

"You're doing it again," he said, interrupting my thoughts, "You zoned out again."

I shook my head in embarrassment, "I'm sorry, I was miles away."

"I think you need that holiday." He smiled and his eyes searched mine, making sure I was okay, "Come on, let's get you to Jo's, it's getting a bit nippy."

"Hang on, buster, we haven't all got legs as long as a freakin giraffe!"

"Buster?" he asked, making me laugh at the surprised expression on his face, at which point I started laughing as well.

Chapter Sixteen

"Hey, Ab...errr *guys*." Jo's surprise at seeing Jake with me interrupted her greeting. However the stunned expression on her face turned to one of excitement almost instantly.

"Close your mouth, Joey, there's a bus coming," I said, shaking my head as I strode past her, followed closely by a grinning Jake. Her mouth snapped shut, the grin that began at the corner of her mouth simultaneously spread across her face. Her overactive imagination getting the better of her and Jake quickly diverted her attention.

"I'm not staying, Jo, don't worry, I was just walking with Abbie. I wouldn't dream of cramping your style." He winked at me, making my stomach flip.

"It's fine, I don't have a problem with you tagging along," Jo said, battling the amused smile plastered to her face. He looked over at me with a raised eyebrow.

"Hey, I don't mind," I said, leaving it up to him.

"I'll head home in a while. Want me to make you two beautiful ladies a drink while you get on with your planning?" he offered, moving towards the kitchen, making me blush profusely.

"Thanks," Jo said, her eyes widening at Jake's gesture.

"What's it to be? Hot or cold?"

"I'll have a coffee please," I said.

"Make that two and whatever you're having. The cups are in the wall cupboard, the coffee is in the pantry," Jo said, all the while beaming at me, making me blush, "Oh and there are chocolate cookies in the pantry as well."

I sat down on the shag pile rug covering the den floor, getting comfortable at the coffee table. Jo joined me and laid out a folder in front of us, containing information about the house at the lake with spectacular photos of the surrounding area. Jo produced a writing pad and jotted down a few notes as we talked. We worked out times, what to pack and organized our meals for the trip. Pam was going to shop for food on Friday during the day while we were at school.

"I know this is going to sound ludicrous to you, Abbie, but we really should think about taking some work with us. We're miles behind on our assignment, if we don't work on it this weekend we'll never get it done in time for Wednesday's deadline," Jo said as Jake entered, balancing three cups and a plate of cookies.

"Here you go, ladies." He placed the drinks carefully on the coffee table in front of us and offered round the cookies, a cheeky grin playing at the corner of his mouth.

"Thanks."

"You're a star."

Jake helped himself to one of the cups and a couple of cookies before sitting with one leg tucked under the other behind me. He took a sip of the hot drink, picked up the TV remote, pointing it at the huge flat screen on the wall and changed the current news program to the sports channel. I chanced a look his way and he met my glance with a wink, causing me to tingle and flush bright red, again. I turned back to Jo, keen to finish what we had started and noticed a smirk painted across her face. My eyes widened spontaneously, threatening decapitation if she opened her mouth in front of Jake.

"Don't forget to bring a rain coat, the forecast says rain," Jo said, hiding her smirk behind her hand.

"Okay."

"So…I think that's about all," she said, closing the folder. "Should be good."

"Did I hear someone mention doing our assignment while you're away?" Jake asked, his curiosity getting the better of him. He took another slurp of his coffee, glancing between us as he waited for a response.

"Erm…yeah, Jo thought it might be a good idea, we're a bit behind and what with going away we're not going to be able to meet up until next Monday," I explained, catching Jo deep in thought. "What?" I asked, thinking that she was about to contradict me.

"Well... This might be a bit left field, but..."

"But what?" I asked, cringing, not sure whether I wanted to hear her latest suggestion. Jo usually dropped me in it big time when she had that gleam in her eyes.

"How about Jake and Callum come with us to the lake?" I just about choked on my coffee.

"It makes perfect sense, guys, we'd get our assignment done completely and have a great time as well," she said, waving her arms round in emphasis as she spoke.

Jake and I were equally shocked at the proposition at first, but looking at him I could see that he liked the idea. My stomach on the other hand felt like the inside of a washing machine. We had only just gotten over the first hurdle of our very new and sensitive friendship. I didn't know whether I would be able to cope with him being so close for an entire weekend. Why did my overly analytical thinking complicate everything? My frown didn't go unnoticed and Jake looked quite deflated.

"It's okay, Jo, you guys go. It was supposed to be a girlie weekend. You don't want us two crashing the party," he said, not taking his eyes off me. I could hear the disappointment in his voice.

"It's fine. Jo's right it's a really good idea. We could finish the assignment completely," I heard myself saying, while still looking at Jake as my stomach commenced a triple somersault with a twist off a cliff into deep water.

"You sure?"

"Yep, sure. It'll be good," I said, giving him an encouraging smile.

His eyes narrowed slightly, not completely convinced, "Well, if you're both sure we won't spoil your plans, I'd love to. It sounds great."

"Don't you think we'd better give Callum a call to see if he can make it?" Jo said, picking up the empty cups and walking into the kitchen.

"I'll call him now," Jake offered. "Hey!" he whispered, reaching for my hand as I cleared the table, forcing me to look at him, "If you'd rather I didn't come along…just say, Abs. It's okay."

I could tell he meant it and I smiled, "I'd love you come with us." Reaching up on my tiptoes I touched my lips to his lightly before pulling my hand from his and taking the empty plate to Jo.

Walking into the kitchen she immediately pounced on me while doing her happy dance across the room. I laughed quietly at the ridiculous expression on her face.

"You're mad," I said, laughing at her craziness.

"I'm so happy for you, Abbie," she said after calming down a notch.

"I can see." I smiled at my friend and totally understood her reaction. I'd been a nightmare to deal with over the years and I suppose the beginnings of a *normal* relationship with Jake spelled a simpler life for her. "Come on, let's finish up, I want sleep at some point tonight," I said through a yawn, dragging her back to the den.

Jake had his back to us and was talking on the phone, "Yeh? That's great, Cal… No problem, man. I'll speak to you later… Okay, bye." He turned to us, looking pleased. "We're on!"

"Yay!" Jo cheered while bouncing up and down, clapping her hands like a performing seal. "This is gonna be so cool."

"Listen, Jo, I'm going to head off, I felt like shit this morning. I need my bed," I said, remembering how tired I'd been when my alarm went off for school.

"No problem, don't forget to pack."

"I'll drive you home, give me a minute, I'll get my truck out of the garage, and I'll not take no for an answer," Jake insisted, easing past me in the doorway.

I smiled at Jo's obvious excitement, "See you tomorrow."

"All set?" he asked as I climbed into the truck.

"Yep."

Just as my mind began to wander, Jake interrupted my thoughts.

"Abbie?"

"Hmm," I said, drifting out of my daydreaming.

He seemed torn and rather anxious, "You sure you're okay with Cal and me tagging along this weekend?"

I smiled reassuringly, "It's absolutely fine, honest." He seemed pacified and his body language relaxed for the remainder of the short journey. Just as we pulled up in front of my house I heard him suck in an anxious breath.

"Okay, so I know I'm risking a verbal dressing down by even suggesting this but..."

A slight smirk pulling at the corner of my mouth, "What? It can't be that bad."

"Well, the weather is going to be absolutely crap for the next couple of days and last time it rained on a school day, you got soaked."

"What are you trying to say?" I asked, finding his nervousness amusing.

"I'd like to pick you up for school in the morning." He looked relieved that he'd got the words out and that made me giggle. "What? What you laughing at?" he asked, his eyes twinkling when he realized I wasn't going to go all psycho on him.

"You! You looked terrified. Jeez, am I really that scary?" I giggled some more at the idea of it. In a flash he reached over and dragged me towards him along the beach seat, a small squeak escaped from my throat at the sudden movement. My arms found their way up to his shoulders as we stared into one another's eyes.

"You're not scary at all, Abbie. I just don't want to scare you off now that I have you back again." His eyes took in my features and lingered on my mouth for a second then traveled back to my eyes, as if asking for permission.

I moved my hands to the front of his shirt, pulling him gently towards me. His mouth found mine and his arms tightened. There was no longer any doubt in my mind that I belonged in Jake's arms. My hands traveled slowly up his arms, across his broad shoulders and then around his neck as he held me close. I could feel his heart beating wildly against my chest as our lips moved slowly together, caressing and responding to the connection we both felt. I wanted to kiss him forever; I loved the feel of his firm, yet soft lips on mine. Jake's hand moved slowly up to my hair as the other pulled me closer. His fingers gently held my head so he could deepen the kiss and I responded by gently nipping his bottom lip, following with the tip of my tongue. A gasp escaped his lips and he pulled away suddenly, his eyes torn and questioning.

"Fuck me, Abs, you're killing me," he groaned, resting his forehead against mine and breathing heavily. My heart slammed against my chest and my mind crashed in response to the sensations I felt coursing through my body. I couldn't look at him. I squeezed my eyes shut, recognizing the feeling. Shame flooded my soul, my body had betrayed me, I wanted to be in control and I'd nearly lost it. I couldn't be a slave to those types of feelings.

As if sensing a shift in my mood Jake cupped my face in his strong hands and caressed my cheeks gently, "Hey? It's okay..." he soothed, encouraging me to look at him. "Abbie? Sweetheart, it's okay." He kissed my cheek gently as his thumbs caressed my jaw. My body trembled with embarrassment and I desperately wanted to get away from him, but he continued to hold firm.

"It's n-not okay."

"Abbie? Abbie, look at me, please." As my eyes met his, the relief I saw was quickly followed with concern when he saw the shimmer of unshed tears in my eyes. I felt completely defeated, unable to speak and pressed my head into his shoulder. Jake's hands came up my arms and round me as the tears fell down my cheeks. He wrapped me so tightly in his arms; I realized it was to satisfy a need in him as much as to console me.

"Baby, what's wrong?" Jake's voice trembled with emotion, but I couldn't speak, I couldn't put it all into words. I didn't want to.

After what seemed like an eternity and when I was sure I could hold it together, I eased myself away from him. He wiped the remains of the tears from my face. The concern I saw in his eyes was heart breaking. I reached up and placed a hand against his cheek.

"I'm sorry, it's just…I don't want to hurt you…"

He looked puzzled at my words, "What do you mean, you don't want to hurt me?" He took a deep breath and blew it out before continuing, "Is…Is there someone else?" His jaw tensed as he released my hands.

"No! No there's no one else!" I cried, shocked at his assumption that I had a secret boyfriend or admirer that he was unaware of, "What the fuck, Jake!"

"I'm sorry…it's just… Oh hell, Abs, I feel as though you want to be with me but…you don't." A wry smile crept onto my lips because that was exactly how I felt.

"I *do* want to be with you, more than anything."

"But?" he asked and I knew he was expecting me to say I couldn't be with him.

"But I'm scared I'll never be the girl you want."

"I don't understand what you mean…you keep saying things like that. It's madness to me that you think that, Abbie. You already are the girl I want. You're the most important, beautiful, special girl I have…or will ever want in my life," he paused, his eyes searching mine for a reaction, "We can do this, Abs… I want to be with you… I want you to be my girl." I gulped and closed my eyes, needing a minute to take in everything he'd just said. "Abbie, did you hear me?" he asked carefully, urgently almost. I looked up and smiled, nodding silently not trusting my voice. "So does that mean…" he began narrowing his eyes, "You will…you'll be my girlfriend?"

I nodded, blushing profusely, "I think so."

"Seriously?"

I nodded again. The beaming smile that spread across his face warmed me to the pit of my stomach. He pulled me close and kissed me with such tenderness I thought I'd burst, his lips lingering as if soaking up the moment. I'd made him happy. I felt good about that.

"I'll never hurt you again, Abbie, I promise."

I placed a finger quickly on his mouth to silence him, "You didn't, it wasn't you…" Realizing quickly what I was about to say, I broke off, hoping he didn't question me further. Jake stared at me as I quickly continued, "Let's just see how we go? Let's not make any promises." I leaned forward and kissed him lightly on the lips while running my fingers gently along his jaw. Before he had the chance to react I pulled away, "I have to go."

My hand trembled as I struggled to unlock the catch on the door. Jake leaned across me and released the lock then turned quickly to give me a quick peck on the cheek.

"You're a shocking sneak, Jake Ashton," I teased, grinning at him before climbing out of the truck. "What time in the morning?" I asked, turning to face him when my feet hit solid ground.

"Erm…8:15 okay?" I nodded and threw him another grin heading towards the house as he started up the truck, waved and sped off down the road.

"You took your time," Martin said with a wicked chuckle as I ran past him upstairs to my room.

Chapter Seventeen

Torrential rain slammed against my bedroom window, the front yard was already flooded and water gushed into the storm drains lining the footpath. I smiled; satisfied in my prediction and turned towards the bathroom, happy I'd offered to call for Abbie this morning.

At 8:15 I pulled up in front of Abbie's place, the endless rainfall and thunderous skies, showing no signs of letting up any time soon. Dressed in an oversized winter coat Abbie dodged the rain, hauling herself down the front path towards my truck. I slid along the seat and popped open her door.

"Argghh!" Water sprayed in every direction as she clambered inside.

"Morning, beautiful," I greeted as she pulled off the hood and unzipped her coat a tad.

"Hey," she smiled, her face blushing scarlet.

"How you feeling this morning?" I asked, watching her intently. The glow of pink to her cheeks from the cold stirred a familiar sensation deep in my gut.

"Yeah, I'm really good thanks. I slept so well last night and that's unusual for me" Abbie's expression puzzled me.

"Did you hear from Callum again at all last night?" she asked, changing the subject before I could ask why she usually had difficulty sleeping.

"No, but he'll be at school when we arrive. He's got training early today. I said we'd see him in the cafeteria at about 8:30, hope you don't mind."

"No problem, I think Jo will be there by then as well. She usually gets a ride in with her mom when the weather's bad. I'll treat you to a hot chocolate before lessons start." She blushed again, "Call it payment for the ride."

"You're on."

We weaved our way towards the cafeteria through the hordes of damp students crammed into the confined undercover courtyard. I was disappointed to note that Abbie had avoided any physical contact with me since arriving at school. The return of her self-erected barrier and her need to hide behind her well-practiced anonymity frustrated the hell out of me, but I understood, to a point. She had spent years avoiding people and not drawing attention to herself. This new relationship was hard for her and I would have to earn her acceptance and trust again.

Abbie's body tensed as we approached the cafeteria and I knew it had a whole lot to do with Jess and Becca. I spotted Jo as soon as we entered the steamy canteen and tapped Abbie's arm, nodding to where her friend was seated.

"Yep, I see her."

I gripped Abbie's hand and pulled her gently through the crowd.

"Hey, Jake," a voice called as we neared our destination. My stomach dropped at the realization Jess had seen us.

"You coming to my party, babe?" the skank screeched, and everyone in earshot turned in our direction. Abbie wrenched her hand from mine and made a beeline for Jo who in turn stood opened mouthed at the nerve of Jess.

"I wouldn't go to a party with you if you were the last girl in school," I growled, eager to catch up to Abbie.

Jess smirked and turned to her groupies, "That's not what you said the other day."

My hackles rose on my neck at her sluttish jibe, my eyes searching Abbie's distraught features, begging her not to acknowledge the comments. Becca and a few of the others erupted into childish giggles. I saw Abbie swallow and hoped she didn't believe Jess. Doubt crossed her face and I knew I had work to do.

"I hope you're not paying any attention to that worthless tramp," Jo asked, at Abbie's subdued reaction.

As soon as I reached Abbie I placed my hand on the small of her back and leaned in so only she could hear me.

"There is no way in hell I would ever go there, Abbie. Honest. Don't listen to her; she's just trying to get a rise out of you. It's just us now, baby." She smiled in response to my words, but still, I felt a twinge of discomfort with the whole situation. Then just for good measure. Callum strode towards us.

"Hey, guys! So… how are we getting to the lake this weekend?" I thought he was going to spontaneously combust, he was that excited. We all looked at each other before bursting into laughter.

"What?" He frowned, looking between us.

"Oh, nothing," I said with a smirk, "You don't get away much then?" Callum's frown turned to amusement and he punched me in the arm, taking a seat.

"How was practice?"

"Yeah, not bad. Bit more like boot camp than regular practice though. Coach reckons we need to get some serious fitness training in if we are going to make it in the A Grade this season."

"I'll go grab the drinks," Abbie said, getting up from the table.

"Okay." I gave her a wink and a supportive smile.

"I'll give you a hand," Jo called, following Abbie to the kiosk. The queue wasn't too long; most people had drifted off with only twenty minutes left until the start of lessons.

Cal's enthusiasm for football practice rippled off him in waves, but my mind replayed Jess's snide interaction and my heart raced at the consequences of her cruelty. I was really pissed she'd once again, succeeded in making Abbie feel like shit.

I could see Jo giving Abbie a talking to while they waited for the drinks. Abbie intermittently dropped her gaze to the ground and then looked over at me. My stomach lurched at the sadness in her eyes.

"What you gonna do, man?" Cal asked, following my gaze when I left too long a pause in our conversation.

"She shouldn't have to put up with that crap, Cal," I muttered, shaking my head. "I'm fucking livid."

"Do you want me to have a word with Jess?"

"No, I don't want them thinking they're getting to her or to me, not yet. I need to give it some thought. I just hope Abbie can cope in the meantime." I racked my brains for ways to help my girl, watching as she and Jo headed back with four hot chocolates. *The bullying might be one problem, but it isn't the only issue here. Jo's already hinted at more.*

"You'll do what you need to do, Abs. Just as long as you know I'm here if you need me, yeah?" Jo said as they took their seats. Jo's sideways glance at me made my stomach churn with increasing frustration and worry.

The rest of the day passed without incident, I'd more or less zoned out for the majority of the afternoon and was relieved to be climbing out of my truck at home. I'd dropped Abbie off at her place, where her less than animated goodbye left me sitting in my truck openmouthed. She hadn't even turned to wave, opting instead to simply close the door behind her.

"Why is everything so fucking difficult?" I growled, slamming my hand on the steering wheel stamping on the gas pedal and hurtling down the street.

It took me less than five minutes to reach our driveway and I skidded to a halt inches from the garage door, my heart still crashing against my chest.

"Hey, Jake!" Jo called over the fence separating our two houses as I climbed down from my truck. "Has Abbie gone home?"

"Yeah." I answered, frowning at the thought of how Abbie had been since the incident in the cafeteria this morning. "She's not in a good place, Jo. I don't know what to do." I hoped for a suggestion or explanation from Jo that would help me understand Abbie's mood swings.

"I don't know what to tell you, Jake." Jo leaned on the fence between us, her eyes showing her inner turmoil, at holding onto a confidence she ached to reveal. "She's worth the fight. Please don't give up on her." I frowned at her statement. Why the hell would a teenage girl need such careful handling? It was seriously doing my head in. I didn't know how much more of this I could take.

"I get mixed messages, Jo. My head feels like it's going to burst. One minute she's screaming at me, then she's all over me and then the next, she's an emotional wreck. It tears me apart to see her so upset, especially when I don't seem to be able to help. All I manage to do is to make her feel worse."

"That's not true!" Jo cried, laying a comforting hand on my forearm, "She's been happier since you arrived than I've ever seen her."

Jo closed her eyes and rubbed her face as if tormented by something. Though whatever it was, it was clear to me she wasn't going to share it with me, not tonight anyway.

"I don't know whether I can help her... I can't stand to see her hurt. She needs help. I don't know what to do." I blew out a long sigh, "You must think I'm terrible."

Jo shook her head slowly. I could see the understanding in her eyes as she smiled, "I don't, not at all. It's just... I guess I've seen a glimmer of the old Abbie since you two hooked up. It's been nice."

"I miss her, Jo."

"I know you do. She's still Abbie deep down. You can get her back, Jake... if you want to. I know you can."

I nodded with renewed determination, not quite ready to give up on Abbie yet. Perhaps this weekend would help. It was just the four of us; maybe that's what she needed. Maybe that's what we both needed.

"I'm not making any promises. Abbie has always been special to me, but if she doesn't want it to work between us then nothing I can say will change her mind. She was always stubborn." I raked my hands through my hair. "Let's just go away and enjoy the lake. At least we'll get the damned science assignment finished."

"That we will...and it's a fabulous place." Jo smiled as I contemplated a whole weekend with Abbie.

"Okay, well, I guess I better get going. Packing to do."

"See ya tomorrow, Jake. It'll all be okay, you watch," she said before turning towards the house, leaving me standing there pondering over what to do next.

***

"Hi, Mom. You home?" I called as I closed the front door behind me.

"Hey! How was school?"

"Yeah, Okay," I said, convincing no one as I walked into the kitchen where she was preparing dinner.

"What's up?" Mom put down the knife she'd been using and turned to face me.

"Nothing."

My mom raised an eyebrow.

"I don't know," I paused, breathing in and then out slowly, "I'm trying to say the right things, but how do I know what the right things are?" I sighed in frustration.

"Abbie, right?" I nodded. "Listen, sweetheart. Teenage girls are complicated, just listen to her, you'll know what to say if you listen. Don't assume too much." Jeez, my mom was ace.

"I love you, Mom," I said, pulling her into my arms for a big hug.

"I love you too, sweetheart, just be careful. You have your whole life for girls," she said, rubbing my back as we stood in the middle of the kitchen.

"I know... Thanks."

"How are you all getting to the lake this weekend?" she asked, moving back to chop the vegetables for dinner.

"Dave's driving, we're taking the SUV. It holds seven plus luggage, so we should be okay." She nodded looking happy with that information.

"What's the plan, have you got much organized?" I knew she was genuinely interested, not just snooping like some moms. My mom trusted me; I'd never given her reason not to.

"I think we're gonna get settled tomorrow night, late dinner and bed. Saturday, well…we want to get that science project finished first. It's been hanging over everyone's heads a bit, what with me being sick. Then I think Jo mentioned something about fishing or canoeing. Sounds good, hey?"

"It does, just go steady. I can do without a call from the emergency room," she said, raising her eyebrows in emphasis.

"Yeah, yeah. Don't stress, I'll be fine."

"I take it you guys will be alone most of the time?"

"Hmm?" I waited to see where this line of enquiry would lead.

"Look, honey, just be careful." she said, knowing full well that I knew exactly what she was suggesting.

"It's not like that, honest."

"Hmm, it never is… It never is."

Chapter Eighteen

Jo, Callum and Jake were all in the thick of the loading operation when Martin and I arrived at Jo's house on Friday evening. Conveniently for Martin, Mom was working double shifts at the hospital this weekend and had agreed to let him stay with Howie. Callum held open the tailgate of the car, balancing what looked like a duffle bag on one shoulder while Pam loaded groceries into the back. Jake stood at full stretch holding the fishing gear above his head so Dave could secure it to the roof rack while Jo was shouting orders at Howie who was struggling to cram another bag into the already overloaded vehicle.

"You could always do it yourself, you know!" He said.

On the way over, I'd been sure to remind Martin what good friends the Johnsons were to us and how it would be disrespectful to abuse Pam and Dave's trust. We watched for a second, soaking up the humor and pandemonium surrounding the loading of the car. I giggled, trying my best to hide my amusement. Jake caught me and grinned, rolling his eyes as he acknowledged the chaos. I sauntered towards the car, dropping my bag on the driveway before reaching up to give him a hand.

"Hey," he said, winking at me.

"Hey, yourself."

"Abbie, is this all you're taking?" Pam asked.

"Yep, that's it." I'd packed the basics which looked to have been a blessing. I couldn't imagine how we were going to get everything into the SUV.

"Now you two…" Dave began, turning to Howie and Martin, "I know you're excited to have the house to yourself while we're gone…" Howie looked to Martin as he tried to second guess his dad, "But…if I hear of any damage or complaint lodged with the local police due to unruly behavior during your planned gathering tomorrow, mark my words, boys, you will be paying for it for the next twelve months. Do I make myself clear?" They nodded in rapid succession, much to the amusement of the rest of us. The expression of shock on Martin's face was priceless.

"As crystal," Howie said, absolutely gob smacked that his dad, by some miracle, had guessed about the party planned for Saturday night.

"Good," Dave said before continuing to load the last of the bags into the back of the car. "Have we got everything? I'm not turning back once we're on the road. Girls, have you got your makeup, hair dryers, manicure sets?" he said with amusement, knowing full well that none of us were into all that shit. "Okay, you have ten minutes and then we leave."

After a quick bathroom visit we headed back to the car. Pam followed behind us, armed with an ice chest. Dave shook his head, "There are plenty of stop off points along the way, woman. You don't need all that. It's just taking up room."

"Well, you don't have to eat or drink any of it," Pam said, climbing into the passenger seat, placing the small cooler between her legs.

The journey was long but entertaining. After three hours of joking around, scenery watching, listening to Pam and Dave sparring with each other and finishing the snacks that Pam had packed, we turned off the highway. On approaching our destination, the road narrowed to a winding country lane lined with dense trees; the foot of the property came into view as we rounded a bend onto a gravel driveway. Through the darkness we saw the lake twinkling in the moonlight.

"Oh my God," I whispered, casting a glance sideways at Jake. He beamed back at me.

"Good, hey?" he said, giving my hand a gentle squeeze. I nodded in reply before turning my attention back to the house perched on the water's edge.

"This is so cool, Pam. I can see why you spend as much time as possible up here in the holidays."

"Yes, we love it. You'll have to join us more often."

We all clambered out of the car and spent a moment stretching our cramped limbs.

"Come on," Jo squealed, rushing towards the door of the lake house, "Let me show you round."

On entering the house we found ourselves in an impressive great room dominated by a huge stone chimney breast topped with a high mantel; a fire roared its welcome in the hearth.

"Fuck me!" Callum said, prompting the rest of us to burst out laughing. After a moment our eyes were drawn to a magnificent view of the lake through the floor to ceiling French doors. Several soft leather sofas, all in natural shades of tan, covered in textured throws and cushions provided a welcoming seating area. A luxurious, Native American rug spanning the width of the room complemented the setting.

Totally lost for words, I ran my fingers along one of the sofas, taking in every detail of the room. Even the vaulted ceiling with its naked beams spelled history and splendor. The spacious country styled kitchen was no less impressive; from its huge range cooker to the flag stone floor, it oozed sophistication. Positioned in its center was the largest island bench I had ever seen.

Jake placed a casual arm across my shoulders. "This place is freakin awesome."

"I know. It's pretty special, hey?"

"I'll say."

We followed Jo upstairs to inspect our rooms. Jo and I would share one and the boys were bunking in together. After exploring the bathrooms and several other nooks and crannies we headed back outside.

David was just on his way inside with the fishing gear, "I think you guys can manage your own bags."

We spent the next thirty minutes or so unpacking and organizing our rooms. After which, Jo and I headed down the hallway to the boys' room.

"You guys sorted?" she asked, walking through the open doorway. Jake grinned at Jo's forwardness. Our eyes met momentarily as she pushed her way past him into the room. I often took his looks for granted. He was just Jake to me, his appearance was secondary, but in that moment I couldn't take my eyes off him. He smiled and held out his hand. I took it willingly and entered their room.

"This is a bit posh," I said, walking towards double doors. Pushing open the French doors I covered my mouth in shock.

"I know. It's pretty cool." Jake whispered as we took in the view across the lake. His arms circled me from behind and he rested his chin on my right shoulder. Unable to speak, I nodded. Jake kissed my jaw softly, causing a warm glow to ignite deep inside me.

"Thanks." I said simply, turning towards him.

"What for?" he asked, narrowing his eyes. He lifted a hand and brushed his knuckles along my jaw.

"For being here with me."

"You're welcome."

Jo and Callum were deep in conversation when we rejoined them.

"Hey, you guys done sucking face?" Callum asked with a smirk. Heat flooded my cheeks and I headed straight for the door, followed closely by a slightly pissed off Jake.

"Seriously, Cal," Jo grumbled, punching him in the arm, "Try a bit of tact for once would you?"

"What? What did I say?" he said, throwing his hands in the air in exasperation.

The mouth-watering aromas wafting through the air led us to the kitchen where Pam had put a pasta bake in the large oven.

"Mmm mmm," Jo said with her nose in the air, "That smells good, Mom. Anything we can do?"

"No you're okay, all done. It will be about thirty minutes. Why don't you show your friends the lake?"

"Okie dokie," Jo said, dragging me towards the door and past the boys. "Come on, you two."

With an almighty groan, Callum agreed to tag along and nudged Jake towards us, "Go on then."

In the pitch black of the night the bright glow of the moon provided our only light source. The crunch of the gravel under our feet was punctuated only by the sound of a distant wolf howling and the lapping of the water at the lake's edge.

Stepping onto the boardwalk we followed it down to the lake. Contentment spread through my body in ripples and a stupid grin took over my face. I felt grateful for the dark so no one would see.

"Jeez, I wish it was the summer," Callum said with a shiver, "Can you imagine legging it down here and diving off the end into the water?"

"It's been done," Jo said and from the sound of her voice we all assumed correctly that she had been the one to do just that.

"Seriously?" Jake asked.

"Yep! It's awesome. You guys will have to come back in the summer. It's so amazing here when the weather's hot." I started to visualize strolling along the water's edge on a glorious summer's day.

"Hey…you okay?" Jake asked with more than a hint of concern.

"Yeah, I'm good." I said, smiling up at him. With the moon directly above us it made it hard to see Jake's face. "I can't see you in the dark." I said, squinting. I lifted my hand to his cheek, reveling in the feel of his skin under my palm. Jake tilted his head, bringing his lips dangerously close to mine. Instead of closing the distance I grinned and ducked quickly under his arm, giggling as I ran off down the wooden pathway.

"Oh, like that is it?" he shouted before chasing after me. He soon caught up and bent down with his hands in the lake, threatening to splash me.

"Don't you dare, Jake Ashton! I swear, you do and I'll…" I said, grabbing at Callum's jacket trying to avoid a dowsing.

"You'll what, baby?" he challenged. I took off again down the gravel beach screaming like a child.

"No! Jake! Arggh!" I felt the icy coldness hit the back of my neck as he let loose with a wave of water. "Oh my God! I c-can't be-lieve you did that," I said, shivering from the shock of the cold water now trickling down my back.

He grinned widely in front of me, leaning over with his hands resting on his thighs as he caught his breath.

My slightly wet appearance was obviously amusing to him and the others. "Well, I'm glad you all think it's funny," I said, allowing the humor of the moment to force a smile onto my lips. "I'll get you for that!" I said to Jake, grinning at him as he laughed with me. Grabbing my hand he pulled me towards him and wiped the water from the side of my face and neck with his sleeve.

"Sorry, I couldn't resist."

"Really?"

"Well, you started it!"

"How?" I asked, still giggling.

"You set the challenge by running away from me." I could tell he was smirking from the tone of his voice.

"So you thought you'd drench me in icy water and wreck the weekend by causing me to get pneumonia?" I asked jokingly. Jake didn't answer and I felt him stop walking. I waited until Jo and Callum walked past before turning to face him. I frowned.

"Jake?" Still he didn't answer. "I was joking, Jake?" I reached towards him and tried to touch his arm, but he pulled back and moved to walk towards the house. I swallowed past the anxious lump forming in my throat, wondering what was wrong.

"Jake? Jeez, I was only joking." Jo and Callum turned to see what I was shouting at just as they reached the porch of the lake house. Jo pushed Cal inside as if sensing we were about to need some privacy.

Jake turned round cautiously, running his hands through his hair and I braced myself.

"I'm sorry," he said simply, his voice lacking any real emotion.

"Why are you apologizing? I said I was joking." I shook my head slowly, finding the situation confusing to say the least. I couldn't work out why he'd gone all weird all of a sudden. "*I'm sorry*, it was funny. I was only joking," I said, taking his hand and squeezing it gently.

"I know," Jake replied, but didn't say anything else. We walked slowly up the steps at the end of the gravel drive before I plucked up the nerve to say anything else.

"Jake?" I said, pulling slightly on his hand so that he would have to hear me out.

"What is it, Abbie?" I inhaled sharply at the harshness of his tone and dropped his hand, forgetting what I'd been about to say. Unable to look at him I turned to lean on the hand rail. I heard him take a deep breath before he placed an arm round my shoulders and pulled me into his side.

"I'm trying so hard to say and do the right things around you." My stomach tightened at his words. I didn't want him to struggle to be with me. I wanted it to come easy to him, to us both. This relationship was already causing problems for Jake. I looked up at him wondering what to say, feeling lost. He was staring across the lake, deep in thought.

"Do you…do you want to finish it?" I asked and I felt the familiar prickling sensation at the back of my eyes. He turned to face me, his eyes narrowing as if contemplating my question. I moved away, trying to give him physical space.

"No!" he said sharply, "I don't want to finish it." I looked into his eyes as he spoke. "But, I don't know how to be with you… I don't know what you need from me." he said, lowering his head. He sounded ashamed.

"You don't have to be anything but you, Jake," I said, lifting my hand to cup his face so that he would have to look at me, "I just need you to be you. I like being with you. You're my best friend… If this is too hard…I'll understand."

I'd been on my own that long if he decided to walk away from this, I'd be okay. I chewed my lip at the thought, not wanting that to be the case. My heart was beating so fast it felt as though it was moving up into my throat.

"It's not." He pulled me towards him and wrapped me in his arms. I breathed out a sigh of relief and held onto him like my life depended on it, taking in a good lungful of his comforting scent.

"You know what?" I said, reluctantly pushing myself away from him.

"What?" he asked, brushing my damp hair behind my ear then lowering his head to kiss me, "What do I know?" He kissed me again and I felt him grinning against my lips. I could have stood there all night but dinner was ready.

"I think we'd better go eat, before they send out a search party."

Chapter Nineteen

The relaxed atmosphere at dinner with its mouthwatering aroma of garlic, cheerful conversation and background music was reminiscent of an Italian café. Sitting at opposite ends of the huge table, Pam and David held our attention as they shared memories of their visits to the lake over recent years. Intermittently, each of us dropped into the conversation with tales of memorable holiday destinations, highlights at school and most embarrassing memories.

Abbie appeared relaxed, relishing the casual chatter and easy ambience over dinner. She leaned forward in her seat, resting her elbows on the table and seemed to be genuinely enjoying herself. Together with Jo, she participated in playful, gender warfare whenever the opportunity presented itself. She'd become an enthusiastic participant in the conversation and I loved that she was in a better frame of mind.

It was easy to be distracted by her beauty. My mind wandered as I stole glances of my girl whenever I could do so without it being too obvious. Her long hair flowed like a silky veil around her shoulders, framing her perfect features; I imagined running my fingers through it while kissing her soft lips.

Excitement swelled deep in my gut as shades of the old Abbie began to materialize. I took in a deep breath as I recognized the dry humor clearly visible in her eyes as she laughed and joked with Callum over his fashion sense. She was the most stunning girl I had ever seen and now, at last, she was mine. In fairness she'd always been mine, but agreeing to be my girlfriend was the icing on the cake. Just as my eyes moved to her lips a smirk appeared at the corner of her mouth, drawing my eyes back to hers. I knew she'd caught me staring and we each grinned.

Jeez, I love this girl. I couldn't resist throwing a wink her way and as soon as I did, the blush that spread across her face triggered a warm glow in my lower regions.

"This is good, Mom," Jo said, her mouth full of pasta. I smiled at Jo's random comment.

"Good, I'm glad you like it. There's more if anyone wants it," Pam offered.

After finishing off the pasta and copious amounts of garlic bread, we offered to help clear away the dishes.

"Well, if you don't mind," Pam said as Callum and I moved the dishes while the girls headed into the kitchen with the glasses.

"Your mom's a great cook," Abbie said as Jo loaded the dishwasher.

"Yeah, she's not bad." Jo set the dishwasher to start and was about to close the door when Pam appeared with the large pasta dish.

"Thanks, guys," she said, nodding approval as she looked round, "You can all come again. We're going to head on up, Jo. If you need anything give us a shout," she said, pouring two glasses of brandy for her and David. "Your dad will be up early. He's meeting John at seven for fishing. So please keep the noise down. Okay?"

"Yep, we won't be too late." Jo gave her mom a kiss, "Thanks for dinner, Mom."

"Night all," Pam said before turning and pushing open the door with her behind, "Oh, there's ice-cream in the freezer if you want any."

"Your mom's ace," Callum said and headed straight for the cooler while Jo took four small dishes from one of the many cupboards in the huge kitchen.

"Yeah, she's cool," said Jo, smiling at Callum.

"Who wants fudge sauce?" Jo asked, grabbing a squeezy bottle from the pantry. No one refused and soon we were all tucking into a generous bowl of choc chip with fudge topping.

"What should we do now? It's early; what about a movie?" Jo asked, taking a mouthful of dessert.

"Movie sounds good. What you got?" I asked.

"What *haven't* we got?"

We all piled into the huge living room.

"Have you seen this one?" Callum asked after a few minutes of browsing the vast collection of movies. He held up a copy of *The Lake House*.

"Seriously?" Jo said, her eyes wide at the obvious irony of his suggestion.

A lonely doctor who once occupied an unusual lakeside home begins exchanging love letters with its former resident, a frustrated architect. They must try to unravel the mystery behind their extraordinary romance before it's too late. A thoughtful expression crossed Cal's face as he read the blurb on the back. I raised my eyebrows, but didn't pass comment.

"I don't mind what we watch," Abbie said and she sprawled on one of the sofas in front of the open fire. I decided to join her rather than worrying about having a say on the movie choice. Let Cal and Jo fight it out over that one.

"I don't think you guys would appreciate that one, it's more of a chick movie," Jo said, turning her attention back to the shelves.

"Are you implying that we are insensitive to the needs of you young ladies, Jo?" Callum asked, his hand on his heart as if upset by her suggestion.

"No..." she said, giggling, "It's just...that movie is a love story and well...you know?"

"Know what?" he taunted.

By now both Abbie and I were leaning back enjoying the floor show. Whether we got to see a movie tonight or not this interaction between Callum and Jo was getting interesting. I cast a glance sideways and grinned at the chocolate sauce running down Abbie's chin.

"What?" she asked, wiping randomly at her face.

"Here," I said, reaching over and removing the offending fudge from her chin with my thumb and sticking it in my mouth.

"Thanks," she said, blushing scarlet.

"I've heard it's a great movie!" I said, but I was more interested in the fact I got to spend an evening with Abbie; it didn't matter much to me what we watched.

"Whatever! If you want a chick flick, who am I to argue?" Jo said, throwing her arms in the air.

"It's not a chick flick. Plenty of the guys have seen it," Callum said, doing his best to sound serious.

"Who with? Their moms?" she asked, shaking her head in frustration.

"Hey!" Abbie said, trying to get some semblance of order, "Are we watching it or not?" Both Callum and I shrugged.

"Why not," Callum said, grinning widely at a dumbfounded Jo.

"Jeez, you two never cease to amaze me," Abbie said, taking the DVD from Callum and passing it to Jo as she stood up to take her empty bowl into the kitchen. "Guess you'd better do the honors then, Joey. You finished, Jake?" Abbie asked, holding out her hand to take my dish as well.

"Yep, thanks." I settled back into the leather sofa while Jo muttered under her breath as she sorted out the DVD. Callum slumped down on the sofa furthest away from the fire. He kicked off his sneakers and leaned back, putting his feet up on the foot stool.

"Comfy there, Cal?" Abbie grinned at him and shook her head in disbelief as she sat back down beside me.

"Is it getting hot in here?" I asked, leaning forward to pull off my sweatshirt. My T-shirt traveled up with it and I heard a gasp beside me. I gave Abbie a cheeky wink, acknowledging her reaction before leaning back and raising my arm so that she could move a bit closer.

"Lights on or off?" Jo asked.

"Off!" Callum demanded.

"More of a cinema atmosphere," I whispered in Abbie's ear as Jo turned out the lights and sat down on the same sofa as Callum.

About thirty minutes into the story Callum began muttering under his breath, "So hang on a minute. How can they be talking to each other when they..." he asked with such a look of confusion on his face that Jo and Abbie burst into fits of giggles.

"That's the whole idea behind the story," Abbie said, leaning forward to explain the plot to Callum. "Their love transcends the boundaries of time."

"Oo err," Callum said, mocking Abbie's choice of vocabulary.

"Sandra Bullock's character lived there after Keanu's character. There's a two year time difference. It's the whole point of the story," she said, laughing and threw a cushion at him. Callum's face reflected that of a reprimanded child; his forced pout was hilarious. "It's a good movie, Cal. I've seen it before, stick with it. It all falls into place in the end," Abbie said, smiling at him. He grinned and relaxed into the sofa, hitting Jo with another pillow because she was giggling.

"Anyone want a drink?" I asked, squeezing Abbie's knee as I stood up, causing her to inhale sharply. *Jeez, I wish I was alone with her right now.*

"Want any help?" Callum offered, getting to his feet.

"I'll get a soda please," Jo said, still glued to Keanu.

"Abbie?"

"Huh?"

"Would you like a drink?" I asked, screwing my eyes up as I tried to clear my mind of the vivid thoughts of thoroughly kissing her until she moaned my name.

"Err…yes please, I'll have whatever everyone else is having," she said, blushing scarlet. Nodding, I left her and Jo watching the movie.

"I don't know what to say about you guys?" Callum said, shaking his head slowly while I pulled four cans from the cooler.

"Me either."

"It's like, she's a split personality. One minute she's all over you, the next; she's like all psycho. Don't get me wrong, Jay, I like Abs. She's cool, but I'm glad I'm not you."

"Hmm, thanks."

"You gonna try cranking it up a notch?" he asked with a smirk on his face.

"I don't know, she keeps giving me the come on then she's super cold. I think maybe I'll just see how it goes, enjoy the weekend and get the assignment finished."

"Whatever, dude. Hey, I have a feeling young Jo might have a bit of a thing for me. What d'you think?"

"Is there no end to your womanizing? Jeez, you're a man whore." Callum laughed and grabbed two of the sodas before heading back to the girls. Picking up the remaining two cans; I followed him into the den.

Callum passed a can to Jo then slumped onto the sofa next to her. A fountain of fizzy drink erupted from his can and we all dissolved into fits of laughter.

"Shit!" He held the can away from himself and the furniture as Jo dashed back to the kitchen to grab a towel to dry the mess.

"Dude! You're a classic," I said, shaking my head as I walked past him and offered Abbie a cola.

"Thanks," she said, reaching for the drink. She curled up in the corner ready to enjoy the rest of the movie.

"Hey…come over here," I said, moving a loose throw from next to me to make room for her to scoot a little closer. Holding my breath momentarily, I hoped I wasn't expecting too much. Pleasure washed through me when she wriggled closer and curled up at my side. I felt my heart swell at the ease of her reaction and draped my arm over her.

By the time the closing credits came on the screen Abbie had fallen asleep beside me.

"Come on, sweetheart," I encouraged, stroking her cheek so that she'd wake enough to get up to bed.

After a quick tidy round we headed towards the oak stairway. I'd managed to keep a physical connection with Abbie throughout the movie and now climbing the stairs, my arm was draped casually around her shoulders. She had her hand tucked in my jeans pocket and leaned sleepily into my side; the sensation in my groin, driving me crazy. I imagined what it would be like having her hand against my ass without the denim as a barrier.

"Night, guys," said Jo, winking at me as she went into their room. Callum continued on down the darkened hallway, leaving me with Abbie.

"Don't be all night, lover boy," he growled with a smirk as he entered our bedroom. I turned to face Abbie and placed my hands on her waist.

"Bend down a bit then," she said with a tired grin playing on her mouth. "What's your mom been feeding you anyway?" I didn't need asking twice and pulled her into my arms as she brought her lips up to mine. It was a kiss that said *thanks for tonight, I love being here with you, sorry about earlier* and *see you in the morning* all rolled into one. Abbie ended it by bringing a hand to my cheek before leaning against my chest. My heart was beating so hard I was convinced she would be able to feel its pounding.

"Night, Jake," she said, giving me one last squeeze.

"Night, baby, sleep well." We shared another tender kiss before she turned and opened the door to her room. One last glance over her shoulder as she entered and I smiled before she closed the door behind her.

Chapter Twenty

"You're so lucky, Abbie," Jo gushed. I shook my head while grinning at her analysis of mine and Jake's relationship. I felt anything but lucky as it happened; my life being so complicated.

"You reckon?"

"I do! Jake really cares about you, Abs. Then there's having me as a friend! I mean… how lucky can you get?" She ducked under the covers away from the pillow I launched at her head.

"God, you're so sure of yourself," I said, shaking my head as she peeped up from beneath the sheets.

"You know you love me." She grinned. I gave her a hug before fluffing up the biggest pillow I'd ever slept on.

"You and Callum seem to be getting rather cozy." I turned onto my side, propping myself up so I could see her properly. The slow blush crept up her face at my words surprised me. Jo wasn't usually easily embarrassed.

"I like him. He's good fun." I was quite sure she could handle Callum. If anything, I was scared for *him*. "What you grinning at?" she asked, through narrowed eyes.

"Just thinking about you two hooking up, I think he needs to be very careful."

"Yeah, yeah! I'll have you know I'm quite a catch!" Jo fluffed her hair around her shoulders and batted her eye lashes at me dramatically. I burst out laughing and buried my head in my pillow at the thought of her and Callum getting it on.

"I wonder if he realizes what he's getting himself into," I said after wiping the tears of laughter from my eyes. Jo was quite naïve at times; she'd flirt with anyone for her own ends without once considering the guy's feelings.

"I can't help it if I'm irresistible, Abs."

"Do me a favor… You've already said he's a fun guy. I actually think you like him a bit more than you're admitting, but that's your business. I like him too; he's okay, kind of a gentle giant. Very different from the character he gives off at school. Anyway, what I'm trying to say is…enjoy, but don't hurt each other?"

"Oh my God, Abbie! When did you get all philosophical?"

"Well, you're my best friend. If you like him like that…just go steady, hey? I don't want either of you getting hurt and ending up enemies."

"We aren't talking wedding bells followed by divorce here, Abs! We're just having a bit of fun!" Jo's mood shifted and I sensed she was getting pissed at my opinion.

"I'm sorry, it's none of my business, forget I said anything." I lay on my back, pulling the covers up to my chin. She could do what she liked with Callum.

Jo turned towards me beaming, her eyes sparkling with mischief. "You know something? It's awesome having these chats with you." I understood what she was getting at. Jo had recognized from an early age that I was uncomfortable with anything to do with boys or relationships.

"Can I ask you something?" My eyes probed hers. I wanted her to take this seriously.

"Sure, what is it?"

"Before I told you about... You know? We never talked about boys and stuff. How come you never brought it up? How come you've hung out with me all these years?" Her eyes widened at my words, she looked completely shocked and quite hurt.

"I don't know, Abs! Maybe because we were best friends and that's what best friends do!" She sat up and looked straight at me.

"No, I didn't, mean it like that, I love you too. It's just... Well... You've always had guys falling at your feet and we've never talked about them."

"Well, you weren't into that shit. I saw how you reacted around boys. I just assumed that you were recovering from your mom and dad breaking up." Her eyes teared up and she looked away.

"I'm sorry Jo, really I am." I said, pulling on her hand.

"You have nothing to apologize for," she said, frowning at me. "The whole deal makes sense now and I'm so glad you trusted me enough to confide in me."

"Well, I didn't really have much option under the circumstances, did I?" I rolled my eyes, grinning at her.

"I guess not, but I'm still glad you told me"

"Me too."

"What time is your mom leaving for that course tomorrow?" I reached for my cell so I could set the alarm.

"Oh, I think she mentioned a nine o'clock start," Jo said, shifting down under the covers. "We don't need to get up when she does."

"Yeah, but we're only here two days."

"True. Better get some sleep then."

"I guess. Night, Joey."

"Night, Abs."

***

Jo's snoring reminded me of a jack hammer and after a restless night of tossing and turning I finally gave up and hit the shower.

The early morning sun streamed through the open shutters, pulling me towards the stunning view of the lake. This place was amazing and the sooner we all finished our assignment, the sooner we could explore.

"Oi! Joey! Up!" I shouted across the room, reaching for a cushion from the floor. I had every intention of whacking her with it if she didn't get her ass out of bed. No way was I going to waste a second more of this weekend, tired or not.

"Argghh! We haven't been in bed two minutes."

"It's time to get up, Jo, come on. We've work to do and then... *Party!*"

"Let me come round. Jeez, Abs! I'll see you downstairs." She turned away from me, grumbling under her breath. "Why don't you check on the boys? Go see if they're awake." That wasn't a bad idea. I didn't particularly relish the idea of getting to dinner time tonight and still having an incomplete assignment. We needed to get it done and out of the way so we could enjoy the weekend.

"Okay, I'll see you in ten minutes. Please get up."

"Yeah, yeah."

The usual sounds of bathroom activity and guy banter drifted through the door so I knocked and leaned against the wall facing their room. Callum opened the door with a huge grin plastered to his face.

"Jeez, you're cheerful in the morning."

"Morning, Abs. Just off for a run, back in a tick," he said and with that he'd gone, leaving me standing in the hallway with my eyes wide and my mouth open.

"Hey."

My insides turned to molten gooeyness at the sound of Jake's sleepy voice.

"Hey, yourself," I said as he approached me and reached out to pull me towards him. His arms came about me and I found myself inhaling his glorious scent. I lifted my head and smiled at him, reveling in the warmth of his embrace.

"You smell nice," I said, dipping my head again to steel another breath full of his freshly showered aroma. As I did, his grip on me tightened and I felt his breath on my neck as he too inhaled deeply.

"You aren't so bad yourself," he said, kissing my forehead. Jake's eyes searched mine momentarily before his mouth found mine with a tender kiss and I was lost.

Inching away from the doorway he continued his exploration of my mouth. Butterflies sprang to life in my tummy as a warm tingling sensation spread downwards from my stomach. Jake's arms wrapped me in a tight embrace, his fingers splaying across my lower back. He hesitated momentarily and stilled his lips, breathing heavily. One hand held me steady as his other came to my face; his thumb caressing my cheek. I ran my hands down his sides and round to his back. He tasted of toothpaste and with that thought I was brought back to the here and now. I slowed the kiss and gently placed my hands against his chest, smiling against his lips which were now still.

"Morning," I whispered against his mouth before pulling away so I could look at him properly. His eyes seemed to soak up every inch of my features; his eyes twinkling like a young child on Christmas morning.

"Morning, beautiful. You okay?" He stroked a strand of hair from my face and I nodded in response not trusting my voice. "Come on, let's see who's up."

"Okay" I whispered.

He kissed the tip of my nose before taking my hand. I was still regaining the use of my legs as we walked along the hallway.

"Did you sleep okay?" he asked, his thumb running idly across the back of my hand.

"Jo snores," I said, shaking my head. "But that's okay. I slept pretty well. How about you?"

"Not bad, Callum snores too, but I'm sure I do also."

Downstairs was deserted. Callum would likely be a while and Jo would probably still be in the shower so we had a free run at breakfast.

"What's it to be?" Jake's eyes widened suggestively. "For breakfast." I said, grinning. I turned towards the fridge to gather eggs and butter just as he grabbed from behind. I froze and inhaled sharply. His hands stilled on my stomach and then pulled away. I couldn't help but tear up. I squeezed my eyes closed, trying frantically to slow my breathing which had accelerated to warp speed in two seconds flat. On opening my eyes I turned tentatively towards Jake, searching his face and willing him to accept my apology.

"I'm sorry... I..." I lifted my hand to his arm, but he pulled away and spun towards the sink, resting both hands on the drainer. He sucked in a deep breath before blowing it out slowly.

"When will you trust me?" He sounded defeated.

"I'm so sorry."

"I don't want an apology from you, Abbie. Fuck me, one minute you're all over me and then..."

"I didn't expect it... That's all... You startled me."

"That's bullshit and you know it." With that he stormed past me and out of the house. I was still in shock when Jo bounced into the kitchen.

"Morning." She was oblivious to what had just gone down between Jake and me.

"Hey," I said and continued my search for butter. I didn't say anything about what had happened. I was still in shock and trying to work it out in my own mind. I didn't need Jo getting all mushy.

"You cooking eggs? Cool," she said, grabbing the kettle and filling it at the sink.

"Yep," I said and proceeded to gather the items necessary for breakfast for four.

Callum arrived back from his run and hit the shower just as the aroma of bacon began to fill the air. I spotted Jake wandering along edge of the lake in front of the house as I helped prepare breakfast. It wasn't long before two large plates of steaming food sat on the island bench ready to be consumed. Jo decided we needed freshly squeezed orange juice to go with our breakfast.

"I'm just gonna get Jake," I said, leaving her to juice the oranges.

The butterflies in my stomach fluttered uncontrollably as I approached him.

"Hey." My eyes narrowing thoughtfully as I looked out across the lake, pushing my hands deep into the pockets of my jeans. Jake remained silent and continued to search through the pebbles at the water's edge with the toe of his sneaker. "Breakfast's ready."

"Kay," he said and turned towards the house.

"Is that it?" He glanced back at me, a look of bewilderment in his eyes then shaking his head, turned away again. "There's stuff you don't know about me!" I called out, unable to stop myself.

"No shit!" he said, but carried on walking.

"Jake!"

"Jeez, Abbie, I can't deal with this, *on one minute, off the next*, situation."

"Situation? Is that what this is to you?" I asked, my eyes filling with tears.

"Don't do that. Don't turn this back on me, Abbie."

"I'm sorry."

"And stop saying you're fucking sorry!" he said, running his hands through his hair, "I'm sorry! We're both sorry! Why? What are you sorry for? For being with me? For kissing me with that much passion I wanted to make love to you just now!" he shouted, gesturing towards the house. I gasped at the admission. I wanted to be with Jake in every sense of the word as well. I never thought I'd have feelings for a guy and want to do *that*, but with Jake I felt safe and loved. I didn't want to lose him, but right now, losing him was a strong possibility.

"I want you too, Jake," I whispered as a tear trickled down my cheek. I sucked in a deep breath, realizing if our relationship stood any chance of moving forward I was going to have to talk to him. If I didn't, I'd lose him for good. We'd moved past being just good friends with fond memories of a few happy months from our childhood. Jake stood just a short distance away from me, waiting. I took in another deep breath and closed my eyes. "Can we talk later?" I asked, wiping the tears from my cheek with the back of my hand.

"That's all I want, baby," he said, his eyes searching mine and he held out his hand. "It doesn't have to be today, or even tomorrow, but I want you in my life...all of you, good and bad. We have to be able to trust one another, Abbie." I nodded, taking his hand.

Chapter Twenty-One

For close to three hours the dining room hummed with our productivity. We each had tasks within the assignment and individual accounts to write. Abbie had collated the whole thing into chapters. Jo compiled the bibliography and appendix, leaving the evaluation to Cal and me.

"Woo Hoo!" Jo cheered. *Jeez, that was a chore.*

Satisfied with the finished product and with the onset of rumbling stomachs we headed into the kitchen.

"Fuck! I'm glad that's out of the way," Callum said, slumping against the bench.

"You can say that again," I said, laughing.

"Fu…"

"Don't!" Abbie interrupted, slapping a hand over Cal's grinning mouth as he was about to repeat himself.

"Okay then. Lunch then the kayaks," Jo announced.

After polishing off a mountain of sandwiches and fries washed down with copious amounts of soda we headed down the boardwalk; wearing life jackets, hauling the two antiquated kayaks towards to the water's edge. For weight ratio reasons we decided it would be safer to pair up; a boy and girl in each craft. I'd join Abbie and Cal would share with Jo.

The task of carrying the heavy two man craft with Abbie was awkward because we had to hold it away from our legs and she seemed hindered by her massive life jacket. Under normal circumstances it would have been easier to carry the cumbersome kayak above our heads, but our height difference was too great to be able to do that comfortably.

"You okay, Abs?" I asked as we neared the end of the wooden pier. I'd done my best to lever the kayak's weight off the front end to make it easier on Abs. She'd not said much about her hand since we'd arrived yesterday.

"Yep, I'm good," she said, struggling to get air into her lungs but showing bags of grit and determination.

"Okay, set it down." Abbie heaved a sigh of relief and I rubbed her arm, "Good job. How's your hand? You going to be okay?"

"Yeah, it's fine. The bruising's almost faded now." She held up her hand, "I took a painkiller before we left."

This left me unimpressed, but questioning her at this stage wouldn't get me anywhere. She knew her own mind and my interference would only spoil the afternoon.

We sat on the edge of the narrow pier and waited for Cal and Jo to catch up.

"Have you done this before?" Abbie asked.

"Nope. Have you?"

She shook her head and chewed on her lip as she looked out across the lake.

"You okay?"

"Bit nervous."

"I'll look after you." I winked, acknowledging her anxiety; she was probably still upset about our confrontation earlier. I couldn't help the nagging unease in the pit of my stomach in anticipation of the chat she'd promised at some point.

Jo and Callum shuffled to a standstill next to us. "Right, let's go," Jo said cheerfully.

I grinned at her enthusiasm. We lowered the kayaks into the water at the edge of the pier; I held the side of ours steady while Abbie negotiated the rim and eased herself inside the front compartment before tightening the waterproof skirt around her waist. She hung onto the pier while I climbed in behind her. The kayak rocked violently side to side, evoking a nervous giggle from Abbie.

"Whoa!"

"We're okay, hang on," I said, steadying myself and pushing us away from the pier. "Okay?"

"Yep."

We eased out towards the center of the lake. Progress was slow but measured and we soon got the hang of paddling in time with each other. Jo and Callum performed like naturals even though they sounded like an old married couple; I was sure the residents over the other side of the lake would be able to hear them shouting mock abuse at one another.

After almost an hour of paddling, Jo and Cal challenged us to a duel. They flicked paddles of water at us before taking off across the lake. My competitive nature kicked in aided by Abbie's screams of encouragement and we sped after them with all the determination of a war ship going into battle.

"Faster!" Abbie shrieked at the top of her voice.

"I'm going as fast as I can!" We gained on them with every stroke. The look of horror on Jo's face as we drew level was too great a temptation; I swiped the surface of the water, cascading it over our horrified opponents.

"Nooo!" she yelled, trying to pull away. Abbie's raucous laughter filled the air and warmed my heart.

In an attempt to turn the craft about Abbie plunged her paddle straight down, deep into the water; big mistake. The momentum of the craft against the choppy water so far out, coupled with our uneven weight ratio resulted in an instant capsize.

"Arrgghh!"

The icy water took my breath away, but after a second my sense of direction returned. Unable to right ourselves I pulled free from the spray skirt sealing my compartment and surfaced a few feet from where we'd capsized.

I searched anxiously for Abbie, but couldn't see her anywhere; my core temperature plummeting as the freezing water lapped around my frantic body.

"Abbie!" I thrashed about unable to find her. "Where is she? Callum?"

"Fuck!"

Jo's screaming filled the air around us as she and Callum paddled to our aid, "You've got to find her! Jake! Do something!"

Sudden realization hit me; I remembered Abbie fastening the protective skirt round her waist. Time slowed and panic set in with the force of an avalanche pressing against my chest, my eyes filling with tears.

"Oh my God! Abbie! Please, baby…"

I tore the life jacket from my shaking body and plunged under the water. Pure terror pierced my chest as I reached her. Stuck fast inside her protective skirt and thrashing wildly, her terrified eyes found mine. *Come on baby… pull free.* My numb fingers found the seal around her waist; her desperate hands fighting with the cord, but failing to release the restraint. An adrenaline fueled rage took over my body as the utter horror of losing Abbie took over every inch of my body.

No! Please! Fuck! Help me, Abbie. Please pull! Please, Abbie!

My head pounded like it was about to explode under the pressure. I tugged and tugged on the rubber membrane until it broke free from the rim. Not wasting a second more, I grabbed her around the waist and hauled her to the surface, tremendous relief gushing through my body. Abbie gasped for air and lashed out, grabbing at me; distress etched across her face, half the lake spouting from her mouth.

"It's okay… Abbie, it's okay…" I choked out, pulling her towards me. "Here, baby, hold on to me."

"You guys okay?" Callum cried, reaching for the end of our kayak.

"Yeah… We are now," I replied, keeping my eyes firmly on Abbie before pulling her closer. "I thought you were never coming up."

"The skirt…was…too tight; I couldn't…undo the damn thing." Still coughing, she kept her eyes fixed on me. "I'm okay…" My heart crashed violently against my chest as adrenaline pumped through my veins.

Fuck! She almost drowned! I froze in a state of catatonic shock until Abbie clutched my arm.

"Shit! Scary!" She struggled to speak. Relief and terror coursed in unison through my entire being and I rested my head on the underside of the capsized kayak.

"We're okay, Jake. Come on, we need to move. I'm cold." Abbie sounded scared, but her eyes held the same strength I'd grown accustomed to over recent weeks.

After a moment I guided Abbie towards Jo's outstretched paddle. Together Cal and I turned over the kayak without capsizing theirs. After attaching the clip at the bough to a hook on Cal's, he and Jo proceeded to tow our death trap back to shore with Abbie and me in slow pursuit. Numbness brought on by the near freezing temperature of the water swept my entire body by the time we reached the steps of the pier.

Abbie clung to the side rail while I heaved myself onto the boardwalk. I reached down, grabbed her wrists and hauled her up beside me. Her breathing was labored and I tugged at the clips fastening her lifejacket, eased it from her shivering body and tossed it to one side. I slumped to the ground, relief flooding my body and turned my head to face her; the horror of what just happened wrenching at every nerve in my body.

"Fuck! Never...a dull...moment." The half-smile playing across her oxygen starved, blue lips as she tried to make light of the situation didn't quite clear the fear from her eyes.

Lifting a hand to her cheek, I made a conscious effort to slow my breathing and closed my eyes, swallowing past the emotional lump restricting the air flow. After a moment I pulled myself upright using the railing to the side of us. The aftershock of what had happened brought graphic images of Abbie's terrified face to my mind's eye. I rubbed my face, sucking in a deep breath before turning to Abbie and holding out my hand.

She placed a cautious hand in mine and I helped her to her feet. Frozen to the spot for a second and a little unsure of our footing, I wrapped an arm round her waist, holding her tight.

"Close call, hey?" she commented, trying to lighten my mood. I closed my eyes again, taking stock. She didn't seem to see the seriousness in what we'd just been through.

"Jake?"

My gaze found her shivering lips and I pressed a kiss to her forehead before guiding her to the house.

As soon as we reached the kitchen Jo ran upstairs to grab dry towels and robes. Exhaustion kicked in and we both sat on the stools at the island bench. The warmth of the house contrasted the freezing temperature of the blood running through our bodies and along with the strong possibility of shock, our shivering grew more violent.

"Get undressed!" Jo shouted, tugging at Abbie's drenched hoodie. Callum helped remove my wet clothing before grabbing a towel from the stool beside him.

"Fuck me!" Callum said, throwing the towel my way, "You really know how to kill a party, dude."

My eyes never left Abbie's, her teeth chattered as I pulled the towel across my exhausted muscles.

"Here, sweetie, drink this," Jo said, holding out a mug of sweet tea and for the first time since we got back Abbie's eyes moved from mine leaving me with an instant sense of loss.

"Thanks," she whispered through trembling lips.

"You okay?" Jo's face reflected the fear and relief I sensed flowing through my body.

"Yeah, I'm fine, just cold," Abbie whispered.

After a moment Abbie frowned in my direction, placing her drink on the bench before taking my cup from my hand.

"Jake?"

I snapped out of my trance, my eyes flying towards hers and I let out a long breath. I frantically searched her face for any sign of lasting injury before pulling her into my arms; relieved to find her okay.

"I thought you'd drowned." I rubbed her back, squeezing her body close to mine, scared to let go. The fear of losing her was incomprehensible. "I thought I'd lost you."

"You didn't though, I'm okay."

She reached up and wrapped her arms around my neck, her cheek touching mine as she embraced me tightly. My hand found her hair and held her close. After a moment I eased slowly away, brushing my knuckles along her cheek.

"Don't do that again!" I said, my eyes locking on hers.

"Okay," she whispered, snuggling into my neck. I ran my hands over her back through the robe as I fought to regain a little composure.

"Thanks guys, that was close."

"Don't sweat it; you'd have done the same, man," Callum said, slapping me on the shoulder.

"I think that's enough excitement for one day," Jo said, bending to pick up our wet clothes.

"Leave those, Joey, I'll do it." Abbie said, blushing for the millionth time so far this weekend and moved towards her friend.

"It's done, don't worry."

With her palms resting on my chest she glanced up at my face, her eyes narrowed as if assessing my state of mind. She smiled warmly and kissed the side of my jaw, sending tingles of relief and desire soaring through my veins.

"I'm hungry," she said. I couldn't help the broad grin that took over my features, and I pulled her into my chest.

"Me too, must be all the fresh air and exercise."

Chapter Twenty-Two

I found Pam and Jo busy in the kitchen, preparing salad ingredients when I emerged fresh from my shower.

"David? Can you bring the fish inside please? I need to prep them," Pam called from the back door. "Hi, Abbie! We were just talking about you. Goodness me, girl, you know how to raise the adrenaline levels. How are you?"

"I'm fine. It was a bit scary, but we were never in any real danger." I felt guilty for causing her so much concern.

"Yeah, I tried to hold her head under a bit longer, but she was too strong," Callum said, smirking as he walked past me. I swiped at him, but he managed to dodge my flying fist just as David appeared at the door. At least everyone saw the humor in it. I was keen to move on and enjoy the rest of the evening.

"How'd you get on, Dad?" Jo asked her father as he pulled two large fish from the cool box.

"Pretty good, actually. Stick these in the sink, Joey would you?" His success rate in the past cast doubt on his true ability as a serious fisherman, but David enjoyed regular trips out with his friends. It was more of a guys' catch up than anything else; male bonding at its best.

"That's good, have we got enough fish to barbeque or are we using steak as well?" she asked, grinning at her dad.

"Maybe a couple of steaks as well, the boys will have big appetites I bet," David said, heading back outside to where he'd been working on the barbeque with Jake.

David's fishing friend had invited both him and Pam over for dinner and cards. They'd decided to stay over so they could indulge in a drink or two without worrying about the drive back. This meant we'd be free to enjoy the outdoor feast without adults cramping our style.

After helping to prepare the salad I was keen to check on Jake. I followed the aroma of charcoal and marinade drifting in through the open door to the patio area. Though the light had already begun to fade the seating area was illuminated with dozens of fairy lights and candles. I was surprised to see an open fire smoldering in a custom fire pit in the center of the large, circular stone patio instead of a simple gas fired barbeque. The steaks lay suspended above the hot embers on a grate and several foil wrapped potatoes lay among the coals. Jake and David were deep in conversation as I approached.

"Hey," I greeted the two chefs, hoping that Jake was feeling better as well.

"Good to see you're still in one piece, Abbie. Jake was just filling me in on the finer details of your near miss."

David winked at me as he spoke. Jake winced at the joviality in David's comment. Not wanting the conversation to take a nose dive into the depths of negativity I gave David my biggest smile.

"That I am," I said, attempting to quash any further discussion around the kayaking incident. Jake stoked the fire, clenching his jaw as David headed back inside the house. I placed a hand on the small of his back.

"How's dinner looking?" I asked, eyeing him cautiously.

"Won't be long." He lifted his arm to my shoulders and I let out a sigh of relief as his body relaxed.

"Good, I'm starving."

"What a surprise? You're always hungry."

"Am not." He raised an eyebrow questioning my reply. "Well I have a fast metabolism. I burn food faster than most people." He smirked and I leaned into his chest, feeling happy that my diversion tactic had worked.

"So…is this the first time you've done this outside chef thing?" I asked, biting my bottom lip in mock concern.

"Nope. Hey, cheeky! I'll have you know I'm the king of the fire pit steak."

"Good, because I'm ready for the best you've got."

"Oh, you are, are you?" he said, winking at me. The heat flared in my face and I slapped him in the chest for causing yet another flush to color my cheeks.

"Jeez, you're cute when you blush," he said, a broad grin spreading across his face.

"Hmm."

"What do you guys want to drink?" Callum called from the back door.

"I'll get a soda thanks," Jake shouted.

"Yeah, soda's good. I should go see if there's anything I can do to help." I pulled away from Jake's side before heading back to the kitchen.

"Abbie?"

"Yep."

"Erm… Tell Cal, I'll have diet soda."

"Sure thing," I said, grinning as Jo pushed past me in the doorway with the prepped fish.

"Here we go," she said, placing the large platter on the table. With the food almost ready Callum crashed onto the patio armed with three large bottles of soda.

After collecting knives, forks and a pile of paper napkins I arranged various items on the table, making room for the grilled food. I sensed Jake approaching and gasped when his arms circled my waist and pulled me into his chest. The breath left my lungs slowly and I relaxed into his embrace.

He dropped a kiss to my shoulder, "Now…that was a better reaction."

"That's because you didn't grab me like a madman from out of nowhere," I said with a smile. His eyes narrowed slightly at my comment. "How's the fish?" I asked, in a feeble attempt to change the subject, again.

"Erm… Yeah, should be ready."

The food tasted amazing. Whether it was because of eating outdoors or our magical surroundings, I wasn't entirely sure. The fire glowed in the pit as we cleared the last of our feast. True to his promise, Jake's steak delivered on flavor and tenderness. Groaning with satisfaction we relaxed into the soft seating lining the edge of the patio. The hypnotic glow of the embers pulled my gaze and I soon relaxed into a state of complete contentment.

Callum and Jo resumed their usual banter; it amused me that they had such a great rapport after only a couple of weeks of being friends. Jake, although calm seemed quieter than usual. He was uncharacteristically distant and it bothered me.

"Now, you're sure you're going to be okay, kids? We don't want any more emergencies this weekend," David quipped, leaning out of the back door and casting an eye around the group. As David joked about our mishap on the lake, Jake lowered his head as if distracted by the fire in front of us. I squeezed his knee gently and he forced a smile in return.

"Of course we will, Dad. Don't worry about us, we'll be fine." Jo said, "What's the worst that can happen?"

"Don't even joke about it, young lady!" Pam said, widening her eyes at her daughter.

"We'll be fine, Mom, honest."

"Don't stay up too late…and lock up when you go to bed please."

"We will. Have a good night. Love you."

"Love you too," Pam replied as they climbed into the SUV and drove off up the gravel driveway.

I stretched my arms above my head, inhaling deeply as a wave of tiredness passed through me. I slumped into a large cushion on the floor beside Jake and snuggled up to him, resting my head on his knee. Jake lifted his hand to my shoulder and ran his fingers gently through my hair as we sat enjoying the warmth of the fire.

"Hmm, I could just fall asleep, that's so relaxing."

I turned my face towards him and smiled. Jake lifted his hand from my shoulder, his eyes searching mine before running his thumb across my cheek. My eyes closed involuntarily at his gesture, a sudden wave of butterflies taking flight in my tummy.

"I like watching you sleep."

"When did you watch me sleep?"

"Well, there was last night…and then there was last week at your house." His fingers drifted along my jaw and across my cheek.

"I know about last night, although I thought you were watching the TV, but what about at my house? You were asleep as well."

"Only for part of the time, I woke up before you. I watched you for a while before your mom came downstairs."

"Jake!"

"Sorry, but you looked so peaceful. You'd had a tough evening and I wanted to let you rest." I frowned at the memory of the night at Jo's house and my resulting meltdown.

"Yeah well, you shouldn't stalk people when they're sleeping. It's rude." I said with an amused grin.

"Well, forgive me if I continue to act in a manner considered rude. I refuse to stop stalking my girlfriend while she looks so stunningly beautiful in her sleep."

"Shush! Stop it, you're making me blush."

"What do you guys think about a short stroll to work off this feast?" Jo asked, climbing onto her feet, making her way towards the pile of dishes.

"I think that's a great idea," I said, looking at Jake.

"Where do you have in mind?" Callum asked.

"There's a lookout about twenty minutes' walk from here. We can take a couple of lamps. It'll be cool."

"Sounds good," Jake said, pulling me to my feet.

We quickly cleared the table and took everything inside. Jake raked the fire so it was safe to leave while Jo and I cleaned the bench tops and stacked the dishwasher.

"I'm just gonna grab a jacket and change my shoes," Jake said, leaving us to finish in the kitchen.

"I might do the same," Callum said, following his friend.

"You two okay?" Jo asked as she threw the cloth she'd been using into the laundry. I closed the lid to the dishwasher before turning to face her.

"Fine, why?"

"Oh, just that Jake seems a bit quiet."

"Well, I guess he's had a weird week one way or another. Hospital, the assignment, my mood swings *and* today's little mishap. He's probably over all the drama."

"I guess so," she agreed with a shrug, "Come on, let's get ready."

Apart from the light of the moon, the whole area was blanketed in complete darkness; only the crunch of the gravel under foot hinted at where the trail began and ended. After pointing out the direction, Jo pushed Callum forward leaving me and Jake to bring up the rear.

"Hey, who you pushing around, young Jo?" Callum grabbed hold of her wrist and tugged her towards him. I smiled wistfully at the intimate interaction between the two of them.

"You need pushing, you big oaf!"

They continued their relaxed conversation as we trailed behind. After walking for about five minutes I cast a glance sideways at Jake. The track was easily wide enough for two people to walk comfortably side by side, but I sensed an invisible barrier between us. I was used to him being approachable and supportive; this Jake was guarded. Just as I thought of giving up on any interaction Jake put his arm around my shoulders.

"I'm sorry," he whispered, rubbing my arm.

I tucked my hand into the pocket of his jeans, "You have nothing to be sorry about."

"I'm so out of my comfort zone right now, Abs. I feel like I'm losing it."

"I know what you mean. I'm used to getting on with stuff on my own without anyone paying much attention.

It's been a bit weird having you care." He stopped suddenly and swung me around to face him. The glow from the lamp gave me enough light to see the frustration in his expression.

"Of course I care! Fuck, Abbie, you came so close to drowning today. You were under the water for ages. When I couldn't see you I…"

"Hey, I'm okay." I lifted my hand to his cheek, "Really, I'm fine. I'm sorry I scared you."

"I know…"

"But?"

"There's no but," he said, kissing my forehead, "It's just well…oh I don't know, Abbie. There's been such a mix of emotions running through me I feel like my head's up my ass." He looked down for a moment as if gathering his thoughts before continuing. "Having you relax enough to fall asleep on me makes me real happy. You can't even begin to know how I feel when I watch you sleep. It's like I have my old Abbie back, the one without the anger."

This conversation was beginning to move along to a place less than comfortable. Not wanting to think about the old Abbie I took in a deep breath and placed my hand on his chest.

"I am relaxed around you, Jake, but its early days. Let's get to know each other again, hey?" We stood in silence for what seemed like ages as my suggestion hung above us.

"You bet," Jake said, smiling warmly at me.

"Good. Then can we concentrate on enjoying the rest of the weekend instead of dwelling on any other shit?" I pulled away so I could see his face.

"For sure. Come on," Jake replied, curling his fingers around mine.

It didn't take too long to catch up with Jo and Callum.

"We could ride round tomorrow. We have bikes in the garage." Callum threw his arms in the air in exasperation at Jo's suggestion.

"Seriously? You've dragged us out in the middle of the night, for a walk in the freezing cold we could have done tomorrow on bikes?"

"Yeah? So?"

"So? Women!"

Chapter Twenty-Three

Much of the weekend had centered on consuming copious amounts of great food. At this rate we'd all be spending the next month in the gym working off the extra pounds.

Even so Jo played the hospitable hostess when she came back in and the room carrying a laden platter, "Anyone for nachos and the guacamole Callum made? And if you want a drink there's a few beers in the fridge - Dad won't mind as long as we don't go crazy."

I took some just to be polite and was impressed. "Hey Callum, this guacamole is awesome. Not bad at all." Callum grinned at the compliment as he munched.

"This is really good," Jake agreed his mouth full of cheesy chips. He had salsa down his chin and I reached over to mop it up with a nacho of my own before popping it into my mouth.

"Hey, that was mine," he said, grabbing me and kissing me full on the mouth even though I was still chewing.

"Eww, gross," Jo groaned, "Get a room." I blushed scarlet as Jake moved away and continued to eat his chips while guarding his bowl, but keeping one eye on me.

"Don't worry, Jakey, I won't eat your food." I giggled and popped another chip into my mouth.

Callum almost spat his mouthful all over Jake, "Jakey?" I wondered how Jake would handle my faux pas.

"You're only jealous," he said before turning to me, giving me a wink of approval.

"You're right, dude, I am," Cal said, casting a glance over to Jo.

"Well what you gonna do about it then, big boy?" she challenged, striking an alluring pose that raised howls of encouragement from the rest of us.

Jeez, I wished I had an ounce of her confidence.

Callum backed off. "Oh, I'm still working on that one…still thinking." He shoveled another dollop of salsa and sour cream into his mouth with the largest nacho in his bowl.

"Well, you might want to speed up the old gray matter a tad before the idea wears thin." Her quick-witted come back had Jake and me in stitches. Jo and Callum were definitely made for one another. It was going to be entertaining to see how their relationship played out.

"Jake tells me that you guys used to go to the same school. Even though he denied ever knowing you and made up some lame excuse for why he called you Abbie that time in the cafeteria," Callum scoffed.

"Erm, yeah, that's right, we did," I said as a sudden vulnerability seeped into my system.

"So I guess you must have thought *Oh Shit not Jake Ashton!* ...when you bumped into him again... hey?"

"I guess, at first anyway," I stammered, embarrassed at the memory of mine and Jake's reunion.

"Jeez, Cal, you can be a nosey fuck." Jo shook her head and headed to the trash with her empty bottle.

"What? It's not every day childhood sweethearts reunite ten years later and end up getting it on. You've got to admit, it's like a scene from a frickin' movie."

I wriggled with discomfort in my seat wishing the ground would open up and take me away.

"I used to be a jerk. It's not surprising she ran a mile." Jake jumped in to help me out, winking at me and trying his best to pacify Callum and move the conversation on before it got too personal. He knew the subject of our childhood upset me, though he'd no inkling why.

"Well I think it's sweet. You've turned out okay, Jake. You have my permission to date my very bestest friend in the world." Jo smiled at me before whacking Callum as hard as possible across the chest.

"Gee thanks, Jo," Jake said and leaned over to kiss me, "But Abbie's always been my girl."

"How to set the bar high, dude," Callum shook his head as he watched us.

"You've got to work hard to impress these girls, man. There's no easy way to the right girl's heart," Jake said, smiling at Callum squirming on his stool.

"Yeah, yeah. You just watch," Cal joked, licking his lips as he ogled Jo. Cal's remark earned him a serious glare from Jo.

"Oh yeah? In your dreams, buster." There was an undeniable chemistry between our friends, but they were enjoying the hunt as much as the attack.

Mopping up the last of his salsa, Jake moved to gather up the empty dishes and headed over to the sink.

"Another beer?" he asked with his hand on the refrigerator door.

"I'll have one. I need to cool down a tad," Callum said with a smirk.

Jo shook her head, "Not for me thanks, I'll have a soda instead."

"Yeah, me too," I added. The whole discussion about Jake and me had left me a bit nervous; the last thing I needed was to get drunk. I watched closely as Jake fetched the drinks and iced the glasses before pouring our sodas and placing them in front of us with a fat grin on his face.

"There you go, ladies."

"Jeez, man, give me a break here!" Callum threw his hands in the air in disbelief at Jake's chivalrous gesture. The room erupted into fits of laughter as Jake sat down and took a long pull of his beer. He winked at Jo; loving that he'd set up his friend. There was no question that Cal and Jo would not get together at some point; if not this weekend, definitely sometime soon.

It amazed me that Jake was sometimes so relaxed, strong and caring and then at other times he'd be uptight, angry almost. How could one person be so different? I frowned at the realization it was because of me. My actions and moods were being reflected back at me. Jake had invested such a lot into our relationship already and I had consistently thrown hurdles in his way. On every occasion he had successfully smashed through each barrier and now we were officially boyfriend and girlfriend.

With our new status came new possibilities. I expected his understanding, although as yet, he was unaware of what he had to understand. His support was important to me, but again, he didn't know what facets of my personality required that support. I needed to be cared for, but how could he do that if I continued to push him away. Love came top of my wish list, but I was scared that I would never allow him to love me, at least not in the physical sense of the word.

The thought of a physical relationship made me shiver; the fear of it rising from my core. This beautiful boy sat beside me had asked nothing more of me than any other boy anywhere else would ask of his girlfriend.

He can't give me what I need because I can't tell him, and he doesn't realize why I can't give him what he wants.

"Excuse me a sec," I said, turning to Jake. I needed a minute to clear my head. My emotions were getting the better of me and I had a sudden urge to be sick.

"You okay?" Jake asked, placing his hand on my lower back as I stepped down from the stool.

I nodded, "Won't be long." He smiled, but the concern in his eyes was plain to see. We'd always been in tune with one another.

The bathroom door clicked into its casing as it locked behind me. I leaned over the sink, watching it fill with water then splashed my face several times before holding a towel to my glowing cheeks. I frowned at my reflection in the mirror, seeking a simple answer to my dilemma.

What am I going to do?

I've fallen in love with Jake.

It hurt all the way to my core that I was unable to move forward into a physical relationship with him. I wanted to… Jeez, I wanted to show him just how much I loved him. How much his kisses electrified my entire body, and how much they left me aching for more.

As quickly as the thoughts of a tender moment between us entered my mind more sinister memories of Peter seeped out of the hidden recesses of my memory. The pounding of my heart echoed in my head, bringing a throbbing ache to my temples as I relived the sound and smell of his breath on my face. The measured touch of his hand creeping up my leg caused my lungs to constrict with overwhelming fear. I felt his fingers inside me again, his... The bile rose to the back of my throat halting my breath. I slumped onto the edge of the bath and grasped at the sink, my heart crashing against my ribs. Tears welled in my eyes and spilled over. I couldn't steady my breathing; the burning in my chest took over and I began to gasp. This hadn't happened for a long time. A full blown attack was the last thing I needed. Silent tears poured down my cheeks as the floor came up to meet me.

My confused mind registered the sound of banging and someone's panicked cries. It was a man's voice, but muffled and distant, "Abs, you okay in there?" Muddled and dazed, the tiles on the floor of the bathroom swirled beneath me. He pounded again, but still I couldn't answer. Nausea gripped me as my stomach tightened and tried to eject its contents. Spots of color and light flickered to the beat of my heart and I gasped for breath as the fog closed in on me.

"Jake! Get up here, man! Abbie's in trouble!" The echo of Callum's booming voice filled my head. After what seemed like an eternity the rumble of pounding feet vibrated beneath me and Jake's voice drifted into my numbed consciousness.

"Open the door, baby! Jo get the door open!"

Jake sounded frantic; I could hear the fear in his voice, but it was getting harder to stay in the moment. Clouded with confusion and regret my mind began to wander.

It's okay, Jakey. Don't be scared.

More tears trickled from my eyes and ran into my ear as I lay on my side on the cold tile, my heart still pounding in my head.

"Break it down!" I thought I heard Jo scream. The explosive sound of a door smashing into the wall beside me roused my awareness.

A hand came to my face. A familiar scent, "Oh my God, Abbie! Come on baby, breathe," Jake urged and his fingers moved the hair from off my face, "Come on, sweetheart, slow it down. Please, Abbie... Come on... Abbie, please..."

I dug deep to reach him, to find the control to do as he asked, but reality faded with every failed breath.

"Get me a cloth," he yelled.

"Abbie! What the fuck?" Jo shrieked from somewhere behind Jake, "I knew she wasn't okay! She should have gone to the hospital!"

"Get her out of here, Cal," Jake said, keeping his attention on me all the while.

"Shall I call an ambulance?" Callum asked. I caught a glimpse of Cal holding Jo around her waist, fighting her off maybe, I wasn't sure.

"No, not yet, she'll be alright. Just take Jo downstairs."

"Okay, cool, shout me if you need me, man."

A soothing coolness caressed my cheeks, my brow, the side of my neck and then back to my cheek as the room came back into focus. I closed my eyes, trying with all my might to steady my breathing.

"Abbie?" Jake said, resting a comforting hand on my waist, "Come on, baby. You're okay. That's my girl."

I opened my eyes and found Jake smiling back at me. He ran a gentle thumb across my cheekbone, his eyes searching mine.

"What am I going to do with you?" he asked, his expression filled with fear.

"I-I'm s-sorry," I managed between breaths.

"Don't say that, Abbie." he said, shaking his head, "Don't say sorry."

Jake continued to wipe my brow with the damp cloth and I felt myself calming down to a more comfortable state. My heartbeat slowly returned to its regular rhythm and after a few minutes I had to get up from the floor before I lost all sensation in my legs.

I placed a hand on the edge of the bath to hoist myself upright, but Jake was quicker and soon had me on my feet, his firm hands gripping my waist. I clung to his arms uncertain whether or not my legs would take my weight.

"Sorry," I said again.

He sat me on the side of the bath and knelt in front of me. "Abbie, I can't help you if you don't tell me why you're sorry or what you're sorry for." He ran his thumb along my jaw, his eyes locked on mine. I reached my hands to his shoulders and grabbing his shirt, pulled him towards me. He responded and wrapped his arms around me, holding me tightly against his chest. One hand stroked my hair as he soothed me.

I didn't cry. "Just hold me, Jake, please." His arms tightened and hauled me close. His heart beat against my cheek; his scent encasing me as we clung to one another in the middle of the lake house bathroom.

I knew my next request was pointless, but I made it anyway, "Please don't leave me."

"I'm not going anywhere. Why won't you believe me?" Jake eased back from me to look me in the eyes, "I love you, Abbie. I always have."

I shook my head frantically, panicking at the thought, "You can't love me, Jake. You can't!" A lone tear trickled down my cheek and I lowered my gaze wondering how or whether to continue this conversation.

"Well tough shit, because I do and no matter whether you like it or not I'm here to stay. So make up your mind," he said, running his hands through his hair, "Do you want me or not?"

My stomach was on the verge of turning inside out and my pulse throbbed in my neck as I tried to get some distance between the two of us.

"It's not that simple."

"So you don't want me." Jake became still, dropping his hands to his sides with a look of defeat on his face.

"I do, I really do, but…" I held my head, rubbing my eyes with the palms of my hands.

Fuck, this is it!

"But what?" he asked as he came towards me and circled me in his arms, dipping his knees so we were face to face.

"I want you more than anything…" I said as a tear rolled down my cheek, "I need you to understand…I need to tell you something."

Chapter Twenty-Four

Abbie's nervousness showed in her grip on my arm as we left the bathroom.

"Everything's gonna be okay," I did my best to hold onto the last remnants of my control. The contents of my stomach churned uncomfortably, I was far from calm, but Abbie needed my support and that's what she'd get.

I frowned at the memory of our reunion. Far from being the most wondrous encounter of my life; she'd rejected me outright, leaving me shattered and wondering why? A father leaving his family would be traumatic for anyone and she'd mentioned it a couple of times. The absence of a boyfriend or love interest gave me little clue, but she must have been dumped by someone; causing her to be distant and cautious of my advances. I shuddered at the thought of her with anyone else.

She rested her head against my arm and I placed my hand to her cheek briefly.

"Do you want to go outside?" Abbie lifted her head, her eyes questioning my suggestion. "I mean…if you want some air or to talk…it'll be quieter. What do you think?" I lifted my hand, moving her hair from her face.

"Okay," she whispered, forcing a thin smile.

I grabbed a couple of hoodies before we headed back downstairs.

On entering the den, I sensed the waves of anxiety radiated from Abbie. I squeezed her hand in an attempt to ease her nerves, hating that she was so different now. The once strong, confident little girl whom I had loved dearly had gone; to be replaced with this timid, self-conscious shell of a woman. I longed to find her hidden strength. The confrontations we'd shared gave me hope that I could resurrect my Abbie. Her self-esteem had taken a battering, but her passionate side lay dormant and I had to bring her back. My stomach churned at the strong possibility she might back off altogether after tonight.

Jo flew off the sofa when she saw us at the bottom of the stairs and wrapped Abbie in a tight embrace.

"Abbie! Fucking hell, girl... Are you okay?"

"Yeah, I'm alright," Abbie said, squeezing Jo, "Sorry, guys. I don't know what happened there."

I pulled on my jacket, "We're just heading outside to get some fresh air. We won't be long," I said, placing my hand on Abbie's lower back and guiding her towards the kitchen door.

The sympathetic look Jo gave Abbie followed by the forced smile and acknowledgement from Abbie sent chills down my spine. Memories of my chat with Jo after Abbie fled from my house the other night flooded back. I realized it was possible Abbie and I were about to have *that* conversation.

"I'll keep Jo busy," Callum said, putting his arm round her shoulders, but Jo shrugged off his advances.

"You won't!"

The cool night air filled my lungs as I followed Abbie onto the deck. I loved her so much. My heart crashed against my ribs at the horrific memory of Abbie sealed in the capsized kayak, struggling to get free. We'd recovered from that, but seeing her fighting for her breath just now on the bathroom floor had scared the crap out of me.

Abbie walked towards the railing, gripping it tightly and stood looking out over the lake. I placed the other hoodie around her shoulders. She turned and smiled up at me as she dragged her arms into the sleeves of the oversized garment, wrapping the extra fabric around her shivering body.

"You cold?" I asked, reaching out to rub her arm.

"Not really," she said, lowering her eyes to my waist and appearing to look right through me. She lifted her hands to hold onto the edges of my hoodie where the zipper met the fabric; running her fingers up and down the fastener. I kept my hand on her arm, searching her face for a hint of what might be coming; every inch of my body tense in anticipation of the worst. She grasped my jacket, squeezing her eyes closed to shut back the tears. I had an overwhelming urge to protect her from any further hurt, but did nothing, and for a moment we stood in uncomfortable silence.

I couldn't stand the utter sorrow emanating from her and pulled her close. I placed my hand at her nape and as I breathed in her delicious scent, longed for a simple resolution to the heartache seeping through her body and into mine. I pressed a gentle kiss to her neck, tightening my hold in desperation.

"Oh, Jake, I've missed you so much," she whispered, grasping the back of my neck.

"Me too, Abs, but I'm here again now, sweetheart. I'm not going anywhere." I kissed her head and held her close, hoping for a happy ending. A sob escaped her throat and she hung onto my sleeves as if her life depended on it.

"I don't want to hurt anymore, Jake…I don't want to see…" she said, sobbing into my chest.

"What baby? Tell me what happened?" I eased away just enough to place my hands either side of my angel's face. Wiping the tears from her cheeks I searched her eyes for the source of the torment I'd seen since the day I came to Casey.

"Jake…I'm scared."

"Of me?" Gripping the shoulders of my hoodie she shook her head, her eyes closed.

"No…I'm scared of…of losing you all over again," she whispered. Her body trembled as I held her to my chest. A wave of complete helplessness flooded through me as she clung to me.

"How many times do I have to tell you? I'm here to stay, Abbie."

"But…you…won't…want to be," she whispered, lowering her head.

"What?" I asked, confused by her comment.

"I have nightmares." She peeped up at me briefly from beneath her hair.

I pulled her closer, "What nightmares?" She gagged as if struggling to elaborate. "What nightmares?" I bent my knees and dipped down so she had to make eye contact. My heart began thumping so violently I thought it might come crashing through my ribs at any minute.

"I see the removal truck pull up and the driver…" she choked out, "It's like…it's in slow motion…he…" Abbie shook her head her eyes were awash with torment; I couldn't work out what she was trying to say.

"Hey, hey… Who baby?" My pulse rate ramped up another notch.

"And my mom…she…"

"What about your mom?" I frowned in confusion.

"She…she wanted me to look after Martin, make sure he was okay."

"Yeah? Well you did, Abs…you always looked out for him, I can remember…and you still do. Why would you have nightmares about that? Martin's fine."

"You don't understand…I didn't though…" she said, shaking her head frantically. I eased back slightly, giving her a bit of space to work out what she wanted to say. Reaching for her hand I tucked her fingers through mine, needing to maintain some physical contact as she continued. "I left him…and sneaked off…to play at Claire's." A tear fell down her cheek and her lip quivered as she stared through my chest into her memory. "Claire wasn't home…" I swallowed to rid the lump in my throat as she rubbed the back of my hand nervously and I took a deep breath.

"Claire? Claire from Raven?" She nodded.

"Whoa, that was years ago," I said, narrowing my eyes. I took both her hands in mine and whispered, "Easy baby…Where's this going?" Her body continued to tremble under my touch and I squeezed her hands, trying desperately to bring her comfort.

"She'd gone out...but...her dad was home..." she said, dropping her gaze. My grip tightened ever so slightly.

Please, no...

"I...I should have stayed away..."

Please, God... I felt myself losing control as all the pieces started to fall in place.

"What? Tell me, Abbie." I urged, struggling to hold back the raw emotion in my voice. "I don't understand. What are you saying?" The tremors running through her body increased as she slumped down onto the top step of the deck, pulling her knees towards her chest. My mouth became suddenly dry.

"I went into her apartment to wait for her...and he..." I backed up to the railing, my knuckles turning white with the force of my grip. Abbie took a deep breath as silent tears fell from her eyes. I closed my eyes, shaking my head slowly, willing her not to say what I already knew in my heart she would.

"He raped me, Jake," she whimpered, swiping at the tears flowing endlessly down her cheeks.

"No...Abbie...no..." I wanted more than anything for her to take back the words she'd just spoken. "No!"

The bile hit the back of my throat as I digested the depravity my beautiful girl had encountered. I'd tried to imagine what had caused her to change so radically, but this was beyond anything I'd envisioned. It was too much to comprehend. In that moment I had to get away from her. The most uncontrollable rage rumbled deep within me. "Arrgghh!" Tears welled in my eyes and the pain in my chest became unbearable as I staggered down the steps and onto the patio. I crashed into the solid table we'd previously used for dinner. I needed to calm down, but all I saw was the vision of that evil pervert with my Abbie.

"You…were only…a baby!" I choked out, pressing my fists into my eyes. My pulse raged at the thought of that bastard touching her. I wanted him dead. I sucked in a ragged breath and braced myself, my hands gripping the wooden edge of the table, my head pounding; trying to slow my breathing.

"Jake, please!" she sobbed.

My chest tightened violently when I heard Abbie's cry of deep despair. I growled in desperation and spun towards her, lifting my hands to my head. I couldn't take this away or make it better.

I stood frozen, my eyes fixed on the girl that I loved unconditionally. She'd been violated by that fucking animal, robbing her of any chance of loving me as a consequence; she couldn't want me now, not after going through that, I was too late. My heart dropped into the pit of my stomach. It was all I could do to resist the violent urge to vomit right there on the patio.

"I'm sorry," she whispered, her head on her knees.

"Sorry? You're sorry? Fuck me, Abbie!" I yelled, slamming my fist against the table, sending the remaining barbeque utensils flying just as Callum and Jo burst through the door.

"What the fuck is going on?" Jo screamed at me when she saw Abbie crying on the ground. Jo ran to Abs and wrapped her arms around her friend, and glared at me. "What did you say to her, Jake?" Callum launched himself at me as I made a move towards Abbie, grabbing my arm in an attempt to stop me.

"Come on, Jay, calm it down." I threw Callum's hand off and swung towards Jo.

"Why didn't you tell me? Why, Jo? Why?" I needed someone to blame, anyone.

"Hey, that's enough, Jake," Callum said, placing both his hands firmly on my chest, "Don't do this, man. Jo didn't do anything."

"She fucking knew...and...she didn't say anything..."

Callum now had me encased in his arms, "Come on, man, it's not Jo's fault...and you know it." He looked over at Jo to see she was also in tears.

I heaved in a deep breath and closed my eyes briefly before nodding. Callum's hold loosened and I dropped to my knees in front of Jo and Abbie. She cowered away from me, sobbing uncontrollably. Shame flooded every cell of my body; she'd needed me to be strong and I had fallen apart. Abbie flinched and withdrew even further towards Jo when I placed my hands on her legs.

"Oh my God, Abbie, I'm sorry." My throat tightened as tears fell from my eyes, "I'm so sorry… I would never hurt you." I placed a gentle hand on the side of her head and waited for her to look at me. "Please, Abbie…I love you." My voice crackled with emotion.

The fear I saw when she opened her eyes ripped out my heart and tore me apart. Pushing gently away from Jo she lifted her hands to my shoulders then around my neck. I felt empty and utterly helpless, holding onto her for what seemed like an eternity.

"Here, Jo…come on, leave them. They'll be okay now." Callum said quietly. Jo reluctantly followed him into the house leaving us clinging to one another.

"I had no idea… I should have been there," I said when I regained the ability to speak; "I'm so sorry, baby." I continued to rub small circles on Abbie's back until she began to relax in my arms. She took a deep breath and eased herself, albeit reluctantly away from me.

Her eyes searched mine, "I'll understand if…"

"Hey, none of that," I said, taking her face in my hands. "I love you, Abbie. Nothing…will ever…change that. Do you understand? Nothing." Doubt and confusion clouded her tear filled eyes.

"But…"

"There's no but. We'll get through this. I promise you. We'll get through this. You and me, together!"

"Okay," she whispered.

"Okay." I brushed the hair from her face and leaned down to kiss her tenderly. Her face looked as blotchy as I imagined mine to be and Abbie lifted her hand to my cheek, forcing a smile.

"Thank you," she whispered.

Chapter Twenty-Five

Agonizing images flooded my subconscious mind and were driving me insane. Minutes seemed like hours since Cal and Jo left us alone on the decking. I'd just learned that as a child barely out of grade three, Abbie had been brutally raped. To say her revelation came as a surprise was an understatement. Each vicious word Abbie had uttered tore out my heart from my chest, leaving a gaping, bleeding wound in its wake. My adrenaline fueled rage passed away slowly leaving an inexplicable numbness spreading through my body.

My beautiful girl had lived with the trauma of horrific and repeated abuse for two years and learned to cope with its gruesome effects. Her entire existence from then had encroached on no one; she'd withdrawn from any social interaction and thrown herself into her studies. Abbie possessed strength and resilience unmatched by anyone. That was my answer. That was why she had changed.

Fuck! I brought it all flooding back. No wonder she was pissed to see me. Out of anger and fear of reliving the most horrific pain any child could possibly encounter, she'd pushed me away at our reunion. I remembered the frustration and confusion I'd experienced that day. All our conversations and interaction since now made sense. I'd reacted selfishly to her less than enthusiastic response to my advances. All I felt now was shame.

I sensed Abbie's anxiety radiating through her trembling fingers. She would surely be over thinking numerous outcomes at having divulged her deepest secret.

What fucking monster would do that to a baby?

I fought back the emotion threatening to reveal itself, blinking back my tears. Abbie seemed to snap out of her imaginings and turned towards me. A sympathetic smile tugged at my mouth, but didn't make it to my eyes; an overwhelming heartbreak and disgust left me unable to give Abbie what she needed. An expression of resignation crossed her face and she smiled, squeezing my hand. Her eyes met mine as if searching for a scrap of hope. I almost choked on the lump lodged firmly in my throat and closed my eyes, my brow furrowing into a frown as I struggled to respond to her unspoken question.

"I don't have the words, Abbie. I'm sorry, but I can't think of one thing that remotely fits what's going on in my head right now."

Abbie shook her head, "I don't need you to say a thing. It's fine. Just so you know…that aside from my obvious issues; I'm actually okay, Jake." I wrapped my arm around her shoulders and pulled her snuggly into my side. "But…" she said, fidgeting uncomfortably, "I could really do with standing up a while. My legs have gone to sleep."

"Come on then. I'm sure Jo will be going loco inside."

I hoisted myself up using the handrail and pulled Abbie to a standing position just in front of me. My hands supporting her tiny waist until the blood flow returned to her legs.

"You're an amazing woman, Abbie James." I lifted a hand and stroked her flushed cheek gently before leading her back to our friends.

Abbie's exaggerated inhalation at the back door reflected the anxiety running rampantly through my body. She paused briefly with her hand on the handle.

"I can't be in there too long, Jake. I…I don't want their pity…I just want them to see…*me*."

"No one is going to be any different, honest. You know what Cal's like. It'll be fine. Anyway, I'm here." I wondered at that point whether I meant it literally or whether I was worthy of this remarkable girl. I placed a supportive hand to her back as she opened the door to the large kitchen.

On entering the house we were faced with a totally unexpected scene. Well, apart from expecting it eventually.

"You two don't waste any time?" Abbie said, an ear splitting grin spreading across her face. Jo and Callum, who were locked together in a passionate make out session, launched themselves apart, levering themselves onto two bar stools at opposite ends of the island bench. Callum tried to hide his smirk behind his beer.

"Oh fuck!" Jo muttered under her breath looking extremely embarrassed. Abbie giggled, which in turn led to everyone laughing.

"Want a beer, you two?" Callum asked.

"I think that would be mighty fine, Cal, thanks."

"Abbie?" I liked Callum a lot. He'd already proved himself to be a great friend and I smiled at the normalcy of his offer.

"Thanks, Callum, I will," Abbie said with a smile.

The conversation revolved around the new couple for the next fifteen minutes or so before Abbie climbed down from the stool and placed her empty bottle in the trash.

"I'm sorry, guys, but I really need my bed. I'm exhausted. Sorry." She attempted a smile, but at best it was one of acceptance. "Thanks…for before." Her eyes locked on mine briefly, and I felt utterly incapable of offering adequate support. I frowned at the anger in my heart. I'd let her down when she needed me most. Abbie had suffered irrevocably and the surge of emotion in my stomach at the realization she was still hurting held me prisoner in my own grief.

"Night, Abs, I won't be long," Joey said. The smile of understanding on Abbie's face nudged at my overriding sense of guilt and inadequacy. Jo had been a great friend and I hoped Abbie would always have her in her life.

I reached out a hand to her as she turned to leave. "Night, Abbie," I said, lowering my mouth to her temple, kissing her gently. She closed her eyes, disappointment radiating off her in waves.

"Night, Jake."

Callum and Jo waited in silence as Abbie climbed the oak stairs to bed. Draining my beer and playing mindlessly with the empty bottle I frowned, frustration and anger still coursing through my system. I felt physically sick to the stomach, a vile taste lingered in my mouth; the like of which I'd never had to deal with before tonight. Putting on a brave face for Abbie's sake had failed badly. She wasn't a stupid girl.

How the fuck had I managed to become the victim? The guilt of my reaction seeped through my soul. How could I so cruelly turn my back on her needs? I shook my head at the sudden realization that I'd been an absolute tosser. She'd had to endure the most horrific ordeal imaginable. Not as an adult, as a child, and I'd just slapped her where it hurt.

How to add insult to an already devastating injury, Jake? I flinched at the memory of her words, *"He raped me Jake."*

"How you holding up, big guy?" Callum asked, his voice full of the brotherly concern I'd grown to recognize in this friend sat beside me. I shook my head, covering my face in a feeble attempt at hiding my shame from both Jo and Callum.

"I let her down. Jeez, Cal… Anyone would think that bastard raped me the way I carried on. As if she wasn't fucked up enough."

"Hey," Jo whispered, reaching for my arm, "It isn't your fault, Jake. None of this is yours or Abbie's fault."

"Maybe not, but I just managed to pull the rug from under her big time. How do I come back from that? She needed me to support her and love her in *that* moment and I turned my back on her, Jo. You saw what happened. You saw me. I'm a fucking loser!"

"Don't be such a dick, Jake. She's lived with what happened for so long it's almost normal to her now. I haven't known all that long, and to be honest my reaction wasn't the best. Well…a bit better than yours, but that's not the issue. I'm not the one head over heels in love with her. There's no right or wrong way to react to something like that."

I took a deep breath and slowly rubbed my face with both my hands, trying to rationalize all the shit flying around in my head.

"Dude, I'd have been the same if my girl had been…well…I'd have been the same," Callum said, giving my shoulder a quick shake of support.

"What do I do now? I don't know how to be there for her. I don't know the right thing to say or how I'm supposed to be?"

"Well one thing's for sure. You have to decide what you want from her," Jo said and I frowned at her comment.

"What the fuck, Jo… I don't want anything from her."

"No? So you don't love her?" She raised her eyebrows.

"Of course I love her. I've always loved her." Jeez, Jo could be fucking annoying.

"Well if you love her, you *do* want something from her. You want to be with her; or at least you did. Has tonight changed that?" I ran my hand through my hair as Jo's words registered in my one and only working brain cell. How had I been so fucking stupid?

"No!" I blew out a long breath, "Of course not. I want to be with her more than anything."

"Well I guess you're having this conversation with the wrong people then." Jo smirked. Callum looked similarly amused as he draped an arm around Jo's shoulder.

"Yeah, I guess I am... I should check on her. Do you think that'll be okay?"

"I'm sure she'll like that. Hey, and Jake, don't worry about being in any rush. There's another bedroom down the hall. If you need to talk, I mean," Jo said and blushed at her unintentional double meaning.

"Thanks, guys," I said and I left both Jo and Callum standing in the kitchen. One thing was certain, they would both be taking full advantage of the fact that Abbie and I were indisposed. A wry smile hit my lips as I climbed the stairs to Abbie's bedroom.

Nervousness presented itself in a variety of ways; I knew this from science at school. The clamminess of my palms, my racing heart rate and inability to catch my breath was indication enough of my state of mind as I came to a stop outside Abbie's room. I placed my hands on the frame, sucked in a calming breath, exhaled slowly and then knocked on the door.

After a moment the door opened to reveal Abbie fresh from the shower, "Hey," she greeted, looking concerned, "You okay?"

I shook my head while forcing a slight smile. "What?" she asked, grinning back.

"I should be the one asking you if you're okay. Not the other way round, but anyway, erm…"

"Do you want to come in?" Abbie seemed calm and well put together, considering what had happened.

"Erm… Yeah…sure. If that's alright." I stepped inside and hesitated, realizing there was nowhere to sit other than the bed. Abbie however, headed in that direction and proceeded to climb under the covers.

"It's not as elaborate as your room. We don't have a couch or a spa." I took in an anxious breath and walked towards her. "Jeez, Jake, just sit on the bed. It's fine. I'm not made of glass."

With everything hinging on this one conversation my pulse rate elevated to fever pitch. I took a seat beside her and lifted my hands to my face, attempting to rub away my overwhelming embarrassment.

"I'm such a fuckwit, Abbie. I can't even say what I'm thinking right now." She reached for my arm and grabbed onto my sleeve. I turned to face her, covering her hand with mine, "I want you in my life no matter what. I care more than you'll ever know about what happened to you, Abbie… I intend spending the rest of forever making up for the shit crazy way I reacted…I'm sorry, I love you so much. I can't even think of being on my own now that I've found you again."

Abbie shuffled forward onto her knees and tugged at my shirt, sliding her arms around my neck, leaving little room for misunderstanding. I blew out a massive sigh of relief and gathered her into my arms, reveling in the feel of her as I pulled her onto my lap. Inhaling deeply, I pressed my mouth to the soft skin of her neck.

"I'm sorry."

"Hey...shh now, it's done." Abbie ran her fingers through my hair and I soaked up the moment, the contact, and the need in both of us to be close. Our love for one another filled the air around us. It seeped into every pore as she placed a gentle hand to my cheek.

I leaned my forehead against hers and smiled, "I love you, Abbie James."

She eased back slightly and blushed as she dropped her gaze, "I love you too, Jake."

"You do?" I lifted a hand to her chin, tilting it up so I was sure to see her confirmation. My heart pounded against my chest at her response, not quite believing my ears.

She nodded, "I always have."

Chapter Twenty-Six

Why is it, no matter how careful I am when closing the blinds or curtains, the sunlight still finds a gap and streams in at the crack of sparrows and wakes me? Jeez!

The stiffness in my back served as a reminder of my underwater adventure yesterday. I wriggled my toes before carefully assessing the rest of my body for any other aches; wincing at the crick in my neck. I smiled as I realized whose arm lay beneath my head. It certainly didn't resemble any pillow I'd ever slept on.

I inhaled deeply and snuggled closer to Jake, feeling comforted and safe in his embrace. I ran my fingers down the firm muscles of his arm. His left hand which up until a moment ago had rested on my waist tightened as he stirred beneath me.

I continued my early morning exploration, my hand tracing the slight regrowth of his fair whiskers along his chin then down his throat to the sprinkling of chest hair. Jake's heart rate quickened under my cheek and I realized that I was no longer the only one awake. Chewing my lip I attempted to carefully remove myself from under his arm.

"You, my girl, are going nowhere," he grumbled, his arm tightening, making me squeal in surprise.

I looked up to see him gazing down at me, "Hey," I said cheekily.

"How are you, beautiful?" he asked, pulling me up to kiss me. My eyes closed briefly when his lips made contact with mine and his knuckles stroked the side of my jaw.

"Better." I pushed myself onto my elbow so I could take in the glorious view in front of me and smiled. Jake rested his hand on my waist as I lay beside him. I placed my hand to his cheek and caressed the skin beneath my touch. Jake brought his hand to my hair and pulled me towards him.

I pushed him away lightly, "We need to get dressed."

"You okay?" he asked.

"Uh huh, just don't want to miss a minute of our last day." We really needed to get dressed. Jake smiled and eased away just enough to rest his forehead against mine.

"I don't want to move," he whispered, smoothing the hair back from my face.

"We have to though."

"Really?" he asked, dipping his head enough to kiss the corner of my mouth gently.

"Mmm, really." I pushed him away halfheartedly. Jake lay back against the pillows with his head resting on his hands as he watched me intently. "Do you always stare at the girls you take to bed?" I asked with a smirk on my face.

"Hey! I resent that…and anyway…I've never slept with anyone else so the question is redundant."

I was astounded at Jake's admission, "Oh." I blushed at my assumption, but continued on towards the bathroom. Jake jumped off the bed, blocking my way. He turned me round to face him and I could still feel the heat in my cheeks. He tilted my chin, his eyes searching mine.

"There hasn't been anyone, Abbie. I don't want anyone but you."

"I-I thought…I thought you'd had lots of girlfriends." I felt uncomfortable with the subject of Jake being intimate with anyone else.

"I have. I've dated and messed about a bit…but I've not…you know," A smirk pulled at the side of his mouth.

"Jake Ashton, you're blushing." I said, grinning widely. I was super pleased that when we did sleep together properly it would be his first time as well.

"You know what this means don't you?"

"What?"

"If you don't let me go to the bathroom right this second, I'm gonna pee on your feet.

"Arrgghh! Abbie, you're so gross!" He dropped his hands immediately.

"Yeah, but you love me," I said, winking at him as I closed the door behind me.

***

My stomach churned a little at the prospect of uncomfortable questions from Cal and Jo as we headed down to breakfast, but instead we were faced with a comical sight on entering the kitchen.

"How many beers did I drink last night?" Callum asked, gripping his head in his hands while Jo cooked pancakes for breakfast.

"Oh I don't know," she said, grinning at us, "More than four. Morning, guys."

"Morning."

"Hey," Callum greeted in a less than enthusiastic tone.

"Morning, pal. Bad head?" Jake asked, grinning at his friend before slapping him firmly on his back.

"Pounding. Got anything for it, babe?" he asked Jo. She turned from the stove with the fry pan in her hand and tipped its contents onto the large plate on the bench.

"I'll grab a couple of painkillers for you in a sec," she said, serving up the last of the breakfast. "Eat something, it'll help."

Callum had never needed too much persuasion when it came to food, whether he had a hangover or not.

"Jeez, I'm surprised your mom keeps up with you, Cal," Jo said, placing the two tablets and a glass of juice next to him as he helped himself to a mountain of food.

"Thanks." He downed the painkillers and winked at Jake. "Well, now that we've all become better acquainted. What are we doing today?" My jaw dropped about two inches at Callum's comment and I turned slowly to face him just as Jo threw the dish towel at his face.

"Callum!"

"Oops, sorry," he said, lowering his head in an attempt to avoid any further vicious stares from Jo or me.

"Well, Dad's fishing with John again today and my mom's back at two." Jo said, pouring more coffees.

"How about exploring the lake? Didn't you say you had bikes, Joey?" I asked, remembering the conversation last night.

"That's right, *babe*, you said something about that when you dragged us half way round the lake in the dark," Callum said, his voice dripping with sarcasm.

Jo threw him a killer stare, "Yes we do."

"That's settled then," Jake said, grinning.

After sharing the more than adequate breakfast we all headed back to our respective rooms to get changed into more appropriate clothing for cycling.

I quickly braided my hair so that the safety helmet would fit better. I stepped out of our room while still in the process of fastening my hair and was met with a thoughtful looking Jake leaning on the wall opposite.

"What are you mulling over?" I quickly finished the tie and slung the braid over my shoulder.

"Nothing much."

"Jake?" He lifted an arm and draped it casually across my shoulders. When we reached the top of the oak stairs I turned to face him and planted my hand firmly on his chest.

"What is it?" I asked, narrowing my eyes at the distant expression on his face. He paused a second before his eyes cleared and his lip twitched with the beginnings of a smile.

"I'm glad you told me… I'm glad you trusted me enough." I smiled and stretched up on my tip toes to kiss the corner of his mouth.

"Me too."

"Are you guys coming or what?" Jo shouted, holding the door with one hand while balancing a back pack in the other.

"Jeez, Joey, where's the fire?"

"Come on," Jake said, pulling me alongside him down the wide staircase.

"About time," Jo said, her eyes twinkling as she threw me an, *I know what you've been doing* look.

***

The breeze caressing my face as we pedaled leisurely around the lake had a therapeutic effect on every inch of my being. The last couple of weeks had taken their toll and as I took in the surroundings I could feel the stress and anxiety melting away. The gravel track was only wide enough for us to follow one behind the other.

"Anyone need to pee?" Jo shouted over her shoulder after about thirty minutes as we approached a picnic area. The question created a ripple effect from the front to the back of our group. Joey's choice of words amused me as I remembered threatening to do just that on Jake's feet earlier this morning. From the wink he threw at me over his shoulder he'd had a similar thought.

We pulled into the rest area and leaned our bikes in the purpose built racks before taking a seat on the grass beside the lake.

"So, I've had a thought," Jo said, looking rather pleased with herself, however her words caused my stomach to flip a loop with impending dread. I knew how her thoughts usually panned out. "I was thinking…"

"You already said that once, Joey," I said, grimacing, "Get to the point."

"What's that look for? My ideas aren't that bad!"

"Hmm."

"Well anyway, before I was so rudely interrupted…" she took a deep breath, "I thought it would be great if we all went to the Halloween Dance together."

As soon as the words crashed out of her mouth I flipped on to my stomach and buried my head in the crook of my arm.

"Arrgghhh!" I groaned.

To my amazement Jake and Callum were in favor of the idea.

"Sounds great to me, babe. Any excuse to partayyy!" Callum said, demonstrating an exaggerated shimmy.

"I'm in," Jake said before he leaned onto his side and placed a comforting hand to my shoulder, "It'll be fun, Abbie. Come on I'll look after you."

I rolled over onto my back and rubbed my eyes with the palms of my hands. I really didn't want to go, but I didn't want to spoil the fun for my friends either. I groaned, visualizing the chaos, the crowds *and* the jibes.

"Come on, Abbie, please." Jo begged.

"Oh Okayyy if I have to, but…" I said, sitting bolt upright, "One loser comes near me or any skank pisses me off and I'm out of there."

They all sat wide eyed at my outburst for a second before Joey snorted like a pig and fell back laughing.

"O*kay*," Callum lowering his head to hide his smirk. Jake pulled me into his side and kissed my temple.

"This is gonna be so much fun," Jo said, climbing back onto her bike. I rolled my eyes at her enthusiasm and followed her and Callum onto the track that would lead us the rest of the way round the lake.

The light mist lingering just above the water's surface was enchanting and with the early-morning sun casting a shimmering reflection on the ripples my mind drifted, lapping up the stunning view. As we rounded a bend I was vaguely aware of Jo swerving to miss a rock on the track, but unfortunately a little too late.

"Watch out!" she shouted over her shoulder as my front wheel hit the boulder full on.

"Arrgghh!"

The collision gave me a fright more than anything. I skidded over to the side of the gravel and fortunately, landed clear of the bike on the grass.

"Fuck!" My ass hit the ground just as Jake screeched to a halt and dumped his bike on the track.

"Abbie!"

"I'm fine." I blushed at my clumsiness, "Only I could hit a boulder the size of a house."

"Here…" Jake held out his hand to pull me to my feet.

"Is she okay?" Jo shouted from where she'd stopped. Callum hadn't even noticed the commotion.

"Yeah, she's good." Jo nodded and headed off up the track to catch Callum.

"You sure, you're okay?"

"I'm fine, Jake, stop fussing will you?"

"Fine," he said, lifting my bike so that I could climb back on.

"I'm sorry, it's just… the whole fucking weekend seems to have revolved around my fucking mishaps and fucking issues!" I slammed the seat with my fist at the ludicrousness of it all, "I'm such a klutz."

By now Jake was trying his best not to laugh. I blinked back the tears of embarrassment and punched him hard in the arm before giving in to the grin tugging at the corner of my mouth.

"Come on, let's catch the others," Jake said, leaning forward briefly to kiss me before straddling his own bike. I pulled onto the track in front of him again glad he hadn't dwelled too much on my latest mishap.

The rest of the "Tour De Lake" went off without incident and I was relieved when we pulled up in front of the lake house a little after two.

Chapter Twenty-Seven

I hated packing at the end of a vacation, even a short one. Despite having divulged my biggest secret last night to the most special person in my life, I felt a strange sense of calm coming over me. Jake's reaction turned out to be a little more animated than I'd expected, but the result topped my wish list by a mile. He hadn't run in the opposite direction and still wanted to be with me.

"How long are you guys going to be?" Pam shouted from the bottom of the stairs, "If we don't hit the road soon we'll never get home in the daylight."

"You thinking about lover boy?" Jo teased with a huge smirk on her face.

"Actually…no. I was thinking about running club next Thursday."

I'd not been for a run in the morning for over two weeks. Coach Jackson would bust my ass if I didn't meet his high expectations at this week's cross country trials. I'd missed out on selection for last year's team due to an ankle injury and it took me all season to get back to full strength. Coach Jackson assured me that with hard work and determination this year I stood a good chance of getting through to state level.

"Oh Wow! Jeez, you're weird. I don't get what's so great about running round and round a track for hours?"

"It's stimulating," I said, closing the zipper on my bag, "I love the adrenaline rush of winning. Plus, it's something I can do on my own and do well." She smiled and I saw that my explanation and the source of my motivation made more sense to her now.

"Hey, you ready?" Jake asked, hovering by the doorway to our room.

"Yep, all done." I glanced round the bedroom to make sure there were no stray personal items lurking for the next guests before picking up my bag and joining him.

"Are you okay, Jake?" I asked, loading my bag into the car. He seemed withdrawn and quieter than usual.

"Yeah…I'll be fine."

I wasn't convinced. He definitely had a gray cast to his complexion and seemed a bit lethargic.

"Seriously, you don't look good." This time I turned him towards me and placed my hand to his forehead. "Jeez, Jake, you're burning up!" My stomach leapt into my throat, my heart almost joining it. *Fuck, this boy will be the death of me.* I vaguely remembered him telling me that the doctor recommended he left out exercise until next week and he'd also been told to avoid stressful situations. "Fuck!" I said as the weekend's events came back to me in a rush.

"Calm down, Abs, I'm fine. I'm a bit tired, that's all." The guilt of having dumped my shit on him pressed heavily on my shoulders.

I felt awful, "You're sick, Jake."

"Abbie? Seriously…I'm okay, I've been taking my meds. All I need is a good night's sleep." Jake's expression reflected all the seriousness of a well-informed patient. He understood his condition better than anyone else and I had to trust his judgment. I nodded as he placed a hand on my lower back and guided me to our seats in the car.

By the time we pulled in at Jo's house Jake had fallen asleep on my shoulder. Perhaps his analysis of the situation had been accurate? The weekend had been pretty full on.

"Hey, Jakey," I whispered, "We're home."

"Hmm?" He slowly stretched himself to an upright position, "Oh yeah."

"How you doing?"

"Mmm, not bad. Bit tired."

"Okay you lot. Hit the road," David said with a grin as he slammed his door closed and headed down the drive to where my mom and Callum's dad were waiting.

"Text me," I said as he kissed me lightly on the lips through our car window.

"I will," he said, throwing me a wink before my mom sped off down the street.

***

Jake took the next day off school. His mom had insisted, saying she wanted to be sure he made a full recovery before returning to normal duties. She'd been less than impressed with the state of him at the end of our weekend break.

That was two weeks ago and the state of Jake's health had now faded into insignificance, for Jo at least. All her energy over the last couple of days had centered on the infamous Halloween Dance.

"I hope you all have your costumes sorted," she said over lunch on Wednesday.

We'd decided to go as Abba. My mom had swayed our choice in the end. She'd apparently seen the famous group in concert in New York back in the day. So after looking up some photos on the internet we agreed the costumes would be easy to source.

"Just wait, you won't be able to keep your hands off me, babe," Callum said, wriggling his eyebrows at Joey.

"Yeah, yeah," she muttered under her breath.

"You got training tonight, Abs?" Jake asked, looking up from his phone.

"Yeah, I'll be about an hour."

By coincidence running club was the same night as football training so we usually grabbed a soda on the way home. With three weeks to go until the first meet of the season I'd been training every morning. My body was stronger. Muscles definitely had a great memory and I was now hitting my target lap times. The buzz I got from competing contrasted significantly with my normal insecurities.

I'd just hit the shower after training when I sensed someone behind me. I pulled a slow breath into my lungs, trying to steady my racing heartbeat.

"So…*The Freak* is back in action!" Jess said, leaning on the tile to the side of the communal shower. I put my hand on the wall in front of me, contemplating my response to her intrusion.

"What do you want, Jess?" I asked, keeping my tone neutral and my head down.

"Oh, I don't know. Maybe I want to discuss the fact that you and your sidekick don't appear to have listened to a word I said the other week." My stomach flipped at the tone of her comment. I really didn't need this right now.

Things had been moving along pretty well lately and I had all but forgotten about Becca and Jess.

"Oh yeah, and what was that again?" I just couldn't resist stirring the frickin' pot. There I was stark naked, face to face with two of the biggest skanks in school, asking for a confrontation. *Will I ever learn to keep my mouth shut?*

"Keep the fuck away, Abbie. I don't know what you think you have in the way of goods, but who'd want to be you?" Jess said scathingly, "You're nothing. Why would Jake look twice at a piece of shit like you when he can have me?" I was relieved to be under the shower while she had her say. Not wanting a reaction to the tears pooling in my eyes. The truth in her comment hit me in the stomach harder than a physical punch. She smiled at my lack of a comeback and left me to wallow in self-doubt.

As much as Jake had managed to build up my confidence in the last month or so, I didn't really believe everything he said to me. Peter had left his mark. There was no getting away from how much I hated myself. Whether I stood tall, slim and attractive or not, none of that mattered. The internal me couldn't be changed. Jake helped me to forget for a while, that's all. It only took a second for reality to come crashing down again. Jess and Becca seemed to have the ability to do that with great expertise.

I stood for a moment after they left before taking a deep breath and exiting the showers. I dressed quickly and dried my hair trying my best not to dwell on what Jess had said moments earlier.

"Hey, beautiful," Jake said, his face lighting up with the most radiant smile I could have wished for. I dropped my bag at his feet, looked into his eyes briefly and moved my hands up and around his neck, pulling myself into him. He responded immediately by wrapping his arms around my waist and holding me close. I sighed deeply as Jake nuzzled my neck; his arms soaking up every ounce of self-loathing that threatened to consume me.

"What's this for?" he asked, "Not that I'm complaining or anything, but…"

Moving away from him slightly I looked up at his concerned face, "Nothing. Just felt like it," and stretching up onto my tiptoes, I kissed him lightly on the lips before picking up my bag and turning towards his truck. Jake paused and narrowed his eyes not at all convinced at my brush off but seemed to think better of questioning me further at that particular moment. Instead, he took in a quick breath and climbed into the truck.

"Still want to call at the diner?" he asked as we neared our usual hang out. He sounded uncertain; I'd been quiet in the truck so far, where usually I'd be chatting about training or asking him about football.

"Sure…why not." I said, managing a small smile.

"Abbie, what is it? What's happened? And before you say *nothing* I'm not blind." He looked concerned and I could hardly bear to look him in the eyes. I hated lying to him, but I knew he'd retaliate and I didn't want that.

"I'm fine. Honest. It was just a really hard session, that's all." I leaned over to him and placed my hand to his cheek before stretching that extra inch to kiss him. He pulled away and took my hand in his, looking down as he laced his fingers between mine.

"Really?"

I nodded and squeezed his hand tightly, "Really." He seemed to force the smile that followed and I knew he was just pacifying me, but I left it there and made a move to get out of the truck.

"You do know I can read you better than anyone else don't you? I'm not a fool, Abbie." I dropped my hand to the seat beside me and turned slowly around. I could sense Jake's eyes boring into the side of my face as he waited patiently for me to give him an explanation.

"I…"

"For fuck's sake…just tell me!"

"Can I ask you a question?" I asked, not making eye contact with him; while nervously twiddling the fabric of my sweatshirt between my fingers.

"Go on."

"If I hadn't been here…would…erm…"

"If you hadn't been where? What's this about?"

"If I hadn't been here at Casey when you arrived…"

"But you *were* here." Jake lifted his fingers to my chin and was about to lean in to kiss me when I placed a hand to his chest. I needed to hear why he wanted to be with me. What the outcome would have been if I'd not been a student at Casey.

"You'd still have bumped into Cal wouldn't you?"

Jake's eyes narrowed slightly and he nodded his head slowly, "Yeaahh, why?"

"You'd probably still have made the football team."

Again he nodded. "Abbie, where's this going?" he asked, moving further away from me, gripping the steering wheel in frustration.

"Well…" I said, turning to face him, "Do you think… Do you think you would have dated one of the cheerleaders?" There, I'd said it; I'd asked him that burning question branded into my mind since Jess planted the seed half an hour ago. Well actually, since we'd hooked up. I didn't understand what he saw in me. Jake looked away and I swallowed, waiting for an answer.

"I'm right…" I whispered, "I'm not really your type at all…am I? She was right." I quickly climbed from the truck and left Jake with his jaw nearly on his knees.

Chapter Twenty-Eight

"What the fuck now?" I smashed my fist against the steering wheel as Abbie disappeared round the corner. "Arrgghh!" After sucking in a deep breath I grabbed the keys from the ignition and flew out of the truck. I wouldn't let this stand; she was going to hear me out. The pulse in my neck throbbed violently as I watched Abbie pushing through the crowded sidewalk.

"Abbie!" I shouted, "Hold up!" She appeared resigned to me catching up and slowed to a standstill. I grabbed her arm and turned her towards me; the emptiness in her eyes delivering a punch to my gut.

"Leave it, Jake. Your silence said enough." I pulled her over to a nearby bench seat; reluctantly she sat beside me, but kept her eyes focused on the passing pedestrians. I ran my hand through my hair, frantically trying to make sense of her meltdown and how to dig us out of this latest hole.

"Abbie, look at me." I didn't shout, though it was a struggle to appear calm. "Have I given you reason to doubt me?" My voice was shaking, and I swallowed, trying to clear the lump from my throat. "If you hadn't been here when I arrived…no doubt I would have eventually hooked

up with a girl or two, just like I did the last few years…
That's not to say I would have jumped into bed with every
member of the fucking cheerleading squad! Jeez, Abbie." I
took in a deep breath and turned away while my heartbeat
slowed to a more comfortable pace. I didn't want to make
things worse by losing my temper. "They aren't my
type…I have better taste…I thought you had a higher
opinion of me than that."

After a moment she placed a hand on my leg and I
turned slowly to see a flushed, but slightly calmer looking
Abbie. I took her hand in mine.

"You've nothing to worry about, Abs. I love you. I
always have," I said, pulling her into my side. "Now, are
you going to tell me what happened?" Abbie went rigid
and I sensed I'd hit a nerve; something or someone kept
unraveling her.

"I'm sorry," she whispered, "It's just…" She stood up
and stepped towards the park leading away from the
shopping mall. "I don't know what to say."

"Just tell me how you feel… I'm beyond upset at what
you went through. I can't begin to put into words how
fucking angry I get thinking about it, but I want to help.
What's going on in your head, Abs?"

"I get confused…" Abbie paced slowly along the wide
path leading through the manicured grounds of Casey

Park, her hands rammed deep into her jacket pockets. "You guys lift my spirits so much I start to think…maybe I'm…" She shook her head trying to make sense of her thoughts, "I'm comfortable with you all, but…" Abbie glanced up at me. "I don't know…it's so hard to explain."

"You're doing okay, baby…go on…"

"When I'm running…" She scanned the park as if searching for explanations hidden in the trees, "I get such a rush it makes me soar. I'm the best, I love winning. No one can touch me." I smiled at her confidence. "School's okay; I do alright with my work and get reasonable grades…" Her mood began to darken, her eyes narrowing, "I'm better when I'm alone, Jake. When I kept to myself no one bothered me; there was no pressure."

I shook my head in confusion, "What…what are you saying?" My heart accelerated and my eyes began to itch.

"I don't know…" she said quietly, shaking her head.

"Abbie…I have never…nor will I ever…love anyone as deeply as I love you. You have to believe in yourself…I believe in you." The strength of my commitment couldn't be denied.

"I understand what you're saying, Jake, I do."

"But you don't believe me!"

"I do, I'm trying, but…"

"Baby, you have to keep moving forward. You are an amazing person with so much to offer. You've come so far." I lifted my hand to cup her tear stained face, "Please don't shut me out, Abbie. I want us to be together. I don't want anyone else."

A lone tear trickled down Abbie's cheek as we stood under the canopy of red oak trees lining the pathway. I wiped it away gently and dipped my head, kissing the trail it left behind before pulling her into my chest.

"I'm sorry, I'll try harder, I promise."

"Hey…It's not about it being hard. Trust me. I'm not here to put more pressure on you. I want you to enjoy your life."

"Me too; I don't want to be like this!" She pulled out of my embrace. "It's hard though, I just don't feel whole. I haven't for years. I can't promise how long it will take, Jake," she whispered, moving her attention to kick away the crisp leaves around our feet.

"I have all the time you need, but it kills me when you push me away. You're a part of me. Don't you see that? You were the first person outside my family to show me any affection. Those months we spent together as kids were the best months of my life, until now."

As I poured out my true feelings to my beautiful girl the tears I'd held at bay trickled over and ran unashamedly down my cheeks. I sniffed and tried to turn away from her.

"Fuck!" Abbie had been through a tragic period and there I was, comparing a lonely childhood to what she'd had to endure.

"Jake? Oh my God, I'm such a bitch."

I swung round and swept her into my chest burying my face in her neck; desperately inhaling to find comfort in her scent. We clung to one another in silence, holding and soothing each other. Moments passed before I cradled her face between my hands. I lowered my mouth to hers; kissing her with such tenderness she *had* to see the truth in my words. My heart pounded in my chest, sending an ache through to my soul.

"I'm sorry," she whispered against my lips, her icy fingertips brushing the side of my cheeks.

"Hey, you're freezing," I said, swiping at my face and taking her hands in mine, blowing my warm breath onto them before kissing her fingers.

Abbie closed her eyes and smiled, "I'm fine. It's getting cold." I nodded, holding her hands.

"You don't want to grab a hot chocolate, do you?" she asked, a glimmer of contentment sparkling in her eyes.

"Yeah, that would be good," I said, pulling her close as we headed for the diner.

The warm air hit my head as we stepped inside the retro diner. Abbie's body relaxed instantly making me smile.

"I'll get the drinks. Go grab a seat. Why don't you give Jo a call and check if they're still coming." Abbie nodded and made a move towards our usual booth, pulling her cell phone from her pocket.

Joanna Johnson was an angel in my eyes. The gratitude I had for her couldn't be measured. I couldn't even begin to contemplate what the outcome would have been without her in Abbie's life.

Abbie closed her cell as I placed a steaming mug of hot chocolate on the table in front of her.

"Careful it's hot."

"Thanks," she said, stirring the frothy liquid with the spoon. "Jo's outside already."

"Hey! Jay," Callum's voice echoed, following the bell above the door.

"Speak of the devil," Abbie said, beaming at our friends. "Jeez, Joey you look as though you've just run a marathon. What's going on?"

"Nothing, just Callum being a dick!" They exchanged knowing glances before sitting down in front of us. Abbie shook her head at the pair and took a sip of her drink.

"What are you two up to?" Callum asked. He leaned against the padded bench seat and casually slung his arm across the back behind Jo.

"Not a lot, just finishing up and heading home. What about you guys?" I asked, knowing full well that Cal had made plans to take Jo to the movies later.

"Not much." The slight smirk at the side of his mouth gave him away.

"What's going on?" Abbie asked, looking confused, "Why do I feel like I'm out of the loop here guys?"

"Cal and me well we're…" Jo's face blushed somewhere between rose and scarlet, "We're, well, you know."

Abbie squealed and almost knocked me off the end of the bench as she threw herself at Jo. "Since when?" she asked, pulling Jo to her feet and dragging her off in the direction of the bathroom.

"Don't mind us." Joey giggled as very determined Abbie manhandled her through the swing doors.

Heaving a sigh of relief I took a gulp of my drink and slumped back against the seat. Callum's grin faded as he noticed my expression.

"What's the go, Jay?"

"Oh, you know…usual."

"Bad day?"

"You could say that," I said, looking over to the restroom, "I'm sure Jess has been at her again. Something's up, but she's not saying." I rubbed my face slowly out of frustration before turning my attention back to Callum.

"So… You and Jo?" He gave me a smirk and raised his eyebrows suggestively. "Man whore!" I shook my head just as Abbie and Jo appeared again.

We spent another hour giving Callum and Jo heaps before they had to leave.

"You ready, Jo?" Cal asked, looking at his watch.

"I guess. You guys sure you won't join us?"

"Nah, we're good. Wouldn't want to cramp your style," Abbie replied with a wink.

"Home?" I asked and Abbie nodded, smiling over at Jo and Cal.

"See you tomorrow, Joey."

"Night," Jo said, linking her arm through Callum's, "Don't forget we're sorting our costumes after school tomorrow for Saturday.

"Yeah, yeah," Abbie groaned. I smiled, tucking her into my side as we rounded the corner to where we'd parked the truck earlier.

"Are you running in the morning?" I asked, unlocking the truck.

"Yep. Why? You going to join me?"

"Sure. Why not?" The reappearance of a twinkle in her eyes brought a grin to my face. Fuck me, if I'd known all it would take to lift Abbie's spirits was an early morning run I'd have suggested it weeks ago.

"Not long now."

"Huh?"

"The competition. How's the training going?" I asked, trying to move her focus.

"It's going well; I'm hitting my goals and passing them most days. I'm stronger this year."

"How do you reckon you'll get on?"

"I should do well. The girls I'll be up against haven't beaten me yet." She oozed confidence; the strength in her voice filled me with pride.

"What's Coach Jackson said?"

"Yeah, he thinks it's a done deal."

"That's great. I'm so proud of you, Abs." I said, reaching over and squeezing her knee gently. She quickly placed her hand over mine.

"So you set for Saturday?" Abbie asked when we pulled into her driveway.

"Yep, all sorted. Cal's got the suits. Just need to collect the wigs from the hire shop on Saturday morning. It should be a great night." It would be an opportunity for us to enjoy a night out together before the next round of assignments and Abbie's running commitments.

"Okay, baby, I'll be here in the morning. Don't leave without me." I turned off the ignition and climbed out of the truck.

Abbie was already half way up the path when I circled my arms around her waist. I buried my nose in her neck, inhaling deeply. I longed to spend another night with her in my arms. The lake had been awesome but unfortunately we hadn't had the chance to spend the night in the same bed since then. Now visibly relaxed I turned her in my arms, dipping my head so she could reach to meet my kiss.

We maneuvered over to the porch and I leaned her against the railings. Abbie's hands traveled around my neck. The renewed urgency in our kiss had my heart pounding wildly in my chest. Her hands moved cautiously to my arms and I sensed her need to slow things down. She smiled against my lips before lowering her forehead to my chest.

"I'd better go before your mom throws a pot of water over us."

"Yep, I guess…" I sensed a slight reluctance in her as she stepped away from me. "I wish you could stay, I slept so well at the lake." Abbie frowned as if struggling with the idea of sleeping alone.

"Hey, I'll come over whenever you need me. Don't ever be scared, baby. Okay?"

Abbie nodded, "Okay."

"Please call me if you need me." It killed me that she had nightmares, and I wasn't there to comfort her. She'd mentioned her mom would be going on night shift soon and asked me if I'd stay. "Got to go," I said, kissing her again before she climbed the steps of the porch.

"Bye, Jake."

"Night, sweetheart."

Chapter Twenty-Nine

"You look frickin' hilarious, dude," Callum jibed through a huge grin as Jake paraded up and down the kitchen, sporting a pale blue, seventies style suit with a frilly shirt and wide lapels. I'd never seen trousers look more ridiculous. The wide bottoms had enough fabric for two pairs. My mouth hung open in shock at the unnatural pleasure rolling off both Callum and Jake dressed like seventies porn stars.

"That's awesome, Jake. Where's your wig?" I scanned the vast array of makeup and hair products covering the bench top. He pulled on a glossy light brown collar length wig and swung around.

"Arrggghh!" Jo roared, "Seriously?"

We all fell about in fits of laughter, prompting Cal's mom to put in an appearance.

"What do you think, Mom?" Callum asked, holding his arms up as he strutted his stuff. She gave him a wide eyed grin and shook her head. After taking a few photographs she left us, laughing under her breath.

Jo and I had straightened our hair, applied copious amounts of glitter eye shadow, highlighted our cheek bones and emphasized our mouths with a lip tingling, bright pink gloss. Sequined headbands across our foreheads provided the perfect complement to our silver and blue spandex cat suits.

"Want a drink?" Callum asked as Jo struggled to fasten her belt.

"I'll grab one please," I said while tugging Jo towards me, "Here let me help, Joey." I clipped the elastic belt at the back, "How's that?"

"Yeah, good thanks."

"Hey? What about mine?" I asked, holding up the wide elasticated belt that had an ornate butterfly buckle encrusted in glass stones on its front.

"Come here, baby, I'll do it," Jake said with a twinkle in his eye. I narrowed my eyes suspiciously as he tugged me towards him. He turned me so he could clip the belt secure before lowering his mouth to the exposed skin of my neck.

"You look gorgeous," he whispered in my ear, dropping another kiss to my flesh, his hands squeezing my hips. He slowly wrapped me in his arms from behind. I breathed in deeply, closing my eyes, savoring the contact and wishing we were alone.

"Jeez, guys, get a room will you?" Jo groaned.

I giggled and turned to face Jake, placing my hands on the lapels of his not so stylish suit jacket. He lowered his head and kissed the corner of my mouth, dropping his hands to the soft satin covering my backside.

"Later." My breath caught in my throat in response to his hushed promise.

My mom's nightshifts at work began tonight. She'd reluctantly agreed to let Jake stay as Martin was away with Howie. I think she realized it was pointless arguing; Jake would have stayed anyway.

Looking into Jake's eyes the passion was plain to see and though it scared me to death, I wanted him too. My lips parted as my breath hitched again in response to the unspoken words hanging in the air between us. Jake lifted his hand to my face and ran his thumb along my jaw. His eyes twinkled like crazy and I all but melted into a quivering mess in the middle of Callum's kitchen.

"We ready?" Jo asked, oblivious to the intimate display going on behind her.

***

The aroma of caramel apples, candied corn and apple cider drifting through the air heightened our senses as we approached the school gymnasium. The organizers had again surpassed themselves. The spectacle greeting us when we entered *The Crypt* was breath taking. The high ceiling of the gym lay hidden beneath a canopy of spiders' webs and skeletons. Artistic head stones, depicting students past and present lined the walls. Mock coffins doubled as seating areas and serving stations covered in an abundance of Halloween goodies. A variety of traditional and contemporary characters swarmed into the hall followed by our resident school rock band.

"This is fucking amazing," Jake said, taking in the scene before us, "Jeez, this has got to be the best effort I've ever seen for Halloween."

We all looked at one another doing our best to hold back the smirks and giggles. Casey students were renowned for making an effort with celebrations and tonight proved no exception.

"Come on, let's grab something to drink," Callum said, dragging Jo over to the bank of coffins on the left of The Crypt. Jake was careful to keep contact with me, his hand at the small of my back, sending tingles up my spine as we followed closely behind.

"You okay?" he asked, handing me a putrid looking, blood red punch.

I took the cup and nodded, "Yeah, I'm great."

We claimed one of the many graveside booths. Within moments I noted the arrival of two particularly unsavory characters I'd have preferred to avoid, but I was determined they'd not get the better of me tonight. I'd had enough of being victimized and belittled.

Not surprisingly Jess and Becca had on the shortest outfits imaginable under the pretext of resembling Snow White and Cinderella. Their dresses looked like old fashioned baby doll pajama sets, leaving nothing to the imagination. I rolled my eyes in disgust, bringing my attention back to my friends.

"Alright?" Jo asked discreetly.

"Yeah, I'm cool. They're not spoiling my night. Fuck that," I said loud enough that Jake and Callum heard me. Both followed the direction of my frown and shifted uncomfortably in their seats at the sight of Jess and Becca flaunting their wares on the dance floor.

After I'd told Jake and the others what had happened, they'd assured me they weren't prepared to stand by any longer while I put up with the bullying. Jake had been less than impressed and quite hurt that I'd been subjected to repeated attacks by the two of them. He was disappointed that I'd kept the full extent of my feelings on the subject hidden from him, but reluctantly accepted my reason for doing so. Still unsure of my value as a person was one thing, but taking a shitload of abuse was another.

The evening began to heat up and alongside dancing and eating, the more traditional activities such as bobbing for apples proved popular. With my face covered in sugar frosting after trying to eat a donut suspended from a string, Jake grabbed me and tried to lick it off.

"Eww, Jake...don't!" I squirmed, trying to get free from his craziness.

"Give me a break. I'm gonna vomit," sniped a less than friendly voice from behind us, "Why don't you just screw her senseless right here, Jakey? Bet the Freak would love that."

I'd reached my limit, my blood hit boiling point in a split second. Before Jake could react I'd wrestled myself free from his grip and swung around without stopping to consider where I was at. All the abusive interactions I'd suffered at the hands of Jess over the years flooded back and fueled the anger flowing through my veins. With a rush of adrenaline I let my fist fly at her face.

Chaos followed; her friends flocked to examine the damage to her nose, hidden beneath the bloodied hands now covering her face. She whimpered as they dragged her away; her friends throwing, *I don't blame you* glances over their shoulders while I stood frozen to the spot.

"What the fuck?" I whispered, silent tears trickling down my cheeks. Jake quickly pulled me into his side.

"Abbie, let's go." He, Jo and Callum quickly led me back to our booth before any of the teachers could get wind of what had happened. By the time we sat down the tremors running through my body were almost uncontrollable.

"Fuck!" I said again, a little louder this time.

Jo wiped my face, careful to preserve my well applied makeup and smiled while Jake clutched my hand.

"Hey…it's a good thing, sweetie," she said, doing her best to pacify me, "I don't think you'll get anymore shit from her."

Jo patted my arm as I looked up and saw expressions of pride mixed with concern on the faces of my friends. I took in a huge breath and exhaled slowly. I forced a thin smile and nodded, acknowledging an end to the bullying which had been a part of my school life for years.

"Jeez, you're one scary mother when your pissed, Abs," Callum said with a smirk.

"She's awesome," Jake said, squeezing my hand as my worried eyes found his. "She had it coming to her, baby. You have nothing at all to be sorry for, okay?"

I took a sip of my drink, giving my body time to recover from the shock of turning on Jess in such an uncharacteristic, violent manner.

Callum broke the tension first, "I'm starving. All the action has made me hungry."

He headed in the direction of the food before anyone had a chance to react.

"You okay?" Jake asked again. I blew out a slow measured breath before forcing a tight smile. "Dance?"

"Erm." Still shaken from punching Jess, dancing was the last thing on my mind.

"Come on, Abbie, dance with me." Jake's expression proved my undoing. I couldn't resist the puppy dog eyes for long.

"Go on then." I grinned as he pulled me up from the seating and led me towards the now crowded dance floor.

We were joined by Callum and Jo who had seemingly fallen into a seventies role play. Unable to resist the hypnotic temptation of the music our hips and arms took on a life of their own. Cal and Jake strutted about disco style and gradually the party goers began to form a circle around us as we got into the groove. The music morphed into Abba's Mamma Mia and the roar from the crowd almost lifted the roof. The euphoric sensation spreading through me was unlike anything I'd ever experienced. This friendship thing seemed to be the way to go; I'd never had this much fun.

By the end of the song the incident with Jess had all but faded and I was left in Jake's embrace. As I made a move to head back to our seats the mood of the music shifted and crept across the dance floor seeping into my very soul. Jake pulled me back into him and wrapped his arms around me.

"Just one more, baby," he whispered and I nodded. Jake turned me around to face him. He lifted my hands so that they were around his neck before resting his own on my waist. Our bodies soon molded together, mirroring the sensual rhythm of the music. The warmth in his touch and the scent of his skin through his opened shirt soaked into me like a drug, reaching every inch of my being as we moved as one. Jake held me close while he hummed along to the melody and I closed my eyes, smiling against his chest. His heart beat joined mine in time with the music. His hands ran up my back, one finding its way to my hair then round to cup my face. He brought my chin up to meet his lips, kissing me tenderly as we swayed sensually together. I stretched up to meet his lips and he responded, pulling me closer, wrapping his arms tightly around me. When he ended the kiss he buried his face in my neck and inhaled deeply.

"I love you," he whispered, squeezing me even tighter.

I brought my hands to the sides of his face and leaned away so I could see his eyes. The raw emotion there blew me away, "I love you too."

He smiled and held me close until the song faded.

Taking my hand he weaved between the many costumed party goers now filling the dance floor. Jo and Callum were deep in conversation when we reached them. Still numb from the intimate moment Jake and I had just shared, the blush crept across my cheeks, serving as an embarrassing indicator of where my mind was at and Jake winked at me knowingly.

The rest of the night passed in a blur. The highlight of the evening was a wicked limbo competition which Callum and Jake insisted on entering even though they had no chance of winning. They both stood over six feet tall and spent the majority of their recreation time throwing their weight around on the football field. An obvious lack of flexibility hindered their progress but the sight of them bending over backwards to pass under the bar was the funniest thing we'd seen all night. After more dancing we agreed to meet up for coffee in the diner in the morning and headed outside to the pre-booked cab.

"Night, guys," we both called as Jo and Cal waved when we dropped them off. I sighed, leaning into Jake's shoulder and he stroked my arm as the cab driver did a U-turn and made his way to my house. To say I was nervous was an understatement. The butterflies using my stomach as a flight path had me gripping the edge of Jake's suit jacket as he skimmed his hand intermittently across my arm. Jeez, we weren't even home yet and I was a wreck.

"Hey…" Jake said, leaning down to kiss the top of my head, "We're gonna be fine. I promise."

Something about his tone of voice helped ease my nerves. We hadn't discussed tonight. I guess with where our relationship stood and our already passionate public displays of intimacy; taking the next step seemed inevitable. Whether we would be ready when it came down to it concerned me. My biggest fear was that I'd back out at the last minute and leave Jake hanging.

I chewed my lip nervously and remained silent.

"Abbie?"

"Hmm." I lifted my eyes to his briefly.

"We don't have to do anything, baby, okay?" he whispered.

I swallowed the sudden, overwhelming sense of disappointment at Jake's words and kept my eyes firmly on his, "But…I want to."

Chapter Thirty

We backed into my bedroom locked in a tight embrace, Jake's lips firmly attached to mine. I kicked off my ridiculous platform shoes and struggled to free Jake from his jacket. His hands came clumsily to my face as he deepened our kiss, the taste of him exploding into my mouth. I grabbed at his shoulders trying to rid him of more layers.

"Too many," I whispered against his mouth and he pulled away his eyes searching mine.

"What, baby?"

"Too many clothes." I smiled and lifted my hands to the buttons of his shirt. He quickly grabbed the top two and then stepped back so that he could pull the garment forwards over his head.

I fumbled with the belt around my middle and grew increasingly frustrated at my attempt to remove it.

"Arrggh!"

"Hey…Abbie…it's okay." Jake placed his hands on the top of my arms before turning me around so he could remove the belt he'd earlier secured. He placed it on the cabinet next to my bed before sitting down to remove his shoes.

"These outfits are fucking crazy. There's no way I'm going to get this damn thing off on my own," I said, blushing at my predicament.

"Come here, I'll do it." Jake did his best not to laugh.

How the hell girls had managed to dress and undress themselves in the seventies was beyond me. I swept my hair over one shoulder, enabling Jake to unfasten the small hook at the back of my top. He slid the zipper down to where it ended at my lower back, but instead of removing my top, he stopped.

"Turn around," he whispered. I did, careful not to uncover myself too much just yet. I swallowed nervously and waited for Jake's next move. I placed my hand subconsciously over my heart in an attempt to keep it from crashing out of my chest, looking anywhere but at Jake. Sensing my nervousness he raised his fingertips to my chin, tilting it until I made eye contact. He placed his hand over mine and moved it to where his heart pumped violently as well.

"I'm nervous too."

I felt a sudden urge to go to the bathroom, "Jake I...I need to pee."

"Jeez, Abbie, how to kill the moment." He laughed. "Go on, I'll use Martin's bathroom."

I was relieved to hear his laughter. My life had changed immeasurably over the last month. He'd almost mended a broken soul and now I was ready to love him completely.

I closed the bathroom door, grateful for a minute to gather my thoughts and prepare myself. I moved towards the sink and carefully removed the many layers of makeup. I brushed my teeth and ran a brush through my hair, undressed and pulled on a stretch cotton camisole top and panties from the pile of clean laundry in the corner. My heart rate picked up a notch as nervous tension rumbled inside me.

"Hey," I said climbing into bed, wriggling over to where Jake lay propped up on his side.

"Hey," he replied as I leaned into him and kissed his slightly parted lips. I lifted my fingers to his cheek as I ran the tip of my tongue the length of his bottom lip. Hearing a moan escape from his mouth; I looked up to see his eyes had darkened slightly. He seemed in two minds about something. I smiled, tracing his lip with my index finger as Jake's eyes searched mine. For the first time in my life I knew without uncertainty what I wanted.

"Jake..."

"Mmm?"

"Would you please make love to me?"

"Are you sure you're…" I placed a finger to his lips.

"Please."

Jake let out a steadying breath as he stroked his knuckles along my jaw. The hunger in his eyes was unmistakable as he gently lowered us both to the pillow.

"We don't have to do this…we can wait." Jake gently stroked my hair from my face.

"I want you, Jake," I whispered as he continued to caress the skin of my jaw and neck with the flat of his hand. He lowered his mouth to the junction between my neck and my shoulder, running his tongue over the pulse point. I inhaled at the unexpected sensation deep in my stomach which in turn ignited a pathway downwards.

"You taste so good," he said, dropping kisses along my shoulder and back up along my jaw. Jake's fingers found the edge of my top and slipped underneath, skimming the naked flesh of my waist. I lifted my hand to pull him closer, deepening our kiss.

He gripped my waist gently and moved his hand upward; I gasped loudly as he cupped the soft mound of my breast. My hands ran over his shoulders and down his back, pulling him as close as I could. The heat stirring in my stomach, becoming more intense as the moments passed. Our breathing grew heavier; I could feel Jake's heart pounding against my chest as our mouths and hands continued to arouse each other's senses.

"You feel so good," Jake whispered in my ear as his hand moved over my thigh and round to gently squeeze my bottom.

My hands slipped slowly down his back; my fingers dipping inside the back of his shorts and over his butt. The muscles tensed under my touch and I smiled against his mouth.

"Oh fuck," he whispered and I squeezed some more. Keeping one hand on his butt I moved my other back to his neck, gripping the hair at the back of his head, wanting him closer.

"Please, Jake…" Jake inhaled before lowering his lips to my throat. I struggled to hold on to any sense of control.

"You okay?" Jake asked, breathing heavily. I nodded, not trusting my voice and grinned up at him. "You sure?" His eyes reflected the deep love I had for him.

"Yes," I whispered and ran my palm across the defined muscles of his chest, down to his side and towards his form fitting shorts. He closed his eyes as my hand grazed the top of his underwear.

"Oh, Abbie," he said breathlessly, grinding his body into mine. Jake lifted me up, pausing briefly with his hand at my bottom, "Can I?" he asked, wanting my permission to get me naked. I nodded cautiously. He sensed my uncertainty and removed his hand immediately.

"No...Don't stop...I want this Jake," I said, taking hold of his hand and guiding it back to my panties, "Help me..." I bent my knees, lifting my butt a touch and without further encouragement Jake slowly pulled my pants down the length of my legs before removing his as well. Placing a hand at my hip he leaned down and kissed me with such tenderness, the nervousness threatening to halt our progress melted away. As Jake's tongue slowly caressed mine I became aware of his hands slowly easing my top up towards my shoulders.

"I think...we can lose this as well," he whispered between breaths and I leaned up towards him so that he could pull the cami over my head. With his hand splayed across my lower back he then carefully lowered me to the bed. I closed my eyes and automatically covered myself.

"Hey...don't..." Jake said, placing a gentle hand on mine, moving it to my side, "You're beautiful, Abbie...Don't ever hide." I smiled shyly as his eyes skimmed my figure. "You're stunning," Jake whispered against my lips while taking in every inch of my naked body with his tender touch; his fingers, holding and caressing, moving to my shoulder and down to my breast.

With a touch so light I barely noticed it, his thumb skimmed across my nipple.

"Oh, God." I groaned at the affect his touch had on the sensitive flesh and Jake kissed me again, his hand cupping my face.

"So beautiful." He grinned and pressed his mouth to mine, easing his tongue into my mouth with such tenderness the embers between my legs suddenly burst into flames; our bodies melding with a love deeper than I'd ever imagined. "Stunning," he said after a moment, smiling with admiration as he brought his eyes back to mine.

"Thank you…" I whispered, a tear forming at the corner of my eye.

Jake lifted his hand and used his thumb to wipe it away before dipping his head to kiss the corner of the same eye. My stomach came alive with the million butterflies at the inevitability of this moment, promised since the day we met. I placed my hands on his waist, my eyes asking more than my words were able; Jake sensed my need and his hunger reflected mine.

The heat between my legs became unbearable. Jake continued to arouse my senses. He found my breast again, but this time lingered, kneading it gently before lowering his mouth, suckling urgently.

"Oh, Jake," I whispered, "Please…" His hand inched towards my inner thigh; his thumb edging closer to my most intimate part. I closed my eyes, my heart racing with the anticipation of what was about to happen. Jake continued to devour every inch of my body, but his hand at my thigh grew more urgent and needy. His palm rested at my apex, his fingers dipping into the heat; causing my breath to hitch violently in my throat. "Ah!" I gasped, "Fuck…"

I opened my eyes to see Jake smiling down at me in awe, "Do you like that?" he asked as his fingers continued to work their magic.

"Mmm," I managed as I arched my back to meet his touch, my eyes wide. His thumb continued to circle my sensitive spot. "Can I…can I touch you?" I asked breathlessly.

"Baby, you can do what…ever…you please…" Jake's mouth came to my neck as I slowly moved my fingers down his stomach pausing briefly before taking him nervously in my palm. His eyes closed and he took a huge gasp of air as I tightened my grip. "Aww…mmm…that's so good," Jake moaned as I began to move my hand slowly up and down his length, feeling his pulse through my fingers.

"Is that okay? Am I doing it right?" I asked, uncertain of what to do next.

"That's…per-fect."

We continued to touch and explore one another, our surroundings disappearing as we became one; pulses and breathing synchronized.

"Oh, Jake…"

"Abbie…oh, God…" Jake groaned breathlessly as I pulled and pushed my hand all the way down.

"Jake, please…"

Jake's swift movement brought him above me. He hovered momentarily, his body trembling before lowering himself down and easing forward into me. I gasped at the tenderness of his movement.

"Okay?" Jake waited for me to open my eyes. I nodded, though my eyes pooled with tears. "I'm sorry, baby… Slowly okay?" I nodded again and he stroked my cheek before kissing me softly.

Not taking his eyes from mine he began to move. With shaking hands I gripped his arms as he filled me more with each careful movement. His hand caressed my cheek as his mouth consumed mine, our passion, buried for so long, building with every sweep of our tongues. I reveled in the feel of his naked flesh beneath my fingers; his back rippling with every move, fueling a burning fever only he could extinguish.

I lifted my hips to meet his and soon we moved together effortlessly. Every nerve in my body ignited as Jake increased the tempo. I lost my grip on reality; wrapping my legs around him desperately trying to get even closer.

Our eyes locked as I loved him from the inside out. I threw my head back at the budding fiery sensation deep inside me.

"Oh, fuck...what's happening?"

"It's okay...let it go..." Jake encouraged as his hips slowed to a sensual pace. I became lost to the animalistic beast growing within me.

"Oh, Jake... Oh God!"

He kissed and sucked at my shoulder as his hands gripped my bottom while he continued to plunge vigorously into me, "Come on, baby...that's it..."

Gripping him tightly around his waist with my legs, I pushed myself down onto to him as he came into me one more time. I grabbed onto his ass tightly as my insides erupted and he sent me soaring.

"Ahhhhhhh! Oh, Jake!" Tears spilled from my eyes as Jake pushed even further, holding still as he pulsed his release deep inside me.

"Fuckkkkk!" Jake cradled my face between his hands, resting his forehead against mine; both of us completely overcome with the emotion of our love making.

After a while he carefully eased off me but kept his hand at my cheek, his thumb running down the length of my jaw. He leaned towards me, covering my trembling lips with his. Our breathing eventually calmed and our pulse returned to normal. I opened my eyes and met his gaze.

"Thank you," he whispered as a tear trickled down his cheek.

"Hey…why are you crying?" I placed a gentle hand to his chest.

He swiped at the tear and shook his head before answering, "I've never felt like that before… I didn't know it could be like that."

"Me neither," I leaned into his shoulder and kissed his neck softly, "I love you so much, Jake."

Jake wrapped his arms around me and kissed the top of my head, "I love you more."

Chapter Thirty-One

The clattering downstairs roused my interest, making me smile as I stretched out my sore limbs. *What's he doing?* I quickly ran to the bathroom, cleaned my teeth and pulled on a loose T-shirt before following the sounds coming from the kitchen.

The sight of Jake's rippling muscles as he busied himself at the bench aroused more than my hunger for breakfast. I leaned against the door frame for a moment, taking in the delicious sight before me. His naked back, broad and tanned, his perfect ass just covered by loose fitting jeans, down to his bare feet. *Oh my!*

I caught my lower lip between my teeth and sneaked up behind him. I snaked my arms around his waist, nuzzling up close to the spot between his shoulder blades.

"Hey! You're awake," Jake groaned, "I had a surprise for you." The flexing of the muscles of his chest under my hands had me inhaling deeply.

Jake turned carefully around in my arms. He lowered his head just enough for me to reach his sexy as hell lips. He pressed his mouth to mine, stroking my cheek with his thumb. "Morning, beautiful," he whispered, "Did you sleep well?"

"Mmm I did...thank you." I smiled shyly, another blush creeping up my neck.

"I thought you'd enjoy breakfast in bed." He sounded a little disappointed.

"We could...take it back upstairs...if you like..." The thought of any further physical contact with Jake had my mind spiraling and he noticed the shift in my body language.

"Yeah?" A cheeky smirk played with the corner of his mouth. I reached my arms up and around his neck as the throbbing need in me took over my desire for food. Pulling him back to my hungry mouth I nipped at his slightly swollen lower lip, running the tip of my tongue along its edge. Almost immediately, I found myself in his arms, my legs wrapped around his waist and his hands at my bottom, heading towards the stairs.

"Jake, you'll fall!" I giggled uncontrollably as he reached my room.

"I already have," he said, giving me a wink as he navigated the stairs. In moments I found myself being lowered to the same crisp sheets of our first intimate encounter.

"Mmm," I groaned as Jake's mouth pressed against the naked flesh between my shoulder and my throat. In that moment my stomach lost all desire for food, switching to a more passionate hunger as the tingles of a more lustful need spread through my body; fueling the inevitability of a second round.

Jake pulled away from me and searched my face. I smiled up at him, my lips parted slightly and my bottom lip snagged between my teeth as I caught a glimpse of hunger flash in his eyes. He placed the palm of his hand to my cheek and moved it slowly down, pausing briefly at the pulse point of my neck before resting it against my throat. He caressed my super sensitive flesh without taking his eyes from mine for a second. I thought I'd burst into flames right there. My fingers gripped the back of his hair and pulled his mouth towards mine.

"I can't believe you're mine," he growled before clamping his mouth over my parted lips. The taste of him exploded across my tongue and penetrated my soul as I arched my body up to meet the intimate caresses of his free hand.

Our remaining clothing quickly ceased to be a barrier as Jake responded to my moans of pleasure. Wrapping me in every inch of him we made slow, tender love; savoring the newly awakened pleasure of joining together completely. I became aware of Jake's fingers drifting gently up and down my spine as he dropped kisses to my shoulder.

"Mmm, that's so nice," I whispered, smiling peacefully as my eyes fluttered open, "I must have fallen asleep...sorry."

"That you did," Jake said against my bare flesh.

"I could lay here with you all day. Do we have to get up?"

"Not if you don't want to." His hand came to rest on the small of my back.

I rolled over and gazed up into Jakes beautiful eyes. Confusion trickled into the moment as I contemplated how I had landed this amazing guy.

Noting my shift in mood he brought his hand to my cheek, "You okay?" I nodded, smiling as I lifted my head from the pillow and leaned my mouth to the corner of his lips. Holding still, I closed my eyes and allowed myself to be grateful for the moment. Jake brought his hand to the back of my head, holding me steady and returned my kiss.

"I love you, Abbie," he whispered and I soaked up the moment; I'd never tire of hearing those words. "What do you want to do today?" he asked, leaning up onto one elbow while he casually traced his fingers up and down my arm.

"Didn't we say we'd meet up with Jo and Cal?"

"Hmm."

"What's that?" I laughed at his less than enthusiastic response.

"Can't we make some excuse and see them later or tomorrow or something?"

"Jake!"

"Well it's not like I wake up with my girlfriend every day after having the hottest sex ever. Then have the chance to spend all day together as well," he said with a massive grin across his face.

"Oh my God, Jake, you did not just say that." I covered my face, trying to hide my blush. Jake jumped on top of me immediately, sitting astride my waist and grabbed my hands, pinning them above my head in one of his. He was careful not to rest his weight on me but instead of a kiss, which is what I'd expected, he proceeded to tickle me like he used to as a kid.

"Arrgghh, Jake! No please! Don't…Jake…seriously, I need the bathroom!"

The expression of mock horror across his face made me snort with laughter as he jumped clear.

"You're a monster chick, Abbie James."

***

"How did you get on at the party, sweetheart?" my mom asked when Jake dropped me home just before dinner.

Thoughts of us making mad, passionate love sprung into my mind and my face flushed another variation of bright pink. Fortunately Mom was too busy to notice.

"It was awesome! You should have seen the gym. They renamed it *The Crypt* for the night. Jake and Callum tried the limbo. Jeez, they were funny."

I remembered my run in with Jess at that point and had a sudden urge to head up stairs to my room to avoid any further discussion about the party.

"I'm gonna go shower before dinner, okay?"

"Sure, honey. Good idea," she agreed before turning to face me. "How was Jake?"

Shit, so much for a quick exit, stage left.

"Erm, yeah. He's cool," I said, glancing at my mom on the way out of the kitchen. She had an, *I know what you've been up to* look on her face and I couldn't get out of there fast enough.

"Please be mindful, Abbie…it's all too easy to forget yourself. I'm too young to be a grandma just yet."

Seriously? She did not just go there! Oh my fucking God!

"Mom!"

"I don't care, Abbie. You aren't a little girl any more. These things happen. Just be safe, okay?"

"Okayyyy!" I was out of there.

***

The next few days followed a rigid routine of early morning training before school with Jake tagging along. We spent our evenings after school hanging out with Callum and Jo at the diner before heading home for homework and dinner. My mom left for work around nine each night and not long after that Jake arrived, even though Martin was back from Howie's.

Sleeping with Jake had quickly become a wonderful addiction. The comfort I found in his arms and the dreamless sleep left me invigorated. I couldn't believe how my life had turned around so remarkably.

Friday arrived and along with it...winter. The race was text book perfect. I led from the front and still had enough in the tank to kick away from the pack on the home straight. After crossing the finish line I leaned forward with my hands on my knees, breathing heavily as a marshal draped a foil blanket over my spent frame. The pride emanating from Coach Jackson had me grinning widely. He'd predicted that I'd smash it and I was happy in the knowledge that it had been a comfortable win.

"Guess who's going to State?" I announced as I walked into the diner.

"Really?" Cal replied with surprise.

Jo smacked him hard on the chest before turning back to me, "That's great news Abbie, but I'm not surprised."

"Where's Jake?" I asked, frowning at the absence of my boyfriend.

"Right here," he said, wrapping his arms around me from behind, "How did you get on?"

"Won by a mile."

"That's fantastic, Abs. State next?" I nodded and took a seat facing Jo in our usual booth.

"Then two weeks after that will be Regionals if I get through."

"You will," Jo said, passing me a drink.

"Hey, you seen much of Jess this week, Abs?" Callum asked, slurping on his soda.

My stomach dropped at the random mention of her name. I hadn't been up close and personal with either Jess or Becca since Saturday.

"No." I lowered my head as the festering guilt of punching Jess took hold again.

"You do know you broke her fucking nose?" The look of utter pride on Callum's face astonished me. Maybe it *was* the case that the abused become abusers? I swallowed the lump forming in my throat. Jake sensed my discomfort and placed a hand across my shoulders.

"So you think humiliating someone in public is okay? That's awful Callum. It's not something I'm proud of you know?" I said, lowering my gaze to the glass of soda on the table in front of me.

"Yeah, well, she deserved it in my book. I hate bullies," Jo muttered and forced a tight smile as I looked up at her.

"No one deserves that shit, Jo. Fuck!" I pushed myself away from the table and slammed through the door of the diner. My heart pounded against my ribs as I fought to hold back the tears of anger threatening to burst forth. I don't know how long I stood alone outside until Callum joined me.

"Hey… I'm sorry, Abs. I didn't think. Fuck, I'm such a dumb ass. I just reacted. Jess has torn you apart for years, Abbie. You're my friend, I didn't think about anything else…any of the other shit… Sorry," he said, placing a hand gently on my upper arm, "I'm sorry if I upset you."

"You didn't." I let out the breath I'd been holding, "I know you all care. It's just a bit soon. That's all."

Cal nodded, "Yeah, I know." He put his arm around my shoulder and we headed back inside. Jake's face looked pained when he lifted his gaze at the sound of the door opening. What I'd been through affected him too, but being with him and having these great friends had helped me heaps.

"I'm fine… It's all good. Don't look so worried."

He smiled and pulled me into his lap kissing me on my cheek, "You sure?"

I nodded, "Sure."

"Tell us about the race, Abbie. What happened? I wanna hear how you kicked ass," Jo said, grinning at the two of us.

***

I glanced at the clock before locking the back door then crossed the kitchen to grab a drink. My mom and Pam were going to the theater and staying in some fancy hotel. Jake's mom had arranged a family dinner with an old friend; some vet that Jake's dad knew from way back; a great opportunity to get a valuable insight into the life in the day of a veterinarian. He'd invited me, but I really didn't feel up to socializing with strangers and he understood. Instead he'd promised to come over as soon as dinner was finished. I'd given him a key in case I was already in bed when he arrived.

I grabbed the throw from the back of the sofa and snuggled into the cushions to watch a movie. I didn't want to go to bed until Jake arrived. I hated being in the house alone; it always freaked me out. As the opening credits moved up the screen I settled down and pulled the throw up to my chin. Try as I may, I couldn't keep my eyes open and soon fell into a restless sleep.

My dream was punctuated with visuals from the week's events. Halloween costumes merged with my victory in cross country. Jo and Callum joking around at the diner and pictures of Jake flickered before me like the pages in a photo album. Reminders of times gone by lulled me into a restful sleep as his smile accompanied the memory of his gentle caresses this morning. I watched as my dream moved in a more sinister direction. A familiar panic rose in my stomach as Jake's face and touch morphed into the one from my worst nightmares. My heartbeat quickened as an acrid taste filled my mouth.

"Please don't…No…Please don't…please…" I whimpered, trying to escape him.

Sleazing towards me, Peter's hands came to my shoulders and he leaned in to…

"Abbie! Abbie!"

I could hear Jake's voice, but I couldn't see him. I searched the room frantically, but he was nowhere to be seen. Peter gripped my shoulders and sneered, his eyes full of contempt and lust. His breath crawled into my nostrils and I tried to scream, but his hand covered my mouth. I couldn't breathe.

"Abbie! Wake up, baby."

Yanked from the vicious scene I flew upright on the sofa my heart beating violently in my chest as the tears from my dream poured down my cheeks. My hands clawed at my throat and chest in an attempt to rid his touch from my body.

Jake's face came into focus and I threw myself into his arms, "Oh God!" My body trembled as Jake wrapped me in a tight embrace, pressing his mouth to my neck.

"Hey…Abbie, it's okay," he said, his touch soothing; calming the panic threatening to hold my body captive.

"Just a dream, just a dream," I murmured, resting my chin on Jake's shoulder, trying to bring myself down. Jake hadn't seen the effects of one of my dreams before and I knew he'd be upset. "I'm fine," I whispered, forcing a tight smile as I eased myself back from him, "I'm okay."

He placed his hands to the sides of my face and rested his forehead against mine, "My God, Abbie. Fuck!"

"I'm okay." I leaned forward and kissed him lightly. "I'm okay, Jake." Visibly shaken by what he'd just encountered Jake pulled me into his side, his heart still racing as I snuggled up to him on the sofa.

Chapter Thirty-Two

"But it's so hard to see you like that," Jake said, sitting on the edge of the bed running his hands through his hair. I frowned at the distraught expression on his face. He looked tired; I realized he probably hadn't slept much last night. I knelt down on the floor in front of him and rested my hand on his knee.

"Listen to me, Jake," I said, pulling his hands down from his head before he had no hair left, "I know that you don't want to hear this, but... yes, I *have* nightmares... and no, they aren't great, I hate having them... but for now, that's just the way it is. You being here with me helps heaps. I've not had a bad one for ages so yeah... it's getting better." Jake's eyes searched mine. "You're strong, Jake. Don't fall apart on me now." I forced a tight smile as I held the palm of my hand to his face, "I've been dreaming for years, it's no big deal. Honest."

Jake pulled me into his arms and squeezed me so tight I thought I'd pass out. Breathing in deeply, his hold on me relaxed and he eased away a touch, tipping my chin upward.

"Sorry," he said, leaning forward and kissing me softly.

"That's okay," I whispered.

"So, are you going to tell me about your dinner date with Mr. Vet man or do I have to tickle it out of you?" I said as I pushed him back on the bed and sat astride his legs.

Jake moved so fast I gasped as he flipped me over. In a split second I found myself lying beneath him, my hands braced at his chest.

"Not fair, you're stronger than me," I said, panting at the sudden rush of adrenalin flowing through me.

"And faster?" he asked, smirking. I nodded reluctantly. "And hot?"

My lips parted at his random search for a compliment and my heartbeat picked up its tempo. In my eyes, his hotness was not in question. Jake sensed the shift and grinning widely at my flushed cheeks, he pressed his lips firmly to mine. I returned his kiss gladly and ran my hands down his back before gripping the belt loops of his jeans.

"If I don't stop right now this is going to end badly," he whispered against my mouth as we heard Martin clattering about outside my bedroom.

I giggled and pushed him off me, "You better get up then, Mr. Ashton because I'd love nothing better."

Jake groaned, moving reluctantly away from me, "You're killing me, Abbie." I laughed at the frustrated expression on his face. He slumped against the pillows, throwing his forearm across his eyes.

"I'm killing *you*?" I continued to dress, bending to pick up my sneakers. Jake caught me off guard and hauled me up into his arms. I squealed at the random attack and tried to wriggle free.

"Don't tease me, baby," he whispered at my neck, "You might regret it."

"You guys coming out of there today or what?" Martin shouted through the closed door as he walked past my room. I giggled at my brother's observation. It was true, Jake and I could quite happily spend the day in bed, but I had plans.

"I'm meeting Joey in an hour, Jake, let go of me." He feigned hurt, making me pout, "Aww is Jakey wakey gonna miss his girlfriend while she goes shopping?" I asked, fully expecting some form of retaliation for mocking him.

"Jeez, you're cruel," Jake said in defeat as he dropped his arms to his sides, but I didn't miss the twinkle in his eyes and leaned up to kiss him briefly on the cheek before slipping into my shoes.

***

"This is hopeless, Joey," I said as we trailed out of the second boutique, "I'm just not cut out for all this girlie shit."

After trying on yet another rack of cocktail dresses and not finding one that looked as though it belonged on me my mood was slipping. My eighteenth birthday had produced the unwanted pressure of having to find a dress of all things. I'd have settled on a new pair of jeans and sneakers, but Mom had flatly refused. She'd told me if I didn't get sorted I would have to wear one of hers. The churning sensation in my stomach wasn't helping and I longed for a break.

"Want to grab a soda?" Jo suggested sympathetically, noticing my waning enthusiasm.

"Could we?"

Jo nodded and grinned widely, "Sure. Don't worry, you'll find one today. If it's the last thing I do." I frowned at the determination in Jo's voice and groaned at the idea of being in the mall, shopping for God knows how much longer for a fucking dress. Jo had already convinced me to purchase a pair of killer black, high heeled shoes. How the hell I'd be able to walk in them let alone dance, I had no clue.

"These are ridiculous," I said, pulling one of the shoes from the bag, "The heel makes me nervous."

"They're awesome *and*…They will go with any dress you end up buying, providing of course you stick with sexy and black." Jo wriggled her eyebrows suggestively at me. I couldn't help but dissolve into fits of laughter at the thought of us both wobbling into the party wearing four inch heels and figure hugging cocktail dresses. We'd be laughed out of the place.

"Whatever," I said, putting the shoe away and shoving my drinking straw into my mouth before I said something that would upset Jo. Her excitement for dresses and make up bordered on manic and made me cringe.

"So…how's it going with you and Jake?" she asked after we'd exhausted *shop talk*. We hadn't really had much chance to catch up since the lake, what with school and her new relationship with Cal.

"Yeah, it's going great," I said, unable to keep the twinkle from my eye as I thought about Jake.

"Great?" she asked, "And?"

"What?"

"You know? How great?" she asked, doing her best not to fall apart in the middle of the diner.

"You're asking me if he's a good fuck?" I asked my eyes wide.

"Well…is he?"

"Jo!"

"I'll take that as a yes then," she said, a satisfied smirk pasted across her face as she pushed her chair away from the table, "Come on let's get you a *Fuck Me Dress*."

I stared open mouthed after Jo as she left me sitting in the middle of the busy diner. *She didn't just say that?*

***

"That one is stunning, Abs," Jo said, her eyes twinkling as I turned slowly in front of the full length mirror in the third boutique of the day.

I'd already tried on at least a dozen cocktail dresses. I stared at my reflection in the mirror at the black strapless chiffon dress that skimmed across my hips and ended mid-thigh. The beading crossing over one breast down to the waist subtly pulled the eye to the sexy sweetheart neckline. The Grecian heels complimented the look perfectly with their diamante straps. I couldn't help but imagine what Jake would think.

"I love it," I whispered. Jo's grin lit up her face as I took in the detail at the front of the dress and turned to look over my shoulder, examining the back. "Do you think…"

"I do…he'll totally die when he sees you in it." Jo's eyes glowed with appreciation, "You look hot."

"Really?"

"Yeah…really. It's perfect," she said, grinning widely.

I wasn't sure. I'd never owned anything like it. Jeez, it was rare I was seen out of my jeans and hoodies. This was unfamiliar territory for me. I had to say though, Jo was right; I did look hot and I wanted to buy this dress.

"Okay," I said, nodding cautiously, my bottom lip clamped firmly between my teeth, "I'll get it."

"Yay!" Jo squealed, bouncing up and down.

"Come on. Let's pay and get out of here."

***

The dress was safely hung inside my wardrobe and the shoes tucked away in their box when I heard a knock at my bedroom door.

"Yep?"

I turned to see Jake grinning at me from round the door frame, "Hey!"

"What you doing here?"

"Charming," he said, faking hurt.

"I didn't mean it that way." I slipped my arms around his waist, "I just wasn't expecting you until later."

"Yeah, well, football finished and I wanted to talk to you." I narrowed my eyes and my stomach flipped at the possibilities behind his serious tone. Jake noticed and pulled me to the edge of the bed where he took a seat.

"What is it?" I asked, doing my best not to let the wobble into my voice.

"I have to go away," he said carefully, not taking his eyes off me for a second, "I have an interview for university."

What the... "Is that all?" I said, my voice so full of relief I could almost see it swirling around the two of us. I let out the breath I'd been holding and gave him a huge smile. "That's great news, Jake, I'm so happy for you."

"Really?" he said, "Because I'll have to go away for three or four days." The thought of Jake being away for any length of time made my heart drop into my stomach, but if he had any chance of achieving his dream, of becoming a vet, he would have to go to uni. I swallowed at the idea of not seeing him for four days.

"That's okay," I whispered, not trusting my voice and giving him a smile of encouragement, "When?"

"Erm...two weeks on Thursday."

"Okay." My heart raced at the thought of him being away, but I knew he wanted this. He'd worked so hard to get to this point.

He nodded and heaved a sigh of relief, "I can't believe it's finally happening. It's been my dream for that long." Jake lay back on my bed with his hands behind his head. He turned his head towards me, his eyes searching mine. Pride bubbled inside me and I reached over, placing a hand on his cheek.

"I'm so proud of you, Jake." He hauled me on top of him and reached a hand behind my head, pulling my mouth to his. Jake rolled me onto my back and swept my hair from my face as he continued to drop kisses to every part of my face.

"You're amazing, do you know that?"

"What do you mean?" I asked between giggles.

"I don't know anyone as strong as you, Abbie."

I breathed out slowly as the serious tone in his voice drained the humor from the moment and left me considering everything that had happened over the last month. We'd come a long way I guess. Our eyes fixed on one another and I could see Jake trying to work out what was going through my mind.

"Stop over analyzing," he said, kissing me lightly. "Now… Did you get a dress?" I blushed at the image of myself in the little black dress and heels. Noticing the sudden scarlet cast to my cheeks he leaned back. "What? Did you get one or not?"

"I got one."

"And?"

"You'll have to wait and see," I said, chewing my lip.

"Oh yeah?"

"Abbie?" my mom shouted from downstairs, "Is Jake staying for dinner?"

Jake dropped his head to my shoulder, grinning at my mom's interruption. Mom had a reputation for her timing and this was no exception.

"Do you want to stay?"

"Can I stay all night?" he asked, raising an eyebrow. My breath caught in my throat and I swallowed at the butterflies suddenly launching in my stomach.

"Can you?"

"If you want me to," he said, running his thumb along my lip. I nodded and blushed again making him smile.

"Yes please, Mom," I shouted. "I have training early though. Is that okay?"

"I'll come with you."

"Okay." I laughed.

Jake rested his forehead against mine. "What's for dinner?" he asked as his stomach growled.

"Jeez, you boys and your appetites."

Chapter Thirty-Three

"So you got everything?" Mom asked for the hundredth time since breakfast. Today marked the end of a rigid training regime when hopefully all my preparation would pay off at the state cross country championships. Jake sat at the bench, grinning behind his coffee while Mom flitted around the kitchen in a state of maternal nervousness.

"Yes, Mom."

"You've got your registration paper?"

"Yes, Mom."

"What about a change of clothes for after?"

"I have everything, Mom."

"Okay, well...good luck, honey. I'm sorry I can't be there." She gave me a hug of encouragement.

"It's okay, I understand. There won't be many parents."

"You ready, Abs?" Jake asked, grabbing our bags from the floor near the kitchen door, "Time to go."

"See you tonight, Mom. Thanks for breakfast."

"Good luck, sweetheart!"

My churning stomach emphasized the enormity of the challenge I was about to undertake, but I'd prepared well.

I'd already finished the race a dozen times in my head, each with the same outcome, victory.

"How you doing?" Jake asked as we neared school.

"I'm okay. I'm ready," I said, smiling over at him.

"That's cool," Jake turned off the ignition and leaned over to give me a kiss, "I'll be thinking about you, baby."

"Me too. Thanks," I said, placing my hand to the side of his face as his mouth covered mine.

A loud banging on the truck window had us gasping for breath.

"Hey! Get a room why don't you?" Callum shouted, laughing so loud everyone passing by had a pretty good idea what he'd interrupted.

"God you're *so* funny, Cal," I said as I climbed out of the truck.

"I know. It's my calling," he said with a smirk.

"Listen, guys, I know you've got more important shit to deal with today than what's happening over the weekend, but we're going out tomorrow night and wondered whether you wanted to come along." Jo found it almost impossible to contain her excitement. Jake appeared happy with the idea.

"Sure, where are we going?" I asked.

"We've booked a table at Don's," she said, a huge grin on her face, "I thought it would be ace to celebrate your win and also Jake getting his interview."

"I haven't even been offered a place yet," Jake said.

"And I haven't won."

"Yeah, yeah, technicalities," she said, shaking her head, "Dad offered to take us. We can grab a cab home."

I loved Don's Italian restaurant; I'd been a few times with Mom and Martin on special occasions in the past and always enjoyed the meal. A warm wave of emotion flowed up from my stomach as I soaked in the moment.

"Okay so… Good Luck. Break a leg. Whatever it is we're supposed to say," Jo said, doing her best to encourage me as only she could. She gave me a hug which was followed by a quick rub on the head from Callum before Jake slung an arm across my shoulders.

"Thanks, guys. See you later."

"Right. This is it," Jake said, walking with me to the gym. I nodded and my stomach flipped with excitement. "Good luck, baby." Jake kissed me, "Enjoy it, yeah?"

"I will. See you later." I turned towards the gym door just as Coach Jackson appeared.

"Hey, Abs… You ready, girl?"

"Sure am, Coach."

***

The hum of anticipation at the starting line ran like an electrical current through the competitors. We all pushed and shoved for prime position. My stomach tingled with excitement as I leant forward ready and focused, waiting for the starter's gun.

On the crack of the gun we surged forward en masse. I focused on not ending up boxed in. If I kept up with the front runners it would allow my strong finish to guarantee me a decent finishing position.

On rounding the first bend clear ground opened up before us. I estimated at this point I was about tenth. Not wanting to get swamped by the rest of the field I made a decision to kick up a gear to get clear of the field. I'd happily sit behind a couple of runners for the majority of the race, but equally, I'd be happy to lead from the front if the situation arose. I just needed to have the option to do either.

On settling into my rhythm I began to plan my next move. The strong and steady beat of my heart drove me forward. My breathing remained smooth and controlled. My body ran like a machine; well-oiled and prepared for its debut at state level. The confidence I'd gained and the condition I'd developed over the last month began to pay off. I eased into third position as we ran up a muddy incline through a wooded area. As I approached the half way mark adrenaline pumped through my entire system and all negative thoughts disappeared. All I could see was the end result.

I am going to win. I am the state champion.

With this new mantra flowing freely in my mind I smiled and kicked up another notch like changing gear in a rally car. The uneven terrain proved difficult to navigate, but benefited my preparation. The running round the lake had been great training as this course had similar features, but wasn't quite as far.

I felt a sudden firm push in my back as we came over the brow of the hill and stumbled slightly to the side almost losing balance, but I managed to pull it back. Strategic cheating was to be expected. Marshals were stationed along the routes of all cross country meets, but they couldn't catch all under-handed behavior. Unfortunately it was common to lose a race because of bad sportsmanship. Coach Jackson's training sessions had given me the tools to avoid those types of situations.

With about a mile to go I decided to hit the front. After working so hard I wouldn't risk losing this because of a crowding issue or being intentionally pushed out of contention.

Accelerating came naturally to me; I'd been working on my sprint finish as well as stamina. I kicked it up a notch and sensed the gap between the rest of the field and me widening. Careful of my footing, I held the pace steady and remained focused. Only half a mile to go; my heart pounded in my ears, the cold air burning the back of my throat as I sped home. The end of the course was lined with cones and I entered the last section clear of the field.

Final sprint!

With the end in sight I hit the accelerator and pushed myself to my limit. *This is mine. I've got it.* As I crossed the finish a huge sense of achievement as well as overwhelming exhaustion swept through me. The mammoth effort had clearly taken its toll on my body and I slumped to the ground covering my eyes with my arm. I lay in the dirt gasping for breath, but with a huge sense of happiness and relief. An official approached me with a foil blanket just as Coach Jackson appeared at my side.

"Abbie! That was amazing, girl," he shouted, "Fantastic race. What a finish!"

I struggled for enough breath to respond to his enthusiasm, "Th-thanks." I said, still panting.

After cooling down and making sure to stretch we made our way to the presentation area. As my name was called, the competitors and their supporters all cheered. Instead of being nervous and awkward I actually enjoyed the moment; it marked yet another step forward. My confidence continued to increase on an almost daily basis; I liked the new me.

"So…what do you have on for the weekend, Abbie?" Coach asked as we drove back to school.

"Oh, you know…usual stuff. Except I'm going out with friends for a meal tomorrow night at Don's, so that's something different."

"Sounds good. You deserve it. You did great out there, Abbie. Now make sure you take the weekend off. No training at all. Okay?"

"Okay," I said, happy for a break. My body had hit its limit for one day.

"Then we'll hit it hard on Monday. So no morning run before school Monday either, right?"

"Right." I smiled at the seriousness in his tone.

"You may well smirk, but you can go all the way if your preparation is right."

"Okay, I'll do my best." I looked out the window as we neared Casey. I couldn't wait to break the news about the race to my friends.

After the forty minute drive we pulled into the school parking lot. Coach Jackson wished me a great weekend before heading inside to finish up for the day. Lessons were still in session so I strolled over to Jake's truck and sat on the hood. I stuck my ear plugs into my ears and turned up the volume on my MP3. With about ten minutes before the bell I found myself lying back on the hood, closing my eyes and relaxing as my latest mix swirled around my head.

The next thing I became aware of was someone removing my music from my ears and kissing me lightly on the lips.

"Hey, beautiful," Jake said with the widest grin, "I hear you may be a star of the future."

"You heard correct," I said, blushing at his assessment of my win.

"That's great, baby, I never doubted you." He said, pulling me from the truck and into his arms.

"Diner?" I asked.

"Of course, my treat."

***

After my usual Saturday of window shopping with Jo I was now faced with the unenviable task of dressing for a night out. I had no clue what to wear. *Pants and top or dress?*

I showered quickly and wrapped my hair in a towel. My wardrobe consisted mainly of jeans, T-shirts and hoodies, but I did have a couple of items for more formal occasions, though they didn't get an outing very often. In the end I decided on a pair of tight black pants and a long, flattering cashmere sweater in pale gray. I pulled the outfit from the closet and laid it on my bed. It took no time to dry and straighten my hair and to apply a little mascara and lip gloss. I pulled on a pair of ankle boots, grabbed my purse and headed downstairs to wait for the others.

"You look nice, Abbie," Mom said as I sat on the sofa.

"Thanks. I wasn't really sure what to wear."

"Well, you did good."

"Thanks, Mom," I said as a car horn sounded outside, "That'll be David. I'll see you tomorrow."

"Be careful!"

"I will," I shouted on my way out of the door.

"Hi, guys," I said, climbing into the back of the SUV, "Thanks, David."

"No problem, Abbie." Jake pulled me over to his side as I sat next to him.

"Hey, beautiful," he whispered in my ear making me blush. His hand ran appreciatively down my back before coming to rest at my waist.

"Hey. You look good," I said, smiling widely, noting his black jeans and snug, black V neck T-shirt under his leather jacket. *Very nice in fact!*

"You okay after yesterday, Abs?" Jo asked, pulling my train of thought from Jake's great dress sense.

"Yeah not too bad; a bit stiff, that's all."

"That's easily remedied," Callum said with a smirk, earning him an elbow in the ribs from Joey.

David pulled up outside Don's and turned to us, "Okay, kids. Now, you're sure you're good to get home?"

"We'll be fine, Dad. I booked a cab." He nodded and waved before driving off, leaving us to clamber inside out of the cold.

Our table was towards the back of the bistro and had already been laid out for four with a basket of fresh bread and jug of iced water. The atmosphere at Don's had a ranch feel to it; the aromas of seared steaks and mouthwatering sides filled the air around us making my stomach growl in anticipation of the treats to come.

"Jeez, I'm starved," Callum said, looking at the menu.

"Yeah, I'm pretty hungry too," Jake agreed.

They weren't the only ones. Jo and I usually had big appetites. I certainly wouldn't have any trouble polishing off a steak and salad tonight. My body needed refueling after the battering I'd taken at cross country yesterday.

Laughter and delicious food filled our evening; from steaks to sharing jokes, my insides ached by the end of the night. My friends insisted on hearing a blow by blow account of my win and I gladly filled them in with every miniscule detail. Jake then spoke about his ideas for his presentation at his interview. He usually kept college talk to a minimum so his expertise had us all gaping by the time he'd done. After packing the last inch of our stomachs with pudding we all decided enough fun had been had for one night.

"Tired?" Jake asked as we climbed into the cab.

"Yeah, I guess so," I said, stifling a yawn.

"Any plans for tomorrow?" Jo asked.

"Nope, I'm resting all day. It's gonna be a full on two weeks leading up to Regionals and then my eighteenth. I think I'll take a break from life tomorrow," I said as another yawn took hold.

"Fair point," Jo said, giving me a massive hug as the cab pulled up outside Callum's house. "See you Monday then, Abs."

"Yeah. Thanks for the invite tonight. It's been great," I said as she closed the cab door behind Cal.

Cuddling up to Jake once we climbed into bed was the best end to a brilliant day. I took in a deep breath as I maneuvered my aching body over onto my side.

"You still sore?" Jake asked, squeezing my shoulder.

"Yeah, a bit…my calves mainly."

"Have you got any muscle rub?" Jake asked, climbing off the bed.

"Yeah. It'll be downstairs in the medical box in the kitchen though." Jake winked at me before heading down to get tub of magic relief from the kitchen. By the time he returned with the rub I'd already flipped onto my stomach and moved over to the edge of the bed.

"Oh…you want *me* to ease your discomfort then?" I turned to look at a very smug Jake and put on my most pathetic expression.

"Yes please."

"Jeez, call yourself an athlete. What you gonna be like after the next round?"

"Heyyy," I said, swiping at his chest as he kneeled on the floor next to me. Jake scraped a good dollop of the gel into his hand. I tensed in anticipation of the cold gel hitting the warm flesh of my aching calves.

"Here goes," he said and I could definitely detect a smirk in his voice.

"Arrgghh! Fuck that's cold."

"Seriously?"

"Yeah," I said, relaxing slightly under his touch. Jake's fingers moved carefully over my right calf. He used his thumb to press firmly into the muscle; pushing the gel into the tightness radiating through my lower leg. The sudden increase in pressure caused me to wince. "Fuck!"

"Sorry, baby, but it'll feel better for it later."

"You sure about that?" I asked, throwing Jake a glare over my shoulder, "Fuck!"

Jake continued to work on my calf, ignoring my squirming and complaints. Once he'd done with my right leg he repeated the whole process on my left. I drifted into semi-consciousness as he worked his magic on my tired limbs.

The sound of running water in my bathroom roused me from my near sleep state. Jake climbed back into bed beside me and wrapped me in his arms.

"Better?"

"Uh huh," I said, snuggling into his side, "Sorry, Jake, I'm really tired."

"Yeah…me too." He pressed a kiss to my head. "Night, baby."

"Night."

Chapter Thirty-Four

I saw Callum first, leaning against the gate outside the office.

"No Jake yet?" I asked as I perched on the low wall beside him.

"Not yet, he said something about going to the library after lunch."

"I thought he'd be finished by now." I frowned at the thought of Jake having spent the whole afternoon in the library on his interview prep, "I'll go see if he's ready." Discomfort bubbled in my stomach every time I brought Jake's departure to mind. I'd had trouble thinking about anything but Jake for the last three days.

I crept into the vast library, scanning the reading area for Jake. I found him in the medical section, fully engrossed in the journal in front of him.

"Hey, you," I whispered into his ear as I leaned over his shoulder, kissing his cheek.

"Hey. What you doing here?" Jake asked, surprised to see me, "What time is it?"

"It's late," I said, sitting on the vacant chair next to him. "You've been in here hours."

"Sorry. I didn't realize."

"Have you finished?"

"Yep, I'm done," he said, closing the book. I strolled towards the exit while Jake took the medical journal back to the shelf.

Jake grinned as he approached me, "So… You gonna miss me, baby?" He leaned his arms on the wall either side of my head.

"You know I will." I pulled him down by his shirt and planted a kiss on his lips.

"I'll be back before you've even noticed," he said, resting his forehead against mine. I raised my eyebrows questioning his statement. "Well…maybe not, but I will be back on Monday morning."

"I want you to do well, Jake," I said, struggling to keep my emotions in check.

"I'll do my best… Come here," he said, pulling me close and kissing the top of my head. He slung an arm across my shoulder as we headed over to the truck.

"So… Are you ready?"

"I guess I'm as ready as I'll ever be."

"What about your presentation? Have you finished it?"

"Yeah. I'm happy with it."

Jake's interview comprised of a presentation which he would deliver to the committee and the other candidates tomorrow; Saturday was his formal interview. Tours around the campus and the opportunity to ask current students about life at college were scheduled for Sunday. It sounded nerve wracking to me but then again, anything that involved selling myself terrified me.

"What time you leaving?" I asked as we took our usual seats near Cal and Jo in the busy diner.

"After dinner, my Dad reckons we can be there in three hours. He's booked us into a motel close to St. Mark's. That way I'll get a decent sleep and fresh start in the morning ready for the presentation." As Jake spoke a familiar nervousness crept into my stomach. My mind drifted back to a time when he hadn't been around. I chewed my lip anxiously and toyed with my coffee as Jo and Callum soaked up his every word.

"I can't believe you're going to St. Mark's, Jake. It's such a great opportunity." Jo voice was full of admiration, "Hey, Abbie?"

"Huh? Oh, yeah. It's great," I said, doing my best to show Jake some support and encouragement.

"You okay?" Jake whispered, placing a hand on my knee under the bench so he didn't draw any unnecessary attention.

I took in a deep breath, "Yeah, I'm fine...honest. Just ignore me, I'm being ridiculous." I said, rolling my eyes.

"It's not ridiculous. I'm gonna miss you just as much," Jake said, dragging me towards him before turning back to our friends.

***

Jake's departure came too soon. It was hard to believe that only a month ago I hadn't really given a shit about anything. Now here I stood in the arms of the most important person in my life; he wouldn't be around for three whole days and I was gutted. Jake smiled down at me and lifted his hand to cup my cheek. He lowered his mouth to mine and kissed me gently.

"See you Monday," he said quietly as his dad made his presence known by banging about in the garage.

"Yeah, good luck, Jakey," I said with a wink and he kissed me again, hugging me close before pulling away. He climbed into the front of his dad's car and wound his window down.

"Text me," he shouted as they rounded the corner of the driveway.

I stood rooted to the spot for a moment, feeling cold and alone.

***

"Mom, I'm home," I shouted, dropping my bag at the side of the front door and heading into the living room.

"Hi, love," Mom said, "Did Jake get away okay?"

"Yep."

"Listen, sweetheart, can you keep Saturday free this weekend?"

"Erm, I don't see why not. How come?"

"I thought it would be nice to have dinner to celebrate your success. Also, I had a call from an old friend. She'll be in the neighborhood for the night so I've invited her to join us." I frowned at the idea of spending an evening with an old acquaintance of Mom's, but to be honest I didn't really care either way.

"Sure… Erm, I might go to bed if that's alright."

"Okay, love. Sleep tight."

"Night."

Still battling the need for sleep I pulled the covers back on my double bed and perched on the edge, resting my chin on my knees. Two hours had passed since Jake left; already the empty space in my chest ached. Thank goodness for running club and pointless family dinners. At least I'd be able to pacify my ridiculously obsessive brain until Jake came home.

Mine and Jake's relationship had brought out hidden depths in my personality. I'd finally stood up to Jess and Becca. I'd become a permanent member of a friendship group. My relationship with Mom had taken a turn for the better. I'd won the state cross country championship. I had the best boyfriend in the world and obsessive or not we definitely had a positive influence on each other.

My new train of thought brought a smile to my face as I eased under the covers. Just as I reached to turn off my lamp my phone buzzed an incoming text.

You still up, baby?

Only just! I replied, half asleep.

Wish I was with you!

You are!

After a moment my phone rang, Jake's face lighting up the screen. I smiled, hitting answer.

"Hey. What you doing calling at this time of night? Your dad will think you're bonkers. Where are you?"

"We're about an hour away. Dad's just pulled over for fuel so I thought I'd check on you." I detected an unfamiliar edge to his voice.

"Are you okay, Jake?"

"I…I hate leaving you," he said sadly, "I'm stronger around you. I don't know whether I can do this."

"Hey…you're the smartest person I know. Don't you dare lose your edge," I said frantically, "I'd never forgive myself if you ended up blowing your chances because of me." Panic rose through my body as I registered the enormity of Jake's words. I could hear him breathing at the other end of the phone, but he remained quiet. "Jake? You can do this, I know you can. If you can do what you've done for me in the last month this will be a piece of cake."

Resorting to blackmail wasn't fair, but he needed a kick up the ass. I would not be held responsible for wrecking his future. "If you blow this, Jake I will never forgive myself," I said, getting emotional.

"You're right, I'll be fine. I won't blow it. Just wanted to hear your voice. It's hard that's all. You're the only person who has ever believed in my dream and wanted me to be happy. Dad keeps going on about how much money I'll be earning and how I compare to his army colleagues' kids, but keeps hinting about the scholarships available through the reserves as well. It's not about my happiness for him. I'm a trophy, that's all."

"Oh, Jake…I'm so sorry," I said quietly. He needed me as much as I needed him. Fate had brought us together ten years ago and eventually ensured that our paths crossed again.

"I love you, Abbie."

I heard his dad mutter something about Jake being on his phone again.

"I love you more. I'll call you tomorrow night." I said quickly.

"Kay, bye." Jake hung up and I lay back in bed. His family was almost as screwed up as mine. I wished I could stifle the uneasiness doing its best to infiltrate my subconscious mind.

Three days! Jeez, what could happen in a weekend?

***

Mom went to work as normal on Friday night and left Martin and me to fend for ourselves. We'd decided to grab a takeout and watch a movie. Mom and Dad working long hours had forced us to get along and sort out our differences pretty well from a young age.

"Did Mom tell you about tomorrow?"

"Yeah…I guess we haven't eaten together for a while," he said, shoving half a slice of pizza into his mouth.

"I suppose. I'd rather it was just us though. I mean…who wants to sit through dinner making small talk with a stranger?"

"It won't be that bad. I'll be there!"

"Ha ha. That's so comforting Martin."

I'd offered to prepare lasagna as Mom was working. Apart from meeting Jo at the mall it wasn't as though my social calendar was overflowing.

With the credits rolling and my stomach stuffed I was ready for bed. I really wanted to speak to Jake before he went to sleep. "I'm off, night, Mart."

"Yeah, night. Don't be up all night talking to lover boy now will you?" I picked up a cushion from the sofa and lobbed it at his face, but he ducked easily, laughing loudly as I blushed in response to his observation.

"Hmm. Night, Martin."

Are you awake? I text, hopping onto my bed. Moments later the phone rang.

"Hey, baby. How are you?" Jake asked, sounding happier.

"I'm good, thanks. What about you? How was your presentation?"

"Yeah, it went well. They seemed satisfied so that's good. I'm glad it's over." He sounded relieved. "How about you? What's on for the weekend?"

"Oh you know…not much really. My mom's arranged a family dinner for tomorrow and invited an old friend along. Fucking typical if you ask me."

"Why? It'll be good for you all to spend time together for a change."

"Yeah, but what about her friend? If you were here we'd be able to make our excuses and go out somewhere after," I said, huffing loudly.

"Abbie, it will be fine. It's only dinner," Jake said logically, "I'm glad I have my uses by the way."

"You know I didn't mean it like that. Anyway, I'm cooking, so it's your loss."

"I'll make you a deal. Whatever the outcome next Friday, I'll cook dinner for you at my place." Jake said.

"Seriously?"

"Yeah… Don't sound so surprised. I'm pretty hot in the kitchen," Jake said and I was quick to detect the double meaning in his words.

"Yeah, yeah. Don't go getting ahead of yourself. Jeez, you're cocky," I said, laughing down the phone.

"Listen, baby, I'm going to have to go. I've got a really early start tomorrow."

"Okay… What time's your interview?"

"I'm up first. It's alphabetical."

"Figures. You'll do great. I'll call you tomorrow night. If dinner doesn't finish me off," I said, grinning.

"Okay, baby. Speak to you then. I love you, Abbie."

"Love you too. Bye."

I sank into my bed, comfortable in the knowledge that Jake would do well tomorrow and I had a full schedule to fill the entire day. Sleep took me over pretty quickly with dreams of reunions, hugs and kisses carrying me through the night.

***

"Abbie! Are you up?" My mom could wake the dead with her voice after a nightshift.

"Yeah," I groaned. I looked at the clock and saw it was already ten. "Fuck!" I had lasagna to prepare before I met Jo in the mall. Tradition had it that whoever got there first chose where we ate lunch. I flew out of bed and into the shower. I decided to prepare the sauce for the lasagna this morning and assemble it later when I got back.

Martin was of course already filling his face when I walked into the kitchen.

"Why didn't you wake me?" I asked, frowning at the mountain of bacon and eggs in front of him.

"You were out cold, Abs."

"Hmm, I guess. Didn't have anything to do with not wanting to share your breakfast with me then?" I asked, smirking at him.

"I'm hurt that you would think such a thing," he said, clutching his chest.

"Well I need a clear kitchen right now if I'm gonna get dinner prepared before I meet Joey at the mall, so clear off, guzzler."

"Okay, okay," he said, picking up his plate and heading into the living room.

It didn't take me long to chop, stir and simmer my way to a complete meat sauce. I covered it with a lid and turned off the heat before heading back upstairs to wash up and grab my purse. I had thirty minutes to get to the mall and to text Jake.

Hey hope ur okay love u.

Within seconds my cell beeped with a return text…

All good, baby, love u more. Call u later.

"Hey," Jo shouted, interrupting my daydreaming.

We spent an hour browsing in all the usual stores before heading to Jo's favorite burger bar.

"Mom told me about your visitor coming from out of state. That'll be nice," Jo said as we tucked into our burgers.

"Yeah, I guess."

"Has Jake called?"

"Yeah. We spoke last night. He said the presentation went well and that everyone seemed happy. He was nervous about his interview though."

"Is he missing you?"

"I guess," I said, looking down.

"You're blushing!"

"Yeah well, this relationship lark is all new to me. I don't really know what to expect. It's weird not having him around though."

"Well you've got one hell of a week coming up. Jake will be back on Monday, so that's a late night. Regionals on Friday means a week of training your ass off with Coach Jackson and then Partayyy!"

"Yep, that's one way to put it."

"Will Jake be done with his interview yet?" Jo asked.

"Yeah."

"He already text you didn't he?"

"Yep."

"Jeez! Must be love," she said, grinning. "I'm pleased for you, Abbie. You deserve to be happy."

"Thanks. What you up to tonight?" I asked, finishing off my soda.

"Home alone with Cal. Mom and Dad are going to some anniversary dinner and Howie's at the game."

"So Callum's babysitting?" Jo laughed and picked up her drink.

"Listen Joey, I'm sorry but I'm gonna have to cut it short today."

"That's okay, I've got a hot date anyway," she said, wriggling her eyebrows.

"I'll catch you later," I said, picking up the new running shorts I'd purchased.

"See you, Abs. Have a good night. I'll text you."

Chapter Thirty-Five

"Jeez, Mom, anyone would think royalty were coming to dinner," I said, rolling my eyes in exasperation.

"I'll have you know, young lady, three of us live here and it's about time you guys pitched in with the housework a little. I don't need to have dinner guests to have a clean and tidy home thank you very much."

Sorry I spoke!

The aroma of garlic filled the air as I opened the oven door to inspect the food bubbling inside. Happy with the appearance of the lasagna, I lifted it carefully and placed it on the bench top. Mom was busy finishing off the salad and Martin had his hands full of glasses as the front doorbell rang.

"Can you get that, Abbie?" Mom said as she took the salad through to the dining room.

"Sure." I couldn't say I was too comfortable greeting Mom's friend, but at least it would all be over in an hour or two.

I plastered my most cheerful smile on my face, unlocked the door and pulled it open, stepping forward to greet her. I froze.

Please no! My heart smashed against my ribs and my breath caught against the boulder sized lump barricading my throat as my terrifying past flooded back to the here and now. I was conscious of a hand on my shoulder as I stared at the two faces in front of me. The lady's mouth was moving, but all I could hear was the banging of my pulse, pounding like a bass drum inside my head as I took in the image of the man, leering at me from behind his wife. Overcome with fear, a violent urge to throw up seized me.

"God it's so great to see you both. You have no idea," My mom said as she eased me out of the way so our guests were able to come inside.

I stood paralyzed as Mom accompanied Jillian and Peter through to our living room. The most unbearable terror coursed through my veins like a drug burning away my soul. My brain started spinning inside my skull and I pressed my hands against the wall to stop me from falling.

No, no, no…! This isn't happening! Please, God!

My body was shaking uncontrollably on the inside while my face remained expressionless. I didn't know what to do. The shock of seeing him had quite literally taken away my ability to process anything rationally. Mom still had no idea what had happened and as a consequence was oblivious as to how this visit would affect me.

The monster from my nightmares was here in my home. He was back in my life. The bile rose in the back of my throat and I swallowed frantically trying to get a grip on my completely trashed nerves.

Jake what do I do?

Okay!

Calm down!

Breathe!

Fuck me, Jake why aren't you here?

I took a couple of desperate breaths and pressed the heels of my palms to my eyes for a second, trying frantically to work out what I should to do. My chest ached with the pounding of my heart, making it difficult for me to think. I needed to focus quickly; I had to make a move.

Turning towards the door I placed my clammy palm on the handle, struggling to close it. I sucked in another breath, blowing it out slowly before turning back towards the living room. I was a quivering mess and unless I wanted the whole thing with Peter to come out with my family tonight I had to get a grip, now.

Two hours! Two hours!

I forced a tight smile despite my insides turning into a gelatinous mess when Jillian turned to face me, "So, Abbie, you're quite a star! I was just saying, it's a good job you found your talent in cross country or we would never have tracked you down." I frowned with confusion. What was she saying exactly?

"Erm, how so?" I asked quietly.

"I'm on the committee at JCCA. So when you qualified for a spot in next week's regional championship I saw your name and thought it might be you. I was so excited to get home and call your mom."

"Well I'm really glad you did. It's so good to see you, both of you," Mom said, looking between the two of them.

What? It's my fault he's here? Peter fucking Stevens was here because of my running; the thing I did... to help me forget? Anger ignited in my stomach as I absorbed this latest information.

"I hope you're both hungry. Abbie has prepared a great dinner for us," my mom said, gesturing towards the dining room.

"I'm hungry enough to eat anything, especially if young Abbie here has prepared it for me," Peter said, his voice dripping with hidden meaning, causing me to clamp down firmly on my bottom lip. His eyes bored into me with every word that spilled from his foul mouth.

"Erm, help me with the food, Martin, will you?" I needed an escape route; I didn't know how long I'd be able to keep a lid on my fear. Mom and Martin couldn't know. Jeez, Martin would flip. It would kill my mom. Fuck this was bad. This was really bad.

Jake, where are you when I need you?

"What's the go with you all of a sudden? Fuck, Abbie, Mom's been looking forward to seeing Jillian all week. You're not gonna throw a tantrum on her just because Jake's away are you? Jeez, you can be selfish," Martin said, frowning at my astounded expression.

"How the fuck did this all get turned around on me?" I asked, glaring at him, "I am not having a tantrum. I just think she should have told us who was coming…that's all."

"What difference does it make? They knew us years ago. I don't even remember them. That's how important this shit is. Get a grip, Abbie. It's always about you."

"Whatever! Think what you like. I'll eat then I'm leaving. Fuck this circus. Mom can have her catch up. I'm done."

We collected the dishes and headed into the dining room where our so called guests were already seated. Martin placed the lasagna in the center of the table before taking a seat facing Peter, leaving a seat for me opposite Jillian. I swallowed and took in another deep breath, still fuming from Martin's completely misguided interpretation of my jittery behavior.

Mom began dishing out the lasagna, "Martin, can you pass the salad please?" With sweaty palms I took the meals from my mom; the sudden urge to spit on Peter's gripped me as I quickly handed it to Martin. I hated who I'd become because of this man. The bastard had wrecked my childhood and now had the nerve to show up again. *This is fucked.*

"This is wonderful, Abbie. You're not only talented on the track, but in the kitchen as well," Jillian said, smiling at me as she took another mouthful.

I tried as best I could to avoid eye contact with her husband. However the evil undercurrent in the room had me transfixed. I felt terrifyingly connected with him, like he had some sick power over me.

"Thanks," I said quietly.

"I bet there's nothing you can't do when you put your mind to it, Abbie," Peter said, giving me an all knowing evil smile. I trembled with fear as his words opened the vault of memories I'd tried to keep locked and hidden away.

"So how are your three getting along?" Mom asked and I had to admit I was keen to hear news of Claire.

"The boys flew the nest years ago. Both off, doing their own thing...that's boys for you. Claire...well, she's away at college. She moved in with her boyfriend a year or so ago. We don't see much of her," Jillian said, looking down at her food. I couldn't help but detect a little regret and slight upset in her voice.

"You going to college, Abbie?" she asked after a moment.

"Erm, I'm not sure yet, maybe."

"Yeah, depends on whether her boyfriend gets in at St Mark's or not hey, Abs?" Martin said, grinning at me. I shook my head at his ignorance; he really didn't have a clue.

"Boyfriend, hey? Well you are growing into a very attractive young lady," Peter said suggestively, looking over at my mom. "I bet the boys are beating down the door." Mom smiled, lapping up the compliment as though it was directed at her. My stomach lurched at the looks passing between Mom and Peter at my expense. *Jeez, this is getting sicker by the minute.* My mind began drifting to less pleasant memories.

"Abbie...? Abbie? Goodness, girl, what's got into you? Jillian just asked you a question," I heard my mom say, breaking me from the memory, playing with horrific clarity in my head.

"Erm, s-sorry. I erm…what was that?"

"I was just asking what you enjoyed at school, other than sport?" Jillian asked for what was apparently the second time.

"Oh, erm…I don't mind most subjects." I said, hoping the conversation would move along to someone else.

"Yes, I remember you being a bright young thing all those years ago," Peter said, smirking at me as he spoke.

"I bet you do," I muttered and I noticed he paused briefly before biting into another mouthful of his dinner. *Hmm you didn't like that, hey, you fucker?*

The conversation continued back and forth. My growing distress and sense of vulnerability was agonizing, causing my leg to shake violently under the table.

"Jeez, Abbie, sit still," Martin said, huffing, "The whole floor is shaking." I caught the haunting grin Peter threw at me in response to Martin's comment and my heart dropped. He'd recognized my fear and loved it. He grew in stature at the realization he still had an effect on me. I looked away quickly, my hand shaking as I lifted my glass to my mouth.

"Okay you two, let's clear away these dishes. Anyone for dessert?" Mom asked cheerfully as I blinked away the horrid memory thrusting its way into my mind uninvited.

Martin and I began moving plates and glasses through to the kitchen to make way for the next course and coffees.

"Here let me give you a hand," Peter said, placing a hand on my arm. The bolt of repulsion that shot through me as he made contact with my bare flesh almost dropped me to my knees.

"No!" I gasped, yanking my arm away from him, "I mean, s-sorry I can manage." Martin missed the interaction as he'd gone to get the coffee, but Mom looked up briefly from her conversation with Jillian. I scuttled away to the kitchen and threw the plates into the sink before grabbing onto the bench top. I closed my eyes, my breathing labored as tears pooled in my eyes.

"Would you pour, Martin?" I heard Mom ask. I had about thirty seconds to pull myself together before dessert.

"You sure you don't want any help in there, angel?"

Oh My God!

I can't do this...

Fuck!

I quickly grabbed the bowl flew back to the dining room. No way was I risking him getting me on my own. I placed the dessert on the dining table and took my seat near Mom. I looked at her chatting happily to her long lost friend. Here she was, catching up with the source of my fucked up life as though nothing had changed. Here I was ten years on and no closer to being able to move forward with my life.

It's just the same as before.

Peter's here.

Jake's gone.

Nothing's changed.

I cast a glance around the gathering. Martin was slumped in his chair, stuffing his face with spoonful after spoonful of sickly sweet dessert. Mom and Jill sipped coffee and drifted off to talk of days gone by. Peter leaned back in his seat surveying the scene before him; an air of superiority and deception evident in every sleazy move and glance. The shivers running through my body were painful. I'd been holding myself rigid for over an hour and couldn't bear it any longer. I had to get out.

"Shall we head into the living room where it's more comfortable," Mom asked just as I thought I'd lost the plot completely.

Here's my chance. "Mom, would you mind if I headed over to Jo's? She's on her own tonight. I told her I'd ask after dinner." The sudden inspiration I'd summoned from deep within had my insides dancing in silent celebration as I waited for her reply.

"Well...I guess we're done here. Just make sure you say goodbye please before you leave. Okay?"

I nodded enthusiastically, "Okay. Thanks, Mom." I quickly ran upstairs to grab an overnight bag; I didn't even know if I'd go to Jo's house. I dropped my bag near the front door and stuck my head into the living room. "I'm off out now...erm...nice to see you, Jill," I said, frowning as I noticed Peter wasn't in the room.

"Oh, okay, Abbie. It's been lovely seeing you again. Don't be a stranger hey? You're welcome any time, sweetheart," Jill said, giving me a friendly if not hesitant hug. I swallowed, scanning the room for Peter.

"You going somewhere, angel?" he said, skulking up behind me. The air supply was suddenly sucked from my lungs as he pulled me into a claustrophobic embrace. My entire being, flipped to another dimension; the ground, spiraling away from me as I became a nine-year-old again.

"I thought I'd have longer with you. Never mind. Keep in touch," he said as his filthy mouth lingered repulsively at my cheek and his gnarly hands fingered my waist. My stomach lurched with revulsion as I struggled to push him away.

"Night, Mom!" was all I could summon as I fled from the hallway.

"Night, love," Mom called.

I grappled with the car keys, struggling to get the key in the ignition. The fire of pent up anxiety and fear burned in my chest as I pulled the car off the driveway. Tears streamed down my face, making it difficult to see where I was going. I headed towards the freeway as the heavens opened.

My hands shook violently on the steering wheel as I swiped at the tears, trying to clear my vision. My heart pounded in my chest and my stomach heaved painfully. *He touched me! He kissed me!* I smashed my hand against the wheel in disgust.

"Arrgghh!" My fear morphed into anger as I coursed down the road leading to the freeway in the pouring rain.

"He's not wrecking me again! No way! Fuck you, Peter! Fuck! You!"

Just at that same moment the glare of headlights coming towards me hit me full in the face causing me to swerve. I fought against the wheel, losing control as the tires hit the wet gravel and pulled me towards the barrier at the side of the road.

"Arrgghh!" I braced myself against the steering wheel, waiting for the impact. The back end of the car swung towards the barrier as the front wheels gripped at the ground. The noise of the brakes deafened me and time slowed to a crawl as I fought to avoid damage and injury.

"Please no...please no...please no!"

With a whip the back of the car righted itself, but not in time to miss the barrier. The impact was harsh and threw my head to the side, wrenching my neck violently. My face collided with the window to the side of me; sending excruciating pain through my head as the car came to a standstill.

The vomit that had threatened all night was about to make an appearance. I threw the door open and hauled myself clear of the car in time to empty my stomach at the side of the now deserted road. The throbbing at my temple and the ache in my neck had me gripping my head in my hands. I slumped onto the ground, fumbling in my pocket for my cell phone and hit call when I came to Jo's number.

"Hi, Abs, what's up? How was dinner?" Jo asked chirpily.

"Jo...I need you... Car crash... Can't drive." My stomach lurched again as the pain in my head grew worse.

"Oh my God, Abbie! Where are you?"

"I... Erm... Jackson's Road. I don't feel too good, Joey."

"Okay, sweetie, stay on the line we're coming," Jo said calmly, "Listen Abs, Cal's going to call an ambulance, just in case. Okay?"

"Okay." I leaned against the car. My stomach lurched and I threw up again. *Fuck!*

I wasn't sure how long I'd been there when I heard the sound of a car approaching. The crunch of gravel was the next thing I became aware of as Joey ran towards me.

"Hey, sweetie…how you doing?" Jo rubbed my arm. I smiled weakly at her. "Abbie? She's not saying anything Cal," Jo screamed frantically, "Where's the fucking ambulance?"

After a while the sound of distant sirens broke into my thoughts followed moments later by a barrage of strangers moving me from the ground while asking questions that confused the hell out of me.

"She's going into shock. We need to get an IV in."

"We'll be right behind you, Abs," I heard Jo shout from somewhere.

"This will sting a bit, Abbie," someone said before I finally shut down.

Chapter Thirty-Six

"Jake, what do you think about getting away straight after the tour tomorrow and being home for dinner?" Dad asked wistfully, folding a sweater and placing it in his bag.

"Sounds good," I said with a huge grin, happy I'd be seeing Abbie before Monday after all. I'd missed her far more than I ever thought possible. Abbie had become an integral part of me over the last month and it had been hard saying goodbye on Thursday.

It took no time at all to gather up the few clothes I'd worn and throw them into my bag as I mulled over the events of the last two days. My presentation had been well received and today's interview, although nerve wracking had not been too unpleasant. The panel was more than fair; asking questions about my interests, aspirations, skills, beliefs and why I wanted to attend St. Mark's.

I'd just settled down to watch the movie that Dad had selected from the cable menu when my phone vibrated in my back pocket. It was a bit earlier than expected, but I smiled at the chance of catching up on Abbie's news. Flipping the cover I was surprised to see Cal's smirk pasted across the screen.

"Hey, Cal, what's up?"

"Jake, listen, man… It's Abs…she…"

My heart dropped ten feet. "What about, Abbie?" I bolted out of the chair, sending it crashing into the wall behind me.

"She's been in a car accident, Jay." A stabbing pain seared my chest on hearing Callum's words.

"No, she can't have, she's at home with her mom. She…she wasn't going out!" I laughed nervously and the hairs on my neck stood to attention as shivers ran down my spine.

Abbie's hurt!

Car accident!

No, no, no…

She can't be!

"No you've made a mistake…she can't have…"

"Jake… They've taken her to the hospital. She lost consciousness as the paramedics arrived. But listen…they said she'd be okay, she's in good hands," Callum explained, "She's gonna be okay, Jay."

My rational brain spiraled out of control. All I could see in my mind was Abbie hurt, she'd been in a car accident and I wasn't there with her.

"Where did they take her?" I asked, swiping angrily at a stray tear.

"Jake? What's happened?" Dad asked, getting up from the sofa. I held my hand up to him so I could hear Callum.

"She's at Casey Hospital."

"Did you see her?" I asked, running a hand through my hair.

"Yeah, we saw her. She asked where you were, Jay. We thought you should know. Abbie rang Jo from the accident. Jo said she sounded confused as fuck."

In that split second I decided to go to her. Panic rumbled through me like a freight train running out of track. I physically ached with the thought of losing here when I'd only just found her again.

"I'm coming. When she wakes up tell her I'm on my way okay?"

"Okay. We'll stay with her, Jay. She'll be fine. I'll call you as soon as I hear more."

I handed my phone to my dad. I didn't want to have to repeat what Cal had told me. I didn't want to say the words. My body was numb, but my mind flipped into overdrive as I replayed the dramas of our short time together.

When Dad had finished he closed the cover and handed me the phone, a look of concern clearly etched across his face.

"Listen, son, there isn't anything you can do whether you go back tonight or tomorrow as planned. It sounds to me like Abbie is going to be absolutely fine. I suspect it will turn out to be nothing serious and everyone is panicking for no good reason." I couldn't believe what I was hearing. I'd just been told that my girlfriend had been involved in a car accident and was in hospital unconscious and my own father had it down as *not serious* without speaking to any doctors.

"What the fuck, Dad!" I shouted angrily, "She's un-fucking-conscious!"

"Jake! I will not be dressed down by you, boy. Is that clear?" he said, in full blown military mode. He wasn't amused by my outburst, but I didn't care. I'd had it with his rules and regulations. Abbie was hurt and I was going to her. My body began to shake uncontrollably with the fear I might lose her.

"Think of your future, Jake. This is the opportunity of a lifetime." I grabbed my bag up from the floor at the side of the bed and proceeded to throw my wash bag into it before zipping it shut. "Jake...? Jake!"

"What...? What do you want from me, Dad?"

"Where the hell are you going at this time?" he asked, throwing his hands up in the air.

"I'm going to be with Abbie. There's a train to Casey around nine, it will get me there by midnight."

"Are you going crazy? You're not done here. What about the tour?"

"Fuck the tour, I'll come again. Don't you get it…? I love her… She needs me," I said as my voice broke and I slumped into the seat behind me. The tears flowed freely as I leaned into my hands.

My dad paced the floor, breathing heavily. After a moment he placed a supportive hand on my shoulder.

"Well…we better get a move on if we are going to get you there for when she wakes up." I lifted my head and nodded, acknowledging Dad's acceptance.

In no time at all we were on the road. My dad estimated we'd be there in a little over two hours due to the much lighter traffic at this time of night.

My stomach heaved repeatedly at the possibility I wouldn't get there in time. I'd spoken to her last night; she'd text me this morning. Why had she been driving at all? She was supposed to be having dinner at home tonight. She said she'd call me after her mom's friend had gone home. I didn't understand what had happened. Where was she going?

My mind shifted to our last conversation…

"I wish you were here. Then at least we could make our excuses and go out somewhere after..." The memory of her words haunted my subconscious, going over and over in my head until I couldn't hold off any longer. I reached for my phone and searched for Cal's number.

He answered straight away, "Hey, man."

"Any news, Cal?" I hoped desperately to hear it had all been a huge misunderstanding.

"No not yet. Sorry, Jake…she's still out." My heart pounded in my chest; the pulse in my neck throbbing as I took in Cal's words.

"What the fuck happened, Callum?

"I'm not sure… All I know is she rang Jo all confused. Said she'd been in an accident. I called for the ambulance… When we got to her she was still conscious."

"Did you speak to her?"

"She kept asking for you, Jay." I swallowed past the lumped restricting my breathing. I'd let Abbie down again. I'd never forgive myself if I lost her. "Jake, the doctor's just come out. I'll call you back." With that Cal hung up, leaving me hanging.

"Dad, how much further?" I asked frantically as I looked at the clock on the dash again for the hundredth time.

"Nearly there, about twenty minutes." My heart pounded like a battering ram inside my chest as I replayed the initial phone conversation from Callum not three hours earlier, my knuckles turning white as I gripped my cell tightly.

"Jake, listen, man… It's Abs…she… She's been in a car accident… She's in shock…We thought we should let you know."

I looked at the dash again just as my cell phone lit up in my hand. "Cal…Tell me?"

"She's come round, Jay. Abbie's awake." I blew out a lungful of air as relief cascaded through me.

"Oh thank God," I said, my eyes filling with tears, "Thanks, man. I'll be there in about ten minutes…"

"Right, see you then."

"She's awake…" I said, turning to my dad. He smiled, but kept his attention on the road ahead.

"You need to calm down before you get there. You're no good to her in this state."

I swallowed and took a few deep breaths. My girl was going to be okay. Abbie was awake.

We pulled up in front of the hospital less than ten minutes after speaking to Callum.

"Call me if you need a ride," Dad said through the open window of the car, "Give Abbie our love." I nodded and he then drove away, leaving me at the entrance.

Rushing through the automatic doors I was surprised to see Abbie's mom in the foyer, talking to another nurse.

"Beth?"

She smiled widely when she saw me, "Jake? Jo said you were on your way back. Weren't you supposed to be at St Mark's all weekend?"

"I was, but Dad brought my back early when Cal rang about Abbie. How is she?" I asked, running my hand nervously through my hair.

"I left her with Jo about an hour ago. She's going to be fine, sweetheart." Abbie's mom placed a calming hand on my arm, smiling kindly. "They're keeping her in overnight just to be on the safe side."

"Will I be able to see her?"

"Yes of course, go on up. She'll be pleased to see you. Room 10B, first floor."

"Thanks."

I stepped out of the elevator just as Jo rushed round the corner and my heart leapt into my throat. I could barely contain the anxiety threatening to burst open my skull.

"Jake!" Jo said, throwing herself at me, "Thank God."

"What's happened, Jo? Is she…?" I said, gripping her arms tightly, my eyes searching hers.

"She'll be so happy you're here." Jo said, a face splitting grin spreading across her face.

I gasped with relief, "Fuck me, Jo, I thought…"

"No…she's okay," Jo said, wiping away her happy tears, "She's confused mind you, so tread careful, hey? Do me a favor, Jake… Will you tell her Cal and I left and we'll see her tomorrow?"

I nodded, "Sure… Thanks Jo. Tell Cal thanks as well." She smiled before leaving me in the empty hallway.

I sucked in a deep breath and exhaled slowly before pushing open the door to Abbie's ward. The sight that welcomed me took my breath away. There was my beautiful girl hooked up to an IV and heart monitor all battered and bruised. I swallowed hard as I slowly approached her bed. Her eyes fluttered open as soon as the door closed behind me.

"Jake?"

"Hey…" I said, forcing a smile. I leaned down and kissed her gently, my thumb caressing the side of her face. "Can I not leave you for one minute without you ending up in trouble?" Abbie lifted her hands to my chest as the tears began to fall. I smoothed the hair from her brow and cradled her face in my hands, pressing my lips to her forehead as she sobbed.

"You're really here?"

"Shhh…I'm here, baby. I'm so sorry," I whispered, running my hands over her arms and down her sides checking she was in one piece until she stopped crying. I cupped her face in my hands and lowered my mouth to hers; my love flowing into her broken body. "I was so scared…" I said, resting my forehead against hers. Seeing her here, awake, holding her; the relief was immense.

"Are you okay?" I asked, stroking her hair away from her tear stained cheeks.

"I'm fine…but I have to stay…until the morning." she said, grasping my hand.

"I'm so, so sorry, baby…"

"Why?" she said, frowning at me, "It wasn't your fault." Abbie began to cough as her body language shifted.

"I should have been with you," I whispered, filling a glass with water from the jug on the nightstand. Abbie reached for the glass as I held her steady. She took a sip before I lowered her gently back to the propped pillows. "What happened?" I asked, wiping the tears from her cheeks.

"I…I don't remember." She swallowed before gesturing to herself, "But this is the fucking result." I smiled at her attempt at humor, but I wasn't convinced. My gut told me there was more than she was letting on.

"Why were you even in the car? Where were you going? I thought you were having dinner with your mom and her friend."

Chapter Thirty-Seven

The three hours from hearing about Abbie's accident until I could be at her side were the most agonizing of my life. The question of why she'd been driving at all kept going round in my head while watching her chest rise and fall with every breath as she slept. The only sound in the room other than the throbbing of my pulse was the incessant beeping from the machine Abbie was hooked up to.

Relief that she was alive consoled me as I held her hand, running my thumb across her knuckles; my eyes taking in every inch of her swollen face. Her distress when I'd asked why she was driving left me mystified. Her confused state was cause for concern, but she was still here and that miracle far outweighed her reluctance to open up to me.

My eyelids became heavy with the need for sleep; eventually losing the battle to keep them open. I slumped forward, Abbie's hand still in mine.

Why is she so angry?

Abbie maneuvered the car through the driving rain erratically. Powerless to help, terror strained every nerve in my body as I watched her panic, fighting to avoid the oncoming vehicle. The fear in me escalated to fever pitch with her screaming as she careered off the road and I flinch as her body impacted violently with the side of the car.

"Abbie!"

We were suddenly out of the car, surrounded by flashing lights. Abbie lay shivering on the ground next to the car with Jo holding her hand. Her eyes barely open...

"No! I can't leave her...I promised I'd stay! I won't leave her again!"

"Jake?"

"Abbie! I'm here, baby!"

The images in my head faded; replaced by the stark white of Abbie's hospital room.

"Jake! Jake, my head..." I became aware of fingers gripping my hair, "Jake?" In a blind panic my eyes flew to Abbie's. I'd dozed off, resting my head at her side. I pressed my hands to my eyes, trying to banish the nightmare from my mind before looking up at Abbie.

"Jake, my head..."

I grabbed her hand, "What about your head, baby?"

"It really hurts" she said, screwing up her eyes and lifting her arm to block out the light.

"I'll go get someone."

"No...stay... Please...don't leave me," she said, hanging onto my hand. The fear in her voice tore me apart.

"Hey... I'm not leaving you, Abbie...I'll never leave you again, ever."

"Jake, I...I feel sick...I..." I grabbed the bedpan next to her just in time. While rubbing her back I reached for the call button, pressing it firmly. I needed to be strong for Abbie, but I was in shreds. I'd expected when she woke to take her home.

"It's okay, baby... You're gonna be okay... I'm here..." I said as she eased back against the pillows.

"Fuck," she whispered, "I hate being sick."

The nurse on duty rushed into the room as Abbie leaned over to vomit again.

"I'll take it from here, sir," I reluctantly moved away so Abs could get the help she needed, my head swimming with confusion and fear.

Please let her be okay!

"Jake, don't leave me," she cried desperately.

"I'm here," I said, almost choking as fear constricted my throat, "I'm not leaving."

After what seemed like an eternity Abbie's physician arrived to examine her. He'd already arranged for her to have a CT scan in order to rule out any permanent damage to her brain.

"Can you give her anything for the pain?" I asked, swallowing back the emotion.

"No problem, I'll arrange something right away." With that he left and I took my place by Abbie's side once again. Just staring into to her eyes made my heart ache. I couldn't bear her suffering; I hated that she was in pain.

"I want to go home, Jake," she whispered, her eyes pooling with fresh tears.

"I know, love…soon, I promise." I cupped her face in my hand, my thumb caressing her cheek.

The nurse reappeared and injected, what I assumed was some pain medication into Abbie's IV.

"You'll feel better in a minute, baby," I said as I continued to stroke her hair, careful to avoid the severe bruising across her temple and cheekbone.

The next twenty-four hours passed in a blur. Abbie slept for most of it; waking intermittently, but at least the sickness seemed to have subsided. The scan revealed no apparent bleeding or swelling to her brain. Her sickness and headaches on Sunday were symptomatic of a severe concussion; providing she followed doctor's orders he saw no reason why she shouldn't make a full recovery. He arranged to see her again in the morning and as long as her condition improved between now and then she would be able to go home.

"Did you hear that, Abbie? The doctor thinks you will be okay to leave tomorrow," I said, leaning over her to kiss her lightly on the mouth when he'd left. I smoothed her hair away from her face as my eyes searched hers for any sign of pain.

"Jake, I'm okay. You can stop with the whole Doctor Ashton routine. I have a concussion, that's all." She smiled.

"I know, but…"

"But what?" she asked with a smirk.

"You're my girl…and I love you. It's my job to worry… Okay?"

"Okay." Abbie pulled on my T-shirt so my face came within inches of hers.

"Thank you for being here," she whispered, placing her hand on my cheek.

***

On Tuesday morning the doctor arrived as planned and proceeded to examine Abbie. He checked her eyes and read her chart. He placed his hands in his pockets and gave her a tight smile. I sensed she wasn't going to be very happy with the news that followed.

"I've been speaking with your mom, Abbie. I think you will be fine to go home. However…" he said with determination, "It would be dangerous for you to resume sport until you show no further symptoms of the concussion. It's crucial that your brain has time to heal. It could prove catastrophic if you were to suffer another blow to your head whilst still recovering. I would say at least a week followed by another CT scan to ensure complete recovery, before returning to any sporting activity."

My eyes flew to Abbie's which had filled with fresh tears at the news she'd miss Regionals this coming Friday. She nodded and the doctor left the room. I moved quickly towards her and pulled her into my arms as she broke down. She'd worked so hard. I felt her disappointment flow from her and into me as she sobbed quietly.

"Oh Abbie…I'm so sorry." There was nothing more I could do or say to ease her pain.

"What was the point? What a waste of fucking time," she cried as I held her close, running my hands up and down her back, "Look where it fucking landed me…and for what? Now I can't even finish what I started. It's all my fault." I frowned at her words, but left my questions unasked for now. After a while her sobs eased and I lifted my hand to her face, wiping away the last of her tears before kissing her forehead.

"Come on, let's get you home."

Abbie's mom arrived with a wheelchair when we were ready to leave.

"It's procedure," she said, smiling at the expression on both our faces, "I'll be home in about an hour, okay?"

"Okay," Abbie said quietly, still reeling from the doctor's instructions.

"I'm assuming you'll stay, Jake, at least until I get home?"

"Of course, I'm not going anywhere," I said with conviction. This was the second occasion Abbie had needed me and I'd not been there for her. My chest tightened as guilt consumed me once again.

***

"Okay, easy does it," I said, helping Abbie from the car when we got home. She gripped my hand tightly; too tightly as I led her into the house. The sound of her sudden intake of breath bounced off the walls as we stepped inside; something was wrong.

"What is it?" I asked as she froze in the doorway.

Shaking her head she looked up at me and smiled, "Nothing, just thinking about the accident. I should have stayed home, hey?" I nodded my head in agreement before leading her up to her room.

"Okay, you get into bed. I'll grab a drink for you and be back in a tick." Abbie nodded and made her way over to the bathroom.

Abbie was still in the bathroom when I returned. I placed the cup of tea on the nightstand and lay down, exhausted by everything that had happened over the last three days.

I became aware of a gentle touch on my arm and opened my eyes. I lifted my hand and caressed her face gently, moving slowly down her cheek to her neck and then her arm. Abbie flinched; I looked where my hand lay and saw that her face wasn't the only part of her that had suffered in the crash. Dressed in her usual sleep attire of singlet and shorts her injuries were in full view. Her left shoulder, arm and hip had acquired some fierce looking bruises also.

"Fuck! Abbie…look at you," I cried, running my hand gently down her side.

"It's not that bad, it'll fade," she said, forcing a smile.

I lived the horror of the vision of her body being thrown into the side of the car with enough force to cause such extensive bruising. It made me sick to my stomach. I couldn't clear my mind of the blinding guilt. If only I'd come home after my interview she wouldn't be in this mess; the whole crash could have been avoided; I'd let her down again.

I slowly rubbed my face, recognizing how lucky I was to have her here with me. I ran my hands through my hair before sitting up.

"Please do me a favor…" I said, swinging my legs over the edge of the bed, pressing my hands to my eyes desperate to get my point across, "If you ever need me…or are upset, angry, hurting… Anything. Please call me. Please, Abbie, I can't lose you. Not knowing what was happening with you or what I'd be facing when I arrived was the worst…" My words were halted by a sob as my emotions got the better of me and Abbie wrapped her arms around me from behind. I turned towards her and pulled her into my arms, scared to ever let her go; I buried my face in her shoulder as the tears fell from my eyes. Abbie's hand came to the back of my head and her fingers gripped my hair as she held me close.

"I'm sorry. I didn't mean to worry you… I just…" she took a deep breath, "I had to get out…it was stupid. I'm sorry, alright." That was it. That was all I was getting; still no real reason. She'd risked her life driving in that state because she had to get out. She'd been so upset over something to the point where she had to get to Jo's house there and then.

"No! It's not…it's not alright, Abbie…you almost died. I nearly lost you because you *had* to get to Jo's. What could have possibly been so important to cause you to risk your life driving in such a fucking state?" I held her face between my palms so she'd acknowledge the seriousness of her decision.

My heart was now banging in my chest with all the force of a battering ram and I had a sudden epiphany.

"Fuck!" My hands dropped to the bed like two lead weights. When Abbie looked up I saw fear in her eyes; fear that I'd worked it out.

I thought back to all the times we had made love over the last few weeks and my stomach turned at the realization I'd been so thoughtless. We'd never discussed birth control; I'd never given it a second thought. All that had mattered to me was I loved this girl with all my heart and wanted to be with her.

"Are...are you...are you pregnant?" I asked; my eyes narrowed with the shame of my carelessness. My foolishness had led to this. I imagined her shock at finding out she was having a baby at her age. Devastated by the news she'd almost killed herself, rushing to her friend's house because her fuckwit of a boyfriend had gone off for the weekend.

The expression of complete horror on Abbie's face served as confirmation enough and I lowered my head in shame.

"I'm so sorry baby…" I swallowed past the numbing guilt before looking up at her. I froze as I registered the anger and disappointment in her eyes. Abbie was frowning and shaking her head slowly; tears trickling down her bruised cheeks. I considered my reaction and how it must have come across.

"Fuck!" I lifted my hand, but she pulled it away still shaking her head, her lip trembling and I sensed I'd blown it big time. "Abbie… I didn't mean that how it came out baby. I…"

"Jake, I'm not pregnant. I can't be…" she whispered, turning away from me. At that point my brain began to race like a steam train as I processed her words. What did she mean she couldn't be? Why couldn't she be pregnant?

"I don't understand…" I said, frowning.

"I'm on the pill, Jake. My cycle was so fucked up at fourteen because of Peter fucking Stevens, my mom took me to the doctor. So I can't be fucking pregnant okay. Don't worry, sweetheart, you're not about to be a daddy. In fact you probably won't ever have to worry about having kids with me because the doctor told me it's highly unlikely I'll ever conceive. Panic over hey?" After her outburst Abbie flew into the bathroom, slamming the door behind her.

I sat on the bed dazed. What the fuck just happened? The look of pure gut wrenching disappointment and devastation in Abbie's eyes left me speechless and powerless to respond.

We can't have kids?

Fuck!

I hauled myself off the bed, "Abbie, I'm sorry… That all came out wrong… Please open the door…" I leaned my forehead on the bathroom door, willing her to come out. She was sobbing and my heart split in two at the thought I'd caused her even more pain. "Baby, open the door…please. I'm so sorry."

Sorry for hurting you.

Sorry for leaving you.

Sorry for everything.

"Just fuck off, Jake! Take your sympathy with you."

"Abbie, please I'm sorry… I love you." This time I'd royally screwed up. I'd thrown away my chance of happiness because I was too fucking selfish to wait for her to be ready to speak to me. *I had to ask, I had to open my fucking mouth.*

"Just go away, Jake. We're through… I'm done with all men," she whimpered.

"No, baby… Don't do this," I begged in a blind panic.

"Just go!"

Chapter Thirty-Eight

With nothing rational to explain what had just gone down at Abbie's house I flew up the stairs in a blind rage. My heart pounded and my stomach rolled with disgust at my misinterpretation of Abbie's upset on Saturday night. My fear for her safety, then worry over her recovery, was now replaced with an overwhelming urge to throw myself off the nearest bridge at the very least.

How could I have been so fucking stupid? Another few seconds would have seen her open up about her evening and what had caused her to be so distressed that she felt the need to drive in that state to Jo's house.

I threw open the door to my room and slumped down to the floor by my bed. Gripping my phone, I ran a hand through my hair, contemplating my options. Who was I kidding? I'd already completely exhausted my options. Abbie had made it very clear to me that I was no longer welcome in her life. My only hope now was that she's rethink her decision when she calmed down.

She'd been through insurmountable trauma already and I'd taken away the only tangible thing she had left. Abbie had trusted me with her heart. She'd given it willingly. After a matter of weeks I'd repaid that life altering gesture by ripping it from her chest and stomping on it with both feet.

I hoped with all my heart and soul that we would be able to work things out. Life without Abbie was incomprehensible. I'd spent my teenage years dreaming about her coming back into my life. The challenge of convincing her that I was worthy of her affections when we finally met up again just a short month ago had been worth every painful confrontation.

Finding out what had driven her to retreat inside the shell of her former self had broken my heart, but the eventual relationship we had grown out of that revelation had astounded me. It was more than I could have ever thought possible. Our love for each other had surpassed all of my dreams and now without warning it was over.

My heartless response to a non-pregnancy had smashed any future we may have hoped possible. All because I *had* to know what was wrong. I'd learned nothing from her past efforts at hiding trauma. I'd jumped in with both feet and shown no restraint what-so-ever.

That evil bastard took away her chance to have a family. She'd had to live with that knowledge for years and in typical teenaged male style, I'd just responded with repulsion at the chance of her carrying my baby. At least, that was how she'd read my reaction.

I'd single handedly smashed any semblance of a trusting and loving relationship for Abbie. I'd taken what she'd offered and thrown it back in her face.

My hand trembled violently as I flipped open my cell and desperately searched my texts.

Baby, I'm so sorry

I'm such a dick

Abbie, I love you so much, please pick up

I'd already sent a dozen messages in the last ten minutes with not one response.

"Nothing!"

Scrolling through my contacts I found the one I was looking for.

"Jay, how are you, man? How's Abbie?" Cal asked cheerfully.

"Are you free to come over, Cal? I need your help." I hardly had the breath in me to speak. My eyes stung from crying like a baby and my chest felt as though a sumo wrestler had been sat on me for the last ten minutes.

"Sure, I'll be over right away." I threw my cell on the floor beside me and leaned back against my bed.

***

Callum listened to every word I said without commenting until I'd finished and the tears I'd held at bay, betrayed my tough pretense.

"Jay, you guys have been through hell and back in the last month. It was bound to take its toll sooner than later. I don't think for one minute this will see the end of your relationship with Abbie. She's a sensible girl, so hot for you it's ridiculous. Give her time man. She'll come round."

"You didn't see her face, Cal. She was gutted. I could feel the disappointment towards me coming off her in waves," I said, shaking my head.

We cracked open a couple of beers out of my dad's stash and continued to talk about both Abbie and Jo well into the night. He left me pondering my position with Abbie. I loved her so much; I wanted to be with her, to spend the rest of my life with her. Nothing was clearer in my mind.

I tossed and turned all night, trying to get to sleep, but my alarm for school found me exhausted and totally drained. Although school was the last thing on my mind I knew Jo would be going and I needed to find out whether Abbie had contacted her last night.

I'd just stumbled downstairs when someone knocked at the door. My heart began pounding with anticipation it might be Abbie, but was replaced by disappointment when I opened it to reveal a pissed off looking Jo.

"Oh, hey, Jo."

"What the fuck, Jake?"

"Don't start on me, Joey." I mumbled, turning away from the door, "You have no idea what went down so don't start going off on one until you have the facts from both sides. Okay?"

"Well I guess you can tell me all about it on the way to school then, big boy. I assume you're driving."

"Yes…yes I am." I muttered, feeling sorry for myself.

By the time we'd reached school I'd filled in the gaps for Jo and she seemed to empathize with mine and Abbie's situation.

"Well I can't promise anything, but I'll try my best to explain your side of things when I see Abs tonight. She's stubborn mind you so don't bank on a miracle. Abbie will move in her own time, when she's ready. I know it's hard, but try not to worry. It'll work out I'm sure. She loves you."

The day dragged amidst a tide of boring lessons and countless texts to Abbie without one reply. I'd skipped lunch in favor of hanging out at the library, immersing myself in a medical journal or two to alleviate the heavy lump in my gut.

***

Two more torturous days passed and still I heard nothing from Abbie. I'd avoided contact with Cal and Jo since Wednesday in favor of blanking out the gut wrenching pain of mine and Abbie's apparent split. Every time our paths crossed my heart plummeted at the realization things were unlikely to ever get back to how they were before my fuck up. They tried tirelessly to lift my spirits with friendly banter and encouragement, but my mood had slumped to an all-time low. I couldn't bear to be around them, to be reminded of happier times with Abbie, with no imminent sign of reconciliation.

"Jake, hold up!" Jo shouted as I climbed into my truck.

"Hi," My greeting lacked enthusiasm, but I didn't care.

"Erm, any chance of a lift home? Cal's not ready yet and I want to get to Abbie's before dinner."

"I don't know, Jo…"

"Fucking hell, Jake, just give me a lift already!" She didn't give me any opportunity to refuse as she hauled herself into the truck beside me and slammed the door.

Of course I was being ridiculous. Jo was a friend and just because Abbie didn't want me, didn't mean I should ignore her.

I didn't say much on the way home. I didn't have it in me. Jo sensed my reluctance for conversation and stayed quiet as well.

"See you then. Don't worry. She'll come round." Coincidentally Callum had said the exact same thing only days earlier, but I still wasn't convinced.

"I'm not so sure Jo, but thanks," I said, watching as she climbed out of the truck. "Hey, Jo?"

"Yeah?"

"Tell her I miss her and…that I love her." Jo nodded.

I didn't have a clue how long I sat, just staring into space before my mom got home from work. She pulled onto the drive and broke my trance. I climbed out of the truck and approached her, forcing a tight smile, which try as I might, didn't quite reach my eyes. She frowned at my appearance before handing me a box of groceries.

"You look shocking, Jake. Have you two not sorted out your differences yet?" she asked, lifting a hand to my shoulder, "You will have to do something before next weekend, sweetheart. Either that or send your apologies."

"I've screwed up, Mom. I've screwed up big time," I said, heading towards the kitchen door.

"Anything I can help with?" she asked, her voice reflecting all the love of a mother soothing her child.

I shook my head, "No it's too late... I really blew it this time, Mom," I said as a lone tear trickled carelessly from the corner of one eye.

"Jake? Come here." My mom pulled me into her arms.

"I'm sorry, Mom."

"Hey, don't ever be sorry for needing a hug from your old mom," she said with a smile, "Now, sit down. I'll make us a hot drink and you can tell me what has got you so worked up."

Explaining to Mom what had happened whilst omitting the shit about Peter proved tough going. I'd settled for a simple version. She'd often suggested that listening was the way to go in a relationship, however on this occasion her reminder came a little too late. I only wished I'd remembered it three days earlier.

"I spoke to Beth today."

"Yeah? What about?" I asked, frowning at the idea of our mom's having a conversation about us.

"Well I offered to make Abbie's cake weeks ago. Beth wanted to check that I was still happy to go ahead."

"Oh. You are, aren't you?"

"Of course I am. I told her it wasn't a problem and that I'd have it ready by next Friday."

"Okay. Good," I said, doing my best to sound happy with her decision, "I might go lie down for a bit. My head's in bad shape."

"Okay, sweetheart… Jake?"

"Hmm?"

"Don't worry too much about Abbie, darling. I'm sure she'll…"

"Please don't say she'll come round." My stomach churned at the chance that Abbie wouldn't come round.

I pulled my cell phone from my pocket as I climbed the stairs to my bedroom.

Still nothing. I longed to hold her, to make it all go away. With nothing else to occupy my battered brain I headed into the bathroom.

After a punishing cold shower I dried off and grabbed my cell.

Just wanted to check on u. I hope ur feelin better… I love u baby. I breathed in deeply, closing my eyes as I hit send. Then slumped to my bed, holding my phone to my chest as silent sobs racked my body.

Chapter Thirty-Nine

"What are you going to do?" Jo asked tentatively. We'd aimlessly browsed through countless fashion magazines for about half an hour making small talk so her random question floored me.

"What about?" I asked, dropping my gaze from Jo back to the latest text from Jake.

"Don't give me that, Abbie. I see your reaction every time you open a text from him. You're just as shattered as he is."

"This week has been a fucking wake-up call, Joey. The sooner everything gets back to how it was before Jake Ashton showed up the better," I said, my hand tightening on my cell phone.

I didn't want Jo to see me cry. It took all my resolve to keep my voice steady. Jake's persistent texts were keeping my emotional state on a knife edge and although I couldn't bring myself to reply, reading them was a whole different matter.

His latest tugged at my heart more than ever, *Just wanted to check on u. I hope ur feelin better... I love u baby.* How was it possible to be so angry at someone, but still have feelings for that very same person?

Since Tuesday, my nights had been plagued with terrible nightmares. Sleep deprivation was a cruel affliction and had certainly affected my perception of the situation.

Jo remained quiet for once; her obvious discomfort with the direction of the conversation triggered a swift change of subject.

"Erm... We need to sort out the final arrangements for your party," she said, forcing a smile.

Jo's determination for my birthday celebrations to go ahead despite all that had happened floored me. It had been booked for this weekend originally, but because of the accident my mom had rescheduled it for next Saturday instead. The manager at the venue had been very understanding and after checking his calendar, confirmed the new booking.

"What did you have in mind?" I asked, rolling my eyes, "I really don't care you realize?"

"Yeah well your family and friends want to mark the occasion so suck it up, princess," she said with a smug expression on her face.

"Whatever."

It was at this point I zoned out and left Jo to her ramblings. She decided to check the status of my online invites and run through the arrangements. We'd opened the party up to a few people from school that I'd become more friendly with since hooking up with Jake. A lump came to my throat as my mind drifted to happier times. I missed him so much.

I longed to make it right with Jake, but I'd avoided all contact with him for four days. It was getting harder to stand down and admit my reaction had been as over exaggerated as his. With every text my heart swelled and cracked open a fraction more.

"Okay, here we go," Jo said, breaking into my thoughts momentarily, "With extended family and old friends we should be expecting fifty plus guests."

Mom had booked The Tavern, a popular venue for local functions; from birthdays to weddings. Weeks ago I'd decided on a live band in addition to a DJ as Martin had provided a demo of his friend's band. Even Mom had been impressed and agreed they would be suitable.

Karen was down for making the cake and providing the decorations. Even though Mom had confirmed with her only this week I was still uncomfortable with the arrangement. Jo had originally suggested we spent Saturday morning decorating the venue together, go for lunch somewhere and then hit the hair and nail salons.

Horrified was a tame description of how I felt about the whole pampering thing. My idea of getting ready for a night out consisted of having a shower, dressing in a nice outfit and applying a touch of makeup. The biggest decision was usually whether to wear my hair straight or wavy. I longed for the event to be over so that I could get back to normal.

What's normal then Abs?

"Okay…That's the lot," Jo said, looking extremely pleased as I snapped out of my trance.

"I'm glad you're happy," I said sarcastically.

"Yeah, well…it's not like you would have bothered sorting anything if I hadn't pushed it, hey?"

"Nope… Probably not."

Jo closed the lid to my laptop and placed it on my bed just as my cell phone leaped into action for the hundredth time this week. I ignored it, but much to my horror Jo snatched it up and flipped it open.

"Hi, Jake, it's Jo," she said, mouthing at me, *speak to him* as he answered.

I shook my head crazily, refusing to take the phone from her. I threw myself back on the bed and covered my eyes with my arm as she continued her conversation. My heart felt as though it was going to jump clean out of my chest any second. The lump constricting my throat was the size of a small continent.

"Jake, I don't think she's ready to speak to you yet, I'm sorry… Yeah, she's doing much better now… No, no headaches. The swelling round her eye's gone down and the bruises are fading." Jo left a longer pause as Jake was obviously talking at the other end. "Her mom spoke to your mom about it today… Yeah… Jake, you have to come…"

I launched myself off the bed as I realized she was referring to my party. Panic consumed me. Of course I wanted him there. I really did, but… Oh I don't know…the idea of him being there, but us not being together killed me.

I glared at her, trying to get her to switch her mouth off for a second. Jo had this awful knack of dropping me in the shit at every turn.

"Okay, Jay, I will, see ya."

"Abbie…seriously…he's falling apart," Jo said, sitting amidst the fashion magazines strewn across the covers of my bed.

I'd been out of hospital for four days and been watched like a hawk by my mom who had taken the rest of the week off work to make sure I made a full recovery. Jo had visited after school each evening; during which time she'd tried her best to present a comprehensive case for why I should, in the very least, answer Jake's calls. I had to admit, my resolve was taking a beating.

"I'm not having this conversation with you again, Jo," I said, pulling off my sneakers.

"Whatever. Anyway listen, I'll have to get going. Callum's sleeping over and he'll be at my place in about half an hour."

"I'll see you tomorrow?"

"Yep, see you at the diner?" she said, hugging me before we headed downstairs.

After picking at a re-heated dinner in front of the TV while making small talk with Mom and Martin, I headed back up to bed in the hopes of getting some sleep. My head betrayed that need by replaying mine and Jake's confrontation. The memory merged with nagging images of Peter sat at our dinner table last Saturday and him laying his filthy hands on me. After what seemed like hours, I finally drifted into a restless sleep.

***

We took our usual seat in the diner and Joey ordered two hot chocolates.

"So…" she began as she placed the steaming hot drinks on the table, "Have you heard from Jake today?"

"Yep."

"And? Are you going to hear him out? Abbie, you should have seen him at school this week," Jo said, shaking her head slowly, "He's a mess, Abs."

"Joey, I love you dearly, but you weren't there. The expression on his face when he thought I might be pregnant... He was devastated," I said, taking a sip of my drink. My eyes prickled with the threat of more emotion and I swallowed hard, determined not to cry. I'd wasted enough tears on Jake Ashton.

We sat in silence for a minute while I regained a bit of composure, but not being one to let an issue drop and renowned for her determination Jo swallowed. I braced myself for her next effort.

"Abbie, he looks terrible... You both jumped to conclusions. He told me what happened, what he said, but he explained it to me and...well...I have to say, I don't believe his intentions were to give you the impression he never wanted kids," Jo said, her eyes begging me to listen.

"I was about to explain everything to him, but he didn't want to hear me out. He just assumed the worst, which is ironic under the circumstances... Having Jake's baby would have meant the world to me."

"I know that, but..."

"No, Joey, you should have seen his face, he reacted to the idea of having a baby like it was the worst thing ever.

He didn't wait for me to confirm whether I was pregnant or not. He just assumed I was and reacted instead of waiting for an answer. He should have known I wouldn't have been sad about carrying his child."

"How would he have known? Have you discussed kids? He isn't a mind reader, Abbie."

"Jo… If I *had* been pregnant there's no way he would have wanted it. He looked mortified. The color literally drained from his face." I began to gasp with the emotion of having to replay mine and Jake's last conversation. I took a breath, "I…I need some time to think Jo. It's been a hell of a month."

"Well, all I can say is…he's in a bad way… Abbie he's hardly speaking to Cal or me. Please think about seeing him. I'm worried about him."

"He built a fence between us…and he hurt me, Jo…" I said as a tear trickled down my cheek at the thought that Jake was in bad shape too, "I can't keep bouncing back. I'm hardly holding it together here."

I missed Jake so badly it physically hurt. My body ached for him, but I couldn't allow my emotions to get the better of me. It killed me that he was hurting and I wanted nothing more right now than his touch, his arms around me, but I felt torn. No man was going to hurt me ever again.

"Jake's not the bad guy. You have him paying for what that bastard did to you all those years ago. It's not Jake's fault, Abbie. What do you stand to gain from driving him away? You're made for one another. He loves you more than I've ever seen a guy love anyone. He'd do anything to make it right, Abs."

I sat in silence as Jo's words penetrated my skull like a jack hammer. Jake, along with Cal and Jo had helped me to realize it was okay to stand firm in my beliefs and decisions, but not at the expense of hurting myself in the bargain. Was I being stubborn? Was my need to protect myself from Peter again, damaging what Jake and I had created together? Maybe my emotional state *was* irrational and my stubbornness was my defense mechanism. I swallowed, realizing I'd done more damage than good.

A text came through on my phone and as per the rest of the week, my heart rate quickened, but I ignored it. Jake had almost blown up the network with his incessant texting since Tuesday.

"You're going to have to speak to him at some point Abs. You're back at school on Monday and then there's your party next weekend. If you don't break the ice before then it's going to be even more painful."

I'd been blind to the fact I'd have to see him and with that possibility came the fact he apparently looked like shit.

The last thing I needed was to come across him at school on Monday, be faced with an emotional wreck and end up causing a scene.

I took a deep breath and picked up my cell. Jo's eyes warmed as I flipped the cover back and opened his latest message.

I love you so much, baby. I'm so sorry. Please believe me.

My throat tightened as I took in his words and my eyes prickled with unshed tears. I'd come so close to contacting him with each text. The more I considered our break up, the more my spin on the whole thing became confused.

"It's the right thing to do, Abs… Don't let that monster take away Jake as well."

With those final words I found my nerve and hit call.

***

Jo left me to head to the park on my own. Jake's voice sounded so full of hope by the end of our brief conversation that it left me eager to see him. I pulled the zipper on my padded jacket as high as it would go and secured my scarf forming a barrier between the cold and my nose. As I sat watching the last of the leaves fall from the giant trees lining the pathway; I pondered everything that had happened over the last month.

The accident had left a dull ache in my shoulder and yellowing bruises, the worst on my hip and the more

430

noticeable bruises on my face. I worried a little about Jake's reaction when he saw me, but the memory of Peter's arrival far outweighed the injuries I'd sustained; his face had plagued my dreams all week. I chewed my lip nervously as the minutes ticked by and my mind began to play tricks on me.

What if he's changed his mind?

What if he says he doesn't love me anymore?

Maybe I've blown it.

It was on the last thought that a familiar figure approached from around the corner of the diner. My heart began to race and I stood up from the bench. I pushed my hands deeper into my pockets and breathed in deeply, uncertain of what he would say.

Our eyes met, and my breath hitched in my throat at the pain and damage etched into his features. His usual tan complexion had taken on a gray hue and the haunted appearance of his eyes caused mine to fill with tears. He stopped a few feet away and pulled in a visible breath as if gathering himself for trial.

My lip trembled with the fear I'd pushed too hard. My brow creased as I squeezed my eyes shut and clamped down hard on my lip.

"I'm so very sorry that I hurt you, Abs... Please believe me...I want you to know that I freaked out because my lack of care over protection jeopardized your safety…"

I gasped, "Oh Jake…" My voice was barely a whisper.

He paused a second, "I know you said we may never have a baby…but I want you to know I love you, Abbie James, I love you so much…whether we're blessed with children or not… I'll always love you." I swallowed back the emotion coursing through me. Jake and I would never be parents together. Up to this week I hadn't given it much thought, but now it seemed like the bottom had fallen out of my existence. "I never meant to hurt you. My only intention is to be there for you… My interview was about both of us, our future. I'm nothing without you, Abbie. I love you."

"I know…" I whispered as a tear rolled down my cheek. I swallowed past the nervous lump threatening to cut off my air supply. "I've been a fool. I don't want to lose you, Jake. I'm sorry I didn't take your calls."

That was all Jake needed to close the distance between us and wrap me in his arms and his mouth found mine. The tenderness of Jake's kiss blew my mind. I was home, where I belonged. My arms traveled up and around his neck in a desperate attempt to get even closer to him. Our kiss deepened and soothed away the emotional trauma of the past week. I brought my hand to his cheek as we eased apart momentarily, running my thumb along his jaw.

"I'm sorry I didn't trust you. I love you, Jake," and with that he lowered his trembling lips to mine once more.

Chapter Forty

The previous night's love-making with Jake had to pass as the best yet. He'd avoided intimate contact with me for three days after we got back together under the misguided idea I might need a little space. I'd finally confronted him about it and the result had been a night of pure unadulterated passion. *If that was make-up sex then we'd have to break up more often.* I smiled at the thought and looked up to see the brightest of blue eyes gazing down at me.

"Hey, sleepy head?" he said with a half awake grin tugging on his lips, "I thought you'd never wake up."

"How long have you been watching me?" I asked, snuggling into his shoulder.

"Long enough to want you to be awake too," he said, smiling widely as he flipped me onto the mattress and came over me. I ran my hands up his arms and pulled him closer before leaning up to kiss him full on the mouth.

"I've missed you so much," he groaned, stroking the hair away from my face, "I don't ever want another week like last week. Going from the accident straight into the trauma of thinking you'd hate me forever…"

"I didn't hate you, Jake. I could never hate you," I said, taking a deep breath and sitting up. Jake leaned onto his side, watching me. My eyes teared up at the memory of Peter's surprise visit and I hated that I'd been put in this position again by that monster. Jake immediately saw my reaction and reached for me.

"Hey?"

I chewed my lip, not wanting to bring up all the shit about Peter, but at the same time, wanting to do so. I leaned into his chest, swallowing back the urge to spill the whole drama.

"I'm fine, it's just...it's been a long week..." I said, deciding to stick with Plan A and let sleeping dogs lie. My stomach turned with the guilt of the non-disclosure. I couldn't tell him. We'd been through hell and back already. I had a lot of making up to do this week and my eighteenth to get ready for. The party was apparently...*The social event of the year*! Best I forgot about last week and moved on.

"You sure?"

"Yep, I'm absolutely fine again now." I said, smiling at the concerned expression on his face and lifting my hand to smooth away his frown. "Do you think we could go somewhere today?" I asked, tracing the outline of the morning regrowth across his jaw.

"And where would my beautiful girl like to go?" he asked, grinning widely at me.

"Ermm…you okay with skipping school?" I asked, fully expecting him to renege.

"Maybe."

"Can we go to the zoo?" Jake's eyes took on a life of their own as he considered my request. The twinkle made my stomach flip.

"I don't see why not," he said before kissing me lightly, "We'll have to get up now if you want the day there." I faked a pout and he laughed, pulling me up to standing. "Shower?" he asked and I raised an eyebrow at his unspoken suggestion. We hadn't showered together in that sense yet and Martin had already left for school so we were completely alone.

"Okaaayy then." My eyes reflected the desire coursing downwards as he took my hand and led me into the bathroom.

The steam from the hot water filled the air around us within seconds of stepping into the shower, adding to the desire, running through our veins. I lifted my hand to his stomach and traced the water droplets, racing down towards his happy trail before moving towards him and dropping kisses lightly across his chest. I moved slowly around him, letting my mouth trail across his skin, coming to a stop at the center of his back. I lifted my hands and eased them around to his chest as I continued to kiss in between his shoulder blades.

Jake's groan caused the heat to flare between my legs and he turned to face me. He reached for a sponge hanging from the faucet and squeezed some shower gel into it. He ran it along the front of my shoulder, careful to linger momentarily at my throat before lowering his head to kiss me. I moaned into his mouth as he dipped his tongue between my slightly parted lips.

As soon as he heard the sound of desire leave my throat he hauled me into his arms. His eyes searched mine as if uncertainty clouded his mind. I stretched up onto my tip toes to reach his mouth and nipped at his bottom lip encouragingly.

He moved his mouth across my jaw and down to my throat; his lips following the trail of steamy water flowing between my breasts and downward. My breath hitched in my throat as he pulled me closer. He gripped my bottom as his mouth continued its exploration and I thought I'd explode right there in the shower.

"Oh my God, Jake!" I gasped as he continued to work his magic until he sensed I could take no more. My legs almost buckled and Jake hauled me up into his arms, wrapping my legs around his waist. His hands kneaded my bottom as our tongues entwined and deepened our kiss, tasting, caressing, and loving. The water continued to beat down on us and I gripped him closer with my legs.

"God, Abbie, you're something else…"

I loved it when Jake gave in to his feelings. He made me feel whole. I never wanted to lose him ever again.

"I love you, Jake," I whispered as he lowered me onto him, filling me entirely. My heart swelled and I clenched around him causing him to gasp in response.

"I love you too, Abbie…" My fingers dug into his shoulders as my legs tightened. The muscles under my hands flexed with every movement. What began slowly soon escalated to new heights. My head fell back as a wave of desire flooded my body.

"That's it, baby…" he groaned, the tempo building as the fire in us grew to an inferno. Jake tightened his hold as his mouth found my shoulder, his teeth grazing at my flesh as he continued to thrust at a pace matched only by our beating hearts. Still the water embraced us and drove us onward, building to our climax. Jake smiled, his eyes searching mine as he sensed I was there with him, "Ahh…fuck yeah."

I bucked against him unable to control my body's response to the explosion wracking my entire being.

"Oh God," I whispered as his lips found mine.

Our breathing slowed and Jake smiled into our kiss before resting his forehead against mine, "That was amazing."

I reached up and cupped his face in my hands, "You're amazing."

Once dry, we hurriedly dressed in warm clothes and grabbed a quick breakfast of toast and coffee before heading off to the zoo for the day.

"What's going through that gorgeously overly active head of yours miss James?" Jake asked as we pulled into the parking lot outside the zoo.

"Just...how lucky I am."

"You are," he said, as he climbed out of the truck.

"Jeez you're cocky!"

"Nah, just aware of my attributes." Jake pulled me into his arms and kissed my cheek.

"Well...I say you're cocky," I said, pushing him off me, "Where to first?"

The gates to the zoo brought back memories of trips here with Gran and Pops when I was a little girl. It was like entering a whole different world. The animal enclosures had been renovated since then, taking on a more natural vibe. The zoo's developers had been keen to emulate the natural environment of each species as far as possible. In some cases you had to really look in order to spot the animals. I loved the tigers. Their enclosure had a decidedly jungle feel, right down to the humidity. The indoor frozen penguin enclosure took my breath away. The way they slid down the icy slopes and swam about in the custom viewing pool had me gasping with amazement.

Jake took several photos of my childlike reactions to the gorgeous creatures on show before suggesting that we took a break and grabbed some lunch. We shared a selection of fish bites, corn dogs and chips to go with two large sodas.

"So you haven't really said much about school or cross country," Jake said as we took a seat next to the glass enclosed meerkats.

"Yeah well, there's not been that much to say I guess. Coach Jackson's been great. I told you he called me Friday to see how I was feeling. He also said how sorry he was that I'd had to miss Regionals. I was worried up to that point…I thought he'd be angry at me…"

"What the fuck, Abbie? Why would you think that?"

"Well he invested a lot of time in me, Jake."

"Yeah…it's his job," Jake said, shaking his head, "I'm sure he was disappointed for you, but jeez... he wouldn't be angry at you."

"I guess. Anyway, he was cool about it so that's that." I was keen to get away from talk of cross country or anything else that brought back my encounter with Peter last weekend. My knee began to bounce under the table as memories of his mouth on me came back to my mind and I quickly looked up at Jake, working hard at shaking the vision from my head.

"You okay?" Jake asked, reaching for my hand.

"Yeah, why?"

"Oh, you know...zoning out in the middle of the zoo and all that..." he said, making light of my recent absence. I slapped him across the chest and took a sip of my soda.

"Yeah well, the company is obviously riveting," I said, giggling at the look of mock horror on his face. He drained his soda and picked up our empty tray.

"Shall we go see the baboons then?" he asked with a sloppy grin across his face.

"Jeez, you're hilarious!"

We managed to see most of my favorite exhibits before it got late and we had to leave. Jo had sent me several texts during the day but I'd had my phone on silent and missed all but the last one.

"Shit!"

"What?" Jake asked as he saw me look at my phone.

"Joey, she's been texting all day and my phone's been on silent so I've not noticed," I said, chewing my lip.

Turned out Jo had realized I was with Jake pretty early on as he was obviously missing from school as well.

"Tell her we'll see them both at the diner," he suggested, "That's if you want to."

"Sure, that'll be cool."

See you at the diner usual time

"Done."

"Thanks for today, I've loved every minute."

"Me too."

We pulled up outside the diner about ten minutes later than normal. Jo and Callum were already guzzling hot chocolate and eating hot donuts when we stepped out of the cold.

"Well look what the cat dragged in," Cal shouted across the diner with a smirk on his face.

"You're only jealous," I said, punching him in the arm as I sat next to Joey. She gave me a quick hug.

"So…I hope your day trip was worth missing science," Jo said, grinning into her mug.

"It was ace. We had a great time. It was just what I needed."

"I'm glad. Good for you," she said warmly, "Oh, by the way…I've confirmed the hair salon for Saturday afternoon. Nails first…then hair." I rolled my eyes at the idea of the torture ahead of me. "Don't be like that, Abs.

It's not often we get a chance to dress up…and anyways, I bet Jake can't wait to see you in the FM dress?"

"FM dress?" Jake asked before the penny dropped and he raised an eye brow at me. I blushed scarlet as Callum caught on as well.

"Okay, enough already!" I groaned.

Chapter Forty-One

"So you have a *Fuck Me Dress* hung in your closet," Jake said as I walked back into the bedroom.

"It *is* stunning," I said, picking up on his excitement and grinning widely.

"It can't be any more stunning than you, baby." He grabbed me round the waist and pulling me onto his lap.

"You say the nicest things, Jake Ashton. What would I do without you?"

He pressed his mouth to mine and kissed me before running his knuckles across my cheek, "You won't ever have to find out." He kissed me again. "What time did you say we were supposed to meet everyone?"

"Why? Do you have something better planned?"

"I might have," Jake said, lowering us to the mattress. My heart pounded as he lay over me, his eyes taking in every inch of my face before pressing kisses along my jaw.

"Hold on there, buster," I said, bracing my hand against his chest, stopping his advances. The look of horror on his face was priceless, "We have work to do." His seductive grin reached his eyes and I was lost. I yanked him down and kissed him firmly on his mouth before pushing him gently away.

"As much as I would love to spend the day locked up in my room with the hottest boy in school…we really do have work to do. Anyway, *he* isn't here or available, so I'll have to settle for *you* later," I teased before jumping out of his grasp.

"Is that right? We'll see about that, young lady. I'll have you begging for it later. Just you wait and see. You won't see it coming."

The sensations Jake's words stirred deep within me caused my breath to hitch in my throat.

"I'll look forward to that, Mr. Ashton," I said, winking at him. I left him on my bed and headed downstairs.

My eyes went wide as I entered the kitchen. There was an array or food on all kinds of platters strewn across every single surface.

"Holy cow! I thought this was happening later, Mom."

"Well I wanted to have one load ready for you to take down when you go to decorate. Jake can come back for the rest later when you girls go to the salon."

There was no denying my Mom's skill for catering. We'd always joked that she could make a spread out of a jar of pickles and a can of beans.

"Okay, we can do that," I said with a smile, "Thank you, Mom."

"It's the least I could do. My baby girl turning eighteen is quite a milestone," she said, getting emotional.

"I love you," I said, wrapping my arms around her neck.

"Go on, get out of here before you have me bawling." She pushed me away and swiped away her tears.

Jake appeared in the kitchen doorway as my mom turned back towards the sink.

"You okay?" he asked his hand at my neck, pulling me gently towards his chest.

"Yeah, I'm good. Mom and I were just sharing a mother daughter moment. That's all." He nodded and kissed me lightly on my forehead.

"Okay, looking at all of this I suggest we get a move on or this party won't be happening today," he said, scratching his head, "You sure you made enough food, Mrs. James?"

"Get outta here, Jake," Mom said, throwing the dish cloth at him, "Don't be late back. There'll be as much again just after lunch."

"Sure thing, Mrs. J," he said with a salute.

It took about ten minutes to load up the truck with all of the wrapped food platters. Another ten minutes later we pulled up outside The Tavern. My stomach churned with nervous energy. I hated being the center of attention and today promised a shit load of just that.

"You right?" Jake asked, sensing my mood change.

"Yes! I'm fine." Aside from the fact I was uncomfortable with the whole party thing, Jake had already asked me a dozen times whether I was okay or not. I glanced over at him and saw the hurt on his face. "I'm sorry, I guess I'm not okay, hey?" I whispered, "I'm nervous, I hate being the center of attention and I'm dreading everything about today." Jake did his best to hold back a smirk as I looked back at him. "What? What's so bloody funny about that?"

"Did you enjoy the Halloween dance at school?" he asked, raising his eyebrows.

"Well…yeah…"

"This is just the same deal, baby. We're going to be with our friends, having a great time. There'll be music, great food, dancing and later…"

"Yeah yeah, I get it." I climbed out of the truck and into the arms of an extremely hyper Jo.

"I'm sooo excited, Abs. Happy birthday. Are you excited? You should be. Come on, let's get this lot inside. We've got heaps to do," she said, gasping for air.

"Joey! Seriously girl...you need to cool off. I do not want to be all strung out by lunch time. Easy does it."

"Okay," she whispered, taking a deep breath before rushing into The Tavern with a tray full of food.

I turned to face Jake shaking my head, "You were saying?"

"It'll be fine. She's excited. You know what she's like. She loves you. We all do." My heart did a quick flip at Jake's comment and I kissed him on his cheek before grabbing another tray and heading inside.

Approximately fifteen tables surrounded the huge dance floor in a U shape. A large mirror ball hung precariously above our heads and several other smaller fixed lights were set at crazy angles. Our job this morning was to dress the tables and store the food in the cool room out back. Mom, Pam and Karen would set up the buffet just before everyone arrived.

Callum and Jake continued to unload the food while Jo and I set about decorating the tables. I'd chosen a deep purple and silver color scheme. We draped the tables in purple, placed three, weighted metallic silver helium balloons in the center of each table and sprinkled silver confetti around each arrangement. The finished effect looked like something out of an interior design editorial.

"Lunch I think," Callum said as he scanned the finished room, "This looks awesome, girls."

"Thanks," we both said together, grinning at our handy work.

"Who's up for fish and chips at the harbor?" Jake asked as he stuck his head round the main door.

My stomach rumbled as soon as lunch was mentioned. We all piled into the truck keen to get some much needed food inside us. Jake and I had skipped breakfast due to the chaos in the kitchen when we crawled out of bed this morning and I was now paying the price.

After a leisurely lunch Jo and I headed to my place for quick showers before hitting Gianni's Hair and Nails studio, leaving Jake and Callum to shuttle the rest of the food to The Tavern.

Our pampering afternoon wasn't quite as painful as I'd first imagined. The girls at Gianni's were used to dealing with first timers. From the greeting on arrival to their timely conversations during our treatments; their professionalism was second to none. They recommended a clear gloss nail with silver tips and for my hair, a classic up do with soft curls falling over one shoulder to compliment the Grecian style of my dress. I'd been happy to go with the flow. Kerry had just put the finishing touches to my hair when the bell above the salon door rang and in sauntered the boys with not a care in the world.

"Wow, you look good enough to eat, babe," Cal said as he took in Joey's newly styled locks.

"Wait until you see the finished product," she said her smile spreading across her face.

"Can't wait," he said, pulling her into his side.

I turned to face Jake, who still hadn't spoken, "Hey," I said, blushing at the adoration in his eyes.

"Hey, beautiful."

"You done?" Callum asked.

"Yep, just need our jackets," Jo said as Kerry appeared with our coats and scarves.

"Allow me," Jake said, taking mine from Kerry.

"Why thank you, kind sir," I said, giggling at his chivalrous behavior.

After arranging to pick us up for the party later, the boys dropped us at my place.

"Okay, are you ready for your transformation?" she asked as I took a seat at the vanity in the bathroom.

"Hmm." I cringed at the idea of being plastered with make-up, but forced a tight smile.

Ten minutes later Jo had applied a light coverage of blusher to my pale cheeks and given me smoky eyes. A pale pink, shimmer lip gloss finished the look.

"Wow, Abs, I don't think the dress stands a chance!"

"Jeez, you're a lady!" I laughed at my friend's vulgarity.

"What? You don't really think Jake cares what you're wearing when you look that hot in nothing do you?" I shook my head as I stepped into my dress.

"Wow," I whispered as I caught sight of my reflection in the bedroom mirror. The floaty chiffon of the skirt skimmed my thighs whilst the crystals along the top drew my eye to its plunging sweetheart neckline and figure enhancing bodice. Jo had transformed me from an alright looking athlete into a beautiful eighteen-year-old girl about to blow the socks of her stunning boyfriend. I couldn't wait to see Jake's reaction when he arrived.

"Abbie, the boys are here. Are you two ready?" My mom shouted from the foot of the stairs.

"Yeah, coming."

The butterflies I had so often battled appeared again in my stomach. I took one cautious step after another down the stairs until at the halfway point my eyes met Jake's. He scanned me from top to toe before his eyes fixed on mine and a smile of breathtaking proportions spread across his face. He moved forward and held out his hand as I reached the bottom step.

Jo and Callum were already giving one another a playful bashing and had gone into the kitchen to grab a quick drink before our cab arrived.

"You… You're… Fuck me, Abbie… Wow!" Jake said, struggling to make any sense at all.

As soon as my blush faded and my breathing returned to a steadier rhythm I gazed at the vision standing before me. Jake had to be the most stunning specimen of a man I had ever laid eyes on. In his sharp black suit and crisp black, button down shirt he looked like he'd stepped right off a fashion week catwalk.

"I have something for you," Jake said, he voice dropping to a whisper. He pulled a small velvet box from his pocket.

"I want you to know that I will always love you and this is to show you how much you mean to me, Abbie. I know we're too young to get married, but I will ask you one day. I promise you. So please wear this until I get you the real thing."

A lone tear trickled down my cheek as I tore my eyes away from Jake to the tiny box that he held so tightly in his hand. He opened it carefully, revealing a square cut topaz sat on a white gold band. Jake slipped it onto my finger before leaning down to kiss me.

"Happy birthday, baby."

"Thank you, it's beautiful." I swallowed past the lump stuck in my throat, "I love it."

"Well aren't you two the million dollar couple," my mom said, her eyes lighting up with the very same warmth I'd seen only this morning, "Jo! Put Callum down and get your butts in here right this second. I want a photo of the four of you before you head off into the night."

I swallowed back the emotion as Jake pulled me carefully into his side and held me tightly as Jo and Callum joined us.

"Hold it, that's it," Mom shouted then snapped a few dozen photos.

"Here let me," Jake said, holding his hand out to take the camera from my mom, "Let's have one of the proud mom and daughter."

Mom's eyes teared up as I hauled her into my arms, "Thanks, Mom, I want you to know, today has been awesome," I said, blinking back the emotion.

"Well it's not over yet, sweetheart. Let's get you to your party shall we?" she said, holding my face in both her hands before leaning up to kiss me on the forehead.

Jake took a few more photos before we stepped out into the cold night air, expecting a cab to be waiting, Jo and I were speechless when faced with a limousine at the bottom of the driveway.

453

"Your chariot awaits, ladies," Callum announced, looking rather smug.

"You did this, Cal?" Jo asked, her eyes as wide as saucers staring at the sleek limo.

"Yep, Jake and me. We sorted it weeks ago when you two went dress shopping."

"I love it," I whispered, gripping Jake's hand.

Chapter Forty-Two

It took a little over fifteen minutes plus a glass of champagne for us to reach the party venue. The chauffeur opened the door and held out his hand to both Jo and I in turn. Jake's hand quickly returned to the small of my back. We walked up the steps of The Tavern and into the large function room we'd earlier transformed into a rocking party venue.

I scanned the tables as we entered and noted a sea of familiar faces as well as a few I'd forgotten over the years. Mom had told me that cousin Bella would be here with Dean, her fiancé and I quickly found them sat by the bar. I was also happy to see that Tina, Bella's older sister managed to make it as she'd only recently given birth to her third child. I hadn't seen either of them since before we moved away to Raven.

My family had come out of the woodwork just for me, a fact I found surprising, considering the grief I'd given most of them over the last ten years. Fresh tears pooled in my eyes at the out pouring of love towards me and my mom. Pride swelled my chest as I looked over to the tables at the far side of the room where she and Karen were busy arranging the last of the food. I swallowed back the emotion as Jake squeezed my hand.

"You're doing great, baby," he said, leaning down to kiss me, "Come introduce me to your family."

I nodded, "Yep, okay."

"You really have to bring Jake up to visit," Bella said with enthusiasm, "We have horses and the lake in summer. Or you could come for the snow. Whatever you like, but come soon. It's great to see you again, Abbie. It's definitely been way too long and it would we so awesome to keep in touch now we've caught up again. Say you'll come."

Jake appeared to be sold on the idea, "It looks like a 'yes' from the stunned mullet here, so I guess it's a 'yes' from me too," I said, grinning at Jake's obvious enthusiasm.

"Hey! Less of the stunned mullet, missy!" he said, wrapping an arm round my waist and squeezing gently. I giggled as he hit a ticklish spot and wriggled out of his grasp before turning to Bella's sister.

"I'm so glad you made it, Tina. Mom told me weeks ago that you might not be able to come with the baby being so young and all."

"I couldn't let Bella have all the fun on her own now could I?" she said, grinning at her sister, "Anyhow, Tim's mom said she'd have the kids for us so we could have a night to ourselves."

"Well I'm happy she did. I'll come chat some more in a while." I sensed Jake's eagerness to get a little alone time. We'd been making small talk with relative strangers for a little over an hour.

"You want to dance?" Jake asked as we inched towards the DJ.

"I'd love to, please." Jake took my hand and twirled me around as we found our rhythm to the slow soulful sounds drifting across the dance floor.

"You enjoying yourself, beautiful girl?" he asked as his arms came around me.

"I am now," I said, smiling up at him. Jake leaned down and pressed his mouth gently to lips, holding still before resting his forehead against mine.

"I love you, Abbie. Happy birthday, baby." The steady beat of Jake's heart seeped into my soul as I rested my head under his chin. I lifted my arms up to his neck and kissed his cheek before hugging him close as we moved to the sensual beat.

The music faded and the room came to life with chatter as family and friends became reacquainted over food and drinks. We inched closer to where Cal and Jo had set up camp.

"How's the party, Abs?" Jo half shouted so I could hear her above the band tuning up.

"Yeah, it's ace," I said, grinning back at her.

"Hey, your mom's about to say something." I cringed. I'd dreaded this moment.

"I'd like to make a toast." Mom held her glass tightly.

All that could be heard was the sound of chairs moving away from tables as the entire room fell silent.

"To my beautiful, talented daughter...Abbie. Happy birthday, sweetheart."

A chorus of, "To Abbie," rang out as my mom raised her glass and smiled in my direction. I eased my chair back and grabbed a napkin from the table in front of me in the hopes it would soak up most of my nerves. I swallowed hard and took a deep breath. The room went quiet again and everyone sat back in their seats, all eyes firmly pinned on mine. I smiled around the room, taking in the faces of my friends and very distant, in most cases, family members.

"I'd just like to say a big thank you to my mom for making my birthday so special..." The room erupted with applause. "Also thanks to Karen for my beautiful cake which I'll cut in a second. Thanks to Pam for helping Mom with the food all day and to Martin for being his usual brotherly self," I said, raising my eyebrows, "I haven't actually seen that much of him at all today. He's had the sense to stay well clear." I grinned and everyone laughed. "Thanks also to Jo for putting up with my lack of interest in fashion and to Callum for keeping her in check, but…most of all I want to thank Jake, my boyfriend, for being there when things got tough recently."

I sat quickly as everyone clapped. My heart was now pounding in my chest and I sucked in a deep breath before exhaling slowly as I stared at Jake.

"Fuck, I'm glad that's over," I said, still trembling with nervous energy.

"One more then you've done," Jake said, nodding over to the cake.

"Oh yeah," I whispered, "I nearly forgot."

A raucous rendition of Happy Birthday filled the air as I cut into the two tiered purple and silver creation Karen had made. The crowd drifted back to their seats armed with slabs of chocolate cake and dessert forks. The evening had surely been a huge success and I was surprised just how much I'd enjoyed myself. The stresses of the last week were finally subsiding, leaving me with a warm glow in my stomach.

"Hey, baby, I might get Cal to give me a hand carrying your presents out to your mom's car so we don't have to worry about it later. That okay?" Jake asked as the band began to blast out their first number.

"Yeah, that's fine. I think Mom wants me to top up the cupcakes anyways. I'll do it now." Jake nodded, kissed me and headed off to find Callum.

The pounding of the band followed me down the passage to the cool room where Karen had placed the cupcakes earlier. I struggled with the catch on the door, but finally managed to release it so it swung open.

The light inside was dim, but bright enough to see what I needed. I smiled widely when I spotted the cake display sitting on the stainless steel table at the far side of the large room. Just as I reached the table my cell vibrated in my hand. I flipped the cover to see a text from Jake. I smiled and shook my head.

You look stunning. I love the FM dress, baby. I giggled quietly, reading his message. I'd just placed it in my purse when I became aware of footsteps behind me.

"You're in a rush, Jake," I whispered, smiling at his impatience. The sound of my pounding heart echoed in my head as I remembered his earlier promise…

"I'll have you begging for it later. Just you wait and see. You won't see it coming." I closed my eyes and gasped as his mouth found the back of my neck. His hands reached around to my stomach, pulling me into his chest. He

dragged his teeth along the exposed skin at my shoulder before one of his hands moved lower and hitched up the hem of my dress. He squeezed the flesh of my thigh and dragged his hand upward towards my throbbing center while holding me tight around my waist. His fingers dipped inside my underwear caressing roughly before plunging deep inside, making me gasp.

"Ouch!" I swallowed as my sixth sense stirred, my eyes pooling with tears. *This isn't right!* With a sudden switch in atmosphere he pushed me forward towards the solid table and held me down firmly by my shoulder, fumbling to pull my underwear clear. *No!*

I tried to turn to face him, but he held me fast, his grip on my shoulder becoming almost painful and I struggled to shake him off. Debilitating fear coursed through my body as I realized my mistake.

Oh my God!

His hand gripped my throat with enough pressure to make sure I was powerless to fight back. Again he lowered his mouth and bit into my neck. His teeth grazing the flesh aggressively while all the time grinding firmly against my ass, pressing my hips against the steel of the table with abandon. He struggled to part my legs with his thigh as I fought with ever last ounce of determination vested in me to resist. His hand at my throat tightened as he continued grinding into me. I couldn't breathe, my head pounded with the heavy beat of my heart as his vile hand crawled over my flesh.

Please no! I couldn't breathe, or scream, I couldn't make a sound. Utter terror engulfed me, traveling like poison to my heart, burning away my soul.

I felt his breath on my flesh, coming heavier as his hands began to hurt me, tear me, thrust too far inside me. His body pinned me to the table. He wanted to hurt me and I'd let him, my desire for Jake had clouded my senses. His fingers thrust painfully like knives inside me without caution. Hungry for his pleasure alone, not gentle and loving like Jake. My head began to spin as the oxygen I so badly needed was denied me.

"Jake!" My voice strained from my throat, but it was too late.

"Let me in, Angel… Mmm you're so fucking ready for me. Can you feel how hard I am for you, Abbie? You'll love this, my angel… It's been too long…"

A tidal wave of disgust and self-repulsion seared my soul as darkness engulfed me.

Jake I'm sorry!

Forgive me!

Chapter Forty-Three

My mind hadn't stopped spinning since the moment I'd seen her appear on the stairs at her place earlier. The dull, ache in my pants magnified as the evening moved along. I'd spent all night unable to keep my eyes, or hands for that matter, off her fabulous body.

As I scanned the dance floor for Abbie, images of her undressing for me in her bedroom came to my mind, causing my heartbeat to quicken and sweat to bead on my brow. Jo hadn't been joking when they'd talked about Abs having bought a *Fuck Me Dress*. Smoking seemed a lame description for how she actually looked in the sexy as hell outfit. I couldn't wait to get her home later, help rid her of the little black number and run my fingers through her long, silky, curled hair.

I let out a slow, deep breath as I tried to get my head back in the game. The bulge in my pants was neither comfortable nor an appropriate condition for a family gathering.

"Jay! Hold up man," Callum shouted above the band. They'd made a start on their first set of the night.

"Hey, I was just looking for you," I said when he sauntered over. "These guys sound great," I said, nodding towards the band.

"Yeah," Cal agreed, "Why were you looking for me?"

"Oh, it was nothing. Just wanted a hand getting Abbie's gifts into her mom's car. It's done now," I said, raising an eyebrow and grinning at his timing.

"Oops," he said, turning back to the band. I continued to scan the room for Abbie until my gaze fell on the woman talking to Beth.

"I'm sure I know that woman," I said to Callum, my brow furrowing as I tried to place her. "I... wait..." I swallowed as realization hit me. "No!"

What followed was like a sledge hammer to my gut as the bile rose to my throat and my eyes searched frantically around the vast space for Abbie. Callum grabbed my arm as I began to panic; my breath came in gasps as I struggled with the thoughts flying uncontrollably through my head.

"Jay?"

"He's here, Cal! Fuck!" I choked back the tremendous fear for Abbie's safety, streaming through my body.

"What the fuck, dude? Who's here?"

"The fucking child molester! That's his *fucking wife*..." I growled, frantically trying to spot Abbie amongst the crowd. "I can't see *him*... I can't see Abbie... Fuck!"

"Jake, slow down, man. Come on, we'll find her," he said calmly, "Where did you last see her?"

"Erm…" Confusion and fear clouded my head as panic spewed into my chest. "I…she said she was getting more food…for the buffet." At the realization of what might possibly be going down in the storeroom I launched myself across the dance floor. I raced towards the room where only hours earlier we'd stacked plate upon plate of food for Abbie's special day. My eyes began to sting as visions of a horrible outcome raided my mind.

"I'll check outside!" Cal shouted from behind me.

I tore down the narrow corridor leading to the small room furthest away from the party, my heart pounding violently. As I crashed through the heavy door I was confronted by my worst fears.

"Get. Your. Fucking. Hands. Off. Her!" I growled at the vicious monster holding my beautiful girl over the bench by her throat. My world came hurtling down around my feet as I took in the vicious scene before me. Tears of rage blurred my vision as I lunged forward and ripped him from Abbie's lifeless body, throwing him up against the fixed shelving behind us. Kitchen utensils scattered and glass exploded into a million pieces as jars hit the ground.

I rushed to Abbie, dropping down beside her. I placed a gentle hand to her neck, desperately searching for a pulse under my fingers. "Baby?" My sleeve caught the tears dripping off my chin.

"You're too late, Jakey... I had her a long time ago... She's all mine," he snarled as he staggered towards me.

My body began to shake uncontrollably at the image of this monster forcing himself onto my innocent girl. My beautiful girl who'd never deserved the agony his depravity had caused.

"Arrgghh!" I roared, lunging forward. My eyes bulged with rage as I swung my adrenaline fueled fist into his face. The force of the blow threw his head sideways, smashing it into the wall. I swung again, pummeling his lip before he threw my enraged body away from him.

With blood spilling from his temple, he lifted a hand to test his lip for damage, his expression that of a sadistic maniac.

"Nice...you grew up strong, Jakey," he taunted, spitting his blood on the floor. The tone of his voice turned my stomach and fueled my need for blood, his blood; I wanted him dead.

I flew at him with all the force of a freight train, smashing into his vile bulk. The impact crushed the wind from my lungs, causing me to double over, gasping for air. Before I could register what had happened his foot connected with my ribs. The pain radiating from the point of impact brought me to my knees.

"Fuck! You'll pay for that," I growled.

The rage in me pumped violently through my veins, replacing my need for air.

He swung his leg back to repeat the attack, but I grabbed his foot, sweeping his legs from under him. His head made contact with the stone floor with a hell of a smack. I thrust my fist towards his face, but he blocked it and threw me over onto my back.

The image of Abbie's limp body trapped beneath him flashed through my mind and with it an uncontrollable fury burned deep inside me. I had to get up. It wasn't going to end like this. He wouldn't have her. I heaved with all my might and threw his stinking body from mine before clambering to my feet.

Abbie lay huddled on the ground gasping for air, her new dress ripped away from her body. Waves of relief washed over me when I heard the sound of her coughing.

"What the fuck?" Cal growled as he flew into the room. He spotted Abbie in the corner and rushed to her side, "She's okay, Jay."

"Get her safe," I yelled as the pitiful excuse for a human that was her abuser staggered towards me.

My breathing was labored as we stood locked, face to face. His crazed eyes bored into mine and in them visions of Abbie's body then and now. Brutalized and broken by his doing.

"You'll never have her…not really!" he roared, madness pulsing from him as he grabbed one of the nearby knives. He thrust and jabbed the blade at me, piercing my side, but my rage consumed me and I caught hold of the hand clenching the weapon.

"You. Fucking. Piece. Of. Shit!" I yelled; my words punctuating the slamming of his arm against the wall. Each of my senses and every nerve ending heightened by a hunger to finish this.

We struggled for dominance. I fought with all my might to disarm him, my pulse pounding in my head. With a clatter of steel on stone, the knife hit the ground. I grabbed his head between my hands and smashed his face down onto my knee. The need for revenge for Abbie drove me onward and I repeated the action before throwing him to the ground.

"You worthless piece of shit!" I said, wiping the sweat and blood from my face as I took in the filthy animal lying at my feet. Rolling over he grinned up at me.

"Finished already, Jakey?" He spat blood as he dragged his sleeve along the bloodied mess that was now his nose.

His smart mouth sparked a chemical reaction. A renewed hunger for vengeance flooded my soul as I kicked into him repeatedly. Laying boot after boot into his vile body; I was unable to stop the torture. With every impact I saw Abbie's broken body growing stronger.

"No, I fucking haven't! You vicious bastard. Fuck you to hell. I'll fucking kill you!"

He'd long since stopped moving, but I couldn't help the relentless punishment flowing out of my body. I'd lost complete control. Tears of anger streamed down my face as someone launched themselves at my back. My fists thrashed and punched in an attempt to break free of whoever was restraining me. I had to kill the bastard that had tried to destroy Abbie.

"Get off me!" I roared.

"Jake! Enough, it's done…" Callum shouted, wrapping his bulk around me, "Jake?"

I fought to gain control. It felt like minutes passed before I slumped into his arms as the emotion of what had just happened engulfed me. The small cool room, used earlier for storing the food for my girl's special day, had just become a place of torturous humiliation for that same beautiful girl. I'd ended him, right there on the cold stone floor. He lay in his own vomit and blood, as broken as he had left my baby ten years ago and again moments earlier.

Mandy Thomas

"She'll never get back her childhood. She'll never know that innocence. He told me, Cal... He'd said I was too late!"

Callum jerked me back to the present. "Jake? It's done, man... It's over." Bodies poured into the small space. I felt numb as Callum led me away.

"Jake!" Abbie screamed, the agony in her voice piercing my chest.

"Abbie? Where is she?" Then I saw her, staggering towards me, her tear stained face racked with confused repulsion for what had just happened. I stumbled away from Callum and wrapped her violated body in my arms.

We stayed like that for what felt an eternity... Holding, soothing, promising and loving with all we had.

Abbie's hand came to my cheek and her eyes locked on mine. "You're bleeding." She frowned before pulling herself into my chest once more as she began to shake. "I thought he was you..." she whispered, her body giving way to the most gut wrenching sobs I'd ever heard.

I held her tightly as the memory of what I'd seen invaded my mind and I squeezed my eyes shut.

"It's over. He won't hurt you...not ever..."

"Sir? Jake is it?"

"Huh?" I asked as I realized I was being spoken to.

470

"We need to get you both to the hospital, Jake. You and Abbie need to come with us now." The guy in the paramedic uniform smiled kindly as he laid his hand on my arm. I nodded and pulled Abbie into my side as we passed our families and several police officers to get to the ambulance. Beth reached for Abbie on the way outside.

"I didn't know, sweetheart... I never knew," she sobbed as Pam wrapped a supportive arm around her shoulders. Abbie pulled away from me just enough to hug her mom briefly.

"It's okay, Mom, It's over," she said before kissing Beth lightly on the cheek and then turning back to me.

"We'll see you there, Jake," my mom said leaning into my dad's chest and he in turn patted my shoulder.

***

After spending the night being interviewed and photographed by the police and examined by the medical team at Casey Hospital we were cleared to go home. Abbie was showing some early signs of bruising to her torso and legs as well as around her throat where she'd been restrained. I'd received a gash to my arm, a puncture wound to my side which needed several stitches and two broken ribs.

Despite having beaten the evil fucker to within an inch of his life I was released without charge as it was

471

considered self-defense. Stevens was under guard in intensive care somewhere else in the hospital. He would be charged with one count of assault and one count of assault with a deadly weapon with intent to kill as soon as he regained consciousness.

In her interview with the female detective Abbie had heard in depth what the whole process of proceeding with a rape charge would entail. She learned how traumatic it would be if she decided to go ahead. We left the hospital fully armed with the knowledge needed for Abbie to make an informed decision, but more importantly a decision that was ultimately the right one for her.

**

"Mom, it's okay if Jake stays with me isn't it?" I asked as we climbed into the back of the station wagon.

"Of course, sweetheart, if he wants to. He can stay as long as he likes," she said quietly.

It took no time at all to drive the short distance to our house. I leaned into Jake's chest and closed my eyes. A weird sense of finality swept my body as I looked up into his swollen eyes.

"Is that alright with you? Will you stay with me?" He lowered his lips carefully to mine before pulling away slowly and resting his head on top of mine.

"There was never any question."

"How's your side?" I asked as he winced.

"It's fine, baby. It's nothing," he said, stroking the hair back from my face and tucking it behind my ear. I nodded and lowered my head back to his chest as he tightened his hold on me.

"Okay, you two, we're home."

The sun was just appearing over the brow of the hill, casting a warm winter glow across the sleeping neighborhood. The sight of it brought a slight smile to my lips. Jake's arm came around my waist as he climbed out of the station wagon.

"You two need sleep," Mom said when we got inside.

"Yeah, I'm exhausted," I said quietly. The haunted expression on Jake's face killed me. I squeezed his hand and he kissed the top of my head.

I froze as I put my hand on the handle of my bedroom door. A sudden flurry of sensation rushed my body as images of Peter's assault flooded my mind. My breath hitched in my throat and tears sprung to my eyes.

"Abs?"

"I was so scared... I... He... I..." I swiped madly at my tears; anger burned in my chest that he'd taken away another special moment. He'd done it in front of everyone. I felt so ashamed. "You saw..." I cried, shaking my head,

"He… And you saw…" Jake grabbed hold of me and pulled me into his chest.

"I did, I saw a fucking monster hurting my beautiful girl. I promise you…he will never lay…another hand on you. Not as long as I have a breath left in me…" Jake said, rubbing my back. "I wanted to kill him, Abbie. I thought I'd killed him."

"I thought…I…I thought you'd hate me." All my worries and fears centered as a lump in my stomach as Jake eased away from me shock and confusion painted in pain across his features.

"Don't ever…think that…I love you with everything I have Abbie… Everything!" I leaned up on my tiptoes and pressed a kiss to his lips, bringing my hand to his cheek.

"I love you more, Jake."

We spent most of the day asleep. Jake was still sleeping, but even asleep his expression seemed pained. He looked broken. I ran my fingers down his cheek and his eyes flickered open.

"Hey," I whispered, leaning up to kiss him.

"Hey, beautiful girl," he said, taking my hand in his. He swallowed as his eyes locked on mine.

"What?" This was the hardest, knowing the effect last night would forever have on him. I'd been through so much worse. Last night was already tucked away in a sealed box in the recesses of my mind, but Jake wasn't as lucky. He hadn't learned to do that and maybe never would have that ability.

They'd spoken to us about counseling at the hospital. I suspected Jake would need it more than me. My mom and Martin had access to the service as well. This was going to be a tough road. I had to help them all. My family meant the world to me. He wouldn't take them away from me, he'd taken enough already... He wouldn't take Jake. I'd fight for him. Forever if that's what it took.

"Jake?"

"What are you going to do, baby?" he asked, concern etched across his brow. A new hope germinated deep inside me as I realized the enormity of my decision.

"I want him to suffer." My heartbeat pulsed in my neck as Jake ran his thumb across the back of my hand, "I want him to rot behind bars forever. I want him out of our lives for good." Jake took a deep breath and closed the gap between us, pressing his mouth firmly to mine. His love flowed through me, embracing me for all eternity.

"I'm so proud of you, Abbie. I love you so much," Jake whispered, resting his forehead against mine.

"I love you more, Jake." And I did; I loved him with every inch of my being, I always had. Jake Ashton made me whole.

About the Author

Mandy Thomas is an English born mother and teacher, living in Australia on the beautiful Mornington Peninsula with her husband and their two children.

An avid reader as a child, she rediscovered her love of books in 2012 when a friend introduced her to the wonderful world of self-published authors. After enjoying twelve months of fabulous stories by everyday people like herself, she decided to dip a toe into the writing pond. Her debut novel, Hard to Feel Whole, the first in the Hard to Feel series was released in 2014. The series follows Abbie James and her circle of friends through many of life's challenges and possibilities.

Find more interesting facts and updates of future writing projects on **Facebook**-

www.facebook.com/mandythomasauthor

Twitter-

www.twitter.com/MThomasauthor

Goodreads-

www.goodreads.com/author/show/9853873.Mandy_Thomas

Acknowledgments

Special thanks to my amazing editor, Peter Thomson for his incredible patience and proficiency while editing, but also for the support and encouragement he offered, making sure that Hard to Feel Whole made it to publication.

Thank you also to Angela Stevens for sharing her knowledge of all things self-publishing at all hours of the day and night.

Also, thank you to my proof reader extraordinaire, Tina for your friendship and honest, from the hip feedback. You're amazing.

To my beta readers: You are all superstars. Thank you.

Finally…

To my wonderful family, for your never-ending optimism, reassurance and understanding as meal times disappeared in place of creative flow; without you I would never have attempted something as huge as this.

Hard to Feel Series

Hard to Feel Whole ~ Book One

Hard to Feel Free ~ Book Two

Hard to Be Strong ~ Novella

Hard to Feel More ~ Book Three

JꞶ.SM

Printed in Great Britain
by Amazon

63321363R00281